'*Outgunned* had everything I want from a 40K novel: compelling characters, a gripping narrative delivered in crisp, deft prose, and things going fast and exploding. *Above and Beyond* more than lives up to its title, having all these things again but bigger and better, and revealing more of the wider picture merely hinted at in the first volume. Simlex and Shard are rapidly becoming the most iconic double act in the worlds of Warhammer since Gotrek and Felix, and I'm eagerly awaiting their next adventure.'

Sandy Mitchell, author of *For the Emperor*

ABOVE AND BEYOND

More tales of the Astra Militarum from Black Library

OUTGUNNED
A novel by Denny Flowers

SIEGE OF VRAKS
A novel by Steve Lyons

KRIEG
A novel by Steve Lyons

MINKA LESK: THE LAST WHITESHIELD
An omnibus edition of the novels *Cadia Stands, Cadian Honour, Traitor Rock* and several short stories
by Justin D Hill

SHADOW OF THE EIGHTH
A novel by Justin D Hill

THE FALL OF CADIA
A novel by Robert Rath

CREED: ASHES OF CADIA
A novel by Jude Reid

DEATHWORLDER
A novel by Victoria Hayward

LONGSHOT
A novel by Rob Young

KASRKIN
A novel by Edoardo Albert

CATACHAN DEVIL
A novel by Justin Woolley

STEEL TREAD
A novel by Andy Clark

VOLPONE GLORY
A novel by Nick Kyme

WITCHBRINGER
A novel by Steven B Fischer

VAINGLORIOUS
A novel by Sandy Mitchell

WARHAMMER 40,000

ABOVE AND BEYOND

DENNY FLOWERS

BLACK LIBRARY

A BLACK LIBRARY PUBLICATION

First published in 2024.
This edition published in Great Britain in 2025 by
Black Library, Games Workshop Ltd., Willow Road,
Nottingham, NG7 2WS, UK.

Represented by: Games Workshop Limited – Irish branch,
Unit 3, Lower Liffey Street, Dublin 1,
D01 K199, Ireland.

10 9 8 7 6 5 4 3 2 1

Produced by Games Workshop in Nottingham.
Cover illustration by Jan Drenovec.

Above and Beyond © Copyright Games Workshop Limited 2025. Above and Beyond, GW, Games Workshop, Black Library, The Horus Heresy, The Horus Heresy Eye logo, Space Marine, 40K, Warhammer, Warhammer 40,000, the 'Aquila' Double-headed Eagle logo, and all associated logos, illustrations, images, names, creatures, races, vehicles, locations, weapons, characters, and the distinctive likenesses thereof, are either ® or TM, and/or © Games Workshop Limited, variably registered around the world.
All Rights Reserved.

A CIP record for this book is available from the British Library.

ISBN 13: 978-1-83609-162-2

No part of this publication may be reproduced, stored in a retrieval system, or transmitted in any form or by any means, electronic, mechanical, photocopying, recording or otherwise, without the prior permission of the publishers.

This is a work of fiction. All the characters and events portrayed in this book are fictional, and any resemblance to real people or incidents is purely coincidental.

See Black Library on the internet at

blacklibrary.com

Find out more about Games Workshop
and the worlds of Warhammer at

warhammer.com

Printed and bound in the UK.

For Beth, Finn, and Luna the Magic Space Puppy. Love you all.

For more than a hundred centuries the Emperor has sat immobile on the Golden Throne of Earth. He is the Master of Mankind. By the might of his inexhaustible armies a million worlds stand against the dark.

Yet, he is a rotting carcass, the Carrion Lord of the Imperium held in life by marvels from the Dark Age of Technology and the thousand souls sacrificed each day so his may continue to burn.

To be a man in such times is to be one amongst untold billions. It is to live in the cruelest and most bloody regime imaginable. It is to suffer an eternity of carnage and slaughter. It is to have cries of anguish and sorrow drowned by the thirsting laughter of dark gods.

This is a dark and terrible era where you will find little comfort or hope. Forget the power of technology and science. Forget the promise of progress and advancement. Forget any notion of common humanity or compassion.

There is no peace amongst the stars, for in the grim darkness of the far future, there is only war.

PREFACE

My name is Kile Simlex, and I am a liar.

It is an unpleasant realisation. Back when I was a revered propagandist, I saw my duties as imparting truth to the Imperium's citizens and shining a light upon our victories. Because back then I believed in the Imperium.

Or at least, I think I did.

Perhaps I am not wholly at fault. Propagandists are tasked with crafting palpable truths, but, like all of humanity, we build upon the labours of our predecessors. They too were flawed, forced to compromise principles to preserve their modest prosperity. Lies founded upon lies, until the official narrative is a glut of contradictions and truth is a mystery. Our people dismiss the orks as mindless brutes, the aeldari as faded relics, and the t'au as upstarts soon to fall. We claim it is humanity's manifest destiny to overcome such lesser races, to ascend to domination of all.

The Imperium is mighty, our foes weak and corrupt. So far beneath us.

Yet their forces press us, push us ever closer towards extinction.

Bacchus opened my eyes. In those swamps I saw the true threat the xenos presented. Those picts portraying orks as knock-kneed simpletons swiftly dispatched by Imperial soldiers were lies. So I crafted a pict that captured the reality of war. The ugly truth. Whatever the consequences.

I thought they would execute me. I suppose that fear represented the last flicker of my ego, the presumption that my voice carried sufficient weight to warrant such sanction. Instead, my work was vivisected, spliced into a rip-roaring tale of heroism and triumph that found near-universal favour. Acclaim and glory were heaped upon the mutilated pict, while those who gave their lives were quietly forgotten.

My punishment was not death but penitence. I was cast into the deepest pit of the Officio Propagandum, my cell a rockcrete cubicle, my penance trawling through ancient footage for snippets to insert into recruitment picts. Say what you will of the Imperium, but it always finds a use for its citizens. There are servitors to be manufactured, organs to be extracted, and, if nothing else, valuable protein to be reprocessed for the lower classes. And those are merely the ones I know of; I am sure the High Lords have other, more esoteric means of making use of societal detritus.

My sentence did not require solitary confinement, but that was the reality. For although my labours fed into the vast, churning pot of the officio, few spoke to me. I know why. Disgrace and failure could be contagious, and anyone sympathetic to my plight might be labelled as suffering from similar defects of mind and character. None wanted to share in my fate.

I did not blame them. I blamed her.

Flight Commander Lucille von Shard. Prodigal daughter of the von Shard family and fighter ace extraordinaire. She was the one who opened my eyes to the failings of the Imperium, perhaps unintentionally. But once I saw it, I could not go back. For, in truth, our priests praise the God-Emperor even whilst lining their pockets. Our nobles quaff their drinks and dine upon sweetmeats, all the while proclaiming how the citizens must tighten their belts to support the war effort. And our propagandists tell us we are winning, even as we die broken in the streets.

Shard did not share my fall. She suffered no demotion for leading me from the righteous path, instead ascending ever higher. I knew from clips that passed across my desk, snapshots of a Lightning fighter emblazoned with her heraldry dispatching the Imperium's foes with contemptuous ease. Sometimes I saw her face, though it seemed softened somehow, the jagged scar on her lip barely a blemish. When she spoke, the cynicism was absent. In its place, she preached the righteousness of the Imperium's cause, how she lived only to be an instrument of the God-Emperor's will.

I tried not to think about her. But I had limited control over my subconscious. For some time, I had found myself dreaming of Bacchus, of making one last pass over the swamps. Once these dreams had been almost pleasant, a diversion from the drudgery of my new existence.

But that time was gone. Sleep no longer brought solace.

I might have passed quietly away living such an existence, but I was sustained by a last flicker of pride. Isolated, disgraced, and on the cusp of losing my sanity, I drew comfort by proclaiming myself an honest man, any prior deceptions a consequence of ignorance, not malice. I had told the truth and been found wanting, but I would not beg for mitigation or penance. I would sit in my cell, let time do as it would, and allow the God-Emperor to decide my fate in the end.

But even then I deceived myself. For I once said that the final time I saw Flight Commander Lucille von Shard was floating in space, having bested the Green Storm, her vessel about to dock with Orbital Station Salus.

It transpires that that was a lie. For it was not the last time we were together.

CHAPTER ONE

I did not recognise the footsteps. Not at first. But I knew they were out of place, being neither the ponderous trudge of a servitor nor the patter of a scribe. The latter would be hurried, desperate to be free of this sublevel. None lingered here, had they the choice.

No, the footsteps were deliberate. Measured. The stride of someone who walked without fear or the need to match another's pace. There was a familiarity to the tread, and I thought I knew it, though I was unsure from where or when.

And the footsteps had almost reached my cubicle cell.

I rose from my seat, supporting my weight on the armrest, wincing as my twisted left leg protested. The ache was getting worse; my own gait would have sounded like a crippled old man.

The footsteps stopped.

There was a knock – three sharp raps. But before I could reach for the door, it was flung open. The figure framed in the doorway was tall and broad-shouldered. His uniform was partially concealed by a thick greatcoat, but there was no mistaking the skull symbol on his peaked cap.

A commissar. An individual few desire to meet, announced or otherwise. I shrank back, wondering what I had done to warrant such attention, until I gathered the courage to meet his gaze. It had been years, but still I recognised his face.

Commissar Tobia von Shard.

He stood, regarding me and my abode in turn, his expression indicating neither met his approval.

'Propagandist Simlex,' he said, offering a curt nod. 'I trust I find you well.'

'It's just Scribe Simlex now,' I replied, as he strode into the room. 'I am surprised to see you, commissar.'

'Understandable. You are not an easy man to find. Well, tracing you to this facility was simple enough. Locating this room proved annoyingly arduous. Are you aware your personnel file has been mislaid?'

'No, but it's common practice to seal the records of those who have failed in their duties. Some fear that, if left accessible, they could contaminate the records of the loyal and studious through mere exposure.'

'Hmm. And I see your quarters are more... modest than in times prior,' he continued, steely gaze surveying the cubicle.

There was precious little to survey. Besides storage, the furniture consisted of a work desk overlaid with dusty vid screens and stacked paperwork, an iron-framed chair so heavy I could barely move it, and a bed I had neglected to make or, for the most part, sleep in. I could see the commissar bristle at the unfolded blankets, but through titanic effort he withheld judgement. Verbally anyway.

I sighed. 'My last pict was not well received.'

'On the contrary, it has done phenomenally well,' he replied. 'I did not have time or inclination to attend the premiere, but I heard glowing reviews. Though, given the descriptions, it has changed significantly since the rough cut you presented to my family.'

'What was released is not my pict. And I did not present anything to your family. Your sister stole a copy before it was decreed a failure and destroyed.'

'Lucille?'

'No. Your other sister.'

'Ah,' he said, nodding. 'Josephine does like to feel in control. For what it is worth, I thought the original a tolerable work, though I see why others had reservations concerning its impact on recruitment.'

'As can I. Few wish to die ignominiously in a rotting swamp.'

'Yes, possibly. But I referred to the subject. I warned you about the perils of crafting a pict featuring my sister.'

'I recall you also recruited me for the task.'

He did not reply. His gaze was still fixed on the unmade bed.

'Commissar, it is good to see you. But might I enquire why you are here?'

He turned his head, regarding me from the corner of his eye, face shaded by the peaked cap.

'I would prefer to discuss the matter somewhere more secure. And ideally without soiled bed linen. Perhaps a private conference space or meeting facility would be more appropriate.'

'I am afraid I have no access to such facilities. This room is my fiefdom. May I offer you the chair?'

He glanced at the rusted iron frame and frayed synthleather.

'I prefer to stand,' he replied, before once more surveying the room. 'I assume you possess means of projecting a holo-image? What happened to those seer-skulls of yours?'

'One was sacrificed defending Bacchus. Your sister absconded with another.'

'Josephine?'

'No. Your other sister. We met up on Orbital Station Salus right after the conflict. I wished to collect the seer-skull imbedded in her aircraft. But we… quarrelled. And when I left, she–'

'Was there not a third?' he said, cutting me off.

'There was and is. More or less.'

I nodded to the iron-framed cabinet. In the shadows atop it, buried beneath busted servos and stained cloths, a single crimson lens flickered briefly into life.

The commissar stared at it, before glaring back at me. For once, his expression was difficult to read.

'This is your prized seer-skull? You treat a relic in this manner?'

'It's damaged. Prone to misbehaving. When I let it run free, it interferes with my work.'

He did not reply, intent on the flickering red light.

'I was unaware how far you had fallen,' he said at last.

For a moment I thought he would say something more. Perhaps offer his condolences or concede his family's hand in my downfall. But he did neither, instead reaching into his lapel and withdrawing a gleaming silver data-slug.

Then he turned his gaze upon me, eyes bright and cold.

'Before we proceed, let me be clear – what you are about to witness will be treated in the strictest confidence. You will speak of it to no one. Doing so would be to ignore the orders of a commissar, and by extension the will of the Imperium itself. In such circumstances I would execute my duty accordingly.'

He shifted his stance, greatcoat falling open. I found my gaze drawn to the holstered pistol at his waist.

'I believe you.'

I offered my hand. He placed the gleaming data-slug in

my palm, before wiping his gloved fingers on a silken handkerchief.

'The following vid was recently dispatched. Addressed to you, though my family's agents were able to intercept it.'

'Who sent it?'

'That will become clear,' he muttered, folding his arms. 'Just play the bloody thing.'

I turned to the cabinet, taking a deep breath. It had been some time since I had sought to rouse the seer-skull. I reached out to it through my implant, urging it to awaken through a haze of static. But it was like an elderly dog snuggled in a warm bed.

Beside me, I heard the commissar's fingers drumming against his arm.

I tried again, and Iwazar abruptly lurched upright, suspended a few inches above the cabinet, lenses flicking on and off. Its projector flared, and for a moment the room was awash with fractured images. The rancid swamps of Bacchus. Governor Dolos dispensing justice from her insectoid throne. The faces of a dozen aces, none of whom had survived the war. And Shard of course, her visage plastered across both wall and ceiling, her sneer sometimes masquerading as a smile.

'What is this?' The commissar frowned as the images danced uncertainly.

'A failure,' I sighed. 'But one I am reluctant to abandon.'

I tried once more, the command now a plea. Perhaps Iwazar listened, or perhaps it had exhausted whatever subcommand had compelled the display. It came to me, lurching from the cabinet and plummeting towards the floor. At the last moment the anti-grav field flared, the seer-skull rising groggily, surveying its surroundings with a flickering red lens. It regarded the commissar, perhaps recognising him, but made no attempt to approach. Instead, it began slowly tipping to one side, till the skull hung almost horizontal.

It, like I, had seen better days.

I beckoned it closer, and it wobbled towards me, engines hissing under the strain. I held up the data-slug, but paused, looking to the commissar.

'Do you have a backup of this?'

'Why would I create a copy of something I wish to keep secret?'

'What if the original was damaged?'

'Do you intend to damage it?'

'No, I… Forget I spoke,' I said, sliding the data-slug into the seer-skull's data port, praying that it didn't erase the contents, or overwrite them with a compilation of Flight Commander Shard's most biting insults. It was not an idle worry; the latter had happened twice before.

Iwazar's lenses flickered green. It hesitated, before lurching skywards, veering from the ceiling at the last moment and settling into place atop the cabinet again.

'What in the God-Emperor's name is wrong with it?' the commissar hissed, hand now resting on the pommel of his chainsword.

'It was damaged in the conflict,' I replied. 'I've tried to repair it.'

'And failed. A tech-priest should have sanctified it. Or performed last rites.'

'Few tech-priests care to descend to this sublevel.'

He grunted in response, but my gaze was intent on the seer-skull. It trembled, emitting a horrible grinding sound, before suddenly its projector flared, throwing a flickering image into the room's centre. It was little more than a blur of blue and white, vaguely in the shape of a figure.

'I can't see a damn thing!' the commissar snapped.

'Give it a moment,' I murmured, shifting the focus. I still

could not find any colours besides blue, but the blur gradually coalesced into an officer clad in a flight uniform. The helm was missing, and I could now see the pilot's hair was pulled back, a few strands breaking free to frame her ashen face. Though the image quality remained poor, there was no mistaking the scar on her cheek.

Flight Commander Lucille von Shard.

She looked awkward, weight resting on her rearmost foot, arms folded, head turned to the side, avoiding the pict-cam's lens, the image frozen, the vid poised to play.

'Shard?' I frowned, glancing at the commissar.

'Flight Commander Shard,' he corrected, glaring at me.

'Of course. My apologies.'

He nodded, before gesturing to the half-formed image, as though it would provide all the answers.

'Commissar. Is she... Has the worst happened?'

'From her perspective? Possibly,' he replied, a sliver of sympathy creeping into his voice. 'She needs your help.'

CHAPTER TWO

I slumped into the room's only chair, my leg unable to hold my weight. The commissar stood stoically beside me, arms still folded. Together we watched Shard's frozen image flicker.

She wanted my help. Presumably so did the commissar, otherwise he would not have sought me. But she'd always struck me as one who would prefer a slow and violent death to actively requesting another's aid.

I felt too warm suddenly. I was not used to conversing. I had done little of it in the past few years. But I could not take a moment to get my bearings, for the commissar was not a patient man.

'Playback message,' I murmured.

The image jerked into life. Shard glared once into the lens before turning away.

'This is ridiculous,' she sighed. *'I don't even know if the damn thing is recording.'*

She leant forward, reaching towards the screen, the image

collapsing into a blue blur. It vanished, only to be supplanted moments later. Still Shard, though her flight suit was now unzipped to the waist. An undershirt preserved her modesty, though her arms were bare. The flesh was so pale the recorder struggled to accurately capture it. She almost resembled a spectre, skin tinted blue by the lens. She was seated now, the chair reversed, her arms folded across its backrest. A lho-stick rested between her fingers.

She exhaled, the smoke muddying her expression. She looked angry, which was typical, but something else lay behind it. Despair? Resignation?

I found myself leaning closer, willing the image into sharper focus. But Iwazar could only work with what it had.

She took another drag, exhaling a thick cloud the seer-skull depicted as a ghostly haze. Had I been crafting a budget terror pict, it might have been a passable visual effect.

'Will she actually speak again?' I asked, but at that moment the projection chose to break its silence.

'Well, *propagandist*,' she said, addressing the floor. *'I hope you're happy.'*

Whatever the limitations of the pict quality, the audio was clear, as was the recrimination in her voice.

'I never asked to be in a vid. I mean, I never asked for any of this. Did quite the opposite a couple of times. But it was made clear to me that this was my path, and I would not get another choice. I suppose it could be worse. They might have forced me into the priesthood. I couldn't handle that. All the damn singing.'

She smiled. Possibly. It always looked like a sneer.

'I did my bit, though. Lucille von Shard starred in your little pict despite the imposition it placed upon her. And your original cut was amusing for what it was – a child blundering into a warzone and learning a valuable lesson just a little too late. But I enjoyed it even

more when it was hacked apart and turned into a rip-roaring yarn. It's so gratifying to see yourself save the galaxy from the most incompetent orks ever encountered. Some fascinating choices too. Do you remember being trapped in that cave, where Flight Commander Shard fended off an ork horde single-handed, while you lay around mortally injured? So interesting you played that for laughs. Didn't feel funny at the time.'

She hawked and spat, before taking another draw on the lho-stick.

'But thanks to you, everyone wanted a piece of the Imperium's greatest flying ace. A vid, or a soundbite. They're released every day now, so the masses can heed Flight Commander Shard's wisdom and bask in the glory of her countenance.'

She sniggered, then laughed, losing control of the sound, until it was little more than a manic wheeze. She coughed, sucking on the lho-stick as she regained her composure.

I glanced at the commissar. His face still bore that hint of disdain. He carried it like a symbol of office.

Finally she exhaled, the hololithic smoke obscuring her face. When she spoke again there was a hiss of distortion, but I could just pick out her words.

'I made a mistake,' she said. *'A bad one. Rile's fault for throwing me into that maelstrom. But I did something I shouldn't have and… Well, it's all over now, just a matter of time. For me, and perhaps the whole family. I suppose that's a silver lining. What does Tobia always say? Something about it being better to martyr an innocent than risk a heretic going unpunished?'*

The commissar was glowering in the corner of my eye, but he said nothing.

'I suppose you will be safe. For once you made the smart choice in seeking obscurity. In fact, I have no idea if this correspondence will reach you, at least not before someone in my family decides to intercept it. You there, Josephine? Enjoying a bit of voyeurism?'

She had raised her head, addressing the room, as though the spectre of Josephine hovered all around her. Then she sighed, looking back to the cam.

'This is pointless anyway. Nothing can be done. It's a colossal waste of time.'

She hesitated. Or was it an error in the playback? It seemed the image jumped, as though the recording was interrupted, or tampered with. Of course, it was as likely my seer-skull was glitching. Her face flickered before rematerialising.

'I do not expect you to assist me. Frankly, I will think less of you if you do. But this is not a battle I know how to fight.'

She raised her head, staring straight into the cam. I kept expecting that trademark sneer to erupt across her face, or for her to break into laughter and begin mocking me for being drawn into her ruse.

Instead, she gave one last sigh. Her shoulders slumped. Suddenly she looked small, and very alone.

'I cannot do this by myself. I need your help. Please.'

The words were hurried, as though she were anxious to be done with them. And she was already rising from her seat, the image collapsing a moment later.

Silence.

I cleared my throat. 'How long–'

'I ask the questions, Simlex.'

His tone had softened a shade, now closer to rockcrete than adamantine. But he remained a commissar, someone who asked questions and, if the answers displeased him, responded with his pistol.

'Has my sister tried to contact you?'

'Flight Commander Shard? No. We have not spoken since the incident on Orbital Station Salus. We did not part on good terms. There was–'

'What about Josephine? You said you spoke to her?'

'On occasion. But she only sends moves.'

'Moves?'

'We play regicide.'

He stared at me. It was deeply unsettling, especially combined with the increasingly oppressive silence.

'It's a strategy game,' I said, ploughing on. 'Various pieces on the board represent forces deployed–'

'I understand the rules of regicide.' He frowned, clasping his hands behind his back and striding to the centre of my cubicle. It struck me this was most likely a part of his interrogation technique. It probably worked better in a larger room. As it was, he managed two steps before being blocked by the cabinet. He slowed, tilting his head, as though appraising the data-scraps pinned to the wall opposite, his back to me.

'Why do you think Lucille would contact you?'

'To goad me. Or cheat me somehow. But there was something about the way she spoke. She sounded… dejected? Despairing? I'm not sure – the quality of the recording makes it hard to be certain.'

'Indeed. I confess I've never heard her like that before.'

'I have. Once.'

He turned his head, glancing at me from over his shoulder. His face was shaded by his officer's cap, but his eyes shone, piercing and blue.

'Explain.'

'When we faced the ork airship on Bacchus. Before she plunged into battle, there was just a moment. It was like a mask slipped.'

'Disappointing,' he said. 'I detest it when a sibling loses their composure. Makes the family look weak.'

'In her defence, we were facing impossible odds and almost certain death.'

He gave the slightest of shrugs.

'In any event, in that moment she thought it was all over. Perhaps she considers the current circumstances similar?'

'Perhaps. She mentioned a mistake. That is the pertinent question – what calamity has she conjured this time?'

'Shot down the wrong target? Offended the wrong colonel?'

He grunted non-committally, gaze wandering the confines of my cubicle. I wondered if this too was an interrogation technique. Nothing in the room could actually warrant his attention.

'Have you been keeping abreast of my sister's misadventures?'

'Not intentionally. But her face keeps appearing on my screen. Her vid clips seem to be everywhere.'

'Yes. The citizens adore her for some reason. She has become a symbol to the unwashed masses. At least, that is the assessment of the scribes and clerks who monitor such matters. Her pict screenings correlate with increases in productivity, recruitment, and, allegedly, witch burnings.'

He didn't sound entirely convinced.

'All from one rotten pict?'

'No. That was the start, but now clips are released daily. Snippets to be shoved in between psalms and reports. It aids morale, apparently. But she lacks the discipline needed for the role, and her new propagandist doesn't understand this. You cannot be a hero of the Imperium and be beloved by its citizens.'

'With respect, sir, aren't there many such heroes? Sanguinius, the Great Angel, who gave his life for the God-Emperor? Old Man Yarrick, Hero of Hades Hive? Lord Commander Solar Macharius, the–'

'Such legends are remembered for their deeds, not who they were. I'm sure my sister will one day make an adequate martyr. But whilst she still lives, she can falter. And as soon as she does they will turn on her.'

'The citizens?'

'Perhaps. Though I would assume those overseeing the enterprise will intervene before that happens. It takes little to turn a living asset into a dead one.'

'You think they would kill her?'

As soon as I spoke, I realised the foolishness of the question. Of course they would kill her. Advancement within the Imperium involved ascending a ladder built from the bones of those betrayed along the way.

The commissar merely nodded. 'Still,' he said, 'it need not come to that. If we move quickly, it might be possible to resolve the situation before it becomes a catastrophe. That is why you will accompany me to Deighton.'

It was said so casually, the matter already decided.

'I have my duties here,' I said, but he dismissed this with a wave of his hand.

'Inconsequential. You are hereby seconded to my service. My sister has reached out to you and that will be our opening, for she and I are not on the best of terms. When she confides in you, the information will be relayed to me. I can then decide on the proper course of action.'

'And if I prefer to remain where I am?'

I was gratified by his look of shock. He blinked, turning those ice-blue eyes on me.

'It was not a request.'

'I understand that. But I have responsibilities.'

'You prefer to stay?' he said, glancing around the room. 'Tending to data-scraps? Rotting in seclusion? That is your preference?'

'If I learnt one thing from your sister, it is that preferences are immaterial. I have been assigned a task, and my duty is to perform it. With respect, you are not my taskmaster.'

He stared at me.

'Your taskmaster understands his duty. And refusal to volunteer will be considered an act of defiance against the Imperium. I believe you know the penalty for that.'

'So I either accompany you, or face disgrace and execution?'

He nodded.

'May I be permitted a moment to consider the options?'

I'm surprised I got the words out, and that my voice remained level. I thought perhaps he would strike me, or retrieve his pistol and be done with it.

Instead he sighed, rubbing his eyes with thumb and forefinger.

'By the Throne, what is wrong with you? When last in my service, your performance was quite tolerable. Has isolation broken you so much that you seek death?'

'No. But I swore I was done with your family. And I like to keep my word.'

He stared at me as I spoke, perhaps reassessing me.

'What about my sister? She asked for your help.'

'She also said there was nothing I could do.'

'But still she asked for you. Not me, nor a more charitable member of the family like Rile or Josephine. You.'

He loomed over me, confined as I was to the chair. I found I had to look away, but he lowered himself onto his haunches, until his face was inches from mine.

'Do you want her dead?' he asked softly. 'Would that bring you joy? I understand the sentiment. I know better than most how damnable my sister can be, the ruin she leaves in her wake. But I have a hardened soul. Could you live with yourself if you did nothing? If her life was forfeit?'

'Her life and her death are not my business.'

'You do not lie well. Try again.'

'I... think perhaps I could live with myself. But that does not mean I wish her death.'

'Then I suggest you accompany me, Simlex. For my intention is to uncover her sins. And if they prove as egregious as she suggests, then I will be forced to carry out my duty.'

He did not need to flash his holster for me to take his meaning.

'But you,' he continued, 'you are not a stupid man, only naive. Perhaps you can find another solution. One that does not require me to dirty my hands or sully my family's legacy. Sororicide leaves a rather sour taste in the mouth.'

'You task me with finding a way of protecting your sister from dying at your hands?'

He smiled. But his eyes were cold.

'If you like. And if you succeed, I may be able to do something in return. Arrange for your rank to be reinstated. Or have you assigned somewhere a little more pleasant. Perhaps with a window, or even a habitable outdoors. If you help me.'

I met his gaze. His eyes remained cold, but I found no guile behind them. He was not a man gifted at deception. He offered his hand, and I realised it might represent my final chance for a life beyond the cubicle.

Slowly, I reached for his hand. But he seized mine, dragging me to my feet. My ruined leg spasmed, but he held me upright.

'A wise decision, Scribe Simlex. I trust neither of us will live to regret it.'

I nodded, gaze lingering on his holstered pistol.

CHAPTER THREE

'Damn their numbers and damn the odds. I am Lucille von Shard! I have never met my match! Never lost a duel! And never been shot down! When I fly, the God-Emperor flies with me!'

There was murmured approval, and even a smattering of applause from the crowd of indentured workers and soldiers awaiting deployment. They stood enthralled, while I sat incandescent. My stool had been provided by Commissar Shard, and I suppose I should have been grateful he had made allowances for my injury. But he had also selected our viewing material. The port's vast holoscreen, usually displaying shipping manifestos and departure times, was now dedicated to an impromptu screening of the cinema-pict masterpiece *The Glorious Martyrdom of the 2208th*.

Or just *The 2208*, as it had apparently been renamed. Presumably someone had considered my original title long-winded.

On the screen, pict-Shard addressed assorted officers and serfs.

None to my knowledge had served on Bacchus, the alleged setting for this piece of theatre. One bore a sweeping moustache reminiscent of Flight Commander Gradeolous. But I was unsure of the likeness, as the last time I had seen the commander his severed head was being paraded by orkish runts, his whiskers dishevelled and soaked with blood. Whenever I tried to picture his face, this was the only image I could summon.

Onscreen, an unremarkable officer raised his hand.

'But Flight Commander Shard, the treacherous orks are now equipped with our very aircraft!'

'Yes, and it is only by pilfering the superior technology of the Imperium that they stand any chance of opposing us. It was those damned agricultural workers' fault. If only they had been more pious and less curious, this whole sorry mess would already be over.'

The image cut to the various nodding officers. All were, frankly, far too good-looking to be serving on the front lines. And too clean as well; my recollection of Bacchus was that it was one vast quagmire infested with choking vines and insects large enough to vivisect a soldier and use their skin and organs for decor.

'But what can we do?' one bright-eyed young officer asked. *'With our forces depleted we cannot stop the ork threat.'*

Shard backhanded him savagely across the face. The audience winced, I along with them. It did not appear she had pulled the blow. It was the first shot I had found convincing.

'No more defeatist talk,' she warned. *'No matter the odds, humanity will always triumph. Because we are lifted by the God-Emperor's light. Now, who will fly with me?'*

She turned with that last remark, staring into the lens as though addressing the viewer. I rolled my eyes, but the crowd roared their approval, slapping their hands together in rapture.

I shuffled on my stool. I'd have preferred to stand and stretch my good leg, ideally somewhere far from the screening. But

Commissar Shard had an escort of elite Tempestus Scions, and a pair of them were stationed either side of me. I hadn't exactly been instructed to remain in my seat, but the Scions possessed a remarkable gift for conveying expectations with body language alone. I was to sit and I was to watch. Evidently, my new overseer had a lesson to impart. Or punishment to inflict. In either case, we were thirty agonising minutes into the farce, and it was hard to decide what I found more depressing – the deluge of falsehoods, or the way the audience mindlessly gorged upon them.

'But sir, we do not have enough craft. I cannot repair them all in time.'

The statement came from a tall man of proud bearing and impressive jawline, clad in a mechanical's uniform. His resemblance to the real Flight Sergeant Plient was remarkable, but only as far as they bore absolutely no similarities whatsoever.

Shard turned to him, rolling up her sleeve.

'Maybe not alone, Plient, but if we all pitch in, there is nothing we cannot overcome in His name!'

I was unable to contain a snort of derision, but it was buried by the crowd's fervour. They appreciated an officer willing to get their hands dirty, however fictitiously. A series of rapid cuts followed, set to Stadonise's Twenty-Third Symphony, as the impossible task was overcome through graft and editing. The repair crew were not only able to refurbish the craft, but also to provide a quick respray and arrange them in the shape of an aquila. It was an effective if cliched visual, though it somewhat undermined the urgency of the situation.

Then suddenly we were airborne.

And I was there again.

The burnt-orange waters, the sky deadened by the mists rising from the quagmire beneath. Vines, stretching the length of the planet and infested with rotting fruit. The footage was a jumble, the images hastily spliced and assembled with little thought. The light shifted a dozen times during that first leg of their journey. But the crowd did not see it, and I did not care.

This was my pict. The other shots were lazy additions inserted into the narrative. But these moments were mine. My magnum opus. My supposed masterpiece, now gutted, its entrails used to plug gaps in a farcical tale.

Punishment, I decided. The viewing had to be a punishment.

The crowd roared as the explosions came, the planes soaring into battle against the orks. The light was awful, and it took me a moment to realise the original footage comprised night shots. Someone had tried to adjust the exposure, but the cogitator had been unable to detect true colour. Everything was so garish. Not a surprise; the light on Bacchus had a heavy quality. To even–

'Scribe Simlex? The *Traderi* has been loaded onto the *Ilrepuet* and is ready for departure.'

Beside me, Tempestor Rosln had leant in, whispering in my ear.

I nodded, rising awkwardly as I shifted my weight to my cane and my escort collected the stool. My injury had felt so much less of a limitation inside my cell.

I expected Rosln to lead the way, but when I turned I found she was intent on the pict screen. A swarm of orks were surging forward, riding airboats powered by massive fans. They were poised to annihilate a squad of Tempestus Scions when a Valkyrie thundered into their flank, its turbofans and a barrage of missiles scattering the orks.

It was the first mission I had accompanied, the Scions facing an ork raiding force. I could almost smell the foetid waters, the xenos' terrifying battle cries still echoing–

'Scribe Simlex?'

'Hmm?' I frowned, turning to find Rosln staring at me 'Oh. My apologies, Tempestor. I was caught in the moment.'

'I understand, sir.'

There was a note in her voice. Almost inaudible, but I was acquainted with the Scions' reserve. It was not fear so much as recognition. Or even empathy, assuming they still possessed such emotions.

As we turned away, her gaze lingered, just a fraction, on the pict screen.

Commissar Shard's personal transport was an oversized Aquila lander dubbed the *Traderi*. It now nestled inside the transport hold of the *Ilrepuet*, the Gothic-class cruiser that would shuttle us to Deighton. Whatever its original purpose, the commissar had refitted the *Traderi* to match his own specifications. It had a cabin, a small communal space, and little else.

'This will be our base of operations. You'll be granted limited right of access,' the commissar told me, as the Scions loaded our supplies. There was a surprising volume of concealed storage within the craft, most hidden behind false wall panels.

'The prior owner was a smuggler,' he said, as though reading my thoughts. 'I repurposed his vessel.'

'I see. It suits your needs then?'

'Not particularly. The *Traderi* is slow and cramped. But my needs are modest, so why squander the Imperium's resources? Better to be frugal and take from those who have turned from the God-Emperor's light. Are you recording this?'

'I'm sorry?'

'Are you recording?' he asked again, nodding to Iwazar, who was currently inspecting the shuttle. Perhaps it too was struggling to discern how the commissar, five Scions, and I would fit within the space.

'I would not record without permission.'

'Well begin at once,' the commissar replied. 'Officially, you are here as my personal propagandist, capturing footage for my forthcoming biopict. You should look to preserve my every utterance for posterity.'

'I thought that only necessary once we had arrived on Deighton?'

'It would be worth getting into practice. Those in my service are trustworthy, but we do not know my sister's present circumstances. She has no doubt made enemies, and possibly even allies. To move amongst them you require justification, and my patronage will provide some protection and allowances.'

'I understand,' I said, summoning Iwazar. But it was reluctant, tarrying around the shuttle, investigating the tail fin and observation dome. The commissar did not seem concerned, already making for the lowered loading bay. I followed, cane clicking against the railings as I struggled to keep pace.

He slowed, sighing. 'Simlex, what in Terra's name did you do to your leg? How do you injure it in a cubicle?'

'Bacchus, sir. I was injured and the wound became infected.'

'I assume the infection is resolved?'

'Yes, sir. The diseased tissue was cut away. But as it healed, the muscles twisted. They no longer function as they should.'

He nodded. Technically it was a war wound, and thus difficult to hold against me.

'You should get it fixed. Or replaced,' he said as we stepped into the loading bay.

'I lack the means to do either.'

'Well, just try not to fall behind. Now, my cabin is to the rear. You are forbidden to enter it, of course, and will bunk in with the Scions. I trust that will not be an issue.'

My face must have betrayed me. He frowned.

'You object to these arrangements? Expect your own quarters?'

'No. I merely do not… I am not a quiet sleeper.'

'Simlex, these are humanity's finest soldiers. They have endured terrors beyond anything you can imagine. I am confident they can tolerate snoring.'

I nodded, unsure what else to say. Satisfied, he engaged the control panel, and with a whine of servos the loading bay began to ascend into the shuttle.

I glanced at the commissar. He was staring at my good leg. I followed his gaze and found my foot was shaking.

'Are you nervous, Simlex?' he asked, as I tried to steady myself.

'Forgive me, sir. I do not like warp travel.'

'No? I do not recall such reservations the last time we worked together.'

'It is a more recent complaint. I will be fine.'

'Yes, you will be,' he said, his tone one of command, not reassurance.

The bay doors slid open. We stepped through, entering a modest communal space. There was a table, chairs that had been stacked and secured, and sufficient facilities to prepare a hot drink or reheat a meal. But there was no decor, no playing cards or vid facilities. No lho-stick butts. No true evidence of actual human habitation.

The commissar unclipped a panel from the wall and began rummaging within.

'Here,' he said, handing me a data-slate. 'My subordinates have uploaded files relating to the conflict on Deighton. I would suggest you review them en route, though I fear the status quo will have changed significantly by the time we arrive.'

'Do you know the length of our journey?'

'If the God-Emperor favours us, mere weeks.'

I nodded. There was no need to elaborate. If the God-Emperor did not favour us, there was a good chance we would never arrive at all.

'I am concerned about what we will find on arrival,' the

commissar continued, slamming the panel shut. 'I have only perused the initial reports, but if they are any indication of how the war is being conducted, then my sister's failings might just be one of many disasters to resolve.'

'You think the war goes badly?'

'On the contrary – it goes extraordinarily well. At least, if one is foolish enough to believe the propaganda reels.'

CHAPTER FOUR

We flew towards the sun, the waters of Bacchus bloodied by its light.

I piloted a Lightning, though how I knew this was difficult to say. My fingers danced across the controls with surprising ease, though I could not have told you what I was doing. Beside me, on either flank, identical craft flew. Neither pilot wore their pressure helm, and while I recognised their smiles, I could not summon their names.

There were scores of us. This I also knew.

We tightened our formation as the sun bent towards the brackish waters. I glanced right. The pilot was more than familiar. I recognised him, from his waxed whiskers to his self-satisfied smirk. But still I could not recall who he was.

The sky was almost dark now, the sun dissolving into the mist arising from the swamp, shadows encroaching on all sides. We tightened our formation till our wings almost touched, but I could no longer see anything besides the aircraft.

I was scared now, for I knew what was coming. I felt it, even before the hairs pricked on my forearms. Even before the throbbing in my temple. But, like the pilots' names, the nature of the threat eluded me. And I was penned in and could not turn back.

My mouth tasted of copper.

We had to break, pull back before it was too late. I scrabbled for the vox, but I no longer knew how to fly the craft. I glanced left, thumping my fist against the cockpit, and was unsurprised to find a grinning skull staring back at me.

As if on cue, emerald lightning tore through us, a dozen planes consumed in moments. But the survivors tightened, plugging the gaps. Holding me in place with no room to manoeuvre.

I knew their names now. Gradeolous, his severed head hanging loose on his neck. Nocter, his skin greyed and withered. Jaymes, his flesh sloughing from his bones as the fungal blight ate away at him. He had died in the medi-unit, one of the final casualties of the offensive. But still he flew with us.

Another flash tore through the squadron, a score more planes consumed by its light. And the sky was no longer black, the clouds tinted a sickly emerald.

The Green Storm had found us.

I might have fled then, chanced seizing the flight stick and surrendering to the God-Emperor's grace. But I no longer had the controls, instead relegated to the rear of a different craft, the tail fin before me. The path behind us was clear. We could go back. We could flee before it found us.

I could not find the vox but, on turning, discovered that all that separated me from the cockpit was a bundle of orange fabric, hung like a curtain. I drew it back, and there was Shard, her chair swivelled, feet somehow resting on the console.

I tried to scream, but something was pressing on my mouth, and all I managed was a strangled cry. Through the windscreen,

I saw that both sky and swamp had vanished, supplanted by a colossal edifice of brass and steel, obscured by the greenish smog billowing from its chimney. Verdant lightning arced lazily across its copper-plated hull, bright enough to tint the cockpit green.

Shard leant back in her seat, hand cupped behind her head. She glanced at me, frowning, confused by my distress.

She smiled, even as the light grew blinding.

'Chin up, propagandist. We're almost free.'

The light surged, and darkness swallowed us, the plane hurtling into its endless gullet. And I was screaming, or trying to, except a hand clamped my mouth shut. I thrashed, but Tempestor Rosln bore down on me, her forearm pressed to my chest.

'Dream! It was a dream,' she said. 'Breathe. Calm and slow. Just a dream.'

She released her grip, my breath erupting like the last gasps of a dying animal.

'Slow. Hold the breath down and count to five. Then release. Again.'

I caught my breath, slowing it, my heart still hammering against my ribs. I was in the *Traderi*, stretched out in the lower bunk, Rosln occupying the one above. Two more were slung on the opposite wall, their occupants either sound asleep or courteous enough to feign slumber.

'That's good,' Rosln repeated. 'Keep breathing. Now, what was the dream?'

'It was nothing. I–'

'What was the dream?' she repeated. There was an edge to her voice. Her eyes were hard, and her other hand was now tucked behind her back.

'Bacchus,' I said simply. 'I was flying over Bacchus. With the fighters. But they all died. We all died.'

She looked at me, though I could discern little from her expression.

'Bacchus,' she repeated. 'A foul and vile world.'

'Agreed,' I said as she released her grip. I thought I heard the faint rasp of a blade being sheathed before her right hand emerged from behind her back.

'I am sorry,' I said. 'Sometimes I have dreams.'

'It's not uncommon. I can't imagine it was an easy experience for a civilian.'

'It's fine. I'm fine. Usually.'

She nodded, though I'm not sure my lie convinced her. But when she spoke again, the edge had left her voice.

'Bad dreams are not uncommon when passing through the warp. Try and put it from your mind.'

She then rose, clambering nimbly into the bunk above and settling herself.

I tried to do likewise. But when I closed my eyes, all I saw were their faces.

'Tempestor Rosln?'

'Yes?'

'Did you serve on Bacchus?'

There was a moment's silence before she replied.

'You remember your first excursion into the swamps?' she asked.

'Yes.'

'That was my squad.'

'I'm sorry. I did not recognise you. I'm not sure I saw your face.'

'I take no offence. At the time I considered you a burden, but you proved yourself during that mission. You went beyond your station. You have my thanks.'

'And you mine. Are the other Scions also veterans of Bacchus?'

'No. We are from separate squads.'

'I don't understand.'

'We were the survivors. All that is left.'

'...I'm sorry. It must have been hard losing–'

'I would prefer to sleep now. I have duties in the morn.'

'Yes, of course. Goodnight.'

Commissar Shard was already seated when I entered the communal space, his data-slate laid upon a rather cluttered table.

He looked up, raising an eyebrow.

'Forgive me,' I said. 'I had trouble sleeping. I did not wish to disturb anyone.'

'Not a problem. By all means join me,' he replied, gesturing to the stacked chairs. 'I understand. Sleep always feels like the enemy when there is so much to be done. Still, if it's any consolation, I had a personal audience with our captain, and she informed me that despite grumblings from the voidsmen, we are ahead of schedule.'

I nodded, staring at him. I had not realised he was out of uniform, for he still wore his commissar's hat. But beneath was a loose-fitted nightgown of midnight blue, the collar emblazoned with the von Shard crest. A black griffin.

He lowered his head again as I struggled with the chairs, finally dragging one clear and setting it at the rather cluttered table. Files and scrolls were stacked in seemingly arbitrary piles, as though the commissar was constructing a minuscule tabletop fortress. There was a small ceramic cup and matching jug by his elbow. Beside them rested his holstered pistol.

I took my seat opposite, engaging my data-slate. I had already previewed the files a dozen times. There was little to absorb. We were to be assigned to the Láech – a regiment of the Astra Militarum renowned for their expertise in close-quarters firefights.

They were active in a desert region of Deighton, close to the equator, and were supported by an Aeronautica division formerly known as the Nighthawks, but apparently rechristened 'Shard's Daggers'. There were also reams of strategic, tactical and logistical data, all redacted to the point of worthlessness.

From the edge of my vision, I saw the commissar retrieve his cup, then, finding it empty, reach for the jug instead.

He glanced up. I feigned interest in my data-slate.

He rose, turning and rummaging through a concealed cupboard. A second cup, identical to the first, was placed on the table.

'Talgerius tea,' he said, filling both. 'I permit few vices. This is one of them.'

His voice had changed. I could not say it had grown soft, any more than a collapsing star could be described as small. But a little of the sharpness had gone, at least for now.

He handed me a cup. Whatever ceramic it was composed of was parchment thin, and probably part of a set. I handled it very carefully.

The liquid within smelled enticing enough: citric, with just a hint of spice. But when I took a sip, the flavour was disappointing – pleasant, but lacking the promise offered by the aroma. Still, I thanked him.

He nodded, magnanimous, before returning to his data-slate. I did likewise, but I felt his gaze flicker back to me. Perhaps he desired conversation, for the Scions were as taciturn as the table itself.

'Simlex?'

I raised my head. He was no longer looking at me, his gaze fixed upon a sheet of parchment.

'Yes, commissar?'

'What do you know of siege tactics?'

'Precious little, beyond the obvious. You may either attempt to breach the fortress or starve the defenders by cutting off their supplies.'

'An uninspired but accurate answer,' he observed, sipping his tea. 'Would you wager a guess as to the requirements of the former?'

'Well, one would need either a weapon that could penetrate the walls, or sufficient forces to overwhelm them.'

'Correct again. And that's what makes this whole thing so damnable.'

'Sir?'

He placed his data-slate on the side table, rotating it so I had a clear view.

'Industrialisation is focused on the data-fortresses and connecting infrastructure. And the majority of that is subterranean. Beyond that lies desert and little of note.'

I nodded, intent on the report. Unlike my own files it had not been redacted, and I could see our forces clustered around key points, the cartographer making little effort to catalogue the expanses between.

'Any observations?' he asked.

'I'm surprised we fight on so many fronts.'

'As am I. Besieging a fortress merely requires sufficient troops to encircle it. But capturing it is a different story. One paid in blood and sacrifice.'

'Forgive me, sir, but would that not be the Imperium's preferred way of waging war?'

'Yes. But sometimes we are so anxious to prove our piety that we squander lives for zero gain. As it stands, I do not see how the forces deployed have any hope of breaching those walls. And maintaining a siege expends labour and resources, as well as acting as a breeding ground for insubordination and heresy.

I fear by the time we arrive, the situation may have deteriorated significantly.'

He spoke with utter conviction, as though every word were a proclamation of fact, impossible to deny or refute. I had never met a commissar who did not project authority, but he radiated complete certainty.

'The trouble is, Simlex, half the officers are more interested in advancing their own careers than securing victory. And that's before we get to the politicians and the bureaucrats. And the bloody propagandists.'

He caught my expression, and raised a placating hand.

'Not you, Simlex. Your replacement. The limited files I have at my disposal apportion them with significant credit for our scant successes.'

The barest hint of bile lingered behind the words.

'Still,' he continued, 'their ascent will assist in perpetuating our subterfuge.'

'It will?' I asked.

'Our cover will be that I wish you to be mentored by them, to sharpen your skills for my forthcoming biopict. That will provide an explanation for why you do not always accompany me, and an excuse for you to get close to my sister. Once you uncover her crimes, I will take the necessary steps to preserve our family's good name.'

His tone was neutral. Almost pointedly so. But the holstered pistol never left his side.

CHAPTER FIVE

'Flight Commander Shard! The Green Storm draws near!'

Shard glanced up from the grainy holo-image, face adorned with a scowl.

'How long until we are refuelled, Plient?'

'With the current set-up? At least a couple more hours, sir,' the counterfeit Plient replied. I had no idea what accent he was feigning. I suspected neither did he, besides trying to sound like he hadn't been educated at a Schola Progenium academy.

I sipped my recaff. It tasted like engine tar and was so thick that stirring it sometimes bent the spoon. But by the Throne it was potent. Rosln brewed it by somehow bypassing the dispenser's regulators. It had become the high point of my day, and it seemed a shame to waste the beverage enduring such a gutter vid. But I had long exhausted the non-censored files provided by the commissar, and my attempts at improving my stamina by taking modest walks around the hangar had been curtailed due to disturbances on the *Ilrepuet*'s lower decks. I was now confined to quarters, and this was the only entertainment I had. Assuming that was the appropriate word.

The holo-Shard nodded, her expression so grave that I momentarily wondered if the attackers had breached the drinks cabinet.

'Well, if the Storm is at our gates, it would be rude to keep it waiting,' she said. *'We launch in five. I will face the Storm. Alone.'*

I sighed. She had never offered to sacrifice herself. Rather, she had tricked me into acting as her accomplice in stealing a plane, launching an ill-conceived solo attack against the mysterious Green Storm, and almost immediately being shot down. She would have been court-martialled, except by that point the regiment was almost wiped out.

'But sir, it's a suicide mission!' counterfeit Plient said, blinking back tears. *'Besides, if you fly now, you won't have enough fuel to get back!'*

'I don't intend to get back. I only need to slow it down enough to grant our forces time to withdraw and rally.'

'Let me fly with you, sir!'

'One day, Plient.' She smiled, somehow reaching down and ruffling his hair, despite appearing a foot shorter than him in the prior scene. *'But you would last mere moments out there. I'm the only one who has the slightest chance.'*

'You can't do it alone, sir!'

She glanced at him, silhouette framed by the dusk's light. It was a pretty shot, though I could have sworn that moments earlier it had been midday.

'You are right, Plient, but I am never alone. He flies with me.'

Sanctimonious sentiment. The whole piece reeked of it. Except perhaps Shard, though even then I was unsure. I'd initially thought her portrayal a cruel mockery of the whole sordid enterprise, but perhaps I was projecting my own distaste. Perhaps she believed her lies. A bad actor, but not necessarily one acting in bad faith.

Her Lightning was airborne when the image suddenly flickered.

It was not the first time. Iwazar kept malfunctioning, the projection interrupted by random files buried in its data-store. But this time the *Traderi*'s lights also faded. Just for a moment.

I heard a noise from the commissar's cabin, even as one of the Scions rose from his bunk. Their rampant stoicism made it difficult to discern anything from his expression, but to me he looked unsure. Concerned even.

Shard's image flickered back into life, though the colour was off. Too red and too dark. It took me a moment to realise it was not the recording. Something was off about the shuttle's interior lumens too.

The commissar lurched into the room, buttoning his greatcoat and straightening his peaked cap.

'What in the Throne's name is going on?' he asked, seemingly addressing the galaxy in general before pinning his gaze on the risen Scion.

'Unknown, sir.'

'Where are the rest of the squad?'

'Rosln is monitoring the cargo. Brice is conducting reconnaissance. The others are stationed outside the bulkhead in case of a breach.'

Commissar Shard pinched the bridge of his nose between his fingers. His face was stark, the shadows cutting too deep.

'How is the cargo?'

'Unchanged, sir.'

'No... incidents?'

'Not with the cargo, sir. But Brice heard whispering amongst the voidsmen. They say the warp is restless, that something unnatural draws close.'

'In my experience they are always prattling about unnatural somethings and ominous whatevers,' the commissar muttered.

'Still, this sort of insurrection is best resolved sharply, before it escalates.'

He buckled his scabbard into place as he spoke.

The Scion cleared his throat. 'Sir, the *Ilrepuet*'s captain has advised all to remain–'

'I will speak to the captain once the matter is resolved,' he replied, gaze flickering to me. 'Simlex! Remain here.'

'You do not wish me to record the battle?'

'Why would I want footage of us brawling with indentured workers?' he snapped. 'Rosln will remain behind to ensure the *Traderi* is secure. She is attending to a private matter in my quarters. Do not disturb her unless ordered. Even then, shout through the door.'

With that they departed, leaving me in the sole company of the flickering holo-image. I closed it, glancing at the door and wondering what I should do. Did Tempestor Rosln even know the commissar had left?

I stared at the exit leading to his quarters, which lay in the deepest recesses of the ship. I had never seen their interior.

Beside me, Iwazar clicked, something whirring beneath its armoured plating. An image materialised. A cockpit. My hands clutching the tail-gun, even as green lightning struck the aircraft, erasing the plane's rear section. The light arced once more, emerald energies consuming the vessel until the world was torn away, leaving only darkness and pain and my screams forever–

'Off!' I snapped, willing the projection to cease. Iwazar twitched, before crashing abruptly to the floor. But the after-image lingered, just for a moment, despite the fallen projector. Was it a hallucination? A visual effect conjured by the dangers of warp travel? I had heard whispers between the Scions, concerned by the morale of the *Ilrepuet*'s crew. I had not paid them much heed until now.

I was attempting to conduct diagnostics on the projector when I heard a choked scream coming from the rear cabin.

I bent to the door. There was no mistaking the cries. It did not sound like Rosln, though I could not tell if the voice was male or female. Or human for that matter; it seemed to resonate inside my skull.

'Tempestor?' I said, pressing my ear to the door. It felt uncomfortably warm.

Nothing. Would she even hear me over the din?

'Tempestor?!' I repeated, louder this time.

'Get the commissar! Now!'

The door shook at the force of her voice.

'He is unavailable. They all are. There was a–'

'I cannot hear you! Speak up!'

'There is no one else!'

'…Get in here!'

I stared helplessly at the keypad lock. 'I need the code!'

Her reply was strangled. 'Thirty. Seventeen. Forty-Five. Alpha.'

I punched in the keys, forcing it open and stumbling into the room. The commissar's bed lay to my right, but I paid it no heed, for to my left was a concealed chamber, its door flung open. Within, a figure was suspended vertically, and connected to a terrifyingly complex set of machinery, multiple tubes and wires burrowed into the captive's flesh. Their left wrist was secured by a restraint, but the right, despite the seeming frailty of the limb, had somehow broken a steel cuff, and was currently grappling with Tempestor Rosln. The prisoner's head was slumped forward, and he would have appeared unconscious were it not for the wailing emanating from his throat and his thrashing arm.

Rosln's head snapped round to me, even as her hands clasped

the captive's wrist, unable to overpower him. She met my gaze, before glancing down to the spilled medi-kit at her feet.

'Injector! The green one!'

I fumbled for the device, locating it and tearing off the safety cap. I made to pass it to her, but the prisoner's hand was now clamped about her throat. Her eyes darted towards his exposed arm.

'Use it,' she hissed.

I hesitated, before plunging the injector into the exposed flesh. The prisoner shuddered, his grip loosening, Roslyn retreating out of arm's reach, pistol still holstered.

I had expected the figure to slump immediately, overcome by the injector's payload, but he was still twitching, a low murmur sounding from his throat. Rosln frowned, her gaze never leaving him even as she addressed me.

'Where is the commissar?'

'He left to… to do whatever it is that needs doing.'

She glanced up from the thrashing prisoner, perhaps assessing her forces. 'How long ago?'

'Minutes. It sounded as though there is an insurrection below decks?'

'Drassic!'

The sound came from the prisoner. His head had snapped up, gaze meeting Rosln's, though his eyes were white and lacking iris or pupil.

'Drassic!' he repeated, sounding almost plaintive, before his eyes rolled and he slumped again. Rosln seized his arm, once more securing it in the restraint.

'Drassic? Still?' she murmured, before engaging the vox. 'Commissar Shard?'

There was a hiss of static. Then his voice.

'Tempestor Rosln? I hope this is good news.'

'It's Drassic.'

There was a pause. *'Drassic is dead, Tempestor. Devoured by his own hubris and several warp serpents.'*

'Our cargo thinks otherwise. And it would explain the sudden unrest.'

'Then you know what needs to be done. Retrieve the device. Is Simlex there?'

'Yes. He assisted me.'

'Simlex, I would have preferred you remain ignorant of this matter, but there is no time. You are tasked with protecting our cargo.'

It took me a moment to take his meaning. The laspistol Rosln placed in my hand certainly helped.

'Now listen carefully, for your life and soul may depend on it. The cargo is of vital importance.'

'You think he will be attacked?'

'Possibly. But the greater risk is from him. Warp travel can have some unpleasant effects on his kind. If he loses control, it could potentially threaten the entire ship. Before that happens you need to stop him. You understand?'

'I… Yes. But how will I know?'

'Hard to say. If you see odd lights, or taste colours, or feel like your reflection is plotting against you, then there is no immediate cause for concern. If the walls start bleeding for more than a minute or so, then you must do what is necessary.'

I glanced round to Rosln. She had extracted something from the storage. It looked spherical, though I could see little else as she quickly tucked it into a sack. She nodded once and was gone, leaving the twitching prisoner under my stewardship.

My gaze fell to the pistol.

I had never taken a life. At least, not with a weapon. But as I sat there in the dark, I wondered if that made my hands clean. How many had enlisted because of my picts? Perhaps some died as heroes, their lives sacrificed to preserve humanity and the Imperium. Others probably spent their final moments crawling through mud, bleeding out whilst wishing they could return to a life of drudgery in some dull factorum. I would never know.

The captive seemed calmer. His breathing still sounded worryingly close to a moan, but he hung limp and still, the sedative having done its work. I tried the vox, just to ensure I could update the commissar if need be, but the line was dead.

Perhaps they were too.

The thought rose unbidden. I shook my head. No point speculating. All I could do was wait, sitting in the silence and the dark, suspended in a vessel within a vessel within the maelstrom of the warp, trying to shake the sense that something was always behind me.

Maybe an hour passed. It was hard to tell, locked away in the dark. But abruptly the vox spluttered into life.

'–receiving me, Simplex?'

'Commissar Shard? You're alive?'

'Evidently. Can the same be said for our cargo?'

'Yes. He remains unconscious.'

'I am relieved to hear that. Replacing him would have been inconvenient. I believe the matter is now resolved, though I need to speak with our captain. We should return shortly. Remain on guard.'

The line went dead.

I rose, pistol still in hand. It felt heavy, and I was relieved to be freed from its burden.

'Propagandist Simplex?'

The voice was like being plunged into ice water. I stiffened, turning.

The prisoner had raised his head, staring at me with those sightless eyes. In turn I raised the shaking pistol, but hesitated.

I could see no malice in his lined face. Only a terrible sadness. Tears stained his cheeks.

I lowered the weapon. Was he injured? I dared not approach too close; I had seen how easily he broke those restraints. But his head was lolling, he seemed about to pass out again.

Then he spoke one final time.

'Witness her fall. Mourn her death. Seek no more.'

CHAPTER SIX

'Propagandist Simlex?'

'Yes?'

'Why are you awake?'

'I cannot sleep. Forgive me, I thought I was being quiet.'

'You were. Audibly so. At least breathe occasionally.'

'My apologies.'

'If it helps, we have almost concluded our voyage. Commissar Shard has advised it's only a few sleep-cycles more. Then only another day or so for the *Traderi* to reach Deighton.'

'Thank you. I will be relieved when we arrive.'

'You sound unsettled.'

'It was our… cargo. His presence is unsettling.'

'They have that effect. Ignore it.'

I paused. 'May I ask a question?'

'You may ask as many as you wish. My answers are my own.'

'Who was Drassic?'

'I cannot say anything beyond his death serves the Imperium.'

'Will he pose an ongoing threat? Should I be vigilant?'

'Drassic has been eliminated. For good this time. And you should always be vigilant.'

'How close did we come to dying today?'

She was silent for a moment. I thought perhaps our conversation was done.

'That is a difficult question. The forces opposing us were modest – I faced worse odds on Bacchus. But when a vessel traverses the warp, any risk is magnified. There are safeguards and processes, but here an individual can wield power well beyond their station. All it takes is an indentured worker being in the wrong place or making the wrong choice, and it could doom us all. The risk was small, but the consequences potentially dire. If that helps?'

'Not overly. I find myself dwelling on the thought that the lowliest individual on this vessel has the potential to kill everybody aboard.'

'There is little you can do about that. Unless the lowly individual is you?'

'Not to my knowledge.'

'Let me know as soon as that changes.'

I smiled. She almost sounded as if she were joking.

'One final question?'

'Go ahead.'

'Do you know what happened to Governor Dolos after she was deposed?'

'You should rewatch the pict. Then you would know that Governor Dolos gave her life defending the Winter Palace.'

'We both know that is untrue.'

'Perhaps. But that is the official account.'

'I heard she was taken into custody by an agent of Inquisitor Atenbach. By an agent named Rile von Shard.'

'Goodnight, Simlex.'

CHAPTER SEVEN

'We are delaying a full assault in favour of a bombardment of *picts*?'

Commissar Shard addressed the flickering holo-image of Colonel Surling. It was difficult to discern the colonel's expression, partly because I had been forced to compress the hololith to fit within the confines of the *Traderi*'s communal space. It left him looking flattened, his face occasionally expanding to twice its normal width. The rest of the war council were barely visible – renowned warriors and advisors reduced to background shades.

The commissar nevertheless made a point of eyeballing them. Perhaps it registered, for I assume they had access to a superior holo-projector. Theoretically so did we, for the captain of the *Ilrepuet* would have suitable facilities. But the commissar had preferred using the *Traderi* to relay the signal, with Iwazar acting as projector. Perhaps his conversation with her had not been well received.

'Servants of the Imperium,' he continued, 'I remind you that we are custodians of the God-Emperor's armies, charged with bringing Deighton back into His light. Not just for Him, I might add, but for all those who now dwell in darkness. Each day that passes without the rebellion being crushed means more souls are lost to Him. This cannot be permitted.'

He paused, glaring at the indistinct shapes.

'Frankly, when I received this assignment, I was disappointed, expecting that the conflict would have concluded long before I made orbit around Deighton. Yet now I have arrived, my chainsword already bloodied in transit, and I find you have made zero progress. Not a single data-fortress has been reclaimed. I have known worlds burn quicker.'

'Burning the world is exactly what we should do.'

The voice came from one of the background shades. I adjusted the focus, the grim visage of Admiral Desora looming into view. She was clad in the uniform of a Naval officer, and had already interjected several times, speaking with the conviction of one who rarely felt the need to descend to a planet's surface, and therefore saw little issue if said surface was engulfed by a vast apocalyptic fireball.

Commissar Shard directed his gaze like a sniper aligning a laser scope.

'Is that right?' he asked. 'For, as I recall, those data-fortresses are repositories of information. Since the Great Rift carved the galaxy in half, we have been scrambling to recover. So much has been lost. Yet when we are in position to liberate a world only recently freed from warp storms, your first instinct is to destroy it? Each of those fortresses houses data stretching back millennia. Records of Imperial tithes. Regimental histories. The God-Emperor alone knows what else. And you would see it burn?'

'Not all of it. But a small orbital bombardment on one of the

outlying data-fortresses would demonstrate the forthrightness of our mission. I would wager we would need only to obliterate a handful more before they surrendered.'

'And by doing so lose countless tithes?' the commissar asked. 'You could bankrupt worlds. Worse, you could create circumstances where planets are no longer tithed. And believe me, once such obligations are lost, the surplus wealth inevitably leads to decadence and corruption. We do not want a thirst for victory to drown other worlds in heresy. Let us keep the traitors confined to this planet.'

'Separatists.'

The image abruptly shifted, Iwazar focusing upon a new speaker. Wing Commander Prospherous, Lucille von Shard's commanding officer.

He gave no sign he recognised me, or even noticed me. But I lay in the commissar's shadow, perhaps indistinct and certainly of little importance. The commissar stared back at him, expression somewhere between uncomprehending and incandescent.

'Separatists?' he spat. 'What sort of mealy-mouthed gibberish is that? This planet has turned against the Imperium and should be denounced and treated accordingly.'

'Be that as it may, Deighton's rulers claim to be defending the planet from renegades seeking to steal the God-Emperor's secrets.'

'Renegades?'

'That would be us.'

'They falsely accuse us of heresy?'

'Perhaps. Or perhaps they genuinely don't know. Warp storms deprived this world of the Emperor's light for so long that generations have lived and died without contact with the wider Imperium. I gather our initial attempt to re-establish ties was less diplomatic than one would have hoped.'

There was a muttering behind him, too quiet to capture the

audio. Prospherous craned his head round, addressing the speaker.

'Whether they should have bowed down is immaterial – my point is merely that attempting to browbeat the isolated and paranoid into submission does not constitute effective diplomacy.'

Another inaudible mutter.

'If we had done as I advised, their resources might already serve the Imperium. Instead, we find ourselves locked in a war to the benefit of no one.'

There was an outburst at this, the words a garble. Evidently many there were appalled by this very concept. To them, war by its nature was beneficial. Providing you won. I thought the commissar would interject, but he folded his arms and stood very still. Waiting.

Slowly, the voices fell silent. Prospherous first, then the others one by one, until I could only hear Admiral Desora, who was once again advocating the deployment of a sustained orbital barrage. Whomever she addressed must have eventually directed her focus to the pict screen and the commissar's face. One look was enough to silence her.

For a moment nobody spoke, the lull broken only by the whirl of Iwazar's engines.

'Let me make one thing perfectly clear,' the commissar said, his voice dangerously calm. 'War is humanity's natural state. Once, our ancestors on Terra fought the great beasts to rise to dominate the planet. Ultimately we conquered the galaxy. And we fight still, against the xenos, the witch and the heretic. And I hope this state persists, for how else can we grow stronger? But not all wars serve the Imperium. The petty squabble I just witnessed? I do not expect to see it again. If you must squeal like children, have the sense to do so outside my earshot. I would not tolerate such behaviour from front-line troops, and I bloody well expect better from you!'

He gave them a moment to absorb his words, uncrossing his arms, his right-hand tucking into his belt beside his holstered pistol. It should have been a comical threat – a commissar armed with a laspistol chastising officers who commanded armies and armadas. But then you looked into his eyes and saw there was no threat. Only cold certainty.

'Now, as I understand it, there is a planet refusing to bow to the Imperium. A planet whose rulers claim us to be deceivers and themselves His true followers. And your response is to label them as *separatists*?'

Prospherous shrugged. *'The alternative is to brand them as heretics.'*

'As we should!'

'Perhaps. But once the Ecclesiarchy become involved, they will feel the need to conduct purges and burnings. We cannot risk them decreeing the records tainted and incinerating the tomes. Or the datascribes for that matter.'

'I concede the former point. But clerics can be replaced.'

'Not quickly, and fresh recruits will lack an understanding of the data-storage systems. Were we to eliminate the population tomorrow and requisition a few million clerics to take on the vacated roles, they could spend a century merely familiarising themselves with the filing system. The Imperium cannot afford for the population of this world to be deemed as heretical.'

'I should warn you, wing commander, such talk sounds dangerously close to concealing evidence of heresy.'

'Then I must have misspoken. Let me reiterate – I am a soldier responsible for winning a war. In this instance, the enemy have been deemed as separatists. I neither endorse nor refute the grounds for making this designation. I merely have my orders. As do we all.'

The commissar was still staring at him, glare sharp enough to polish steel. Still, I wondered how much of his ire was genuine and how much crafted to facilitate his role.

'We will return to this matter,' he said. 'For now, let us focus on the delay in securing the fortresses. What have you been doing out there? I have served with the Láech regiments and witnessed their brutality. I confess surprise that they have been repelled by duped data-scribes supported by a handful of guards and enforcers.'

'Pah! In open battle we would flow through them, leaving only death in our wake,' Colonel Surling spat. *'But they cower behind their walls. And my men lack the firepower to breach those barriers.'*

'The fortresses are well named,' Prospherous explained. *'Their outer structure comprises multiple layers, and they boast formidable weapon batteries. Anything with sufficient firepower to crack the walls will inevitably damage the records within. We could attempt a breach with melta charges, but it is impossible to get close enough without being cut down.'*

Admiral Desora snorted, rolling her eyes. *'This is a task suited to the Adeptus Astartes. A drop pod assault from the Emperor's Angels would resolve the matter in a day at most.'*

'Not with their orbital defences,' Prospherous countered. *'The spires are festooned with Hydra flak batteries and lascannon emplacements. Unless those can be suppressed, an aerial assault is fraught with risk.'*

'To your pampered pilots perhaps. But I've fought with the Adeptus Astartes before. I'd wager they'd weather the storm with little issue.'

'Do you know of a company of Adeptus Astartes poised for deployment?' the commissar asked.

'Not presently,' Desora said after a pause.

'Then the matter is academic. So, given we cannot breach these so-called separatists' walls, or annihilate them from above, what options remain? Given the collective military expertise gathered about this table, I presume at least one of you has considered the possibility of starving them out?'

'That was our initial goal,' Surling replied. *'But from what we can establish, there is a subterranean network that–'*

Then he was gone, the image cutting out. The commissar rounded on me, but before he could speak a score of hololithic aircraft zoomed into view, their flight set against what would have been a rousing orchestral score if Iwazar's vox-unit had had a suitably tuned speaker. As it was, the music was rather tinny, though still preferable to the manic glee of the voiceover.

'Rejoice, citizens of Deighton! The data-fortress of Edbar has been liberated by Imperial forces led by Flight Commander Lucille von Shard!'

The pict cut to images of cheering citizens and magnificent parades. Stock images, many of which I recognised from my own work. It concluded with a panoramic shot of a towering complex I could only assume was Edbar. It looked in remarkably decent shape. Statues of Imperial saints adorned the walls, and the central tower was finished with a trio of aquilas, above which was the visage of a strange, six-limbed creature that bore a passing resemblance to a grox. A figure rode upon its back, presumably a depiction of the God-Emperor given His stature and the lightning bolt clasped in His hand. I was fairly sure the accompanying soot and smoke had been added to the shot post recording.

Suddenly we cut to a Lightning, its wings adorned with familiar black griffin heraldry. The focus zoomed in, until we were inside the cockpit, closing in on the pilot.

Flight Commander Lucille von Shard.

She lacked her pressure helm for some reason, and her hair was longer, spilling about her shoulders. She smiled. Radiant. Like a goddess of war.

I couldn't quite process it. How had the pict maker managed such a tight shot? And with such clarity? For the first time since the endeavour began, I felt just a tinge of professional jealousy.

Shard opened her mouth to speak, but suddenly the image flickered, and Wing Commander Prospherous' face lurched into view, startling me.

'My apologies, commissar – our signal was interrupted by the Feed.'

'I beg your pardon?'

'The Feed. Our propagandist coined the term. Deighton has an advanced data-veil for disseminating files between fortresses. It provides a steady stream of information, but we can breach it for brief periods. Our propagandist believes it the best means of reaching the serfs within the fortresses and imparting the righteousness of our cause. It feeds an uprising – that's the theory.'

'Sounds like a waste of time. Wars are won by soldiers, not by gutter vids set to bombastic music.'

'I once would have said something similar. But apparently Edbar has now fallen.'

'And you attribute this to a propaganda pict?'

'In part. Though I mainly attribute it to the indentured workers opening the front door.'

CHAPTER EIGHT

The *Traderi*'s transport bay opened, revealing the smoking remnants of Edbar.

The fortress was still structurally sound, its blade-like towers standing in the main. But its epidermis was pitted by blast and bolt, any outer adornment stripped away. The aquilas fronting the central tower had been clipped. The lowest remained mostly intact, but the others were missing wings, only a skeleton of the original structure enduring. As for the strange six-limbed creature, it had been reduced to four, and its rider obliterated. Even at a distance, I could smell the burning promethium. And blood somehow, though perhaps that was psychosomatic, my nostrils prompted by the crimson streaks staining the desert sand.

'Hardly the clean victory presented in the vids,' the commissar muttered beside me.

I glanced to him, but his face was impassive. In fact, he did not appear to feel the heat, his greatcoat still in place, cap pulled low to shield his eyes from the afternoon sun's glare. By contrast,

I had only been on Deighton's surface for minutes and I was already sweating. I pulled my hood up, shading my exposed face.

Between us we surveyed the chaos.

There were troops. And aircraft. And armoured vehicles, though most of those were stationary, hemmed in by an overturned Rogal Dorn battle tank. A vast construction vehicle was attempting to right it, but judging by the volume of sand sprayed by its tracks, it wasn't having much success. Meanwhile, a score of troopers were hard at work excavating a vast pit. Its purpose was, at present, a mystery, but it was certainly causing logistical issues – two Chimera transports, having swerved to avoid it, had collided. Their commanders had emerged from the turret hatches, and given the fervour of their debate, I was glad neither vehicle carried a pintle-mounted weapon.

None of these soldiers paid us a blind bit of interest. Considering the chaos it was unsurprising. But a small welcome committee waited ahead. Two officers, their faces hidden against the sun's glare, but uniforms marking them as members of the Aeronautica Imperialis and Astra Militarum respectively. A small entourage was gathered about them.

The commissar gave no order, simply setting off towards the duo, the Scions deploying around him with perfect synchronicity. Their weapons were drawn, and I could understand why. If one were inclined to assassinate the commissar, the circumstances were ideal.

I hobbled after, unable to match their pace, Iwazar trailing behind. For once the seer-skull seemed content to stay at my heel, though its misaligned lenses swivelled to capture the scene.

The two officers saluted as we approached, arms crossed to form the symbol of the aquila. The commissar returned the gesture with snap and flourish, but I struggled, my movements hampered by my cane.

The Aeronautica officer stepped forward, bowing her head.

'Commissar Shard, I hereby greet you on behalf of Wing Commander Prospherous, Colonel Surling, Admiral Desora, and the rest of the war council. I am Wing Sergeant Keeri Vagbon, and this is Captain Haarol Orlano.'

Orlano offered a curt nod. The commissar eyeballed each soldier in turn before replying.

'What exceptional officers you must be, to have the privilege of welcoming me. I would normally expect such a duty to be awarded to more senior staff.'

'I am afraid the war council is occupied consolidating our position. When the Hydra batteries fell silent we launched a full-on attack, not realising the uprising was already underway. It took some time for us to establish we were attacking the insurgents loyal to the Imperium. The abrupt ceasefire and recriminations have left us somewhat flat-footed.'

'I can see that,' the commissar shot back, his gaze falling on the squabbling tank commanders before shifting to Captain Orlano.

'My apologies, sir,' the officer said stiffly. 'I will resolve it immediately.'

'You should have resolved it before I arrived,' the commissar replied, striding past, hands clasped behind his back. The Chimeras' commanders were too preoccupied by their conflict to notice his approach.

Until he drew his pistol.

The shot caught the brim of the nearer man's cap, tearing it from his head but leaving him unscathed. Both officers turned, anger dissipating as colour fled their faces. The commissar strode on, pistol cocked skywards, though his Scions' weapons were locked on the combatants.

'Dear me,' he said. 'It appears the sun's glare spoiled my aim. Otherwise your head would no longer adhere to your shoulders.'

He sighed, theatrically, before seeming to brighten.

'Still, perhaps this was fated. Perhaps the God-Emperor has blessed you this day, and by His intervention you are granted a second chance. So, in His honour, I decree you have exactly seven minutes to clear this area and return to your duties, or I will pass sentence on the whole bloody lot of you!'

His voice was now thunder, rumbling across the sands. He glared at them each in turn before spinning on his heel, holstering his pistol even as they slammed the turret hatches shut. The vehicles lurched into reverse as he returned. He did not bother looking back to confirm whether the order was obeyed. What other possible outcome was there?

Instead, he advanced on Captain Orlano, only stopping when their noses were inches apart.

'A dead fish rots from the head. But a live one dies when infection takes root in the gut. Get your regiment in line or I may find it necessary to disembowel it.'

Orlano stiffened but saluted, his gaze unwavering. Satisfied, at least for the moment, the commissar turned to Wing Sergeant Vagbon.

'You, Vagbon. Do you know Flight Commander Shard?'

'Yes, sir.'

'Do you know where she is?'

'No, sir, though I would guess somewhere within Edbar. I believe some of the officers have commandeered a space as an improvised watering hole to toast their victory.'

'And you were not invited?'

'I have my duties, commissar.'

'Hmph,' he grunted, turning to me. 'Let us leave these officers to their work. At least they are actually on duty. Tempestor Rosln?'

'Sir!'

'Find somewhere to stow the *Traderi*. I want a private hangar that can be secured and guarded. That will be our base of operations. Simlex and I are going to join the festivities.'

He strode past me, hands clasped to the small of his back, his greatcoat billowing behind him like the wings of a dark spectre, as the sun slowly drew behind the pitted towers of Edbar.

I think even Commissar Shard was surprised by what he found within the walls. At least the mystery of the troopers digging the vast hole was solved. It transpired it was a firepit, one of many being excavated around and within the breached fortress. Vast slabs of a ghoulish-grey meat, bigger than a grown man, were being dragged through the dust in preparation to be seared over the roaring flames. The smoke billowed, all-encompassing as it slowly drifted towards faded sky, where the last daggers of daylight failed to pierce the gloom settling over the fortress, or the long shadows cast by its fractured towers.

Around the pits, soldiers were in various stages of undress. Their unadorned skin was pale, but heavily marked by patterns in blue ink. The light was too poor to identify the symbols, though I thought I saw the odd aquila, the two-headed eagle reduced to a series of stark lines. They were drinking. And fighting, though this seemed relatively good-humoured. Two warriors would wrestle, each attempting to force the other to the ground to the roars and cheers of the onlookers.

I whispered to Iwazar, the seer-skull flexing its lenses. It had been some time since I could fully sync with the device, but I could still borrow its eyes, and through it I watched the figures circling, their comrades cheering them on.

One snarled as he leapt forward, only to be struck down with a single blow.

A flicker. Suddenly, I was back on Bacchus, the orks facing

off in the swamps. The victor roaring skywards, where green lightning split the–

'Disengage,' I murmured, leaving Iwazar to its analysis. But somehow the image lingered. I wondered if the projection was still running, but if it was, the commissar was oblivious.

I shifted the focus to the nearby soldiers. They were singing what I presumed to be some battle hymn, though I could not recognise the words, the sounds alien to my ear. I compelled Iwazar to translate, but was unsure if the command even registered.

Beside me, Commissar Shard stood to attention, hands clasped behind him, expression inscrutable. For all anyone could tell, he might be overseeing a parade or assessing potentially hostile terrain prior to troop deployment.

'Láech,' he muttered. 'A dozen regiments in this warzone, but I had to end up assigned to the bloody Láech.'

I said nothing, assuming he was talking to himself. But he turned those piercing eyes on me.

'You ever encountered the Láech?' he asked, nodding to the combatants.

'No, sir,' I replied, following his gaze. One of the contests had degenerated into a brawl, a handful of fighters sprawled in the mud, trading hammer blows and insults. Further from the fire and half hidden by shadow, I saw two figures locked in an embrace I initially took to be conflict, but quickly realised was precisely the opposite.

I looked away, just in time to witness a modest fireball erupting from the mouth of one of the revellers. All but one of his comrades applauded, and the holdout would have done likewise were he not trying to extinguish the blaze now consuming his undershirt.

'Any initial observations?' the commissar continued, as the man, having finally smothered the flames, arose from the mudded sands to join the others in laughter.

'Is this their typical discipline?'

'Typical?' the commissar replied, considering the question. 'I suppose it depends on what you mean. If you refer to their predisposition towards coarseness and unnecessary violence, then yes. Communicating with them is the biggest challenge.'

'Don't they speak Low Gothic?'

'To a point. But good luck engaging with a non-officer on a topic other than troop deployments and attack plans. To fully converse with them you need to understand their frame of reference – the metaphor and imagery that underpins their, for want of a better word, culture. Excuse me for a moment. I must break bread.'

He strode towards the nearest group, pace neither hesitant nor hurried. As he drew close he barked a series of guttural sounds. They turned as one, glaring at him.

Behind me, Iwazar clicked, its analysis seemingly complete. Without invitation, it began whispering into my ear, the commissar overdubbed by a flat, synthetic voice.

'Honoured Children of the Emperor Beneath the Waves,' it monotoned, even as spittle sprayed from his lips. 'I, Regent von Shard, instrument of His will, hail you and your glorious victory.'

One of the group rose, folding his arms in the sign of the aquila.

'I am Sergeant Xvier. The First-Blade. Bless His name and damn His enemies!' the man roared, his fist punching the air. Several more of his group followed suit.

'Indeed,' the commissar said. 'I gather the hunt was successful?'

'Pah!' Xvier spat, hitting one of his troops in the back of the head, the man either not noticing or not caring enough to react. 'It was no battle! We claimed a paltry tally before they called us back. Half my warriors barely got to wet their blades.'

'Those within are also His servants. They are necessary to His plans.'

'Maybe,' Xvier said, and shrugged. 'But my warriors fight for His glory. They kill in His name, and in death earn their place beside Him in the Black Sea. But they can only do that with a sufficient tally of lives. It is ill advised to leash them before they have earned a kill. It dishonours them in His eye.'

The commissar nodded. 'I understand. I would prefer we were already storming the next fortress and cutting down those who stand against He Who Dwells Beneath the Waves. But to do so we must cross the burning desert. For that, we need time and supplies.'

'I know this,' Xvier replied, gesturing to his troopers. 'But it is hard when their blood is high. They see the sky-hogs strutting in their starched lapels, and speak enough Low Gothic to know that they insult us. And with the bloodlust unsated, it is not ideal.'

'I will address them next. But I remind you that, as First-Blade, you are responsible for maintaining order. And if you raise your blade against any of His servants, however ignoble they might be, I will cut you down and send you to face judgement beneath the Black Sea.'

Xvier laughed. I think. Whatever the sound erupting from his throat, Iwazar could not translate it. He then grinned, crossing his arms again. Presumably in the shape of the aquila, though seeing it a second time I noticed his hands formed mirrored curves as they clashed together. Waves perhaps? Or tides?

'Aye!' he said, bowing his head to the commissar. 'May He wash the lands clear of liars and traitors.'

'May it be so. Now tell me, where do your leaders gather to toast their victory?'

Xvier's smile faded.

'Those Above Us have decided to dine with the sky-hogs,' he

replied. 'They are three layers deeper within and have made a tavern from the conquered-wilds.'

The last word was a garble, Iwazar struggling to translate this concept. Even Xvier looked a little confused.

The commissar nodded, but before he could turn away, Xvier reached towards the fire, tearing off a strip of the ghoulish-grey meat. From what I could tell, it appeared burned on the outside but raw within.

'We eat from His flesh, for all life is He,' he said, before holding out the offering to the commissar.

Von Shard did not hesitate. He took up the scrap, displaying it for a moment before wolfing it down in a single gulp. The warriors roared in approval, arms crossed in salute. Commissar Shard did likewise before turning away and stalking back towards me.

He must have caught something in my expression, for he rolled his eyes.

'Really, Simlex? Do you think I actually swallowed that disgusting thing? A little sleight of hand was all it took to dispose of it.'

'Impressive.'

'Yes, well, regrettably my duties sometimes require me to address the barbarians in a language they understand. The ritual is important – to refuse the offering would be… unwise.'

'I see. So that was akin to an act of brotherhood?'

'Of course not. Not after I had spent so long admonishing them for their wanton savagery and ill manners. But it is customary for their leader to offer his meal to a superior as an act of submission. By eating it, I demonstrate my dominance, along with an implicit threat that I will consume him if he fails. Metaphorically speaking.'

I studied his face, but he seemed as forthright and certain as ever.

'I see.'

'The fraternising was worth it, though. I managed to extract the location of their commanders. Apparently, they are in the company of some officers of the Aeronautica Imperialis and have set up a watering hole in the botanical gardens. We shall head there next. Why are you looking at me like that?'

'Forgive me, sir. I am impressed by your knowledge of disparate cultures.'

'It is my duty to speak to my charges in a language they can comprehend. The Láech's beliefs are rooted in a strong maritime tradition. They value honour and bravery above all. And bloodletting, of course. They are quite fond of that.'

Something akin to a smile almost reached his face. Then it was gone.

'Enough. We have broken bread with the Láech. It is time to face something even more unpleasant. My sister's company.'

CHAPTER NINE

The gilded entrance to the botanical gardens was not unguarded. Two figures barred our approach, though this left us significantly outmatched, in mass if not numbers.

The first guard's pallid complexion and vivid tattoos marked him out as a soldier of the Láech. He was over a head taller than the commissar, his thick neck merging into bearlike shoulders, his massive arms broad enough to crush a skull with little effort.

And he was the smaller of the two.

The second figure stood over eight feet tall, and that was with his back hunched and massive head sloped forward. He was almost as wide as he was high, his scarred hide like leather, his beady eyes staring out from a face seemingly inexpertly carved from stone.

An ogryn, an abhuman subspecies of prodigious strength and minimal intellect. For some bizarre reason this one was clad in a uniform of ochre and midnight blue. I suspected it had once been tailored, but it now sagged from being stretched against his broad frame.

Neither of them looked pleased to see us.

Commissar Shard approached the first man, addressing him in his tongue. Iwazar was poised to translate, but I belayed it. We were too close, and the commissar would have heard. I guessed he would be ill pleased to know I had understood his previous exchange.

Still, the conversation was easy to interpret, even without a translator. The looming guard barely spoke before the commissar tore into him, spittle spraying from his lips. The tirade somehow diminished the towering warrior, and soon his shoulders slumped, his eyes downcast. By the exchange's end, I swear they were equal height.

When the commissar had finished, the man stepped back, chin resting against his chest, head turned away. Was he weeping? Regardless, the commissar ignored him, turning his gaze upon the lumbering ogryn. Before he could speak the brute bellowed, the force of his voice almost lifting me from my feet.

'Private event! None will pass! Esec's orders!'

The commissar stepped closer, examining the ogryn's lapel, where apparently his rank was listed.

'Honorary Sergeant Lanlok?' he asked, only just avoiding Lanlok's crushing salute, the abhuman's hulking arms crashing across his chest with sufficient force to shatter a man's spine.

The ogryn nodded. 'Sir! None shall pass! Orders!'

The commissar rose cautiously to his feet. He straightened his hat before glaring at the hulking brute.

'Honorary Sergeant Lanlok, you have been tasked to guard this entrance so the officers can break bread and make merry?'

'Yes, sir! None shall pass!'

'Indeed. You have done an excellent job,' the commissar said, reaching into his coat. Something silver flashed in his hand, a trail of red ribbon following it. The commissar took the medal and, after a momentary hesitation, pinned it to the brute's ragged lapel.

'I hereby award you this medal on behalf of the God-Emperor for exemplary service.'

'Medal?'

'Indeed. I would also like to inform the other officers of your amazing work. Could you show me where they are?'

'Sir! That way!' Lanlok replied, gesturing through the gates.

The commissar nodded his thanks, walking briskly on as I hurried after, cane tapping, the ogryn glaring at me. But he allowed me to pass, shielded as I was by the commissar's impregnable aura of authority.

I suspect the gardens were never breathtaking, but their mere existence was impressive, given the resources that would have been required to maintain them. The path beneath my feet was laid with slabs of volcanic stone. To my left, a grassy bank proceeded to flowerbeds housing long-stemmed plants with bright blue blossoms, and to my right the grass quickly gave way to a smouldering crater still somewhat aflame. Here and there scrub sprouted from the scorched soil, and the majority of an aged tree still clung to the dirt, though its foliage and upper branches were scattered across the grounds.

But there was something odd about the way the flowers caught the light. I slowed, wincing as I bent my knee, examining the simmering petals.

Glass. At least, that is what they resembled, though given how they had endured the explosions, the material's composition must have been something far stronger. I tested a petal with my fingers and was rewarded with a faint cut.

Were they ornamental? I would have thought so, yet none

were identical, and all seemingly possessed both stamen and pistil. If someone had carved them, they exhibited extraordinary attention to detail.

'Iwazar,' I murmured, willing the seer-skull closer so I could capture some footage of the strange plants.

I felt it tugging at me. Irritated, I glanced back, and found the device's focus on the sky above.

Something was watching us.

I could not see it. Not with my own eyes. But I synced with Iwazar's lenses, grimacing slightly as I struggled to maintain the link. It was hard to make out, for the seer-skull's visual accuracy was not what it once was, and our connection problematic at best. But something hovered high above, the flickering pulse of its systems registering clearly, even if I was unable to discern the device itself.

'Simlex!'

The commissar's bellow echoed across the grounds. I rose, gritting my teeth against a stab of pain and lurching after him, cane tapping against the paving. My gaze kept falling to the detritus of war now decorating the grounds: shell casings, broken architecture, and the occasional limb. There was also a considerable volume of paper and parchment. I had almost caught up when a burning scrap flew past, the commissar deftly snatching it from the sky.

'Look at this,' he snapped, smothering the flames and presenting to me the near-illegible parchment. 'Tithes! The God-Emperor knows how much of the Imperium's wealth is being consumed by flames.'

I followed his gaze. The sky was dotted with them, like tiny falling stars. It was impossible to calculate their worth, for there was no universal currency for tithes. Some planets paid in material wealth. For others it would be agricultural produce, or soldiers for the God-Emperor's armies. But without accurate records it was impossible to know what was owed. Over-tithing could lead to starvation or economic collapse, assuming the planet did not simply refuse to pay. In those instances they might find themselves greeted by the Imperium's forces in the same manner as the separatists.

'Such senseless waste,' the commissar snarled, stuffing the scrap of parchment into his pocket. 'This is worse than I feared, Simlex – the whole thing is already a disaster. Front-line shock troopers expected to show restraint, flames consuming the very assets we are so desperate to secure. Who the hell is in charge?'

I did not reply, following him along the slate-grey path. We did not have far to go; lights glinted ahead, accompanied by a sound that was either laughter or jeers.

The path wound around some undamaged shrubs, their branches blocking our view. We emerged from it to find the commanders of the Imperial forces in recline. Many were draped over wicker furniture, others lounging on the scorched grass. Most had a drink in hand, their uniforms in various states of distress. They blended together, the only illumination provided by flickering promethium lamps.

But one officer stood apart from the group, his back to us, a mallet clasped in his right hand.

He was staring at what could only be a bomb.

I didn't recognise the ordnance, but it was obvious from the shape: a steel tube with a finned rear. It would have been taller than a man, were the bottom half not fully embedded in the ground.

The officer stood over it, the mallet held ready. But he was hesitant.

'Go on, you coward!' someone bellowed, their voice slurred. 'Just let me duck into this trench first.'

'Be silent!' the mallet wielder hissed as laughter broke out. 'I am listening.'

'For what? The fuse?'

'For anything!'

'You don't have to hit it,' the voice continued. 'Just admit that you're afraid it might explode. Then you can stand down.'

'If it was going to explode, it would have already!'

'Then what exactly is the delay?' said another voice. A woman this time. Her tone cutting. Familiar.

The officer swore, rounding on the group. 'I will smash it when I am damn–'

His gaze found the commissar.

He fell silent, the others' jeers quickly evaporating as they did likewise. Commissar Shard stood perfectly still, his gaze fixed upon the mallet-wielding officer. I could see the man was sweating, his gaze flickering to the onlookers, all of whom were suddenly intent on their drinks or the undamaged foliage.

The officer attempted a salute, the mallet smacking against his chest. He looked down, as though seeing it for the first time, before tossing it aside and repeating the gesture.

The commissar stared back. Then, with glacial slowness, he returned the salute, crossing his arms in the symbol of the aquila.

Still he had not spoken.

The officer licked his upper lip, nervous, glancing one final time to the others. But there was no support to be found.

'P-praise to the Emperor of all Seas,' he stuttered in heavily accented Low Gothic. 'Hail the–'

'What in the God-Emperor's name are you doing!?'

The commissar's voice was like an artillery barrage. Even the cascade of burning paper seemed to recoil at the outburst, veering from us. His gaze swept to encompass the group, his eyes blazing with unbridled contempt.

The mallet-less officer tried to straighten, drawing himself up to his full height. In fairness, he was a shade taller than the commissar, even with Shard's peaked cap. But it only took one look at their respective stances to know who held the authority.

'This is how you all fritter away the God-Emperor's hours? Not drilling your troops, or planning the next campaign, or honing your skills? No, you let them run wild whilst you sit up here carousing. That would be damnable in itself, but now you choose to squander your lives by striking an unexploded bomb? Do I even have to outline the idiocy? I'm tempted to relieve you of duty on grounds of chronic stupidity. Based on what I've witnessed, I'm not sure I'd trust you to dig a latrine.'

The officer stepped forward.

'Commissar, they insulted my honour. One of those sky-hogs–'

The commissar rounded on him, exploding into a tirade in the man's native tongue. I have no idea what he said, as Iwazar was still on silent running, but I watched the man's face turn red with fury, white with shock, and finally a faint shade of green.

When the commissar had said his piece, the officer offered a trembling salute before marching stiffly past me. Iwazar trailed listlessly after him. I had to will it back, but still the seer-skull loitered, drawn by the man's distress. The commissar had already turned his attention to the rest of the group.

'If anyone else is an officer of the Láech, I suggest you follow your commander's example and attend to your soldiers. Now.'

His voice held only the faintest edge as he looked to each officer in turn. Then he raised his head, voice echoing as he shouted to the heavens.

'Onairs fírin agus dleastan!'

Three officers repeated the phrase in unison, offering stiff salutes before departing. Those who remained now seemed quite intent on their drinks.

'As for the rest of you,' the commissar continued, 'you should bloody well know better. I expect brutality from those barbarians. Frankly, I am predisposed to encourage aspects of their behaviour on account of their affinity for violence. But you represent a different class of soldier. Yet I find you making sport of your allies, goading them into risking death or injury. Why? For your amusement? Even children would know better!'

He paused, surveying them in turn. He had a gift for silence, employing it with precision, the officers unsure whether they should offer a rebuttal or await the next volley.

Most of them, anyway. For as the commissar drew breath, preparing to lambast them one final time, a voice broke through.

'It wasn't going to explode.'

Somehow, despite none of the seated officers rising, the crowd managed to part.

The speaker sat at the rear, her flight suit unzipped to the waist, its sleeves tied about her midriff. Her undershirt covered only her torso, the exposed flesh of her arms pale as moonlight. Her hair was long, far longer than I remembered. It might have once been tied in a braid, but a sizeable proportion had escaped and flowed freely about her face. She was smiling. Or rather, her lips were as upturned as the scar adorning her cheek permitted. Her eyes were hidden by a rather stylish glare visor, but I thought she looked amused.

Which, of course, is not the same as happy. Or pleasant. Rather, she looked like a cat who had stumbled across a particularly fat and stupid rat.

The commissar stared back, his glare cold enough to freeze a star.

'Flight Commander Lucille von Shard,' he said testily. 'Unsurprising that you are at the centre of this debacle.'

Shard offered a mocking bow from her chair.

'Well, I am a Hero of the Imperium. And in nominal command of the deployed forces, at least according to the vids. So, I have ordered my troops to take a little break and enjoy our success. We did just liberate this sorry place.'

She nodded to the pitted towers looming above, lit primarily by the burning scraps of paper.

'You liberated it? I heard loyal servants of the God-Emperor opened the gate.'

'Oh, they opened the gate. Just not for Him. No, they did it for me. I'm their idol, you see. You must have seen the picts?'

'The sort of idol who attempts to goad a starstruck barbarian into pointlessly risking his life?'

'Like I said, it wouldn't explode. Probably.'

'Probably?'

'There are few certainties in this life. But if it didn't detonate on impact, I doubt a couple of smacks with a hammer would do the job. Besides, it's a krak warhead with an implosive charge. Most of the blast would pass beneath our feet. Nobody would have lost more than a couple of fingers.'

She stretched, the motion once more reminiscent of a bored feline, then rose, swaying momentarily before recovering her balance and striding a shade unsteadily towards the commissar, until they stood face to face.

He was taller by some measure, and his eyes still held that cold fury. Hers were shielded by the glare visor, but she countered his grimace with a well-honed smile.

Silence. It swallowed us all, though I spotted a couple of the more enterprising pilots attempting to slip away. It wasn't easy, for the path lay behind the commissar, but they seemed content to try their luck fading into smoke and shadow as the stare down continued.

I'm not sure either would have broken first. Dawn might have come and gone with them still standing there, had not a scrap of parchment drifted between them, coming to rest on the commissar's shoulder, where it continued to smoulder.

Still, he held her gaze.

'I smell something burning,' she said. 'Tithes, you think? Evidence of heresy? Either way, it smells expensive.'

He glared a moment more, before turning to snatch the parchment from his greatcoat and ramming it into his pocket, his gaze snapping back upon her.

He wrinkled his nose. 'Your breath reeks worse than a distillery.'

'And yours smells like an ogryn's latrine,' she replied. 'I've been drinking. What's your excuse?'

Silence. But not the kind favoured by the commissar. This was the silence of a dozen battle-hardened veterans collectively holding their breath and doing everything possible to avoid attracting attention. At least, those who had not already fled. I've witnessed cornered rats scatter with less haste.

The commissar's face was difficult to read, shaded by both his peaked cap and the gathering darkness. I thought I caught his eye twitching, but before I could be sure he turned away.

'There is no point conversing with you. Not in this state,' he said, before glancing to me. 'Come. We shall retire until the morn. Assuming she's sober by then. Perhaps the afternoon is a more realistic goal.'

Shard raised her hand to her mouth, as though in shock, before clutching her chest as though stabbed.

'Oh brother dear, you wound me,' she said, voice dripping with melodrama. 'I do now swear to forgo my reprehensible behaviour. Starting tomorrow I will be chaste and pure and sober. Or possibly a day after that, though I have yet to decide which.'

He ignored her, striding past me. 'Keep up, Simlex.'

'May I have a moment, sir?'

He slowed. Then sighed.

'I suppose. Once you have discovered the futility of the endeavour, you will find me back at the *Traderi*.'

I watched him leave before turning back to her. She had somehow found a bottle, perhaps discarded by one of her companions, and had set to work at it. I strode towards her, trying to minimise my limp. She raised her head as I approached, but then returned to the bottle.

My face was still shaded by my hooded robe.

'Flight Commander Lucille von Shard,' I said, pulling it back. 'It's been a long time.'

I could not see her eyes, hidden as they were by the glare visor. But she gave the faintest of nods, the bottle still pressed to her lips.

I waited as she drained it, shaking the last couple of drops into her mouth before tossing it over her shoulder.

She belched. Loudly. Then, finally, she seemed to meet my gaze.

'I suppose it has,' she said. 'Been a long time I mean. Ages. Years possibly. Gosh, when did we last meet?'

'On Orbital Station Salus.'

'Where?'

'The station orbiting Bacchus.'

'Bacchus?' She frowned. 'Sorry, doesn't ring a bell.'

'But that is where we met. The war!'

She shrugged. 'I've been through a lot of wars. Did anything memorable happen?'

'...How can you not remember? What we went through? The Green Storm? The deaths? They were wiped out. All of them. And I lost everything, my whole life, because of what happened there. And you claim you don't even remember?'

She winced, teeth gritted.

'Look, I'm sorry. Truly I am. But I meet a lot of people. Kill quite a lot of them too. Then I move on and leave the past behind. So, if we shared a drink or, Throne forbid, some sort of dalliance, then I'm afraid I simply don't recall. Perhaps it meant more to you than it did to me?'

She spread her hands.

I could not speak. My anger was too great. In truth, I had played this moment in my head more than once. Sometimes Shard was pleased to see me. More often, she would utter some cutting remark about our prior adventures, or inform me how awful I now looked. But she always recognised me. Because, awful as it had been, my time with her on Bacchus had shaped my life more than any other single experience.

How could that mean nothing?

My throat felt thick. I feared my voice would falter. But then I remembered the message. Proof. I had proof this was an act – a trick intended to amuse her and belittle me.

I summoned Iwazar.

'If you do not remember me, then why did you beg for my aid?'

'Beg?' she said, voice suddenly hard. 'Lucille von Shard does not beg.'

'Iwazar. Play back message designated *Shard's Request*.'

The seer-skull whirred and whined. Smoke seeped from the cracks in its casing, and for one awful moment I was certain the machine would implode. But then its holo-projector flared, the fractured image of Shard materialising before us.

'This is ridiculous,' it said. *'I don't even know if the damn thing is recording.'*

As the flickering image continued, the flesh-and-blood Shard leant closer, staring at it from behind her glare visor.

She smiled. Or possibly sneered.

'I'm afraid you've been the victim of a fraud. This isn't me.'

I stared at her. 'What?'

'It's not me. Or possibly it is but spliced in a manner intended to deceive. Is that what it's called? When images and words are cut together to perpetrate a falsehood?'

She smirked as I glanced from her to the image.

'You claim this is some facsimile?' I said. 'I was trained as a propagandist. I crafted light and sound as a profession. However poor the transmission quality, this is not some replicated–'

A loud hiss drowned out my words, before a vast holo-image flickered into life high above. It must have stretched thirty feet across. I saw a squadron of Imperial fighters scream into view, Shard's leading, her Lightning easily identified by the iconography of a black griffin adorning the wings.

An irksome voiceover suddenly echoed across the gardens.

'Today we celebrate the liberation of Edbar by forces led by the paragon of excellence Flight Commander Lucille von Shard.'

The image cut abruptly to the lead fighter. The cockpit hissed open, and Shard emerged, removing her helmet, her auburn hair cascading down her shoulders. The colour had been lightened, at least compared to the somewhat dishevelled officer standing before me. Her skin was different too – pale, smooth, and glowing with health.

'Flight Commander Lucille von Shard?' a voice said from offscreen, drawing her attention. She looked to the unseen figure, nodding to them.

'You have freed so many from the separatists' cruel tyranny!' the voice continued. *'Will you now take a moment's respite?'*

The screen-Shard smiled. A real smile, not the sneer she usually wore. In fact, her scar was less pronounced onscreen, the wound smaller and less ragged.

'*Rest?*' The faux-Shard laughed, its smile widening. '*Lucille von Shard will rest only when this world is liberated from the separatists' tyranny. She will rest only when its citizens are once again free to hail the God-Emperor's name. As long as there is fuel in the tank, she will wage eternal war on His foes. He would never shirk from His duty, and neither will she!*'

She raised her fist high, to the applause of teeming hordes who presumably stood just out of frame. The faux-Shard appeared every inch a warrior and leader born, someone who soldiers would follow into a hellscape without pause. Even her voice, familiar enough, had shed its cynicism. She sounded bright, hopeful of a better tomorrow.

My gaze fell to the dishevelled woman loitering in the burning gardens. Currently she was retrieving discarded bottles, checking each for dregs.

'Good advice that,' she said, not looking up. 'About keeping fuel in the tank.'

'Who is that?'

'Why, I believe that's Flight Commander Lucille von Shard, the galaxy's greatest fighter ace. Isn't she inspiring?'

'When was that recorded?'

'I don't know. Yesterday? Last month? Maybe never? Esec pre-recorded a variety of phrases. Often they just splice them together until it makes a pretty speech. It's much easier for everyone if I don't have to try to keep a straight face the whole time.'

'They have created a functional facsimile process?' I asked. 'But it takes decades just to catalogue the necessary pict files, let alone–'

'Don't know. Don't care,' she said. 'But it might explain how you received that little vid of yours. Not sure why Esec would send it to you, though – that bit doesn't add up.'

'Esec?'

'My propagandist,' she said. 'He's very talented. You won't hear me utter a slur against him.'

Her tone did not match her words, and I noted her gaze straying skywards, to where the vast faux-Shard was offering a final very bright smile. Then the image collapsed, the world went dark, and I was left.

With her.

She had secured another bottle and taken a seat within the foliage, brushing aside the razor-sharp petals with her boot. She raised the bottle to me, as though offering a toast.

'You say your life was ruined?' she said, nodding to the sky. 'Well, my life doesn't even belong to me.'

CHAPTER TEN

I left her drunken and wallowing, for the commissar was right; there was little point conversing whilst she was in such a state. She made no effort to stop me, nor gave any indication she even noticed my departure.

I was thankful the path was downhill. I was perhaps halfway to the gates when Iwazar suddenly surged ahead. I could not muster the energy to recall it. No doubt its compromised cogitator had detected something that piqued its curiosity. And it was certainly a curious situation, for Shard's face was everywhere.

Before, I had been too preoccupied hurrying after the commissar to realise. But every vid screen I passed displayed her craft conducting aerial manoeuvres. Every wall seemed adorned with posters of her windswept face. Most were emblazoned with slogans. *Rise Against the Traitorous Overseers! What Have You Done For the God-Emperor Today? Salvation comes from the Skies! Look to the Light of Truth!* They were crude things, roughly hewn and marked, more likely the work of low-born dissidents than an actual propagandist.

Ahead stood the gilded gate, Lanlok still on guard. His back was to me, blocking my view as well as the entrance, where some soldier was seemingly seeking entry. Occasionally, Lanlok would bat at Iwazar, who for some reason was circling him and emitting an unfamiliar whining sound.

'Iwazar!' I said. Verbalising the command sometimes helped, but not on this occasion. The machine spirit was preoccupied by whatever it had discovered.

But when I spoke, Lanlok's head turned. Expressions were hard to read on his slab-like face. Though he had an approximation of human features, his eyes were too small and brow too thick to convey much beyond a scowl. And his cavernous mouth seemed capable only of thunderous bellows or drooling incessantly.

On the latter point I was sorely mistaken, for his suddenly lunging maw also possessed sufficient speed to snatch Iwazar from the sky. I heard the seer-skull's casing crack under the pressure. Not that it was well constructed, the pitiful thing having been subjected to my crude attempts at welding. I think the overlaid plates acted as ablative armour, but it could not endure the pressure for long.

'Stop!' I bellowed with whatever force I could muster, stumbling forward, cane clasped two-handed. I swung it with all my might at the ogryn's head.

The cane snapped, the brute barely registering the impact. But it was sufficient to draw his attention. He turned fully to face me, Iwazar still protruding from his mouth.

'Release it!' I thundered. Or tried to anyway, but I was out of breath and my voice sounded very small.

Lanlok tried to reply, but found his voice restricted by the seer-skull lodged in his mouth. Perhaps this was why he spat it out, the traumatised device limping through the air to hide behind me.

'You hit me,' he said, voice so low I swear the ground shook. He raised one massive fist, far larger than my head.

But the punch never came. He hesitated, brow furrowed, gaze suddenly glassy. Perhaps I'd struck with more force than I thought. More likely he had suffered a momentary mental lapse. Either way he shook his head, studying his clenched fist with some surprise, as though seeing it for the first time.

'Protect the propagandist,' he murmured, presumably speaking of my replacement. Either way, I took the opening, my finger jabbing at Iwazar.

'You were damaging the commissar's property!' I said.

He frowned, the gesture carving a score of furrows into his brow.

'The commissar?' he rumbled, massive fingers caressing the freshly acquired medal.

'Yes! I am his personal propagandist.'

Lanlok stared blankly. I might as well have announced that I was the commissar's personal fruit bowl.

'Protect the propagandist,' he repeated. I pressed on.

'This belongs to the commissar,' I said, pointing at Iwazar. This had some effect, enough to give the brute pause.

'I is a loyal servant of the God-Emperor,' he growled.

'Yes, you are,' I said, stepping quickly past him. 'You guard the gate and keep us out, so we will be going. Iwazar, myself, and whomever seeks entry.'

'Acting Wing Sergeant Plient, sir!'

I froze. Impossible. But it was really him, emerging from behind the ogryn. He had lost a little weight, his cheeks hollowed, lines carved about his eyes. But he had that same infectious smile, even if he did his best to suppress it, instead offering a crisp salute, arms folded across his chest. It was an awkward gesture, as the right limb was now a bulky augmetic of darkened steel and burnished chrome. Still, it moved with fluidity, the joints well-greased and servos painstakingly maintained. I would expect nothing less.

'Plient! By the Throne it is good to see you!'

'Likewise, sir,' he said, beaming as he looked me over. 'You look so... I'm so happy to see you, sir. So this must be, um, Iwazar?'

Iwazar had emerged from behind me and was examining Plient, circling him and making appreciative clicks. He stared back with ill-disguised horror at the device's sorry state. I could not blame him. For a mechanical of his talent, my ad hoc repairs must have resembled the machinations of an unrepentant sadist.

But there was no time to reminisce. Lanlok had faltered during our reunion, his limited focus occupied on following the exchange. Perhaps he had concluded our conversation was unlikely to provide additional medals. A deep growl reverberated in his throat.

'No trespassing!'

'Please, Lanlok, I need to be there!' Plient protested. 'You don't understand, I'm looking for Flight Commander Shard. It's very important. Please, Lanlok?'

The ogryn glared down at him.

'Sorry, Plient,' he murmured, voice softening. 'Can't do it. Not even for you. Orders is orders.'

'It would be best to leave her, Plient,' I said, taking hold of his shoulder. 'She's in no state to accept help from anyone.'

'That's when she needs me the most, sir.'

There was a glimmer of reproach in his eyes, and the words stung. Not because of what was said, but because of who said it.

'You're right, of course,' I replied. 'But she is alone, and I'm sure Lanlok will make sure no one bothers her. Perhaps it would be better to leave her be for now?'

Plient sighed, his gaze falling.

'I'm sorry, sir,' he said. 'I spoke out of turn. I know how difficult she can be. But she's not... It's complicated, sir.'

He trailed off, still intent on his feet.

'Perhaps we should find somewhere to talk,' I said, my gaze falling to the shattered cane. 'Hopefully close by. I fear I cannot walk far.'

'You can lean on me, sir,' he said, offering his shoulder. 'I know somewhere close.'

Perhaps I should have specified somewhere quiet as well as close.

That was probably an impossibility, for the Láech took their post-victory rituals seriously, their enthusiasm as infectious as the blight that cost me the use of my leg. But the firepits were now tamed, the flames receding to smouldering embers, and it wasn't just the Láech who warmed themselves. Aeronautica crew and support staff alike were gathered in small circles, the shadows kept at bay by braziers and the occasional portable lumen. But there were no data-scribes or indentured workers. Occasionally I caught them observing from the shadows, uninvited, or perhaps distrustful of their supposed liberators. Understandable, given the damage our forces had inflicted upon Edbar.

The meat was better than I'd expected. Tough, but flavourful. I was less convinced by the contents of my flagon. It smelt as though it had been brewed using runoff from an engine. Plient had procured it from a server with nothing more than a smile. In the same manner he'd navigated the drunken crowd, exchanging nods and pleasantries with effortless comradery, until he found us a seat with one of the groups.

'To the Throne!' Plient said, raising his flagon in toast.

I did likewise, only to suddenly find my drink tainted by a spray of blood from the fighting pit.

'Don't worry, sir,' Plient said, wiping the rim of his own flagon clean. 'The Láech brewed this themselves. No contaminant can survive contact with it.'

'And this lethality is deemed a positive trait?'

He shrugged, then knocked back his drink. I regarded mine a moment before shifting my gaze to the fighting pit. One of the combatants was being dragged clear while the other unbound his fists. These bouts felt different. Before they had seemed spontaneous, almost jovial contests of strength and skill, brawls punctuated by cheers, curses and laughter. But now, when the combatants stepped into the circle, a hush fell over those gathered. Perhaps the preliminary bouts were precisely that. But now? Now something more significant than bragging rights appeared to be at stake.

'Do you enjoy these contests?' I asked, as we watched the next fighters entering the arena.

'Not exactly, sir. But, as I understand it, it's a long-established custom following a great victory. It's good for morale and helps soldiers settle disagreements before they can become problems.'

Both fighters were stripped of their flak jackets, their undershirts revealing shoulders adorned with those blue tribal marks. One man was clearly the elder, his hair greying and midriff pronounced. But there was no mistaking the width of his shoulders or the iron in his eyes. In fact, there was something familiar about his face.

'Plient, who is that man?'

'Captain Phinn, sir.'

'He was with Shard,' I replied. I almost didn't recognise him without the mallet. It seemed he had followed the commissar's advice and looked to his regiment, though I confess I had not expected to see him engaged in a brawl.

When I asked Plient, he showed no surprise. 'All are equal

within the pit. It is the only place where an enlisted man can strike his commanding officer and suffer no penalty.'

The two men saluted, first each other and then some crude edifice. It was vaguely humanoid and seated upon a throne. I assume it was a Láech artefact, and represented the God-Emperor, though I was unused to seeing Him portrayed with quite as many tentacles.

The preparations concluded, the two fighters began circling, cautious, neither hurried to deliver the first blow.

'It's good to see you, Plient.'

'You too, sir,' he said, intent on the combatants.

'I imagine you were surprised to find me here?'

'Very, sir. Never expected to see you attacking an ogryn like Lanlok. That was a risky move, sir.'

'I meant surprised to see me on Deighton.'

'Oh. Well yes, that too, sir.'

The younger fighter made the first move, unleashing a series of strikes to the face and sternum. Phinn retreated, shielding with his forearms and avoiding the worst of the flurry. The younger fighter stepped back, wary now.

'Do you know why I am here?'

'Can't say I know for sure, sir. But a renowned propagandist like you must go to all sorts of places.'

'Less than you might think.'

The younger man stepped in again, delivering another crisp combination of blows. Several found their mark, but the older man weathered them, like rain on stone. His opponent pressed the attack, halting only when a right cross struck him square on the jaw, snapping his neck back. He staggered but recovered, retreating and raising his guard. Captain Phinn did not press his momentary advantage. Instead, he too stepped back, guard raised. Waiting.

I glanced to Plient. 'I am here because I received an invitation from Flight Commander Shard requesting my aid. Yet, on arrival, I find she not only has no memory of issuing a summons, but also claims to have no idea who I am.'

Before Plient could reply, the younger fighter bellowed a battle cry and hurled himself at his foe. But this time Phinn stepped to meet him, fist hammering into his opponent's face. Now came a brawl of attrition, each weathering the other's strikes as they sought dominance. There was no sophisticated footwork, no feints or tactics beyond enduring punishment and inflicting it in return.

Such an exchange could never last. The older man staggered, his knee seemingly giving out. His opponent surged forward to deliver the finishing blow, only to blunder into an uppercut that lifted him from his feet. As he fell, Phinn had already turned away. He knew he had won.

'That was exciting, sir,' Plient said, gesturing to my untouched flagon. 'Would you like another?'

'Plient, I feel you are withholding something from me.'

His smile faded. His face looked wrong without it.

'Sorry, sir. I don't intend to. It's just that… I made a promise, sir. About keeping certain confidences. Whenever I speak, I worry I will let something slip. And I made a promise, sir.'

'To Shard?'

'I couldn't say.'

'I see. Well, if Shard did not summon me, I suppose I have no purpose here. Perhaps I should return to my prior duties.'

'Please don't do that, sir!'

He blurted the words, before clamping his mouth shut, eyes darting left to right.

'You think I should stay?'

'Yes, sir. You were good for her, sir. Not like your replacement.'

'Replacement?'

'Begging your pardon, sir,' Plient said. 'I am sure Propagandist Esec is a fine servant of the God-Emperor. But since his arrival everything has got worse. And it wasn't great before. Not since Bacchus.'

'Shard said she barely recalled the war on Bacchus.'

'There's a difference between not remembering and not wanting to remember.'

'That, I can understand,' I said, my gaze falling to my drink. 'I would very much like to forget a great many things. But they are always there, whenever I close my eyes. Their faces. I didn't even know most of them. I learned the names when I made the pict. They deserved that if nothing else. Perhaps that was my mistake, because that made them people. Perhaps I should have sought solace at the bottom of a flagon instead.'

'I'm sorry, sir, truly. But you–'

'I lost everything. I can't be who I was. But I don't know who I am now.'

'Sir, you really should–'

'Sometimes I think it would have been better if I had met my end there.'

'Ah. Something we can agree on.'

Her voice was sharp as a knife in the back. I looked at Plient, who was mouthing an apology. I shrugged in response, but did not bother turning. Not that it made a blind bit of difference. She made her way around me, squatting down beside us, her glare visor still in place despite the darkness. She reached for my drink, draining it and setting the flagon down beside her.

'So,' she sneered. 'What are we talking about?'

CHAPTER ELEVEN

It was no joyous reunion. I suppose that was always unlikely, given how few of us survived. A handful more had escaped the orks, mainly due to being in the infirmary when that final wave struck. But we three, we had faced the Green Storm together, and somehow triumphed. There should have been a camaraderie, a bond forged in blood and fire. That's what the stories always claim.

Still, Shard was at least smiling. Plient looked like a child caught between bickering parents.

'This is where you have been hiding then?' Shard said, addressing him.

'Sorry, sir, I tried to find you, but Lanlok was not accommodating.'

'Not your fault. I gather Esec gave him some very specific instructions. He prefers celebrations are kept private. Thinks they could be harmful for my image.'

'Yes, sir.'

'You've been watching the fights, then? When are you going to step into the ring, Plient?'

'I've had my fill of front-line combat, sir. Never was particularly good at it. I'm happier in the workshop. Besides, it wouldn't be fair.'

He raised his augmetic arm, the metal gleaming in the firelight.

'Perhaps we should petition for a separate league catering to those with cybernetic enhancements. Could be quite exciting.'

'If you say so, sir.'

'You in a mood, Plient?'

'No, sir. I was just catching up with an old friend.'

'I assume you mean the skull-thing?' she said, nodding to Iwazar.

'No, sir. You remember Propagandist Simlex?'

'Of course. He was the idiot accompanying my wretched brother.'

'I meant from Bacchus.'

'Bacchus?' She frowned, resting her chin in her hand. 'Bacchus… Was that the void battle where we faced those t'au?'

'No, sir.'

'Hmm. That ugly little war with all the flying lizard beasts?'

'Don't be like that, sir.'

'Really, Plient? That sounds like insubordination.'

'That's for you to decide, sir.'

'Hmph,' she said, shifting her gaze to me. 'Bacchus. Was that the swamp?'

'Yes, sir.'

'With the orks and bugs and so on?'

He nodded.

'I suppose I vaguely recall some of that,' she conceded. 'And now that I think about it, there was a propagandist lurking in the background, snapping voyeuristic picts and generally getting in the way. I take it that was you?'

I shrugged, keeping my gaze fixed on the arena.

'Oh, so now we're pouting. Offering the silent treatment? Is that supposed to annoy or upset me in some way? Because I suspect you are far better company when you do not speak.'

I shrugged again.

'Or are you intimidated?' she persisted, leaning closer. 'I have that effect on most people. It's the blessing and curse of being so exceptional. For me, Bacchus was just another skirmish. Another notch on the bedpost. But it probably meant so much more to you. For a moment, you actually mattered. It must be distressing to go back to your old, sad life. I should have realised that.'

She stepped in front of me, blocking my view of the fight.

'I'm sorry,' she said. 'Truly. I'm sorry that our time together meant so much to you, and so little to me.'

I looked to her offered hand. Then to her face, though her eyes were still hidden behind the visor. Then I shuffled to the side, until my view was no longer obscured, and returned my gaze to the currently vacant arena.

In the corner of my eye, I saw her smile.

'How rude. Are you deaf, propagandist? Or mute? Or too angry for pleasantries?'

I said nothing.

'Would you prefer to settle this dispute in the arena?'

'No.'

'It speaks!' she said, feigning astonishment. 'Can you do any other tricks?'

I did not reply.

'I think you do want to fight me. You just don't have the courage because you know I'd win.'

'Obviously you would win. You are a trained soldier and I am a mere scribe. It would be both predictable and pointless.'

'Ah, but I can tell you're tempted. How about, by way of apology, I let you have one free hit? Let some of the resentment out.'

'No.'

'I know you want to hit me. Most people do.'

'There are many people I might desire to strike. But doing so achieves nothing.'

'I disagree,' she said, rising to her feet.

I foolishly hoped that was it, until I saw her striding towards the arena. At her approach, the crowd's energy shifted, laughter and conversation supplanted by murmured disquiet. Perhaps the contests were over, or should have been, and her presence was an affront to their customs. But Shard never was a stickler for rules. Instead, she advanced into the centre of the circle, basking in the growing unease.

'Friends, fans, and subordinates,' she said, voice carrying across the throng. 'I, as you all know, am Flight Commander Lucille von Shard. Hero of the Imperium. Idol of billions. Ace pilot extraordinaire. Living legend.'

She bowed to scant applause and significant heckling.

'Thank you,' she said, waving. 'As you know, I am the star of numerous cinema-picts, including *The 2208*. You must remember that classic? I gather that in some divisions, it's prescribed as mandatory viewing during leisure periods.'

From their muttering it seemed this was true and not particularly appreciated.

'Well, I have splendid news!' she said. 'The man behind it all? The visionary who heralded my ascension? He is here! Right now! In this very crowd!'

More than a few eyes had turned my way.

'But when I just extended my hand in friendship to him, he spurned it. Worse, he had the gall to talk down to me. To challenge me! Now, I know he is a civilian, and has not earned the right to fight in the pit. But I think this needs to be settled. So, I invite him to face me here. Not to fight, because he is weak. But I'll give you a free hit, Simlex, if that's what's required to settle this grudge. Then we can move on like civilised people.'

She stepped back, spreading her hands, inviting me into the circle.

I looked away, to find more of the crowd staring at me. From their expressions it seemed I was no more popular than Shard.

Plient's hand was on my shoulder. 'Let's go, sir. I'll get you back safely.'

I rose with his assistance, turning away and receiving a chorus of boos. Her laughter carried over them.

'Not so easy to be in the limelight, is it?' she said. 'Not so easy when someone else dictates the terms. That's right, run away, you coward!'

'Just leave her, sir,' Plient whispered. 'You're no coward.'

But I found myself wondering.

Was I a coward? I had never fought, though equally I had no skill or training. And neither had I fled, nor sought to hide. I hadn't soiled myself when the orks struck, nor whimpered and cried. I had risked death in my duties, more than once at Shard's side. What more had I to prove? And she was a trained soldier, albeit an intoxicated one. I was crippled, barely able to cross a room unaided. Surely there was no shame in walking away when faced with impossible odds, particularly as the last time I refused to stand down it had resulted in demotion and isolation.

It was odd. I could barely manage a walking pace, even with Plient's aid.

So why did it feel like running away?

Perhaps that was why I glanced over my shoulder, and saw her grinning as she waved me off. That smile. By the Throne I hated that smile.

I found I had slowed. Then stopped.

I looked back to Plient. 'I'm sorry,' I told him.

Then I turned, unsupported, and took a step towards her. Then another.

It was obvious how limited my movement was, one leg dragging uselessly behind me. The jeers faded, the disquiet returning. There was a hushed gasp as I stumbled, almost falling, but I gritted my teeth and strode on, until I was in the circle of light.

It was bright, my eyes struggling to adjust. I could make out Shard clearly, but the rest was shadows.

Her eyes were still hidden by the glare visor, but something had shifted in her stance, and her smile was gone. She looked surprised, which was gratifying. It struck me she was intoxicated, and had been distracted for the majority of our interactions. She might not have realised the extent of my injury when she issued the challenge. But it was too late.

'Well, you're here now,' she said, defiant. 'Take your shot.'

I said nothing.

'Take your shot or walk away.'

She was close, enough for me to see just how badly she was swaying. Her voice was slurred, and if not for her visor I was sure her eyes would be glazed. But she would not fall. Or be silenced.

'Why?' I said. 'Why does it matter to you?'

'To me? It doesn't matter to me. You're the one with the grudge. You're the one responsible for all of it. You did this!'

Venom had crept back into her voice.

'I have no idea what you are rambling about.'

There was a haughtiness to my tone. I did not care for it, and seemingly neither did Shard. There was a revolting hawking sound as she gathered a wad of phlegm, massaged it around her mouth, and spat it into my face.

I felt it drip from my cheek, even as the crowd gasped in exquisite outrage. And she smiled, lip twisted in a sneer.

I felt calm then, calmer than I had since the whole sorry mess began. Because all my anger, my bitterness, my indignation and my shame? I no longer carried it.

It was now balled into my fist.

It had been years since I'd thrown a punch. And I only had one leg to launch from. But I pulled my arm back and put all I had into that clumsy, lumbering right hook.

I think it caught her by surprise. She certainly failed to dodge or block, swaying into it if anything. My fist crashed against her jaw, knocking the visor from her face. Her head snapped round, shoulders following as she stumbled, the sand slipping beneath her feet. She half tripped and half fell, landing hard on her side.

Silence.

Then the crowd roared. I confess I basked in it, just for a moment, even as I nursed my aching fist.

'Ow.'

Her voice. She was already on her feet, rubbing her jaw. I think she wore a scowl, but to be honest I could not tear my gaze from her eyes. They were bloodshot, harrowed – the lines around them so deep they looked carved by a knife. They blazed with fury and pain and something akin to madness.

She surged forward, and suddenly I was sprawled in the sand, the world tumbling about me, blood on my lips, my jaw numb. I wanted to rise, but couldn't discern which way was up.

My collar. She grasped it and hauled me to my knees. I could see her face, but everything else was dark, the shadows encroaching.

She was smiling. And maybe crying. I could not tell. Her fist was balled, and I wondered if I would remain conscious after the second blow.

'That's enough, sir.'

Plient. He was behind her, his augmetic hand secured about her wrist.

'Plient?'

She sounded puzzled, then tried to pull her arm away.

'Plient? Release me. That's an order!'

'I'm sorry, sir.'

'You are disobeying a direct order? From your superior officer?'

'You're not well, sir.'

She snarled, releasing my collar and rounding on him. But it was pointless, for he held her at arm's length, and she could not bring her shoulder far enough around to strike anything besides his armoured limb. Not that this stopped her from raining blows against it, her knuckles already stained red.

'Sir, you're hurting yourself.'

She slowed, then sagged. I think she might have fallen if he wasn't holding her upright. Her head was lolling, but still she glared at him.

'Release me! For Throne's sake, Plient, you're making a fool of yourself!'

Silence. I hadn't noticed it before, shaken by her punch. But I had recovered my senses sufficiently to realise the crowd was still. In fact, now my eyes had adjusted, I could see it was ebbing away, as the revellers concluded that, one way or another, the evening's entertainment was over.

'Sir?'

Plient was staring at me, head bowed.

'I'm sorry, sir. It's not you. Sometimes she just needs a target. Please come visit my workshop when you have the chance. I would like… I hope it will be better, sir. But you should go now. The Eyes are coming.'

He lapsed into silence. Shard was muttering something, but I could not make it out over the sound of my own laboured breath. As I slowly found my feet, my gaze crept skywards, even as Iwazar chirped a warning.

A score of crimson lights were descending upon us, like bleeding stars.

And now the soldiers fled; there was no other word for it. They ran, as though the lights heralded an invasion by some xenos force. I was knocked aside, trampled in their desperation. I could not see Plient, and Iwazar seemed panicked, attempting to flee from the oncoming lights.

'Propagandist!'

I glanced up at the voice, and was relieved to see Tempestor Rosln. She was clad in her full carapace armour, though the helm was absent, presumably for my benefit.

'The commissar sent me. We must go!'

She seized my elbow, dragging me upright before throwing my arm over her shoulder and setting off at a half-run, my feet barely touching the ground.

'We secured the hangar. Once there I will– Down!'

She threw me to one side, following suit. I did not know why, though I had the sense to trust her, and with good reason. Moments later a score of Scions stormed past. Their livery was unfamiliar to me, ochre and midnight blue. They were running in the opposite direction to everyone else, their pace even, formation maintained. A lumbering figure brought up their rear, the squad's Tempestor accompanying him. It was Lanlok.

'How the hell did she slip past you?' the Tempestor snapped. 'She could barely walk in a straight line?'

'I was ordered to keep them out, not in.'

'Explain that to Esec.'

The ogryn grunted something in response, but they had passed us now. Rosln rose cautiously, motioning me to follow. But I hesitated.

'What?' she said.

'Iwazar. It's still back there. I must–'

The seer-skull suddenly hurtled from the darkness, its engines screeching as it fled. Three shapes pursued it. Ugly, boxlike forms, each with a single unblinking lens. Rosln drew her pistol as they approached, but at the gesture the three shapes recoiled, flittering out of range.

But their unblinking eyes remained fixed upon us, even as we retreated towards the *Traderi*.

CHAPTER TWELVE

Two Scions were waiting for me the next morning.

For once I had slept, perhaps due to the cocktail of painkillers issued on my return. It was Rosln who woke me, and who provided a steaming cup of recaff and a new cane. I'm unsure for which I was more grateful.

'Propagandist Esec has requested your company,' she told me. 'He has sent an escort.'

I rose gingerly from the bunk. My jaw ached, though not as much as my leg. I was still clad in yesterday's clothes, now stained by dust, liquor and blood. I considered changing, until I realised I had nothing else.

'Where is Commissar Shard?' I asked.

'He left before dawn. Said he needed to get a start on restoring discipline. Do you need someone to accompany you?'

'No. The commissar wanted me to ingratiate myself with Esec. It might prove easier if I am alone.'

She nodded before moving on, no doubt intent on whatever

assignment the commissar had issued. I made my way to the transport bay. Iwazar was already there, its lenses pressed to the door, apparently anxious to be let out, its prior disquiet forgotten.

But its newfound courage proved equally fleeting. As we stepped from the craft, it shrank behind me. I could not think why. The commissar had obtained a modest private hangar, remarkably undamaged in the assault. There was space for maybe five small vessels, though only ours was docked. The waiting Scions were just visible through the viewport of the main doors. They wore the same ochre-and-midnight heraldry as the group I had encountered the night before, but they were not the cause of the seer-skull's distress.

That lay beyond the armaglass window.

Our hangar was on a raised platform. Below, I could see the Láech soldiers clearing detritus from the prior night, but Iwazar was fixated on the trio of machines hovering beyond the glass. Perhaps they had been there since the night before. Perhaps they were new arrivals. In any event, they waited. Watching through blazing crimson lenses. They had a classic Imperial design: blocky and boxlike, the chassis marked with a small aquila. But I had never seen their like before.

Behind me, Iwazar screeched, its lenses flashing with images from Bacchus, the display too disjointed to pick out anything besides Shard's sneer and the battle cries of ork warriors.

'Be silent!' I snarled, glaring at the device. It recoiled, the memories fading. As I turned away from it, I spotted three Lightning fighters soaring skywards. They were some distance from us, but I thought the lead had Shard's markings, the image of a black griffin emblazoned upon the wings. I was surprised she was conscious this early, let alone capable of flying.

There was a rapping sound from the door. 'Propagandist Simlex? Are you ready?'

I blinked, turned away from the window, and approached the Scions. 'It's just Scribe Simlex. I understand Propagandist Esec has requested my presence?'

'Yes, sir. Please come with us.'

'Is it far?' I asked as I stepped through the doorway. 'My mobility is limited.'

They exchanged glances.

'That will not be an issue,' the Tempestor said. 'Our destination isn't somewhere you can walk to.'

He turned his head, and I followed his gaze to the colossal airship, suspended high above Edbar, its hull midnight blue adorned with ochre highlights.

Esec was on the vox when I was announced. He smiled at me, nodding to the chair opposite, rolling his eyes even as he conversed. I could see no receiver, only his fingers pressed to his temple. Like me, he must have had a cranial implant.

'Oh, I agree, colonel. Absolutely. Not the sort of thing we want happening again. High spirits are one thing, but–'

He was young. Younger than I had expected, unless his appearance was due to rejuvenat treatments. I was unsurprised to see his robes were midnight blue with an ochre trim, and though they bore no symbol or coat of arms the weave looked expensive. His hair was swept back over his left ear, the right side of his head shaved, presumably to access the various implants just visible beneath the skin.

Behind me, I could feel Iwazar whirling. It had been my shadow ever since we docked. Something about the airship had placed it on edge.

'Listen… I understand, but…' Esec said, struggling to talk over whoever was on the other end of the vox. 'I… Thank you, Colonel Surling, you are too kind. But I have a very important visitor waiting and… No, I'm not saying that! Of course you are important! Possibly the second most important soldier on this planet! I jest! Yes… yes, I would say so too. Thank you, sir, I will have an update before sundown.'

He released his finger from his temple, severing the connection, before turning to me.

'I am so sorry,' he began. 'The last few days have been insanity personified. Edbar fell so much faster than even I expected, and now I find myself running just to remain in place! But that does not excuse my rudeness. Welcome, Propagandist Simlex. I am Propagandist Emulle Esec. Or Emen, if you prefer. May I offer you refreshment? I have some delightful Plesian wine.'

'I sadly lost my taste for wine. But a recaff would be greatly appreciated.'

Esec nodded, touching his hand to a metal stub on his right temple, his eye twitching as he relayed a command. Moments later, one of his devices entered, two steaming cups balanced on its chassis. It glided to me, presenting the drink.

'An unusual design,' I said, taking my cup.

'Yes. I call them my Eyes. I hoped to devise a suitable acronym, but I'm struggling with the "Y"! Any suggestions would be appreciated.'

'Where did you procure them?'

'Well, I was never of sufficient status to be awarded a seer-skull. But these were adapted from an agricultural unit. Mainly used for irrigation and such, but the design was easily repurposed, requiring only a few lenses and an improved cogitator.'

'And that was permitted? I would have thought the priests of the Mechanicus would have raised some objections.'

'Ah,' Esec replied, casting a furtive glance over his shoulder before leaning closer. 'Between you and me, life on a frontier world is… flexible. By necessity. Certain allowances must be made in the name of survival. And if one requires something sanctioned by the tech-priests, there are means of smoothing that process. Let us simply say that by the time I rejoined the more civilised sectors of the galaxy, my devices were fully sanctified by the servants of the Omnissiah. See?'

He pointed to the underside of the machine's carapace, which was admittedly adorned with the cybernetic skull symbol of the Adeptus Mechanicus.

'Impressive. But surely your status has risen since then?'

'Possibly? I have not had the opportunity to check in with my superiors for some time. But I am accustomed to my way of working, and as my methods have brought me this far, I see no immediate need to change them. Unless that is why you are here? To present me with a seer-skull of my own?'

His gaze flickered to the relic hovering behind me. I turned to find it slowly tipping to one side. Esec, to his credit, pretended not to notice.

I shook my head. 'I am afraid not.'

'That is unfortunate,' he said, smile fading. 'I suppose we best get it over with, then. I assume you are here to relieve me of my duties?'

'What? No. Why would you think that?'

He did not reply at first, his gaze resting on the desk between us.

'Because you are you,' he said simply. 'Propagandist Kile Simlex. You were a legend, even before your footage led to the creation of the greatest propaganda pict in living memory. And you have worked with Flight Commander Shard and… I don't know. I guess I just keep expecting this to end. I know I lack your talent, that all I do is cobble together cheap vids. When I heard you were coming, I assumed it was to take my spot.'

He glanced up. He looked worried, embarrassed. It threw me.

'I am not here to take your place.'

'Then, forgive me, but why are you here?'

I paused. 'For your guidance.'

He raised an eyebrow. 'I am supposed to impart wisdom to you?'

'I hope so.'

'Forgive me, but that seems somewhat backward. You are far more experienced than I. Frankly I would not have a career without your work – we both know that. What's next? Am I to provide fencing advice to the Emperor's Champion?'

He sounded sincere, elbows pressed to the desk, chin resting in his hands, expression somewhere between baffled and bemused. I smiled despite myself.

'Be that as it may, I am here to learn,' I said. 'My last cinemapict efforts were… not well received. I am long out of practice. Commissar Shard has commissioned me to complete the second volume of his biopict. I cannot afford to fail again, and given your success with his sister, the commissar thought I could benefit from your insights. He would like me to shadow you and study your methods.'

Esec nodded, leaning back in his chair. He didn't reply at first, his gaze drifting into the mid-distance as he considered my words.

'This is a turnaround,' he murmured. 'My superior requesting my aid.'

'I am not your superior. I don't even share your rank any more. I am but a scribe.'

'I meant in talent,' he said. 'Sorry, this has thrown me. I was all prepared to fight my case, futile as it might be. At one point I even thought the commander might accompany you, demanding you replace me.'

'Why?'

'Honestly?' he said. 'I heard a rumour the two of you were... close.'

'Close?'

'Yes. *Very* close, if you take my meaning. Gossip, I'm sure. But–'

'I assume such concerns have been quashed after last night's incident?'

'Oh indeed! Awful conduct, really shocking. A heroic fighter ace brawling with a crippled scribe is not exactly the fodder of epics. I'm still figuring out what to do with the footage.'

'You were recording it?'

'Not deliberately. One of my Eyes witnessed the brawl. I have the file here somewhere.'

'Perhaps you should erase it.'

'Possibly. But I prefer not to erase anything – footage can always be repurposed, and you never know when something might be useful. But fear not, it certainly won't be released in its current form! Though that reminds me – if you could grant me a moment's grace?'

'By all means.'

He pressed his fingers to his temple, accessing whatever implant interfaced with his Eyes. The nearer, the one that had previously provided our drinks, made for the room's only console, some implement sliding from its hull and interfacing with the screen. An aquila materialised upon it.

Esec was smiling, fingers still pressed to his temple.

'Bear with me.'

I stared at the screen, wondering what he planned to show me. Had he already begun repurposing the footage?

But suddenly she materialised, clad in a dressing robe, glare visor in place, and cradling a cup of something I hoped was recaff.

Shard.

'Flight Commander Shard,' Esec said, smiling. 'Good morning. Again.'

She grunted something in response. Esec continued.

'I'm here with Propagandist Simlex. We're comparing some notes for an upcoming collaboration. But since I have him here, I thought maybe you'd like to say something.'

'Not particularly.'

'Ha!' He grinned, looking at me. 'I do so love your wit. But this might not be the time.'

Something had crept into his voice. More a whetstone than an edge. But any warmth in his smile was gone.

I glanced to the screen, expecting Shard to launch into a diatribe, or simply break the connection. But she was so still I wondered whether the image had frozen.

'Lucille?' Esec warned. 'Don't make me ask again.'

'I... would like to apologise.'

I blinked. I heard the words but found myself unable to process them. It didn't help that she was so still that I could be staring at a picture.

'And what for?'

'Because I conducted myself in a manner unbecoming to my rank,' she continued. *'I had led our forces to victory. My loyal followers felt a celebration was warranted. I indulged them and, in turn, allowed myself to overindulge. Mistakes were made that I now regret. Please accept my apology, Propagandist Simlex.'*

I have encountered servitors capable of more emotive delivery. But it was her voice, and her lips did seem to be moving.

'I... accept your apology,' I said. The screen instantly went dark.

'There,' Esec said, turning to me. 'I felt it best we address the incident upfront and move on. Assuming you consider the apology satisfactory?'

'Yes, I... I confess I'm surprised. I did not think she would express regret.'

'I know how difficult she can be.' Esec smiled. 'But we reached an understanding some time ago. She enjoys her fame, and for it to continue she needs me. And I need her, of course! I cannot confirm her sincerity, but I'm sure, on some level, she understands that she went too far.'

I nodded, still struggling to process what happened. It was telling that my first instinct was the exchange had been falsified, Esec splicing the footage together from offcuts. Especially as I had already seen an aircraft in her colours being launched that morn.

Then again, if it had been a deception, surely I would uncover it quickly enough? So what would be the point?

Had she really just apologised at his request?

Esec smiled. It struck me he did that a lot.

'I suppose we should find some time for you to shadow me,' he said. 'Bizarre as that concept still seems.'

Again, his finger pressed to his temple, eyelids flickering as he accessed the information.

'Ah! There might be something today. A supply convoy that needs to be intercepted. I doubt it will be overly exciting, but perhaps that is for the best, given this is our first proper collaboration. Besides, between you and me, Lucille is supposed to be leading our forces, but she has not been in the best of form recently. There was a mission with her brother that... Well, never mind. She needs support. Guidance. And who knows her better than you?'

'I would hope a great many people.'

'Ha! Perhaps. But few of them are here.'

He was beaming, as though a weight had been lifted from his soul.

'Throne, I'm so relieved! I was certain you would hold a grudge over *The 2208*.'

'Why would I hold a grudge over that?'

His smile faded. He leant back in his chair, gaze shifting around the room and finding everything but me.

'Oh dear,' he said. 'This is awkward. I thought you knew.'

And I did. I saw it on his face. And it was obvious. Shard's meteoric ascent was precipitated by a single pict. One taken from me and finished by another. The work had been anonymised, though I suppose given the inclination I could probably have uncovered the name of the propagandist who had taken over the job. It had never struck me as important until now.

Esec.

The man who had profited from my fall was now to be my mentor.

CHAPTER THIRTEEN

Esec's office was just one of many chambers on his barge. I was given a brief tour of the bridge, abundant corridors, and various engine rooms. The lack of personnel was notable. There were several mechanicals and scribes, but nowhere near sufficient to operate such a vessel. He claimed most processes were automated, hurrying me along until we reached an area designated as his studio.

It featured numerous consoles and workstations, though none were occupied. Esec took a seat behind a throne-like chair, lowering a control helm into place. It was a bulbous thing, and had it not been outfitted with anti-grav units I suspect his neck could not have supported it. Like his Eyes, the design was utilitarian, though it lacked the typical Imperial embellishments. A simple dome around the cranium with a sensor mounted on the side. Despite its bulk it seemed too small to command such an armada of pict-cams.

His Eyes, I reminded myself. That was their designation.

Besides Esec and I, the only other figure present in the studio was Lanlok. He stood behind Esec, arms folded, intent on the myriad screens laid out before us. Most were dark, though the largest, the mainscreen, showed our passage through the rather monotonous desert. We had already set off during the tour, three squadrons of fighters accompanying us.

'Do you have any questions thus far?' Esec asked from his throne.

'I am wondering how you will operate such a fleet of cams. Do you have subordinate commanders housed within the vessel?'

'No. I probably should, but I'm used to working alone.'

'Then how do you do it?'

'Oh, I don't,' he replied. 'They are arranged in units and directed along preset patterns. They have set targets to follow and distances to maintain. I make adjustments on the fly, but the system runs itself. With so many cams I always have great footage, though the challenge is trawling through it all to find valuable shots. Perhaps that's something you can assist with whilst you're here. Providing you don't consider it beneath you?'

'Of course not. The Eyes are deployed in advance of an attack run, then?'

'Yes. Of course, they cannot match the attack speed of our aircraft. Hence the need for this barge to accompany our fighters. Not that it can match their full speed either, but it's closer. They stick close to me, like dogs on a leash. I set the cams in place, and order the attack.'

I nodded, staring ahead at the mainscreen. The desert stretched to the horizon, its bleakness broken only by the occasional boulder.

He sighed. 'It's become awkward, hasn't it?'

'I don't know what you mean,' I said, but it was a lie. A lie so pitiful it could not endure the slightest scrutiny.

'Yes you do.'

I too sighed, glancing to him, though his gaze was hidden by the helm.

'I do not wish it to be so.'

'Neither do I. I have long admired your work, truly,' he said. 'When my superiors first approached me about completing your pict, they made it sound as though you were dead. Or incapacitated – I do recall thinking the details were overly vague. But the footage you had gathered was incredible. And Lucille! Her presence!'

He sounded wistful.

'So, you agreed to take the project as your own?'

'Someone had to finish it. It was your legacy.'

'And your opportunity.'

There was bile behind the words. I'm sure it showed on my face. Whether Esec saw it I could not say, for his own expression was concealed. But when he spoke, there was no reproach in his voice.

'I don't deny it. I laboured in obscurity for years. I might still, had I not seized my moment. But, truly, I thought I built upon the work of a legend. An artist! It was only later that I heard… what I heard.'

He lapsed into silence.

'There is no need to spare my feelings. Tell me what they said.'

'I'd prefer not to. I do not think–'

'I'd like to know what they say behind my back.'

'They said you had become… unbalanced by the war on Bacchus. The more charitable attributed it to neurological damage caused by the various injuries you suffered. Others suggested it was a lack of faith, or weakness of character. Or madness.'

I nodded. Nothing unexpected. Indeed, if circumstances were different, had another taken the assignment and behaved in the manner I did, I might have thought likewise.

'By then I was committed to the project,' Esec continued. 'I thought if I requested to be taken off it, or spoke in your defence–'

'Neither would have been a smart move.'

'I wanted it anonymised, though. It didn't seem right to take credit.'

'Magnanimous of you. Though I'd wager you still received credit for its success amongst our superiors.'

'It did good numbers. Moreover, screenings of the pict were followed by a spike in enlistment. A quantifiable correlation in non-mandatory recruitment. And it's still spreading, far beyond my reach. It has been disseminated across half the Subsector Yossarian. I gather a copy even traversed the Great Rift. And that's all it takes, because one copy can be replicated, dispatched further.'

'Almost like a disease.'

'I suppose. But I see it as one pict changing the galaxy. And the credit for that must go to you.'

I frowned, glancing to him, but his gaze was lost to the helm.

Suddenly, the desert faded from the mainscreen, replaced with familiar burnt-orange swamps threaded with dying vines.

Bacchus. The sight of it made my skin crawl.

'Look at that visual,' Esec said. 'You don't get that in normal picts – it's considered a needless expense. But recruitment drives focus on high-population worlds. When you've grown up in a plascrete hive city, clear skies and uncontaminated waters are almost mythical. Forget the war for a moment, just look at the places a soldier might visit! And those sunsets! The colours! For some, the simple fact that humans can exist outdoors. All wondrous.'

I could see it. That was the odd thing. The images were quite spectacular. This particular shot was from the bombing run, where the craft flew so high it almost breached the void. From such a distance Bacchus appeared almost picturesque.

'Imagine it,' Esec continued. 'You're crammed into an overcrowded cineplex, cheek pressed into someone's armpit, hemmed amongst the unwashed masses. And on the screen flashes this vast expanse. You see the sun glint on the water, insects pirouetting above its surface. It's breathtaking.'

'The stench certainly was. And those insects were colloquially known as banner-bugs on account of their predisposition towards stringing human entrails across their territory.'

'Yes. I saw that footage. I decided it would be best to remove it from the final cut.'

'A shrewder choice than mine.'

'You must have known the effect it would have on recruitment, that your superiors would reject it. Why include it?'

'Because I had set out to show the true face of war.'

'You intended to show Guardsmen digging latrines? Or subsequently using them? Every inclusion and exclusion is a choice.'

'From what I've seen of your pict, significant inclusions were added postproduction.'

'That's not fair. Once I had made the cuts, I had to weave what remained together. That involved splicing a few extra scenes here and there. All of them were based on Flight Commander Shard's recollections of the conflict.'

'And you believed her?'

'She was there. I was not.'

An edge had crept into his voice. I suspect I had struck a nerve. Which was stupid, because I was supposed to be ingratiating myself with him. Fortunately, before the conversation deteriorated further, we were interrupted by a vox-message. Only Esec heard it, relaying it through his implant, but his demeanour changed completely. He half leapt from his chair, striding to the centre of the studio.

The mainscreen flickered. Desert again, but no longer deserted. There was a distant trail of dust and smoke. The supply convoy.

'We're close,' I said, but he shook his head.

'No. A few hundred miles more.'

'Is this footage from an advanced scout?'

'No, merely an advanced lens,' he replied. 'My Eyes see further. But you are correct, we are drawing close. Shard One, is your squadron ready?'

'Yes, sir.'

It wasn't her voice, but by now that was no surprise. Nor was it when Esec performed similar checks with Shard Two and Three. I had seen the fighters launch, each squadron led by a plane adorned with the von Shard family crest. The mystery of Shard's early morning departure was solved. She had not been flying the plane, just as she did not accompany us now.

Ahead, the convoy was visible snaking through the dust. Huge multi-wheeled haulers, each the size of a small building, were chained together, their combined strength dragging the monstrosity on. Smaller buggies flanked the main convoy, aircraft circling above. I believe they were Valkyries, or something equivalent. Either way, their tactical capabilities consisted of infantry support and rapid troop deployment. They were not dedicated fighters; our Lightnings completely outmatched them in speed and firepower.

'Remember the priorities. First, we must surround them. Then I want clean, clear kills. Do not engage until my signal. We don't want to miss a shot.'

He was giving orders.

I hadn't fully absorbed this fact until that moment, because they always felt like suggestions, or requests. But now we were entering a combat scenario. And he was dictating the engagement.

We were close enough that I could pick out individual drivers on the buggies. They wore goggles to shield their eyes from the glare, but they had no real uniform, just scraps weaved together. They had yet to see us. The lenses on Esec's Eyes were extraordinarily powerful.

'Time to unleash our forces.' He smiled, spreading his arms wide, fingers outstretched. He looked poised to conduct a symphony.

Then they were unleashed. Not the fighters as I had assumed, but an armada of Esec's Eyes. The myriad screens lit up, each capturing a different image, some split into multiple shots as the drones flitted in and out of each other's vision. It seemed an impossible mess. Any moment I expected explosions as the devices collided, but none came. Instead, they accelerated ahead of us, their focus the convoy.

Lanlok leant forward, intent on the screens, an almost childlike smile forming on his brutish face.

'Vids,' he murmured.

'Adorable, isn't it?' Esec said. 'He was gifted to me by Colonel Surling as a bodyguard. Loves the picts. Useful too, as he provides a benchmark of accessibility. If he can understand what is happening, then so can the majority of our citizens.'

We had yet to attack, even though it appeared we were right on top of them. The twin occupants of the closest buggy were laughing, perhaps exchanging a jest, when one pointed at the vid screen. He looked surprised rather than concerned, as though he was unsure what he was seeing. From the angles presented, it appeared Esec's Eyes had surrounded the convoy.

Esec was quite still, arms still outstretched. Poised to begin.

'Action,' he whispered.

I heard it even through the hull, the scream of dozens of engines roaring as one. The Lightnings and Avengers surged forward, the myriad screens capturing their assault. The convoy barely had time to register the danger before the first buggy disappeared under a barrage of bolt-rounds. The Valkyries tried to reposition and respond, but they were speared by searing bolts from the Lightnings' lascannons. And then the fighters were already past them, circling about for a second assault even as the Thunderbolts readied their armaments.

Esec's voice came through, calm and deadly as Bacchus' waters.

'Now the convoy. And I want fireworks.'

A barrage of missiles struck the haulers, detonating in an admittedly impressive explosion.

'What are they transporting?' I asked, watching the blasts ripple across the screens.

Esec shrugged. 'No idea. I'm just glad it appears flammable. It's so anticlimactic when they just fall to pieces.'

I watched the unknown cargo burn. Was it supplies? Armaments? Rations? Tithes, even? It didn't matter. Esec had no interest in capturing anything other than a spectacle, and it certainly looked cinematic, providing one was unaware that the targets were slow-moving and, relatively speaking, defenceless.

A couple of the buggies had already sped away. Perhaps their un-uniformed drivers were mercenaries who had decided their pay was insufficient for the task at hand. Or perhaps fear had seized them. As they fled, a trio of Eyes detached and followed, easily encircling the speeding vehicles.

'Shard Two. Intercept the stragglers.'

'*Sir.*'

'Oh, and perhaps you could arrange so they collide? One flipping over the other? Something like that. I'll leave the details to you.'

Most of the screens were now focused upon the fleeing buggies. I watched the Lightning speed towards them, diving low. Too low, and much too steep. I feared a collision, but suddenly the craft was level, speeding above the ground. Its lascannons flared, a bolt of light spearing both buggies, slaying the drivers with a single shot. I don't think the real Shard could have done better.

'Urgh. I wanted spectacle, Vagbon. That was flat.' Esec sighed as he watched the buggies roll to a halt. 'Still, no matter. I have enough to craft what I need. Excellent job, everyone. Another victory for Flight Commander Lucille von Shard.'

CHAPTER FOURTEEN

I heard the commissar before I saw him.

I was propped in front of my data-slate, attempting to review the limited intelligence documents despite the constant interruptions from Esec's doctored clips. Shard besting a score of separatist pilots. Shard gunning down a convoy. Shard handing gifts to cheering children. The Feed cut in constantly, and I could find no means to shut it out.

A personal favourite was her victory in the fighting pit. I missed the initial narration, my focus solely on the visuals. It looked like the prior evening, where I'd faced her and suffered accordingly. But I was absent from the vid, somehow replaced by a burly soldier. And Shard herself had been cleaned up significantly. Esec had smoothed her skin and hair, but more impressive were the changes to her stance. She danced around her foe like a pugilist rather than staggering like a drunken vagrant.

Was it even the same footage? Or the same woman?

I knew how to manipulate images, splice together still picts. But the process was labour intensive, time consuming, and what could be achieved was limited. Yet Esec had accomplished it in a day, and half of that had been spent on our jaunt to intercept the convoy.

It was unsettling. Perhaps, in purely technical terms, he did have much to teach me.

I was relieved, then, when I heard the commissar bellowing outside the *Traderi*. I shut down the data-slate, intent on the approaching voice.

'–grasp the wretches by the throat and squeeze until their eyeballs burst!'

The door burst open, and Commissar Shard stormed into the room. He crossed it in a few strides, but he made no attempt to sit, pacing back and forth like a caged animal.

'Parasites! Vermin fattened on the carcass of our faded glory!'

His eyes blazed. Spittle stained his cheek. I had never seen him so consumed by rage, and thought it foolish to draw his attention. I kept my head low as he continued his rant.

'Those imbeciles. Trying to hammer nails with a wrench. And why? Because that Throne-cursed propagandist wants a spectacle. Well let me explain something to you!'

His hands slammed down on the table, his face now inches from my own.

'Look at me when I'm talking to you!'

I met his gaze, and for the first time saw something of his sister in him.

'War is for warriors!' he spat. 'We fight and die. Your kind captures it for posterity, so the citizens can see the glory of the Imperium and the righteousness of our cause. Now explain something to me, Simlex – when did you people start dictating our conflicts?'

'I was wondering that myself, sir.'

'Were you now?'

'Yes. I spent the afternoon with Esec. Apparently he commands a fleet of our aircraft.'

'Of course he does. What could be more logical?' the commissar said, turning away and ripping open a cupboard, retrieving his tea pouch and a cup. 'What else did you learn?' he asked, back still to me.

'He has some hold over the flight commander, though he claims it is because she relies on him to maintain her fame. But I think it's more.'

'Why?'

'She apologised to me.'

He froze, cup poised before the heater.

'She did what?'

'Apologised. For striking me. I assume you heard of the fight in–'

'I heard and do not care a jot either way,' he said, returning to his preparations. 'But my sister does not apologise.'

His tone was a little more measured now. Perhaps the tea really was calming, for he took the steaming cup with him, settling down opposite me.

'You think Esec is the threat my sister spoke of?' he asked.

'I could not say. But it seems likely. He holds remarkable influence for a non-combatant.'

'That's because this isn't a proper warzone,' he said. 'The real conflict is to the east. That is where Surling and Prospherous are now deployed, along with the majority of their forces. What remains is a token army – a few dozen aircraft and less than half a platoon, their only function to hold Edbar and produce a few more of those abominable vids. Surling favours Esec. He seems convinced he can shatter the resistance in the other fortresses by feeding them a stream of aeronautical victories. Madness.'

'I suppose it did lead to the liberation of Edbar.'

'Liberation?' he spat. 'Innumerable data-records have been burned and half the infrastructure shot. Our attack destroyed most of the air defences, there are multiple breaches in the external walls, and we lost a fifth of the indentured workers when the Láech broke through. And if we can't get the exterior secured, we are going to lose even more. The nights are cold here, and the days far too hot. There was no strategy behind any of it. Who the hell would use the Láech for siegecraft?'

He leant back, cradling his cup. For the first time I saw the bloodstains glistening on his greatcoat.

'The Láech are a liability?'

'Here? Absolutely. They are warriors and hunters. Were I to face a horde of orks in open battle I can think of no better regiment to stand at my side. But they are ill-suited to siege warfare. Storming a stronghold? Just point them in the right direction. But asking them to hold off? To wait around? Madness. Like assigning Savlar Chem-Dogs to parade duty. But Esec personally requested their deployment, probably because their body art looks good on a pict screen. He's caged wild dogs. I've executed three soldiers today, three men whom, if this were a different warzone, I would probably be commending for their bravery. All because some upstart values visuals over strategy.'

He sighed, shoulders slumping, his gaze lost in the steaming cup.

'Please tell me you have uncovered something of use.'

'No. But I am meeting with Plient later.'

'Who?'

'The flight commander's mechanical. And possibly handler. He was the one who assisted us on Bacchus. We would have lost without him. A fine man.'

'Hmph,' the commissar grunted, seemingly unimpressed. 'Has he revealed much to you?'

'Precious little thus far. Apparently your sister has sworn him to secrecy, and he is unwilling to break her confidence.'

'Protecting your superior's confidence is commendable. But I suggest you find a means of loosening his tongue. It would be preferable to me extracting the information. My methods are quite forthright.'

His tone was neutral, though my gaze lingered upon the blood on his coat.

'What if the message itself was a deception?' I said. 'Your sister claimed she had not sent it.'

'She's a habitual liar.'

'Perhaps. But she is not the only Flight Commander Shard I have seen on screen. Did you know she did not fly the mission today? Others operated planes bearing her markings. I'm wondering if she even flies any more, if all of this is mere artifice.'

He frowned. 'The only reason I assigned you to that propagandist was to get close to her, and that will not happen if she stays grounded. Let me see what I can do to get her back in the air – I still wield some influence.'

'With respect, sir, even if she does still fly, it doesn't change the fact that the message could be falsified. I just saw footage of her besting a soldier in the fighting ring, and I'm fairly certain it was cribbed from a vid of her knocking me to the ground. It strikes me that someone with the skill to splice those images together could potentially have fabricated the message, at least in part.'

'But to what ends?'

'That, I don't know.'

'Well find out,' the commissar replied, rising. 'Our contact will be minimal for the next few days. Edbar's fall has granted us access to the tunnels beneath. They were used to smuggle in supplies, but I intend to lead a force through there – see if we can find a path to infiltrating the other fortresses.'

He adjusted his cap, tutting at the blood on his lapel before levelling his gaze at me.

'I expect better news on my return.'

Plient's workshop was opposite the main hangar, where the majority of the aircraft were now maintained. I presumed it had previously been a fabricator of some sort, because he was already settled in, bent over the fuselage of an aircraft, aided by his augmetic limb, which seemed to function as both clamp and hammer.

He looked up as I entered, wiping his brow with his flesh hand and smiling.

'Good to see you again, sir,' he said.

'Likewise,' I replied, as Iwazar lurched past me, seemingly drawn by the activity. But it faltered suddenly, sensors swinging left and right, before surging towards something at the rear of the workshop. An aircraft covered by a drape.

It stared at it, before glancing to me, whistling incessantly. As I watched, it slowly began tipping to one side. Suddenly it toppled, the anti-grav generator momentarily misaligning. It righted itself at the last moment, climbing once more to eye level, before once again slowly tipping to one side.

'It's just an alignment issue,' I found myself saying. 'I just couldn't quite get the balance to–'

'You've done amazing work, sir,' Plient said, intent on the struggling machine. 'But I think this requires more than maintenance. Have you approached a priest of the Mechanicus?'

'No. And I doubt any would touch it.'

'But it's a prized relic, sir! The priests–'

'I am beneath the attention of the Mechanicus,' I replied. 'And were I to come to their attention, I expect my inexpert repairs would render the machine as heretek. And both it and I would be treated accordingly.'

He didn't answer. I think he knew I spoke the truth. Like me, Plient was sanctioned to complete the rituals of repair and maintenance required to keep our charges functional in the field. And like me, he had strayed far beyond this remit. Where we differed was competence. Plient had once cobbled together the means of creating a hololithic armada. I could barely keep Iwazar airborne.

Together, we watched it attempt to right itself again, surging a foot backwards in the process and almost colliding with a servitor hauling an engine carriage. It whirred in alarm, retreating and scuttling beneath the edge of the drape. If I didn't know better, I'd have thought it was cowering.

'Sir, I was wondering…'

'Yes?'

'Perhaps I could have a look at Iwazar? I could try and realign that anti-grav generator and patch a couple of those holes. Also, the leftmost sensor seems to be out. And that lens is cracked.'

'That would be gracious of you, but I fear–'

'Probably need to reboot the cogitator as well, see if that's the reason for the twitching flight,' he murmured, voice fading slowly. I could almost see the cogs turning in his head.

'Plient?'

He blinked, glancing over to me before smiling sheepishly.

'Sorry, sir. Sometimes I get too drawn in. Forget what's going on around me. But I would like to help, if I can.'

'I don't doubt your skill. But I'm not sure if Iwazar would be willing to accept your administrations. It has become wilful of late.'

'Understood, sir, but I can try.'

He slowly lowered himself to one knee, beckoning with his steel hand and cooing, as if he was encouraging a stray dog. I did not know where to look.

But Iwazar's lenses were suddenly fixed upon him, its cogitator whirring, uncertain. Then it bolted towards him, a puppy anxious to greet a long-absent friend. Only, its cracked casing was caught against the drape, and in doing so it tore it clear of the plane. As Iwazar tumbled, unable to compensate for additional weight, and Plient lurched forward to catch it, I found myself face to face with the vessel.

It was *Mendax Matertera*. Or Black Griffin, as some referred to it. The Lightning was famous now. Almost as famous as Shard. Its colour scheme had shifted, sandy-white over the top and a bright blue underlay, presumably to provide some minimal camouflage. It was also defanged, Plient having stripped out the autocannon and lascannons for maintenance, and the hard points beneath the wings were empty.

All but one.

Plient was already dragging the drape back into place, but I still saw the cracked skull grinning from the hard point. It was hard to miss.

'Sorry, sir,' he mumbled.

'What is that doing there?'

'The *Matertera*? Just a tune-up. Lightnings are temperamental and–'

'Not the plane,' I said, pointing to the occupied hard point. 'That.'

Staring back at us was Kikazar, one of my other seer-skulls. It too had seen better days.

'Ah,' Plient said. 'Well, when you met with us and… retrieved Iwazar–'

'It was mine by right. I needed the footage.'

'Granted. But you asked me to examine Kikazar, see if I could repair it. And then you were suddenly gone, sir. Left abruptly. Didn't say goodbye.'

'Yes. I am sorry about that, there was... I had to return to complete my pict.'

'And you forgot your seer-skull?'

'I was angry,' I said. 'Shard and I had a disagreement about the project. She accused me of... It doesn't matter now. My question is why is it still there?'

'She thought it a good-luck charm. I mentioned it in my letter.'

'Yes, I recall. I just assumed she would have disposed of it by now.'

'I couldn't say, sir. Sorry I didn't write more. I meant to. It's just so hard to get a message anywhere once you are out of the subsector. And I must write to my mum, sir. And my sisters. And I kept thinking if I waited longer, I'd have something better to write about...'

He trailed off, gaze settling on his feet, Iwazar bobbing beside him, as though hoping for a treat. I'd forgotten that the device had taken a liking to him on Bacchus, retreating to his hangar when under threat. I had forgotten much, it seemed.

'If you like, sir, I could request removing–'

'No need to trouble yourself. It is nothing more than a broken remnant of a worthless war. If she wishes to carry its weight that is her choice.'

I turned my back on it, my gaze falling on the section of fuselage Plient had been working on when I entered.

'What's this here?' I asked, desperate to change the subject. 'Another Lightning?'

'No, sir. This is a reconnaissance craft. Wrath model.'

'An aircraft with a cam? That would have been damn useful on Bacchus.'

'We had some at the start. But by the time you arrived, whatever was left of them had already become part of the ork fighters.'

I nodded. In truth I barely cared. I just didn't want to look at Shard's plane.

'So, you are repairing it?'

Plient shrugged. 'Not much left to repair. The whole thing was nearly obliterated. The film spools are housed beneath the cockpit, but the hatch is fused shut. I'm still trying to extract it without damaging them further.'

'It was shot down by the separatists?'

'Maybe. There have been some atmospheric disturbances. Not quite sure what's causing it. It seems confined to the Great Glass Plain.'

'Sounds like a region to avoid.'

'Ideally, yes, sir, but apparently navigating it is a necessity. For supplies.'

'Is that why you're undertaking this work?'

'No. To be honest, sir, since Esec arrived the recon planes are no longer valued. But casualties have been light and there is not so much for me to do here, and my mum always said idle hands work against the God-Emperor.'

He did not meet my gaze.

'Did Shard ask you to do this?'

'I can't really say, sir.'

I decided not to press the matter. He was not versed in deception, but he was loyal and kept his word, and I had no right to hold it against him.

But I found my eyes returning to the broken fuselage.

'Sir?'

'Hmm?'

'You… you have a look, sir.'

'It's nothing,' I sighed. 'It's just I seem to recall a previous war where atmospheric irregularities were overlooked. Right up until everyone started dying.'

CHAPTER FIFTEEN

'By the Throne this is tiresome. Do you know why we have been assigned this duty?'

Esec had turned to face me. He was not currently clad in the barge's command helm. It made him a little easier to talk to.

'I thought it was a supply run. Of a sort.'

'It's that commissar throwing his weight around. Why am I on this assignment? And Shard? She should not be flying.'

'Oh?'

'I mean, not a mission of such little significance. Forgive my bluntness, but do you know his motive?'

He asked softly enough. And the question was not unreasonable. But his focus was fixed on the mainscreen, the desert stretching out before us, and he would not meet my gaze.

'I suspect his motives are manifold.'

'Really?' he said, now turning to me. 'He struck me as a rather linear fellow. Well suited to his role, and suitably righteous in the God-Emperor's name. A man of iron, but not necessarily depth.'

'Perhaps. Still, I can discern one motive. Punishing his sister.'

'For striking you?'

'For losing her composure. I doubt the blow itself overly troubles him.'

'I can't say I envy you,' he said. 'Commander Shard presents her challenges, but at least she's captivating. The commissar is so stuffy. He lectured the war council for the better part of an hour last night, bemoaning our efforts and accusing us of abandoning Edbar. Meanwhile his sole strategy seems to consist of marching through the tunnels beneath the fortress in the hopes of stumbling across the enemy. I had to remind him that Edbar fell because of the workers rising up, rather than our soldiers climbing down. That got a few chuckles.'

'You are part of the war council?' I asked.

'Gracious, no!' He laughed. 'No. But Colonel Surling prefers that I attend to provide guidance on the optics of tactical decisions. How to frame the war so its outcome works to our advantage.'

'I see.'

'You do not look convinced.'

'I thought wars were there to be won, and our task was to present those victories.'

'Ah, but just as the maggots feed upon the bird, so too does the bird feed upon the maggots.'

He bowed his head, clearly pleased by this witticism. I suspect it was not the first time he'd employed it.

'If we build the narrative of victory and frame the conflict accordingly, we can end the war almost as soon as it starts. Of course, military commanders would prefer to drag out proceedings to obtain glory or power. But, like you, I think the objective should be to win as swiftly as possible with minimal casualties.'

'Then how does this framing work? What was the secret behind instigating Edbar's uprising?'

'Would that I could tell you succinctly! I analysed innumerable reports of customs, politics, sectarian divides – anything that would assist in the communication of our message. Something as simple as a colour choice, or the tone of voice employed can make all the difference. It was all designed to subliminally reinforce our righteousness.'

'And this was how you inspired an uprising?'

'Yes. It's just a lot of research and attention to detail. Two qualities I sometimes feel are lacking in our approach to warfare. I appreciate ignorance being a virtue for the masses, but those called upon to make decisions should ensure they understand the situation fully.'

I wondered if this was a veiled threat. It was hard to tell. Esec had an earnest quality, almost a desperation. To be liked, perhaps. Or at least admired.

Ahead, the sand was slowly shifting, revealing a blinding glare beneath. The barge was already adapting, filtering the excess light. It was reflected, of course, the sun's glare radiating from the surface.

Glass.

It stretched for miles, and a cursory reading of local history indicated it was a holy place, where the God-Emperor first delivered the 'Light of Truth' to Deighton. According to such tales the people were not prepared for His wisdom, and it burned bright enough to incinerate millions and fused the sand into glass. Since then, knowledge had been carefully guarded, separated, lest too much brought together begat another catastrophe.

When I mentioned this to Esec he laughed again.

'Yes, I think I read that somewhere,' he said. 'Interesting superstition, but I think the Great Glass Plain's origin is a little more pedestrian.'

'Oh?'

'A crater lies at its centre. I am assuming that was the point of detonation.'

'A bomb?'

'Possibly. Or perhaps an ancient plasma reactor overloaded. But it's charming how the locals developed this into some creation myth. They still claim His words haunt the plain, manifesting as multicoloured displays known as the "Light of Truth". A nonsense, of course – what they observe is merely reflected sunlight. Still, it's extraordinary the lies people accept to render an unpleasant truth palatable.'

He smiled, but the expression quickly faded.

'This is such a waste of my time,' he sighed. 'It's not that I'm unwilling to pitch in. The commander has been at the forefront of every meaningful conflict.'

'Sometimes several simultaneously.'

'Exactly! But there must be some benefit to outweigh the risk. I do not see that here.'

'I was under the impression this was not a dangerous assignment.'

'Yes, well, there have been *incidents*. Atmospheric irregularities begetting… accidents. Refracted las-bolts. Blinded pilots. Some odd optical effects. It's the glass, you see. It refracts light in an unusual way, causing visual distortions.'

Ahead, the smooth expanse gave way to what, at first, resembled a vast shimmering wall, a frozen eruption of undulating glass hundreds of miles wide, and stretching high enough to reach for the stars.

'Incredible,' I whispered. 'Is this the blast's epicentre?'

'Possibly.'

'It's astonishing.'

'Yes. That's what I said the first time. Everyone? Keep your eyes open.'

He was leaning forward in his chair now, intent on the screens, his lackadaisical manner absent.

Our vessel began to rise, like a leviathan breaking for the surface, the Lightnings and Avengers storming ahead. As we ascended it grew brighter, though the barge was quick to compensate for the glare. I don't know what I expected at the summit. More glass I supposed, perhaps shaped in some intriguing way by the heat of the supposed detonation.

But not darkness.

For the glass fell away at the summit, a sheer drop leading to a gaping chasm. I could not tell its composition because light refused to enter the gloom. It was blackness, pure and simple.

'Enticing, isn't it?'

Esec was beaming at the mainscreen. It might as well have been switched off.

'What is down there?' I asked.

'I wish I could tell you. The Eye I sent reached sea level before its sensors died, and its final reading gave no indication there was a bottom. It was like it disappeared.'

'Perhaps a subterranean operation could–'

'Perhaps. But we have not the time or resources to squander digging in the dirt. Our business is on the far side, and I would get to it.'

I nodded, but I could not drag my gaze from the screen. The darkness was like some vast maw waiting to swallow us whole. Absurd, for if our vessel were to fall, death would be just as certain over the glass as over the pit.

Still, I was relieved when we passed it, the glittering plains once more rolling out beneath us. But there was vegetation now, flashes of green and blue erupting from vast fissures in the glass. Esec's Eyes were certainly impressive, their lenses able to focus on the individual flowers adorning the shrubs. They were almost crystalline, the petals a vivid cyan that refracted the light, casting tiny rainbows across the glasscape.

'Pretty,' Lanlok said, his voice rumbling. I had almost forgotten the ogryn, who stood so still and silent. But he was right. I had been astounded by the flowers in the botanical gardens in Edbar, but they paled in comparison to these blooms. I wished I had brought Iwazar, but the seer-skull was under Plient's care.

Then the screens cut out. All but the mainscreen, which was focused on a vast shape lumbering across the plains.

CHAPTER SIXTEEN

It was hard to judge scale in the barren landscape, but the creature's size was apparent from the way it moved, six squat limbs rippling under its body's weight, its grey skin sagging and swaying.

And it was not alone. There was a pack – or perhaps herd was a better term, for they seemed to be grazing on the crystalline flowers, their long necks dipping, shovel-like teeth grinding the plants into powder. Their faces were flat and expressionless, and if they enjoyed their meal, they gave no sign of it. The sun still hung low on the horizon, and the shadows they cast might have stretched miles.

'Just how large are those beasts?' I asked.

'Hmm?' Esec frowned. 'The mamutida? Pretty big. I think one could swallow a Leman Russ tank. Probably not whole, it would take a couple of bites.'

'I've never seen anything like it. Are they common here?'

'They are confined to this plain. There is something about the mineral density of the fauna – I forget the details. The locals apparently consider them semi-divine, believing one carried the God-Emperor across the desert when He was wounded by the darkness. Nonsense obviously, but the beasts are nevertheless revered.'

The creatures appeared oblivious to our presence. They seemed docile, despite the curved horns erupting from their temples. As I watched, one brought its head down, smashing into the glass. It rammed its head deeper, emerging clutching a mouthful of crystalline roots that it promptly began to chew.

Then it froze, vast nostrils quivering.

Its head rose, mouth yawning open, but we were far enough away that it took a moment for the bellow to reach us, the sound echoing across the glass plain. There was a violent hiss of feedback, Esec's auditors quickly compensating and filtering the noise into a plaintive cry that carried to my very bones.

'Don't they ever shut up?' Esec was clutching his ears, his fingers stealing to his temple and engaging his vox. 'Flight Commander Shard? Is there some problem?'

'Hmm?'

'Commander? Confirm?'

'Confirm what? And which Shard are you talking to?'

'You, obviously. But–'

'All right, but for future reference I think I should be designated as Shard Prime.'

'Fine. But–'

'Just to avoid confusion.'

'Understood–'

'And needless delays. Over.'

'...Shard Prime, why haven't you engaged?'

The herd was accelerating away, the beasts slowly breaking into a lumbering half-run, the force driving jagged cracks through the glasscape.

'Haven't received my order, acting-commander.'

'Just be done with it. And for Throne's sake don't miss. I don't want a refracted shot hitting my barge.'

'You don't want to deploy those Eyes of yours? Set up some scintillating cinematography?'

'I have deployed a handful. It will suffice.'

Esec cut the vox. He looked at me, perhaps only then realising the conversation had been broadcast throughout the studio.

Panic flashed across his eyes, until I met his gaze and shook my head.

'She can be so tiresome.'

'Exactly!' He smiled, relieved. 'By the Throne, it's not like I'm asking anything difficult! It's not as though the beasts can defend themselves.'

On the mainscreen, the mamutida ran, their hooves kicking up a sparkling cloud of dust.

A las-bolt tore into one's rear.

It barely slowed, redoubling its efforts. But so did our fighters. They unleashed their weapons against the beasts, and Esec was right – they had no defence beside their thick hide. A tank convoy could be crushed beneath their hooves, an infantry platoon reduced to a smear. But their airborne assailants were untouchable.

Another las-bolt struck. And one of the mamutida staggered.

Instantly, the fighters focused upon the creature. Its pace faltered under the barrage, and I could now make out visible tears in its flesh, the blood a violent pink. Was it smaller than the others? It seemed to be, though it was hard to tell as the rest were racing away.

All but one.

It was a huge creature – horns spiralled many times over. It turned, loping back to its dying herdmate, using its bulk to shield it from some of the blasts. But it was no use. The fallen mamutida was bleeding out. It still lived, though, for it offered a horrible mewing sound as loud as thunder. The great beast nuzzled its stricken companion. Then it raised its head, unleashing a cry of pure anguish.

Perhaps the dying creature was its calf.

The aircraft were withdrawing now, leaving the mamutida to mourn its fallen. I doubt it could comprehend what had happened. Possibly the beasts had never been hunted, the indigenous population leaving them to their plodding lives. But we had come, an enemy they could barely comprehend attacking them for reasons they would never fathom. I could see why Esec had little interest in capturing footage; there were no heroes here, only the hunters and the helpless. As the Eyes zoomed in on the gaping wounds, I suddenly realised the origin of those great slabs of grey flesh the Láech had served on that first night.

I did not think I wished to eat it again.

The vox hissed. Not Shard, a less familiar voice. Vagbon?

'Propagandist Esec? A hauler crew is on standby to carve the carcass. But the larger beast refuses to abandon its fallen.'

'And? What would you have me do?'

'There are options, sir. We could attempt to dispatch the beast, or drive it away.'

'Wing sergeant, this is clearly a military matter, so I will leave it to Flight Commander Shard. Commander? Please do whatever is deemed necessary. And if you could make it at least somewhat visually stimulating, that would be fantastic.'

He sounded bored.

There was no reply beyond the gunning of an engine. The mainscreen flickered, and I saw a Lightning spiralling lazily towards the distraught mamutida.

It accelerated. Faster still. Esec leaned forward, touching his temple, and a score of Eyes detached, following Shard, who was now hurtling towards the mamutida, her craft barely a few hundred yards above the ground.

It raised its head, and autocannon fire thudded into its face. The beast roared in pain and fury, swinging its head about with astonishing speed. Shard twisted from its path, coming about before once again surging straight at the creature, who in turn lowered its horns and charged with the pace and grace of an enraged avalanche.

Her lascannons flared. I had seen the weapons puncture a battle tank, but a searing blast barely scorched the creature's skin. She only had time for one shot before it was on her, its huge bulk hurtling towards the aircraft.

She slid from its path, releasing a barrage of flares right into the mamutida's eyes. It stumbled as her craft soared between its legs, rotating on its side. Her wing scraped the glass, throwing a shower of sparks, but she stayed airborne, escaping right as the missiles detonated.

I hadn't seen when she'd released them. I suppose they were dropped rather than fired, for she rode the explosion, the blast propelling her on even as it knocked the already stumbling beast from its feet. It tumbled, the ground cracking beneath it, throwing up jagged shards and a vast cloud of dust.

I assumed it dead, either from the blast or its fall. But it gave a rumbling moan, and slowly hobbled upright, its gaze falling once more upon its fallen kin.

It brayed a final time, before limping off, dragging its hind leg. Defeated.

'Magnificent.' Esec smiled, looking at me, his eyes gleaming. 'I thought this a waste of time, but we can splice that into something memorable. Flight Commander Lucille von Shard defeated a rampaging monster!'

'I thought the creatures were docile and revered?'

'It wouldn't be for local consumption. This would be for the wider Imperium. Or the next world at least.'

He was still grinning as the haulage crew moved in to dissect the calf's carcass.

Esec was in better spirits on the return flight. He was keen to demonstrate his art, dulling the studio's lights as Shard's conflict with the mamutida matriarch occupied the mainscreen. I had to feign interest whilst he attacked the footage with the precision and grace of a back-alley butcher. A pair of Imperial citizens were his first addition to the scene. I recognised the stock footage from older picts. This was followed by a series of explosions, seemingly unleashed by the mamutida. The blasts looked real enough, though the execution was sloppy. Esec made no effort to adjust light or shadow. The aircraft appeared to hurtle east one moment then west seconds later, all as part of the same attack run.

When I noted this, he laughed.

'Honestly, Kile, do you think anyone cares?' he asked. 'You think the citizens will turn away because of the misuse of the backlight? This is a one-minute vid. I will splice it, cut it, release it, and then discard it. It's like casting a stone into a pool. One could smooth the stone, refine the throw, but why bother? The stone is unimportant. What matters are the ripples.'

A second screen flared into life. On it, a plane in Shard's colours was engaging with the separatists, slicing one in half with a las-bolt.

'This thirty-second skirmish?' Esec said. 'Already been round the planet twice. Imagine it – you are one of the many citizens attending your duties, trying to ignore the whispers of war. But suddenly this materialises on your data-slate. You see a hero, you hear her urge you to resist, that your superiors are lying and have turned from the God-Emperor's light. The overseers try to stamp it out, but that just strengthens the message. And more clips follow – Shard saving civilians, overcoming monsters, fighting for the Master of Mankind. Each leaves a ripple in the minds of those who view it. No one cares to examine the stone.'

I nodded. I was supposed to be learning, after all, though the lesson thus far was that Esec had less of an eye for detail than he claimed. Otherwise, he would not have chosen a clip that had been doctored from my own work. I knew it well, for this was Shard defending Governor Dolos' mansion from the first ork attack. I had been unable to capture much, but Esec had done an admirable job cleaning up the footage. Repurposing it.

I wondered how many times he'd used it.

If he could insert new enemies, add whatever visual effects he needed, how many shots of Shard did he really need?

Apparently a few more, given that Esec had instructed our counterfeit Shards to run additional drills. They hurtled past the barge, performing various stunts even as Esec urged them to tighten their turns. With each pass he'd skim away a little more of the backdrop, splicing the images together, the final product a blur hurtling with the force of a fallen star. This was to be the opening shot, the beginning of an attack run culminating in the felling of the beast.

I should have paid closer attention, for in truth the technique was unknown to me. But I caught a glimmer of light on the glass plain below. Faint, but unmistakable. As Esec continued his work, I watched the colours dance on one of the peripheral screens. Its origin was unclear. I have visited worlds whose magnetic fields can produce remarkable visual effects, but such activities are usually confined to the poles. Precipitation was a possibility, except since arriving on Deighton I had yet to see rain. I would have queried it if Flight Sergeant Vagbon hadn't pre-empted me.

'Propagandist Esec, something odd is registering on the auspex.'

'One moment. Shard Three, another pass please, this time with a half-roll?'

The craft obeyed, approaching for another pass, even as a kaleidoscope of light glimmered against its hull.

Esec frowned. 'Hang on, something is wrong with the lens. The colours are–'

Then it was gone. The plane vanished, replaced by a burning cloud of fractured metal. For an instant I wondered if Esec was employing some cinema-pict trick, at least until he bolted from his chair.

'What in His name?' he said. 'What happened? Shard Two, Come in.'

'Sir! I don't know. Shard Three is down, and the auspex thinks something passed us. Or many things. It can't determine–'

Our screens lit up just in time to capture another explosion, the Eyes drawn to the eruptions of light and sound. A second Lightning was struck, a blade of cyan light carving off its left wing. As it tumbled from the sky, the storm of light accelerated towards us, like a kaleidoscope of multifaceted diamonds. I suspect that had the light not been filtered through the Eyes, staring at it would have risked blindness.

'–Thone's name are they? I can't see–'

'Shard Three and Shard Two are both down. Come in to–'

'–around your six. What the–'

I could not understand the gabble of voices. Neither could Esec. He was intent on the screen, mouth agape, unable to process the unfolding calamity. Neither could I for that matter, watching as the storm of light hurtled from us, outpacing even the fastest Lightning as it accelerated away. I thought it was over. But it slowed, the colours coalescing, fractured images folding together.

And for a moment I saw a silhouette framed by the sun.

It looked a little like a hawk, but one almost the size of a Lightning, its beak sharp and wings tapered, nothing like the robust design of Imperial fighters. Apparently, it shared a bird's manoeuvrability too, for it turned on seemingly nothing, and was suddenly hurtling towards us for a second pass. As it accelerated, the hawk-like silhouette became a multihued flock, then a storm of diamonds, its form lost amidst the ever-shifting light.

On another screen I saw Shard rise to meet it, unleashing her autocannon into the dazzling display, perhaps counting on the volley of shells to strike something solid in the maelstrom of colour. But it was not to be. Instead, a single bolt of cyan erupted from the light storm. It struck her craft, the vessel erupted in flames–

'No!'

My voice. I had surged from my seat, and was staring open-mouthed as the Lightning fell.

'–Shard One is down! We have lost–'

It was not her. Just a squad leader bearing the same markings. I lowered myself into my seat, seeking her craft on the myriad screens.

There. She had stolen behind whatever attacked us and was poised to retaliate. Her lascannons flared, but as they did so our attacker suddenly hurtled skywards, accelerating at impossible speed, even as its afterimages danced mockingly in the glass plain beneath us.

Then they too were gone.

I turned to Esec. He was sitting very still, mouth agape, eyes shifting left and right as he tried to comprehend what had happened. It only took a quick glance at the screen to confirm the extent of the casualties.

Each squadron had been beheaded. Shard One, Shard Two, Shard Three. All three squad leaders eliminated in moments. In fact, only one surviving craft now bore the black griffin markings.

The vox flared into life. A familiar voice echoed across the studio.

'Esec? Belay my previous request. I don't think the Shard Prime designation is necessary any more.'

CHAPTER SEVENTEEN

'Still awake, Simlex?'

I glanced up from my data-slate to find Rosln standing in the doorway of the *Traderi*'s communal space.

'Sadly so. There was an incident – I think that's the term Esec prefers.'

She nodded, stripping off gauntlets and helm and placing them on the table before heading through to the commissar's private chambers. I returned to my data-slate. Esec had reluctantly provided copies of footage captured during the attack. I was reviewing them, as well as a few other things I'd manage to liberate from his data-store.

Rosln did not take long. Presumably that meant our cargo was secure. The commissar had not been clear exactly when we would be free of it, and I had elected not to question him.

'How goes the liberation?' I asked, as she emerged from the doorway.

'It would appear the indentured workers of Edbar are less

enamoured by their liberation than one might hope,' she sighed, stepping past me to the recaff machine. She took two cups down, knowing better than to ask me.

'Presumably because many of them were butchered by the Láech?'

'That's not the official position.'

'Perhaps not. But I suspect the survivors will remember.'

I angled the data-slate so she could see the screen before playing the vid. An image appeared: narrow corridors, dark and muddied by smoke and dust. There was no sound, at least none presented, which gave the whole thing an unreal quality. Even when robed figures sprinted past, pursued by pale-skinned warriors in flak armour.

The Láech.

One of the fleeing figures turned, struggling to ready a weapon, but the nearest Láech was on him, knife buried in the man's throat. Blood sprayed across the attacker, who howled silently, even as his squadmates unleashed a flurry of las-bolts to finish off the other fleeing figures.

'It is not the best optics,' I said. 'Frankly, without context, an observer might assume the robed figures were loyal Imperial servants, and the Láech hellbent on murder.'

As I spoke, the knife wielder began smearing blood across his cheeks.

'I assume this footage will not make it into a pict?' she said, placing a steaming mug beside me. A spoon was suspended vertically within, only tipping slowly, the recaff thicker than swamp water.

'Of course not,' I replied as she took a seat at the table, cradling her own cup. 'I gather relations with the indentured workers are tense already. The last thing we need is footage of them being massacred by their supposed liberators.'

'Agreed. The situation is already... challenging.'

There was much unsaid in that pause. I looked up, watching as she blew the steam from her drink. Her expression tended towards inscrutable, like the rest of the Scions. But it had been at least two days since she'd slept, or at least slept on the *Traderi*. Perhaps that was why I could see a hint of concern in her eyes.

'The damage to Edbar's infrastructure is extensive,' she continued. 'And the nights are cold. We have begun constructing temporary shelters, but that involves dismantling more of the infrastructure, making the problem worse. The indigenous workforce, the ones who maintained Edbar? Those who aren't dead seem to have vanished. I suspect they are occupied with their immediate survival, but without them the situation will not improve. Several food stores were destroyed in the attack, and the desert is not abundant with bounty. There is already evidence of cannibalism. Only of the dead thus far. But give it time.'

Her words were addressed to her cup, but I found my gaze drawn to her bloodstained armour. The marks were bright even under the subdued light of the communal space.

'It seems the uprising was not as bloodless as we might have hoped.'

'Yes. When you encourage citizens to overthrow their rulers, you risk them acquiring a taste for it. They deposed their overseers because of a bombardment of half-truths and assurances that, thus far, have led to nothing. What if they take the lesson too well, and decide another uprising is the solution to their current state?'

'You think that likely?'

She opened her mouth but hesitated. Her eyes hardened a shade.

'Forgive me,' I said. 'I should not ask. I know there are limits to what you can say.'

She shrugged, gaze fixed upon her cup.

'You heard of our encounter over the glass plain?'

'I heard several planes were lost due to an atmospheric anomaly,' she said. 'At least, that was what was reported to Colonel Surling.'

'Yes. Even before we completed the return journey Esec was claiming it a natural phenomenon – the crystalline landscape refracting light into something comparable to a las-bolt. Apparently this is not the first time something like that has happened.'

'You think he believes that?'

'Not at first, otherwise he would not have permitted me to review the files. But by the time we reached Edbar, I think he had himself half convinced. It reminds me of being on Bacchus. So much of the early conflict was dictated by a stubborn refusal to face reality, to insist that the galaxy worked a certain way and evidence that challenged that paradigm must be dismissed. Yet I keep coming back to this image.'

I rotated the data-slate, displaying the screen. She watched our planes being consumed by a storm of light.

'This is no atmospheric phenomenon,' she murmured. 'It almost looks like… I can't tell. Is there a shape or…?'

'I thought it resembled a hawk, or some other predator,' I continued. 'I tried researching Edbar legends, those few I can access. There are fables about lights over the Great Glass Plain, legends claiming the God-Emperor once whispered a great truth so shocking that those who heard His voice were incinerated, and His proclamations fused the desert sands into glass. The Light of Truth – that's what they call it. Some say His words can still be seen above the plain, manifesting as a dazzling display, or as jagged flowers that only the sacred mamutida can graze upon without consequence.'

'Mamutida?'

'The creatures we have been using to feed the Láech. They are considered a manifestation of the God-Emperor's benevolence and majesty.'

'Hmm. Then it is probably for the best that the citizens don't discover what we have been using to supplement their diet.'

I glanced at her. 'What?'

'We have limited food. It's better than encouraging cannibalism.'

'Providing they don't uncover what's sitting on the end of their forks.'

'Indeed,' she said, nodding. She drained her cup and rose, retrieving both gauntlets and helm.

'You must return?'

'Yes. I have ensured our cargo remains secure and now I find myself tarrying when there is much to do.'

She slid her gauntlets into place, but she seemed hesitant somehow. Distracted.

'Tempestor?'

'Sorry. I was thinking,' she murmured. 'You said you saw something that resembled a bird of prey?'

'Possibly.'

'I believe one of the data-scribes made reference to a crimson hawk. She used it as a metaphor for an unpalatable truth.'

'You think it connected to what I saw?'

'Perhaps, depending on the expression's origin. Would you like me to make enquiries?'

'If it would not overly trouble you.'

'I can perhaps find a spare moment,' she said with an echo of a smile. 'Brice will take the next shift with the cargo, but I should return within a few days. Perhaps I will have answers to your questions.'

'Thank you. And good luck.'

'The Emperor protects,' she replied, her helm slid into place. Then she turned away and was gone.

I watched as Plient made some final adjustments to the device. He looked up, offering a tight smile, his cheek smeared with grease.

'Think that should do it, sir. Do you want to see how it runs?'

I nodded. 'Iwazar.'

With barely a beat, the seer-skull rose from Plient's bench, ascending to eye level. It still looked a disaster, the metal plating marred by ugly soldering scars. But it no longer hung lopsided, and so far had not emitted that chainblade-like whirring sound.

'Looks like it's level,' Plient said, examining the device critically. 'The alignment was completely off, sir. I'm amazed you managed to get it airborne again.'

I shrugged. 'I studied what data-scraps I could find. I had time – that's one of the advantages of being shunned.'

'I couldn't help but notice you had made a few... alterations to the design,' he said. 'Sir, are you aware the full-spectrum setting is now connected to a modified–'

'I'm aware. Did you remove it?'

'No, though I rewired some of your work. Just enough so it wouldn't explode. Probably. I'm still not sure it's safe, sir. There's a lot going on in there.'

'Thank you, Plient. I will be careful.'

'Understood, sir. You might want to run a general test, then. Make sure the systems are as expected.'

'Iwazar, playback. Random file.'

A whir. But softer. The projector flared. The image was a little indistinct, but I could still make out the swampland and stunted trees, as could Plient.

'Ah, that takes me back,' he said, with something akin to a smile. 'How long has it been, sir?'

'I suppose it depends where you have been stationed. A few Terran years?'

'Seems longer,' he murmured, intent on the device. 'Projector seems consistent. I think it's as good as it's going to be, sir.'

'Thank you, Plient. Once again you have worked miracles.'

'No, sir. Just done my duty.'

'You do not give yourself enough credit. Your ingenuity and engineering skills are what granted us victory on Bacchus.'

'Oh, I doubt that, sir. You and the commander are the heroes. I merely supported you.'

'Without you we would have failed.'

He tried to suppress a smile, with little success. 'I don't know, sir,' he said, grin widening. 'I suppose we all pitch in and play our part. Work together for the betterment of all. My mum always said the God-Emperor has many hands. That's how He wields so many weapons.'

I looked at him. 'You still wish to fight, Plient?'

He shook his head. 'I learnt my lesson, sir. From now on I keep my feet on the ground. Don't want the commander to have to pay for another limb.'

'Quite.'

His gaze flicked to my ruined leg. 'Sir, I know your injury must trouble you. I am sure the commander would be happy to pay for–'

'Are the repairs complete, Plient?'

'Yes, sir.'

'Then I thank you, but I must return to my duties. We lost three Lightnings over the plain, though one of the pilots managed to eject in time. All squad leaders. All bearing Flight Commander Shard's livery.'

'Yes, sir. Very odd.'

'And Esec has the gall to claim it a freak accident, some

distortion from the Great Glass Plain. But I saw something, Plient. Only for a moment. It could have been a hawk. Or even a griffin, were such things even real. When it struck, it was like–'

My voice was drowned suddenly by a roar. I had been lost in my thoughts, and only now saw that Plient was standing against a vast turbofan, the engine muffling my voice. He looked me square in the eye, and slowly shook his head, before nodding towards the window. Beyond lay the ruined buildings of Edbar, its walkways shaded by stretched canvas, its streets cast in shadow.

But above them, something looked down. The gleam of lenses intent on those below.

Esec's Eyes.

They were always there. Watching, Listening. But how? Esec could direct them, assign targets or detection patterns. But when would he have time to review such a volume of footage? He had to sleep. Perhaps he did have a crew hidden somewhere in the barge, each member tasked with the operation of a single unit.

Or perhaps something else was behind the Eyes.

Plient motioned me towards the vivisected fuselage of the recon plane, far from the window and noisome engine. Laid out beside it was a tattered backpack. He lifted it, his augmetic limb masking the weight, for within lay twin canisters, each about a foot and a half in length.

'The film from the recon plane, sir,' he said, mouth pressed to my ear.

'I see. And the backpack?'

'Intended for the pilot to carry it away in the event of a crash.'

'Seems optimistic,' I said, opening one canister, unrolling the film and holding it to the light.

I might have struggled with it when I was a real propagandist. But my recent duties as a scribe involved deciphering reams of such footage. What I saw was sand mostly, interspersed by the occasional rock formation.

Suddenly I had a stark image of only sky. Odd, given the cam was mounted on the aircraft's underside. Then spiralled images, a rotation of sand and sky. Then nothing.

I re-examined the sky. True colour was difficult to assess on a negative, especially given the poor quality of the film. But I knew the light was wrong, the colours distorted. And on a single frame, I found a blurred silhouette.

I suppose it looked a little like a hawk. The same impossibly tapered wings and pointed beak. But from this angle I could see it lacked a tail, the wings mounted at the rear.

The next frame it was gone, supplanted by a burst of light.

It was nothing conclusive. A single image stolen from a damaged roll of film. But I felt it sufficient to prove that whatever had beset our forces, it was not confined to the Great Glass Plain.

CHAPTER EIGHTEEN

Plient had thrust a data-slug into my hand just before ushering me from the hangar. I only accessed it on returning to the *Traderi*, finding its contents to be a disparate tangle of reports and files. Though unredacted, they were so poorly filed and riddled with jargon and coded language that it was hard to make sense of most of it. Still, the prevalence of 'Glorious Opportunities for Martyrdom in the North' suggested the push had stalled, the Deightonians digging in at the mountains. Admiral Desora's demands for the deployment of viral weapons had been met with silence, perhaps because the administrators tasked with submitting the request appeared to be downwind of the offensive.

It took time to identify the documents relevant to the current campaign. Given their sensitivity, I thought it unlikely Plient could have obtained them. That would require someone of higher rank. A flight commander at least.

The first report of atmospheric irregularities related to an encounter with the Desert Wind, a separatist fighter ace Shard duelled over the Great Glass Plain. Both Shard and Vagbon had reported a strange light that seemingly obliterated their foe, though the official report concluded he had been clipped by a stray las-bolt refracted by the glass.

No other incidents followed. Not for months. But there were irregularities. A squad disappeared after passing the saltlands to the east of the Great Glass Plain, their last vox-message complaining that the sky was on fire. Several recon planes had been shot down, though that was not unusual, given their role. And there were unaccounted losses: individuals here and there, scattered seemingly at random across our forces, some from before the Desert Wind. The numbers were not significant, but many were deep within our territory, and it seemed unlikely to be the work of the separatists' minimal air support.

Of course, on Bacchus we had similarly underestimated the orks. Those supposedly dim-witted xenos had somehow cobbled together a teleportation device, employing it to outmanoeuvre our forces. It was feasible the people of Deighton had some secret weapon – a relic from a brighter age that they had kept hidden.

But that would not explain why the Desert Wind was targeted.

Feeling frustrated, I leant back in my seat and used both hands to elevate my leg, placing my twisted foot on the adjacent chair. I was used to the pain, but it remained an irritant, always occupying a little space in my head. Never quite letting me bring all I could to a problem.

Think.

The first confirmed strike had been against the separatists. Against this Desert Wind, who according to the reports was a formidable fighter. So, whatever the threat, it did not serve our foes or us.

A third party? Or some indigenous creature? Perhaps a predator that preyed upon the mamutida, our recent actions having disturbed it?

I might have believed that. The galaxy was inhabited by creatures both bizarre and terrible. But I had seen that image on the film, shot from almost directly below. In that moment, it did not so much resemble a hawk as a blade with wings.

I should review it, I decided. Iwazar had taken a copy of the pict-reel. I glanced to the seer-skull hovering beside me, expectant. I had to credit Plient; it was no longer lolling and seemed less inclined to wander off.

'Iwazar. Display recon vid. Image seventy-three.'

The device purred, the image materialising smoothly. There it was: a knife with sickle-sharp wings. I had never seen–

The image shorted, Iwazar's engine whirring in alarm. Suddenly a Lightning was hurtling through the sky, its wings adorned with Shard's livery. I knew it, for it was the same attack run I had witnessed from my seat on Esec's barge. Where, just for a moment, I thought she–

The craft exploded in a dazzling display. The image cut out, Iwazar's projector going dark.

I sighed. It seemed the seer-skull still had some quirks. Could Plient assist? Whatever afflicted it seemed beyond a pure mechanical issue. I was debating whether or not to disturb him when Iwazar's vox-unit began blaring.

'Receive,' I said.

The holo-projector flared, Esec's face materialising above the table, hair strewn about his eyes.

'Kile? What in the Throne's name was that!?'

'I beg your pardon?'

'Oh, spare me! Only two people on this planet have copies of that footage. From the… incident. And I for one did not just upload it to the Feed.'

'You saw it too?'

'Everyone saw it. Not just Edbar, every data-fortress for miles! We had just breached their wretched data-veil. Tonight was going to be my debut pict. I have worked for weeks for this moment. And that is the first thing they see? Our hero's apparent death? What do you expect to follow that? Her funeral?'

I had never seen him so enraged, his veined temple pulsing in fury.

'I am not responsible. Even with the data-files I would not be capable of such a feat. Besides, I am ensconced in my shuttle, with no access to whatever transmitter Edbar possesses. Surely your Eyes can confirm that?'

He stared at me, still raging. But something in my words must have got through.

'Then who is it? Who has access to my files?'

'Do you have subordinates who–'

'Only I have access. Everything is gene-locked and secure. I reluctantly gave you a handful of vids, and now snippets have been shared across half the continent! How long before someone takes a copy off-planet? I have too much invested in Shard! She can't just die like that!'

'She hasn't.'

'But they don't know that! You don't understand how far I work in advance. I had vids dispatched yesterday for wars taking place tomorrow!'

He was raving, hololithic spittle spraying from his lips.

'You've lost me,' I said.

'You know how long it takes a pict to cross the galaxy? I must plan ahead! It's not like the outcome is in doubt, and the quicker citizens are made aware of our triumphs, the more likely they are to bolster our cause. I have shuttles prepped to dispatch the next month's battles for warp transit. Shard is already booked to clear the insurgents in

the north. It's going to look a little odd if, part way through this campaign, she is suddenly dead.'

'Then put out another vid, confirming she is alive and the previous—'

'I am supposed to use a vid to inform our citizens not to believe the vids? That they might be fabricated? How would that help? Can you not see the eventual outcome of such a policy?'

I took a deep breath. 'Then speak the truth. Some dissident hacked—'

'So now our broadcasts are compromised before they even commence?'

'Perhaps Shard was shot down by enemy forces, but survived through the intervention—'

'Don't be absurd. No, we just ignore it. Postpone a day or two. People quickly forget. It's just a blip. All this. A little blip – some error in the cogitator when we attempted to upload the data. That must be it.'

The anger had faded, leaving a brittleness.

'We need to devise a new pict. Something so inspiring it will erase any memory of this misstep. I'll need your help putting it together. I can trust you, can't I, Kile? I'm sorry for my outburst – I panicked. I couldn't think of anyone else capable of this feat.'

'I think you overestimate me.'

'Perhaps. But you will help, won't you? I need to produce something stupendous.'

'I will assist, but don't you fear another data breach?'

'No chance of that. All passcodes have been reset and a full lockdown of Edbar's transmitter is in effect. I don't know how someone accessed it last time, but they will not be doing it again.'

'That is something.'

'And Kile? Those files I permitted you to take? I need them destroyed. Not because I don't trust you, but because it would seem they cannot be secured. And I would not want someone going after you to retrieve them.'

'I will immediately void them from my data-slate.'

'Thank you! I will see you in the morn.'

The image collapsed, his face fading even as I picked up my data-slate and returned to the files.

CHAPTER NINETEEN

Esec's project was situated in an expanse of desert just outside Edbar. They must have started early, for I arrived a little after dawn to find a score of aircraft had been dragged into place by teams of servitors. Sadly, the lumbering cyborgs lacked the dexterity to perform the next duty, so that was left to the ground crew.

They were repainting the Lightnings. Or had been anyway; the process had seemingly ground to a halt due to a disagreement between the crews, pilots and Propagandist Esec. He was at the centre of the debate, gesturing frenetically, Lanlok behind him, arms folded. I wondered if assuming that posture was part of his training. For, if his arms were crossed, there was less risk of him inflicting an accidental decapitation with an errant limb.

He looked at me, glaring. Despite the raised voices, I was his focus, and I did not like his expression. Had Esec told him to watch me? Was I still a suspect for yesterday's supposed blip?

'You aren't wading in, propagandist?'

The voice came from my shoulder. I turned to find Shard

standing beside me, clad in her flight suit, her glare visor in place, a small metal flask tucked in her palm.

'I'm surprised you're awake,' I replied.

'Haven't been to bed yet. Sleep is for the weak. And you never answered my question.'

'I decided the best aid I could provide was not offering an opinion.'

'Ah, if only you'd discovered this mantra earlier. We'd all have benefited.'

'If only I'd elected to never involve myself in your family's business in the first place.'

'True. There really is no end to the ways you've *básked* up.'

I frowned, glancing at her. 'I'm unfamiliar with that phrase.'

'I learned it from the Láech. I'm sure it's clear from the context,' she said, taking a long swig from her flask. She went to replace the cap, then stopped and offered it to me.

'Is it recaff?'

'Amongst other things. Are you tired, propagandist?'

'I'm not the one hiding behind a glare visor.'

'I do it for the people. We can't have me looking a little delicate. The citizens must believe me invincible.'

'Hence this farce.'

I felt the word apt. Esec's plan involved assembling a faux enemy squadron by repainting some of our aircraft. They were to joust with our forces, before being seemingly destroyed via selective use of spliced footage. From the snatches of conversation I had overheard, it seemed this was not a new initiative. But on this occasion the crews did not appear to be cooperating.

As I watched, a pilot rounded on one of the ground crew, shoving him.

'Flight Sergeant Poskeri,' Shard muttered. 'Good shot, but bit of a temper.'

The crew member would have fallen if not caught by his fellows. Perhaps they shoved him at Poskeri. Perhaps he launched himself. Either way the two fell in a tangle of limbs, though my view was now blocked by the press of bodies. One body, in particular. Lanlok had uncrossed his arms and was advancing with the inevitability of a landslide. Esec was trying to restrain him, arms wrapped around the ogryn's forearm, his efforts having no visible impact on the giant's pace.

'Someone is going to die.'

Her voice was cold. Resigned. She took another swig, then splashed the flask's remaining contents across her face and hair. The smell hit me even as she strode towards the gathering riot, bellowing at the top of her voice.

'Esec? What in the Throne's name is the holdup? Do you know how long I've been having to stand there? Without a chair or anything? And I need a better-shaded area – the sun is awful for my skin. If we are to do any reshoots–'

As her rant continued the scuffle subsided, all eyes drawn to the spectacle, none pleased to see her. Lanlok rounded on her, but Esec had trained the brute well, for he made no move to attack, instead imposing himself between Shard and the group, acting as living bollard.

Esec manoeuvred round him, motioning Shard to lower her voice. I could not hear their exchange. I suppose I could have used Iwazar to eavesdrop, but there seemed little point. The seer-skull waited beside me. So far, it was behaving, having suffered no additional glitches.

One of the pilots was tapping Esec's shoulder. He turned, and Shard took this as her cue to retire, tucking her flask into her lapel as she passed me.

'Did you just break up the fight by being obnoxious?' I asked.

She slowed, just for a moment. Then shook her head and continued, moving away even as Esec approached.

'Throne, this is a disaster,' he said. 'Apparently, we lack sufficient paint to complete the refurbishment. And half the pilots are refusing to fly.'

'They do not wish to play the part of our foes?'

'In some instances.'

'It's Shard, isn't it? They won't fly under her colours.'

'Not the veterans, no. It's considered bad form to fly under another pilot's livery. I'd convinced them this was a foolish superstition. But that was before the incident over the Great Glass Plain.'

'Perhaps the actual Flight Commander Lucille von Shard should do it?'

'Are you mad? Look at her.'

He had a point. Having stormed off, she had found herself some shade under the wing of a Thunderbolt and was stretched out in the sand, her jacket removed and placed over her face as a screen.

'I've seen her in a worse state,' I said.

'I truly doubt that.'

His tone unsettled me. I turned, studying his face. There was sweat on his brow, more than was warranted by the early sun. His eyes were heavy, dark marks beneath them.

'You don't know what it's been like,' he said. 'She was always difficult, but ever since that mission she undertook for her brother...'

'The commissar?'

'No. One of the others. I think his name was Rile? I don't know, I wasn't permitted to escort her, and the Eye I sent to record the battle was destroyed. When she came back she was... Let's say she didn't cope with it well. I had to step in eventually, remind her what might happen if she did not fulfil her duties. But she's still been out of sorts. Sometimes I worry when she gets in the plane that she will just take off and fly away until her engine dies.'

He trailed off, his gaze settling on the counterfeit fighters. His voice was soft.

'What are we even doing?'

'Making a pict?' I offered.

'I don't even make those. Not serious picts like you once did. I just splice together clips and release them like baby birds. I don't know where they land, or if they make much difference.'

'They must do. You said yourself that the only reason Edbar fell was because it was opened from the inside. That is your work, surely?'

He nodded, brightening. 'Yes. Yes, what else could it be? Thank you, Kile. You're right. We will get this pict done even if I must fly the plane myself!'

He squared his shoulders, taking two strides towards the pilots before slowing, glancing over his shoulder.

'Obviously, I won't actually fly it. It was merely an expression.'

'Again!'

Esec's voice seemed to come from all around me, though in fact it merely resonated through a dozen vox-units. The feedback was awful, the hissing sound subsuming his subsequent orders. Presumably the pilots heard it, for they came about, ready to launch another jousting run.

I had no idea what he wanted them to do. Neither did they apparently, for this was the ninth attempt to capture the shot. Our forces and the falsified enemy were supposed to accelerate straight towards each other, before veering at the final moment. Clearly Esec intended to splice in some visual effects, but none of the observers knew what they were, or how they might or might not fit within the context of the scene he envisioned.

All I knew was that at each pass, the planes were getting closer. It made me nervous. Or perhaps my perpetual nervousness caused me to fixate upon it. I could not shake the image of the aircraft coming in just a little too tight, and a fiery collision lighting the sky.

A holo-image flickered beside me: ork planes caught in a maelstrom of flames as they engaged against the shimmering echoes of Imperial fighters.

Iwazar.

I had thought the seer-skull repaired, such outbursts a thing of the past. But apparently something was still off about our link.

'Off,' I muttered, the image fading, revealing Shard sitting a few paces from me. Lanlok loomed over her, holding an improvised parasol crafted from canvas and scaffolding. Behind her was a Lightning. Not *Mendax Matertera*, but a close enough approximation, ready for her dramatic entrance.

'What was that?' she said, raising her voice across the thunder of the fighters.

'Scrap-file glitch.'

'I thought Plient fixed your little machine?'

'Likewise. I will speak to him once we are finished here.'

'If you think it will help,' she said with a shrug, seemingly intent on the simulated combat.

'What?'

'I just wonder if he laboured over the wrong component. Maybe the error lies elsewhere?'

'You mean my implant?' I asked, tapping my temple.

She looked at me, eyes buried behind the glare visor. 'Sure. That's what I meant.'

I said nothing, pretending to watch the craft swing by for another pass.

'Did you hear me?' she asked.

'Yes.'

'And did you understand? Because I was hinting that *you* were actually the problem.'

'I got that.'

'Just checking. It's poor manners not to respond when addressed by your betters.'

'Is that why you feel no need to be accountable to anyone?'

She laughed, throwing her head back. 'Exactly! Y'know, you're more fun this time. Though I do miss that naive idiot pontificating about matters beyond his comprehension.'

'Understandable. I, in turn, miss the high-flying fighter ace. The invincible warrior who has never been defeated. This bitter drunk is a poor substitute.'

'You just know me better now.'

'Do I?' I asked. 'On Bacchus I saw you leading every assault, piloting every plane. You were a one-woman army. But here? Here, you sprawl in the shade watching others labour while waiting to play the part of a warrior, so you can bask in a fabricated glory. It does leave one wondering exactly how vital you are to this operation.'

'I am the face of it.'

'Exactly. The extremity but none of the substance. When was the last time you flew against the Imperium's real foes? When was the last time you fought for your life?'

She took a swig from her flask. 'Every damn day.'

'I doubt you're sober enough to operate your legs unaided, let alone a Lightning.'

'Oh, well consider me shamed into getting off my arse.'

She rose a little unsteadily, straightening and stretching her arms and shoulders, twisting her neck from left to right. She took a deep breath, shuffled from one foot to the other, and then proceeded to bend down and stretch out on the sand again.

'See?' she said, raising her flask. 'Still got it.'

I stared at her. 'You know, I once saw you battle an ork warrior in hand-to-hand combat, right after being shot down and almost dying in the crash. And I still think you were in better shape then than you are now.'

Her reply was drowned by the roar of the Thunderbolts overhead. It was strange. The sound hit us an instant after the planes hurtled past, almost as if it could not keep pace.

Esec's voice came over my vox. *'How was it?'*

'Same as before. Visually it works, but it doesn't sync perfectly with the timings you've given me.'

'I've told them a dozen times! We only need to get this once, then I can replicate it as required, but I need it timed with the explosions we have.'

'Can't you splice in the shots?'

'I don't have time to unpick a scene stitch by stitch! This needs to be released today! It must line up!'

'Then I'm afraid you will have to arrange another pass.'

He cut out mid swear. I sighed, logging the current file. Another failed attempt. It was maddening. Inserting a momentary glitch in the vid could smooth over any discrepancy between the spliced images. And it was hardly as though he was crafting a masterpiece. I'd seen the sloppiness of his prior work. Why did this matter? Why was he so fixated on it?

'I wasn't shot down.'

I frowned, turning to Shard, who was staring at me.

'What?'

'Before. You said I was shot down.'

'And?'

'It didn't count.'

'What?'

'When we were… When I had to make that emergency landing in the swamp. When we regrouped.'

'You mean that time the Green Storm ripped us from the sky?'

She shook her head. 'No. It was an emergency landing. Anyway, that was not my plane. I was flying a subpar vessel under duress to get you your damn vids. And, even then, I would have won if not for the storm. A random bolt of lightning striking your plane does not count as being shot down. It was just bad luck.'

She was sitting up now, about as animated as I'd seen her that morn.

I shrugged. 'I recall it differently. You forced me along on your secret mission, stole an aircraft, refused to retreat when confronted with overwhelming odds and were shot down because of it.'

'I was struck by lightning!'

Her voice was raised. Perhaps that was why the ground crew were neglecting their duties, their focus upon our exchange.

'You were shot down. I don't know why you are arguing. I was in the plane with you.'

'It was the lightning that–'

'It was an ork weapon! For Throne's sake, you were fighting a flying hab-block. There is no shame in being bested by such overwhelming–'

'I have never been bested!'

She was standing suddenly, advancing on me. Lanlok made to follow but was hampered by his parasol. He seemed to find manoeuvring the flapping canvas an intellectual challenge.

'Say it!' she snapped, now looming over me. 'Say I have never been bested!'

I stared at her. 'No.'

'What does it matter what you say?' she said, turning away.

'Half the Imperium knows the story of my victory. And you know what they didn't see? Me being shot down!'

'But I did. I would say I have the footage to prove it. But I don't really need that, because I have a persistent reminder.'

I tapped my leg with my cane.

She snorted. 'So you hurt your leg. Am I supposed to feel sorry for you?'

I didn't reply, for I could not find my voice suddenly. All I could hear was the roar of the plane as we tumbled, the flash of light followed by darkness. Then the swamp, looming from nowhere. It was as though I was there again.

'Simlex? There's a lighting issue. Too much glare.'

'Simlex is broken,' Shard replied. 'Maybe the heat got to him.'

'Sir?' said another voice, one unfamiliar to me. *'Something is wrong with the auspex. I keep–'*

A spear of light tore the sky.

The glare burned the eyes. I turned away, even as Shard screamed something about cover. Then the force of the explosion struck. I was flattened, the sand cushioning my fall but the impact still driving the air from me. I scrambled for my cane, but could not organise my fingers. I saw Shard lurching upright, staggering towards her Lightning, but my vision was swallowed by dust and sand.

I could not rise. But suddenly something seized my chest, the grip sufficient to compress my ribcage. Then I was up and moving, my abductor making no effort to support me. The ground and sky lurched about, until Lanlok's slab-like visage suddenly thrust into view. The brute was carrying me one-handed, the limb swinging back and forth as the ogryn sprinted for cover.

I vomited. I have no idea in which direction. Not that it mattered, for moments later the burning remnants of another plane smashed into the desert a dozen yards from us. Lanlok somehow remained on his feet, though the force nearly tore me from his grip, the sand scouring my skin. I cried out, but my voice was slight against the cacophony unfolding above.

Then there came the roar of an engine. I managed to turn my head just enough to see the Lightning soaring into the sky, its wings adorned with a black griffin.

Shard had taken flight.

My view, however, was soon blocked by Lanlok's bulk. The ogryn appeared, for some reason, to be placing himself to shield me from the attack, his back to it.

'Release me!' I said, craning my neck to meet his gaze. But his eyes seemed unfocused.

'Protect the propagandist,' he murmured.

Perhaps he had mistaken me for Esec. Perhaps we smaller creatures looked the same to him. Regardless, I reached out for Iwazar, attempting to sync with the device. Our connection was still not what it had been, but I managed to peer through its eyes. And the seer-skull was already intent on the tragedy unfolding overhead.

A score of flickering attackers seemed to have struck, flying in perfect unison. But the images glitched as they danced across the sky, momentarily coalescing as the vessels slowed and collapsing into a single familiar silhouette. Iwazar's vision was far better than mine, and I knew now it was a flyer, though one entirely alien to me. And it still swooped like a hawk, expanding into a score of afterimages as it accelerated, until those too broke down into a tapestry of multifaceted diamonds tearing through the blue.

And tear they did, for planes were still tumbling, sliced apart by shining bolts of cyan light. They tried to engage, to strike back. But their foe appeared to weave in and out of reality, counter-attacks passing harmlessly through the ethereal craft.

Shard's Lightning was accelerating towards the attacker regardless. She fired, her autocannon thudding out shells, twin lascannons searing the sky crimson.

Three. She struck three of the flickering images simultaneously. I saw the las-bolts pierce them, one distorting as it was struck by auto-rounds. But none of them was real. And at her attack, the images exploded into shards of light. They turned, impossibly tightly, and hurtled towards her. She met them head-on, firing repeatedly but striking nothing, until the light seemed to consume her craft.

Then it was past her, slowing, the images collapsing once more into a single craft, now on her tail. It fired and she rolled, but I do not think it aimed at her, for each cyan bolt tore another of our craft from the sky. A dozen must have fallen now, more every moment as it continued to fire, still pursuing Shard.

It was faster. And more agile, dancing like a leaf in a breeze. As she dived, it eliminated a score more targets in passing. Perhaps it was this distraction that allowed her to bank hard to the left, and somehow manoeuvre behind it.

She fired, right as it exploded into fractured images. But this time something landed, an auto-shell finding a target amidst the light show.

There was a small explosion. And, as if on cue, our mysterious attacker was gone, the multifaceted diamonds hurtling across the desert at impossible speed.

CHAPTER TWENTY

'It's ruined. All of it. Ruins.'

Esec's murmur somehow carried through the chaos. Haulers had arrived and begun dragging the carcasses of aircraft from the sands, though even Plient would struggle to salvage much from them. A couple of medics were cleaning cuts and issuing stimms, but in truth little treatment was required. Those on the ground, assuming they hadn't been crushed by falling debris, were relatively unscathed. And those who had been piloting the aircraft required only the attention of a priest. Vagbon had been able to eject over the Great Glass Plain, but there were no survivors this time, not from those struck.

'At least Shard drove the attacker off,' I said. 'It could be worse.'

'Until one is dead, it could always be worse. How do you think Colonel Surling will react? I spent so long convincing him what happened over the plains was an accident, an atmospheric anomaly. How will I explain this?'

I had no answer. I suppose I was still in shock. Around me

were the broken remnants of aircraft, but I could not tear my eyes from the horizon, watching for the light.

'What was it even?' Esec continued. 'I have never seen an aircraft move like that. It flowed like smoke, passing through our craft like a spectre, manifested an army from nothing. How can you fight something like that? It could strike down an armada.'

'Nonsense.'

Shard stood beside us, pressure helm clasped under her arm. Neither Esec nor I had heard her approach, the footsteps masked by the desert sands.

'You saw what happened,' she said. 'Lucille von Shard scored first blood. If the coward had not fled they would have fallen. Yes, our foe is fast and adept at deception, but only because these are the weapons of the coward.'

I stared at her, incredulous. 'We lost a dozen fighters.'

'Unfortunate,' she said. 'But our forces were caught flat-footed. Most died before the Black Griffin was airborne.'

She spoke with such certainty. Detached. Almost indifferent. Already, I could see Esec trying to reframe the battle in his mind.

'Yes,' he said, nodding. 'They did flee, after all. But in those first moments, when the light struck? For an instant I thought it something… unholy.'

I did not reply, still intent on Shard. She could not believe her words. Our enemy had outmanoeuvred and pursued her, eliminating several other targets in passing. She might have drawn blood, but our foe had plentiful opportunities to just end her.

Why had they not struck?

'Perhaps… How much of that did we capture?' Esec asked, turning to me.

'I don't know. Your Eyes were everywhere, so I'd assume much of it. But why would we show such devastating losses?'

'We won't. Just one or two. Then Lucille can swoop in and

chase him off. There's intrigue there – that's important to keep them captivated. And the visuals! We need to think of a suitable name for the attacker too. For the narration.'

Had he gone mad?

I could not tell. He seemed earnest enough, brow creased as he ruminated over the optics, his gaze fixed upon whatever vision he had for the conflict. Shard said nothing to refute him. I even glanced at Lanlok, but he had once more taken to glaring at me with suspicion, my miraculous rescue apparently forgotten.

Someone had to speak.

'We don't know what we're fighting,' I said. 'You cannot report a victory against it. As far as we know, it may already be launching–'

'I am the propagandist here, Simlex, not you!' Esec snarled, thrusting his index finger at me. 'I say we can and will. This unnamed enemy will–'

'Greetings, Wayward Children of the Imperium. Forgive this intrusion.'

The voice emanated from Iwazar's vox-unit. Not that I needed it, for it also emerged from the earpiece linked to my implant. And that of everyone else, I assumed, from the way both crew and soldiers were looking around. It was a captivating voice, the words so rich and sweet you somehow knew poison lurked beneath.

Beside me, Iwazar's engine whirred in alarm. Its projector flared, a familiar scene manifesting before us. In fact, it was the very sands we now stood upon, though taken in the final moments of the attack. As we watched, the burning wreckage of a Thunderbolt crashed into the ground. The flames had stripped away the recently applied paint, the craft's original colours visible beneath.

'The invaders came from the void, claiming to represent the God-Emperor. They demanded you bow before them, throw open your gates

and surrender. And when you dared question these demands, they attacked, claiming you as the aggressors, even as they paint their craft in Deighton's colours, and manufacture conflicts to support their lies. Well, their lies now end.'

The image went dark, but it had not faded completely. A figure stood in the shadows, their features etched in candlelight, barely visible.

'My name would mean little to you, my heritage measured in spans beyond your ken. But you may call me Cesh, and I speak with the Light of Truth. They told you Flight Commander Lucille von Shard was a liberator, a hero of the God-Emperor. But once more they lied. She is no hero, or saint. Soon there–'

'Shut it down! Now! Cut the transmission!' Esec barked, fingers pressed to his implant, his other hand gesturing frantically, though to whom I was unsure. Regardless, Cesh continued in the same silken tones.

'–truth of the matter. And in five days, I will duel Flight Commander Lucille von Shard in the skies above Edbar. And she will fall. I do not say this as a threat, or even a prediction. It is an inevitability, a fate writ long before humanity set foot upon this world. Besides, it is hardly the first time I have killed her.'

The image presented was familiar enough. Twice I had seen it. The first from Esec's barge, where for an instant I'd thought we'd lost her. Then again during the abrupt interruption of the Feed. Once more I saw a craft in her colours being obliterated by a spear of light. Then the image cut and another fell, this one eliminated from beneath. Two more craft, each clad in her colours, tumbled from the sky, dispatched with contemptuous ease.

'Is this the second time she has died, or is it the third? One wonders how it is possible. Did she survive each crash only to fail again? Is she a witch, capable of cheating death through foul sorcery? Or perhaps

the legend does not quite measure up to reality. Perhaps others fight in her stead, so she can bask in their glory? Can she even fly? I suppose we will know soon enough.'

The light flickered, just enough to catch the glint in Cesh's eye, before going dark.

'Five days, child. Squander them wisely.'

'It was the aeldari.'

The commissar was even more grim-faced than usual, despite his features swimming in and out of focus. Iwazar was struggling to maintain the projection. His forces must have been deep beneath Edbar.

'You are certain?' I said. 'The pict is hardly clear.'

'Clear enough. There are certain design aesthetics these xenos employ. Once you are familiar with their unsightliness, it's impossible to mistake it for anything else. I take it this was the same attacker you encountered following the supply run?'

'I suspect so. And now they declare the flight commander must die. But I am sure there were opportunities before this. Why make such a spectacle of it? Why mock her first?'

'Do not waste time trying to fathom the motives of the aeldari. Their actions are divined by their witches and soothsayers. They will aid one day and attack the next, all to chase some doomed prophecy.'

His distaste was audible, each word practically spat.

'You doubt their claims?'

'If they could truly divine the future, then why do we rule the galaxy and they slink in the shadows? No, the aeldari are lies and artifice made manifest. Deception and betrayal are their bread and wine, and they prey on fears and desires. Their witches can even influence the feeble-minded, coercing those fools into enacting their will. It is pointless trying to discern their motives – merely doing so may play into their hands.'

'But, if that is the case, surely we cannot take any action without risk of playing into their hands?'

'So they wish you to think. But this Cesh would not be intervening in this conflict unless our current objectives somehow act against his interests. And this alone tells me we are on the correct path. We merely keep going.'

He spoke with his customary conviction. I was not sure it was so simple but lacked the courage to question him.

'What of our attacker?' I said. 'They decimated our forces.'

'Imperial protocol concerning the aeldari is clear. Their craft are fast and deadly, but few in number and with only moderate armour. They specialise in hit-and-run strikes and utilise sorcerous technology to evade and misdirect. But they cannot stand against us in a fair fight. Our positions should be fortified with Hydra flak batteries and missile defences. If the sun merely flickers, if there is a hint of a rainbow, then set the sky ablaze. They cannot evade that.'

His words carried such certainty. Perhaps he was reciting ancient tactica from memory. And I suppose there was a logic to it, though I suspected the majority of the air defences had been redeployed as part of the ongoing offensive, and Deighton's own batteries were crippled during our attack.

'But what about our aircraft?'

'Ground them. What function do they serve? The Aeronautica's only real value was in patrolling supply runs and producing fodder for Esec's Feed. I think this no longer matters. Perhaps this is the incident that will teach Colonel Surling the folly of empowering propagandists. And once I have finished mapping this tunnel network, we can launch subterranean assaults against the other data-fortresses.'

He kept his voice impassive. Or tried to, anyway. And with the poor-quality vid and his cap pulled low, I could not tell if there was a glint in his eye.

'You do not credit Esec's campaign for breaching Edbar?'

'Have you spoken to the data-scribes? Most of them are so dedicated

to their tasks they didn't even notice the attack until the Láech breached their halls. They communicate in some codified tongue and barely understand Gothic. Few have even seen the sky, let alone an aircraft. How much significance could they really attach to some fighter ace? Or the indentured workers for that matter. Besides, the speed at which Edbar fell? The suddenness? Whoever organised the insurgency knew what they were doing. These were not subservient labourers inspired by a vid. There was planning involved. Precision even.'

'You think there was a plan behind it?'

'Forget it, Simlex. For now, just keep an eye on my sister and make sure the Traderi *and its cargo remain secure. When did Scion Brice last check in?'*

'I have not seen him, sir.'

'Most likely he attended whilst you were occupied with this aeldari business. If you see him, ask that he uses the Traderi *to check in. Just warn him the signal may not reach me – we are about to press deeper.'*

'I will, sir, but what about the aeldari's proclamation? Cesh prophesied your sister's death in five days. Four now, assuming it is after midnight.'

'And? Providing wisdom prevails and our forces remain grounded, I do not see the issue.'

'If she does not fight, she will be called a coward. Already her image is tarnished by the revelation others fly in her colours.'

'This xenos wishes to engage in a pointless duel. Why serve his cause? Leave her on the ground, and if Esec still requires a figurehead to rally the people, then I suppose I can record a few short clips capturing our victory over these so-called separatists. I'm sure you can find a way of disseminating them through the current channels.'

His head turned as he spoke. This time there was no mistaking the glint in his eye.

'Yes, sir, I will speak to Esec,' I said. 'Sir, you quoted Imperial protocol concerning conflict with the aeldari.'

'What of it?'

'Have you ever actually faced them in battle?'

'…That will be all, Simlex.'

It was perhaps an hour later when the external vox began chirping.

I frowned, glancing up from my data-slate. The light was flashing, indicating someone outside the hangar sought entry. Brice? No, he knew the access codes. This was someone else.

I waited, in case it was an error, some worker or soldier taking a wrong turning. But the flickering light persisted.

I rose from my bunk, shuffled over to the control panel, and opened the exterior vox-channel.

'Yes?'

'Scribe Simlex?'

I did not know the voice.

'I am he.'

'My name is Scion Selt. May we enter? There is a matter I need to discuss.'

'I am afraid I have orders from Commissar Shard not to permit anyone entry. I cannot therefore grant your request.'

There was a moment's silence before he responded. *'I understand, sir. I am afraid I will have to convey the message via this vox-unit. It concerns Scion Brice. I believe he is part of your crew?'*

'He is.'

'I am afraid there was an attack. He was stabbed.'

'Stabbed? Is he alive?'

'For now, sir. The attacker approached from behind him, and managed to get the blade through a gap in his carapace armour. He is in the medi-unit. The physicians are tending to him.'

'I see. Is there any information regarding who stabbed him?'

'No, sir. The citizens of Edbar are less compliant than one might hope. Most likely it was one of them. An insurgent.'

His voice was steady. And the scenario was possible. Probable even. I had heard rumblings of dissatisfaction, the indentured workers apparently unhappy with the manner in which our forces had captured their data-fortress. And it was hard to ignore the increased presence of soldiers on the streets.

'Thank you for informing me. I will ensure the message is passed to the commissar.'

'Thank you, sir. Until his return, Scion Inger and I will ensure you remain safe.'

'Is there some threat I am unaware of?'

'Not to my knowledge, sir. But, given the current situation, Propagandist Esec has requested we provide you with additional security.'

'Is he your superior, then?'

'No, sir. But our services have been loaned by Colonel Surling. In this matter Propagandist Esec speaks with his authority.'

'I see. Well, you must forgive me, Scion Selt, but I cannot grant you entry. I have my orders.'

'I understand, sir. Your caution is admirable. Do not be concerned, for we do not need access to the vessel. We will secure the exterior. Please use this vox if you require anything. We will be outside.'

The line went dead.

Perhaps the *Traderi* had external cams, but I did not know how to access them. The vessel did have an observation port, though – an armaglass dome through which its commander could assess the vessel's exterior.

I ascended the ladder, raising my head and peering into the gloom. The hangar was empty, but the commissar had angled the vessel so the entrance was visible.

I could see them through the view panel. Two Scions stood on the other side of the door, their ochre-and-midnight armour barely discernible in the half-light.

CHAPTER TWENTY-ONE

At dawn my data-slate blared into life.

I blinked, groggy, dragging myself from some half-forgotten nightmare. The screen displayed a fleet of Lightnings and Thunderbolts, though whether it was new footage or something Esec had repurposed I could not say.

'The vile xenos spread deception to weaken our resolve. But any true citizen can see through their lies, and their attack faltered, repelled by Flight Commander Shard.'

A momentary shot of yesterday's skirmish, Shard scoring a hit upon the attacker.

'Now the xenos seek to challenge the Imperium's might. But why the delay? Why do they not hunger for battle? Because they are liars and cowards, seeking to drag loyal citizens from the God-Emperor's light and down into the darkness.'

Shard addressed the viewer directly here, pressure helm clasped beneath her arm, the Lightning behind her. It was still dark; they must have shot it before the sun rose.

'This morn we sally forth to do battle, to eliminate this xenos threat. I will–'

I stifled the sound, allowing her to mime soundlessly, before scaling the ladder and peering through the observation dome. Esec's guards were still waiting on the other side of the hangar's door.

Despite my misgivings, they provided no obstruction as I emerged from the *Traderi* and approached the exit, even saluting as I stepped outside.

'I… Good morning to you,' I said.

'Sir.'

'I was going to the hangars to speak with a colleague.'

'Yes, sir.'

'You do not intend to stop me?'

'No, sir. Please be about your business. I will accompany you to guarantee your safety whilst Scion Selt ensures the hangar remains secure.'

So, from that point I had two shadows. Iwazar and a Scion. Three, if you counted the Eye that no doubt followed us. I could not be sure, for there were so many of them hovering above us in the streets. Perhaps it was a show of force, intended to quell prospective insurgents. But if Esec had left with Shard, intent on facing Cesh, then who remained to monitor them?

In truth, I cannot pretend I was not thankful for the escort. Edbar had never looked less inviting. Perhaps I was unsettled by Cesh's words, or the early light was particularly stark against the crumbling buildings. It pierced even the supposedly enclosed areas, through the cracked walls and shattered roofs. And I thought there were more soldiers on the streets, both Scion and Láech. But there was barely anyone around, precious little sign of life returning to some semblance of normality. Edbar's original insurgents had presumably risen up and granted us entry on the assumption they would benefit in some way. Such a hypothesis was being sorely tested.

As we manoeuvred through the passageways, passing patrolling soldiers and repair crews, I caught snippets of conversations. Iwazar had good ears.

'–Throne's name are we supposed to repair this with half as many–'

'–soldiers get meat. When was the last time we had–'

'–hope she crashes and dies, and the fire burns that smug expression off–'

By our journey's end I was jumping at shadows, fearful of what I might encounter. And gasping for breath, for it was a steep ascent to the workshop. I composed myself as we approached. The doors were fully open, a pair of rather weathered scrap-servitors stumbling as they dragged an engine block into place.

'Morning, sir!' Plient grinned as I stepped through. 'You're awake early. Did…'

He trailed off as my escort stepped through after me, his mouth slamming shut.

'Pardon me, Plient,' I said, turning to the Scion. 'Would you mind waiting at the door? I believe this is a secure area.'

He hesitated, expression inscrutable behind his helmet's faceplate. Was he unsure whether to grant the request? Or listening for instructions, perhaps?

'Of course, sir,' he replied, nodding and offering a crisp salute before stepping back through the doorway. Plient followed, closing it behind him.

'Those are Esec's colours,' he said, sliding a bolt into place.

'Technically I believe they are Colonel Surling's colours. Esec has co-opted the scheme whilst in his service.'

'Still, sir, it's not a good look. Why are they accompanying you?'

'Esec professes to be concerned for my safety. Requested I have an escort. Apparently the citizens are restless.'

'That's true enough,' he said. 'Ever since that message yesterday. I think it said a lot of things some people were starting to suspect anyway. Not about the commander, those were all lies. But things are not good here, sir. And they're not getting better.'

A sombreness had settled over him. I wanted to ask more, for I recalled on the first night how many soldiers and support staff had exchanged greetings with him. But he looked preoccupied, glancing to the sealed door, unwilling to meet my gaze.

'I wanted to ask about this morning's mission,' I said. 'Flight Commander Shard has apparently set out to face Cesh?'

'Yes, sir.'

'I thought he'd challenged her five days hence? Four from today.'

'He did, so the commander reasoned that, until then, she was invincible.'

'I suppose she would.' I smiled, but he did not return the expression.

'Plient, I am not trying to deceive you,' I said. 'That escort is... I did not choose to–'

He nodded. 'I know, sir. It's just that she was not the one who ordered this morning's flight.'

'Esec,' I sighed. But it made sense. Now more than ever he must have been desperate to produce something, to counter the narrative Cesh was weaving. Perhaps that was why there were continuous updates on the Feed. Shard flying over some bland expanse. Footage of an engagement that I suspected was pre-recorded. Anything to monopolise the Feed, to drown the aeldari's message.

'I see *Mendax Matertera* is still here,' I said, gesturing to the suspended craft.

'Yes, sir. But I'm working round the clock. It will be ready when she faces him.'

'I can see that. Two servitors as well. You must have big plans.'

'I... Yes, sir,' he said. 'She has a plan, providing I can do my bit.'

'You won't let her down, Plient. You never have.'

'You're right, sir. I'll find a way.'

As he spoke, he seized what appeared to be a scrap of metal, his augmetic arm lifting it effortlessly. He slammed it down on a workbench, already lowering a welding visor.

'What is the–' I began, but at that moment Plient set to work, the hiss of the arc welder muffling my voice. I tried again, but he glanced up, shrugging helplessly and tapping his ear, before returning to his labours, welding one scrap of metal to another.

I waited, but it did not seem he would soon conclude his work. In the end I flipped out my data-slate. Esec's Feed continued unabated.

'Though the vile xenos cower from our sight, the God-Emperor has decreed that their existence is an abomination, and no–'

I didn't recognise the voice. It wasn't Shard and sounded woefully generic, and I'd met servitors with greater emotional range. But it continued to repeat snatches of Imperial dogma, the audio set against a montage of ill-defined triumphs. If nothing else, Esec was taking advantage of Edbar's transmitter. No longer was he restricted by only being able to submit short vids, though I'm not sure the deluge of ill-disguised propaganda was an improvement. I think it was looped, repeating, though most was so generic it was hard to be sure.

Until the signal abruptly cut out. For a moment I thought it was Cesh, but a sudden image burst to life.

They were under attack. Not aeldari, but a swarm of enemy Thunderbolts and Lightnings painted in the separatists' colours. They were hurtling towards our fighters.

'Once loyal servants of the Imperium. We implore you to remain loyal, and not be swayed by the lies of the xenos!'

No response. Not a surprise as, assuming these were actually separatists, how were they supposed to hear Esec's words?

Instead, they opened fire, and the tableau unfolded in a predictable manner. The aircraft hurtled at each other at impossible speeds, exchanging flashes of light and autocannon rounds. And I recognised the shots. There was one I had completed yesterday, an aircraft adorned in Shard's colours looping over two attackers before unleashing into their tail. The subsequent explosions were clearly spliced in, though I doubted many viewers would notice. Assuming they had many viewers.

A rough cut. Shard's face, the wind catching her hair.

'A serpent will always reveal themselves, and we now know the rulers of Deighton are in league with the xenos witches. Stand up, loyal servants of the God-Emperor! Reject their lies! Reject their distortions! Know that the–'

The screen flickered.

And there was Shard's Lightning again, swooping low, unleashing a storm of fire. But not against an enemy fighter, or even the xenos.

No, her shots pierced only the hide of a lumbering mamutida.

It was Esec's footage, minus his various embellishments, though I couldn't decide if the beast's plaintive cry had been amplified. It was sufficient to rouse Plient. He almost dropped the arc welder, pulling back his mask as he drew near, intent on the screen.

'Death. It is all the invaders know, promise, and deliver.'

A final screech. Then blackness.

'Will any tally of bodies satisfy them?'

The image faded back in – more of the creatures. Or at least what was left of them. Body parts were strewn across the plains, staining the glass red. The creatures had weathered our barrage, enduring punishing rounds, only their weakest finally succumbing. We had not inflicted this slaughter; they had instead been vivisected by some xenos weapon.

'Why did Flight Commander Lucille von Shard murder these sacred creatures? Did she not know the beasts are the property of the God-Emperor Himself? Or did she not care, seeking only to satisfy her bloodlust? Perhaps she hates what they represent. Knowledge. Wisdom. The Truth. The truth that she is no hero, but a bitter failure with a painted smile. Did–'

'No,' Plient murmured. 'No no no.'

He was by my shoulder, and seemed trapped by that word, muttering it over and over while Cesh recited a litany of failings and transgressions. Some I knew to be true. The rest seemed plausible enough. There were no picts though, at least not of Shard, only the Lightning fighters bearing her colours. The images coinciding with his words were the ruins of Edbar, its infrastructure crumbling, its people huddled in the detritus, clustered round fires in their efforts to ward off exposure or digging into the sand to escape the heat of Deighton's sun.

There were families. Children.

I don't know what their lives were once like. I assume they faced hardship and suffering. But looking at those picts it was hard to argue that they had prospered from our glorious victory.

My vox was beeping. I considered ignoring it, so transfixed was I by the vid. But I had my duty. Whatever that was now.

'Simlex here.'

'It's a disaster! All of it! Why is he doing this to me?'

Esec. I shook my head, muting the data-slate and tucking it into my robes. He was rambling, but I knew better than to interrupt. The Feed had once again been subverted, Cesh's rather unflattering account resonating across most of the desert. Or perhaps further, assuming some of the more distant data-fortresses boosted the signal. I wondered how long it would take for Colonel Surling to see it.

'*–cannot shut it down. Not from here! It's the transmitter itself that's been subverted, and the guards are unresponsive. The damn traitors must have done something to it. It's not just your soldier who has been attacked – my Scions have been forced to dispatch several citizens who refused to comply with their orders. Now those dissidents have been riled up by Cesh. Unless they've been working with the aeldari all along?! I have no idea, but I need someone there who knows their way around a transmitter.*'

A pause. It was clear what was to follow.

'I am not a combatant,' I began. 'If the insurgents have–'

'*You are the only one with the knowledge to do it! You will not be unsupported. A squad of my Scions will accompany you, just as soon as my orders are authorised by their superior. Flight Commander Shard's reputation is at stake, and perhaps the whole of Edbar. You must silence Cesh!*'

The data-spire had, miraculously, survived the initial assault on Edbar. Or perhaps Esec had insisted it was not targeted. But the walkways connecting it to adjacent spires were shattered, or at least damaged to the extent that I had no wish to cross one. We would therefore enter from the ground.

The surrounding area was quiet. Eerily so, seemingly inhabited only by the squad of Scions in Esec's borrowed livery. Their Tempestor informed me that the entrance had been sealed from within, requiring an assault ram to breach it. They had secured the ground level, but their orders were to await my arrival before proceeding.

Selt was the only member of the squad I knew, and beneath his helm he was indistinguishable from the others. Two stayed behind me, the remaining three scouting ahead, hellguns drawn while I hobbled behind. The elevator was unresponsive, either due to sabotage or damage inflicted in the initial attack. We took the stairway, which was little more than scaffold with steps attached. It spiralled like a screw, ascending about a central pillar. Its outer casing was cracked, exposing the frayed cables and wires.

It struck me that I had never seen the transmitter. I had no idea if it operated in a manner to which I was accustomed. And that was before it had been compromised by the aeldari.

My breath was laboured by the time we approached the eighteenth level, where the transmission controls were housed. The Scions slowed only a fraction on entry. I did not know why until I stepped through the doorway and saw the crumpled remains of the onetime guards, their carapace armour cracked and stained. They appeared flattened, as though crushed by a great force.

Suddenly, the Scion squad felt very small.

Two had now pulled ahead, scanning the shadows. It was a wide space, intersected by support columns. Ahead was what could only be the main controls, though I cannot say they looked particularly familiar or intuitive.

The lead Scion slowed, peering into the shadows. I could see nothing, not without syncing with Iwazar, and the device's reliability remained questionable. But the Scion's visor was presumably sophisticated enough to pierce the gloom, for he hissed a command and the rest of them froze, weapons scouring the shadows.

Their view was intersected by the pillars. They were vast in size, wide enough that it would take three people linking arms to encircle one. The lead Scion had not moved, weapon still trained on the shadows. He sidestepped to the left, circling, seeking to bring whatever he had spotted into his line of vision.

He managed to fire moments before he was struck.

If his aim was true, it made no difference. A vast shadow

slammed into him with impossible speed, the impact launching him a dozen feet. He struck the ground and kept moving, limbs tangling over themselves as he tumbled, until he finally skidded to a halt, limp and motionless.

Two Scions leapt in front of me, blocking my view. I saw their weapons flash crimson, and I heard footsteps like hammer blows. There was another sickening crunch, and then someone was dragging me aside. Only they had not accounted for my leg. I tumbled and fell, cane slipping from my grasp. Perhaps for the best, for moments later something whistled over my head. I heard a cracking sound, and hoped it was carapace armour and not the bones beneath.

I rolled, looking up just in time to see a pair of massive hands closing around my remaining guard. I heard his armaplas plate squeal in protest, as the monstrous creature lifted him from his feet. Somehow, he managed to raise his weapon, but he could not aim, the las-bolt searing past his attacker's face.

But it provided enough light for me to recognise our foe.

'Lanlok!' I shouted. I'm not sure why. I suppose it was reflex rather than an attempt to save the Scion's life. The hulking ogryn glared at me, lip twisted in a snarl, eyes hidden by his looming brow. There was blood on his face. And everywhere else.

He tossed the gasping Scion aside, raising an enormous fist.

I tensed, waiting to die. But just as he was about to deliver the blow, he hesitated, massive brow set in a frown.

'Protect the propagandist,' he murmured.

I did not feel inclined to correct him. 'Yes,' I said, rising slowly. His fist was still clenched, but he lowered it, inspecting his hand in a confused manner.

'Lanlok. What are you doing here?'

'Guarding,' he grunted after a moment, nodding to the device. 'I was told to protect it. Propagandist Esec left a message.'

'Has anyone else been in here?'

'Yes! But I crushed him!' The ogryn beamed, looking over his shoulder at the fallen Scions. There were groans, indicating some of the squad still lived.

'What about the guards?'

'Don't remember guards,' he said. 'Nobody was here when I arrived. Not alive ones anyway.'

I wanted to question him further, but there was no time. Gingerly I squeezed past, approaching the device at the room's end. It was an alarmingly complex machine, wires and transmitters jutting from switchboards. There seemed little order to it, and I got the distinct impression that it was not a sanctified device at all, but an assortment of technology cobbled together to perform a function.

There was no obvious means of deactivating it. Or activating it, for that matter, as most of the controls seemed to be little more than circuit breakers.

I glanced to Lanlok. 'I take it you have no idea how this device works?'

'It makes picts. And vids.'

'But not how it is operated?'

He stared at me, as though I'd asked how one operates the wind or sun.

'Is there a way to turn it off?'

He frowned. 'There's one way.'

His broad fingers reached into the nest of wires, tearing a handful clear along with several bits of the panel. I felt the sting of a static charge, and presume he received a fairly significant shock, though it did not register on his face. Either way there came a spark, an alarming whirring sound, and then the transmitter finally fell silent.

CHAPTER TWENTY-TWO

'Idiot. Or idiots, depending on who else is involved. Why would Esec permit such footage to be captured on vid? Madness!'

The commissar's voice was only marginally raised, his tone barely irate. But there was a glob of spittle in the corner of his mouth. I found myself transfixed by it.

'I'm not sure all of it was his footage,' I said. 'I did not recognise at least one shot of Shard's plane being shot down. Cesh may have captured his own, just like he did with the mamutida massacre.'

'Don't remind me. Not only is my sister a fraud and coward, but she is apparently responsible for murdering lumbering beasts that are venerated like saints in this bureaucratic backwater. Did Esec even do rudimentary research into these people?'

'He claimed to have, and that he intended to use that footage off-planet.'

'His intent matters little. The picture is played now. Flight Commander Shard will never be a hero to the people of this world. She

is too tainted in their eyes. It appears we have failed in our quest, Simlex. My sister has already been disgraced. I merely hope the rest of us are not tarred by the same brush.'

'This could not have been the reason for her message.'

'No. But perhaps it is a blessing. This, however bad, is no doubt less disastrous than whatever crime she actually perpetrated. Providing she is banished from the limelight, we might just get through this. I assume, given the day's disasters, that no similar sortie is scheduled for tomorrow?'

'I don't know, sir. Esec is not currently speaking to me.'

'He suspects you?'

'More that he's angry Lanlok demolished the transmitter. He blames me for not preventing it.'

'He was the one who ordered the bloody ogryn to guard the thing in the first place. You cannot leave them unsupervised like that. Not somewhere dark and unfamiliar, where they cannot see the uniforms of their allies. It's basic protocol.'

'Either way, he has banished me from his sight. At least until he needs something.'

'What about his subordinates? Surely, they should be primary suspects.'

'I'm not sure how many he has. When we first met, I thought his talk of controlling fleets of pict-cams was bravado, that he utilised teams of clandestine operators. But I am starting to wonder.'

'Do not lose his trust. Not until I have returned. It should be days at most.'

'Days are cutting it fine, sir.'

'You think I should neglect my duties to resolve this mess? No, we engaged yesterday and it was a rout, virtually without loss. We will break them, hound them until they retreat to the nearest fortress, which we will reclaim for the Imperium. Only then will I

return and resolve matters. Just sit tight and don't let anyone in except the Scions.'

'Understood, sir. But on that note I should warn you Brice is badly injured. He is currently in the medi-unit.'

'That is unfortunate. But I cannot send additional support. You will have to hold out until I return. Has the Traderi *received any communications?'*

His tone was clipped, matter-of-fact, betraying neither sorrow nor anger. He did not even ask the cause of the injury.

'I don't know, sir.'

'Red flashing light on the central control panel?'

'I do not think so,' I said, scanning the room. 'Where would–'

'It does not matter – the cargo won't be collected for at least a few days. I will deal with it on my return.'

'Understood, sir. Good luck with tomorrow's offensive. Might I ask if I could speak with Tempestor Rosln? She was looking into a matter for me that might be pertinent to our situation.'

'Sadly not. She is dead.'

His tone was unchanged, manner calm. But then he caught my expression.

'Oh, for Throne's sake, Simlex, this is war. People die all the time. It is what it is.'

'...What killed her?'

He frowned, struggling to recall. *'Cave-in, I believe? Or an explosion? There have been a few surprises left for us by the separatists. But she did her duty and will be honoured as such and so on.'*

'At His table, sir?'

'I beg your pardon?'

'The God-Emperor, sir,' I repeated. 'Will Rosln have a place at His table? Or dwell with him beneath the Black Sea? Or embrace the Light of Truth and become one with the sky?'

'Go ask a priest.'

The signal cut out.

Dead. I could not quite process it. When had I last spoken to her? Days ago? She had stopped in to check on our cargo. Offered to assist with my enquiries.

It hurt more than I'd have expected. But his reaction was worse. I had barely known her, but she was part of his entourage. There must have been a certain fondness, surely? A respect or comradery.

But it was war. That's what happens.

People die.

CHAPTER TWENTY-THREE

I was unsurprised by Esec's summons in the morn. But I was surprised by the changes to his studio. Scions now lined the chamber, weapons drawn. I was equally surprised to find Lanlok amongst them, but I suppose the commissar was right. He was too simple-minded to be held responsible for what had happened, the injuries he inflicted the equivalent of friendly fire.

Esec sat reclining on his control throne, helm absent. He nodded but did not meet my gaze as I entered, intent instead on the black mainscreen.

'Propagandist Esec,' I said, bowing my head. 'I hope you slept well.'

'Slept? I was awake until the early hours trying to repair the damage you caused. You and this idiot!'

He glared at Lanlok, though I'm not sure the brute registered the insult.

'My apologies. We were desperate. Have you been successful?'

'Almost. Not that I trust anyone to use it,' he said, shoulders slumping. 'By the Throne this is a mess. I'm starting to think Admiral Desora was right. We should just obliterate Edbar from orbit.'

'What of the knowledge lost?'

'If we don't know it already, then what exactly is lost?'

He sounded sullen, bitter. A different look for him. I decided against asking after Shard. After yesterday's debacle I assumed they had given up on attempting to provoke Cesh into battle, or providing a positive narrative to counteract his campaign. Besides, we had a fresh project to occupy us.

'I still don't know why I agreed to this,' Esec said. 'Well, I do. It was a condition for the Láech's assistance yesterday. I suppose there's no harm in dispatching a few Eyes into the tunnels beneath Edbar, though. It's marginally better than providing the Feed with zero output. On screen.'

At first there was only darkness, punctured by the blazing of overhead lumens. But gradually the image adjusted, some cogitator shifting the balance of light and dark. There was the commissar, still immaculately turned out, his collar starched and peaked cap in place. Surrounding him were warriors of the Láech, though in truth I barely recognised them. My first encounter had been with drunkards brawling in a pit. But these soldiers were like a different breed – grim-faced, focused, and utterly dedicated to the mission at hand.

It was hard to get a sense of scale, to judge how far the lumens hung above the soldiers. I would wager the tunnel was around a hundred feet in diameter, but it could have been double that, the screen once more struggling to reveal detail in the gloom.

'Gentlemen. Good morning,' the commissar said, addressing Esec and I. There was no trace of emotion in his voice, no hint of incivility.

'Commissar Shard,' Esec replied stiffly. 'It looks as though you have selected the darkest tunnel possible. It will make capturing the conflict quite challenging.'

'My apologies – our cowering foes have chosen where they wish to die. We can only do our best to arrive promptly and accommodate them.'

Esec grunted something in response, his focus shifting to a control on his console. He clicked a few buttons and suddenly the image was clearer, even if the colour ratio felt a little off.

I glanced at him. 'You did that?'

'They are my Eyes after all,' he said. 'Why would I not give them orders?'

'But they are so far away. How are you–'

'They are my Eyes and I damn well control them!' he said, rounding on me. 'Just because you are incapable of such feats does not make them an impossibility! Unless you have something to say? Some disparagement to fling or accusation to make?'

I shook my head.

'My technology is fully sanctioned by the tech-priests. I have the papers! The deeds! You understand?'

I had never seen him so irate. I assume neither had the Scions. They stood to attention, but I saw a couple tilt their heads during the exchange, and I swear at least one of them turned slightly towards me. His weapon was still trained on the ground, but it felt uncomfortable, as though he was anticipating the next command.

I did not like the look in Esec's eye, and found myself wondering if he could order the Scions to gun me down. They were not truly his to command, his authority borrowed from Colonel Surling. Then again, their squadmates had been willing to risk their lives protecting me the day before. Given the opposing order, I presumed they would be just as willing to perform an execution.

Esec was still glaring at me. 'I am in control. You understand?'

I nodded.

'Esec? We seem to have lost the connection. Are you still there?'

'My apologies, commissar,' he said, turning back to the mainscreen. 'Signal restored. We are ready whenever you are.'

Commissar Shard nodded, straightening his cap one final time before glancing to the soldiers. He said something in their tongue. Iwazar could probably have translated it, but I did not see the point; it would be the same platitudes commanders spouted before sending their troops to kill or die. *You are just. The enemy is evil. Victory both rests with you and is yet somehow assured because of the God-Emperor.*

'Might as well do this properly,' Esec sighed. 'Perhaps there will be something worth disseminating.'

Multiple screens lit up. The Láech occupied the width of the tunnel. Over half our forces were down there, perhaps a platoon's worth of soldiers, though more might have lurked in the shadows. They were supported by a pair of Hellhounds: Chimera-chassis tanks carrying turret-mounted incendiary weapons, perfect for clearing confined spaces. Other vehicles lumbered behind them, though the glare of their lumens made it difficult to discern their form. Still, I had been correct in my assessment of the tunnel's width – there was sufficient space for a tank convoy, providing they didn't mind waiting in line.

The commissar must have concluded his recital, the soldiers in his charge letting out a fierce cry in support. He turned away, and for the first time I noticed Captain Phinn. I hadn't seen him since his brawl in the pits. He delivered a short speech too, with notably less enthusiasm.

'How many commanders do they need?' Esec said, rolling his eyes.

'I believe Captain Phinn is the commander. The commissar is there to maintain morale and inspire the soldiers.'

'Is that so? Look at those screens and tell me who the soldiers really follow.'

It seemed a questionable observation, coming from a mere propagandist who had somehow co-opted an aerial armada. But I said nothing, returning my attention to the screen, where our forces had begun advancing into the darkness.

In less than an hour the first shot was fired.

A sniper, no doubt secreted in a cavity in the tunnel. I assume they aimed for an officer, and perhaps were successful. But the retaliation was swift and precise, for as soon as the soldier fell, a score of lasguns unleashed a retaliatory salvo, bright enough to momentarily light the passage. I did not see the attacker fall, only the convoy continue its advance.

'Scintillating,' Esec said without enthusiasm, fingers drumming on his armrest, control helm now in place.

But further excitement soon followed. A series of explosions rocked the cams, one of the Eyes going dark even as the screens filled with smoke. Esec tapped at his helm, attempting to compensate. Two additional screens flickered into life, figures picked out in red against the grey of the tunnel. There were shouts amidst the crash of rubble.

'Commissar Shard?' he enquired.

'Still breathing. Looks like an attempt to collapse the tunnel ahead.'

We could see his face now as the smoke cleared. The blockade appeared minimal – a cluster of boulders must have been rigged to cascade into the tunnel. But one of the Hellhounds was already rumbling into position, its dozer blade parting the obstruction, the infantry following and clearing the remainder under the commissar's watchful eye. He gave few orders once in the field. His presence alone seemed sufficient, the soldiers striving to excel under his glare.

'Throne, this is tiresome,' Esec said. 'Perhaps we should give up on this project. The business with Shard will soon blow over.'

'You think it will?'

'Bound to. The aeldari are proven liars. They should always be disbelieved, irrespective of evidence.'

I nodded, but my focus was on the leftmost screen. The Eye providing that data-feed had strayed somewhat from its brethren, scouting ahead. I glanced to Esec, but he appeared oblivious, intent on an alternate image, where a medic desperately sought to stem the flow of blood through a torn sternum. The lumens made the blood too bright somehow, as if it was merely paint gushing from the dying man.

The furthest Eye pressed on, seemingly without guidance or direction. My seer-skulls had once been similar, but they were ancient relics with wilful machine spirits, not cams supposedly mounted on automated anti-grav units. The passage was darker here, the overhead lumens no longer supplanted by the additional light provided by the tanks.

Something glinted in the gloom. It moved slowly, creeping forward.

I did not have time to shout a warning. Their weapons flashed, and once more the tunnel was bright, volleys of las-bolts providing all the illumination one could desire. The Eyes struggled for a moment, adjusting for the glare inflicted by the searing beams of crimson, the light's backwash painting the tunnel blood red.

The first volley had caught the Láech off-guard. But they had hunkered in behind their vehicles, which were weathering the worst of it. The separatists had little in the way of heavy firepower, or at least none they could bring to bear in those confines.

'Light them up!'

The commissar's voice rose above the clamour. Chainsword

in hand he had vaulted onto the nearest Hellhound, ordering the tank forward.

'For the God-Emperor!' he roared, and the tank hurtled towards the enemy lines. I do not know the name of the weapon mounted on its turret, only that when it fired, an inferno engulfed the separatists. There was no respite from the flames, no cover proof against the spray of burning promethium. Once again smoke muddied the Eyes, but this time I welcomed it. Anything was better than watching those soldiers burn. Separatist or not, heretic or not, it was a death I would not wish on anyone.

'Blasted smoke,' Esec muttered. But he was engaged now. It was hard to deny the sensationalism of such footage, though I doubted most citizens would enjoy this particular brand of violence.

'We can clean it up, add some context,' Esec murmured, as though reading my thoughts. 'Splice in some footage of the separatists eating human remains. Or abducting children, that always scans.'

It was so simple to him. All that effort I wasted trying to capture the reality of war was a fool's errand. Simply attribute cannibalism to your foe before burning them alive, and your audience will cheer.

And he was right. That was the worst thing.

With the Hellhound breaching their lines, the separatists were already falling back. I saw two tumble, carved into bloody chunks by the commissar's blade. He was still mounted upon the tank, one hand clutching it for support, the other swinging his chainsword and reaping a bloody tally of limbs and heads. His uniform was no longer pristine, now stained by blood and viscera.

'Follow me, you wretches!' he roared. *'The last soldier to reach me will be executed for the crime of sloth!'*

Behind him, the Láech surged forward, lasguns flashing and bayonets gleaming. I think they favoured the latter, the las-bolts but a means of occupying their time before they reached the enemy lines, where they set to work butchering the dying and fleeing.

'He does have something.'

I looked at Esec, who once more was intent on the screen, where the commissar continued to add to his tally.

He turned to me and smiled. 'Relax, Simlex. I'm not seeking to steal your subject. I just never quite understood the appeal. Visually. He seemed too stuffy. Generic. But it's different once the bullets start flying. Just a shame this is not really suitable for our vids.'

'In what way?'

'Well, it's depressing, isn't it?' Esec replied. 'Men dying burning in the sewage, flames roaring all around? It doesn't exactly inspire one to join the fight. Nothing like the clear skies and illusion of freedom. Don't get me wrong, I'm sure we'll find a use for this as supporting material. But I don't think it can replace Lucille.'

The counter-charge was now a full-on assault, the separatist forces routed, their fighters throwing down their weapons in their desperation to flee. But the Láech outpaced them, gunning down the retreating troops or impaling them with bayonets.

'Still, I suppose if they were real traitors. If they had turned from the God-Emperor's light, practised debase sorcery... then surely the punishment fits the crime?'

Esec was intent now, his Eyes soaring ahead of the Láech's charge. It was a rather disconcerting sight to have so many views of the commissar simultaneously. On one screen I saw his back as he hurtled towards the fleeing separatists. On another screen he was coming right at me, the Hellhound tearing through the enemy, several of whom were now impaled on its dozer blade. It seemed almost indulgent that it continued to fire, given the multitude of combatants crushed beneath its tracks, but the gunner persisted, streams of burning promethium arching across the tunnel.

I suppose it improved the visibility. That, or the Eyes had solved the lighting issues, for the images were coming through crisp and clear. The harsh light cast by the overhead lumens gave every swish of cloth or flash of muzzle a starkness, a significance, the colour saturation dominated by the red las-bolts and blazing flames. Through it all the commissar continued, relentless. The left side of his face was blistered by his proximity to the Hellhound's turret, and his clothes were sodden from the blood of the fallen. But no amount of blood or soot could hide the smile on his face.

'Oh. That's good.'

Esec was right. It was the sort of visual you'd build a pict around, the climactic conclusion to a well-fought campaign. Or perhaps a longer piece, for Esec's Eyes now lined the tunnel. They could chart the Hellhound's passage as it thundered onwards, crushing most of those fleeing beneath its weight, before incinerating the remainder, every death captured from multiple angles. And there was certainly an audience for that kind of gutter vid.

'Blast it, they're losing it again,' Esec said, scrabbling at the controls. 'Wretched things. You had it a moment ago!'

The light was glitching. Not darker exactly, but the colour was off, the crimson drifting into violet and lilac, yellows and cyan.

Esec spotted it a moment before me, surging from his chair, mouth torn open to screech a warning. But there was no time for words, only a sharp intake of breath as a spear of light pierced the Hellhound's fuel tank, the explosion hurling the commissar aside like a broken doll. The tank's momentum carried it forward, but now as a cloud of burning fuel and ruptured metal, though no less deadly because of it. Then the image collapsed, the Eyes overwhelmed by the blinding storm consuming the tunnels.

It seemed the Light of Truth now shone beneath the ruins of Edbar.

CHAPTER TWENTY-FOUR

'I don't care. Wake her! It doesn't matter what I said before, she must fly. Tell her every second is precious!'

Esec paced across the studio, vox signals relayed through his control helm. The screens remained focused on the conflict beneath us, where the situation had at least stabilised. Colour and light had returned to normal, and what remained of the Láech were hunkered down amidst the rubble, sheltering behind cover provided by the smoking wreckage of their tanks. A few brave souls had attempted to press on. A few cowards had attempted to sneak back. They all met the same fate.

'Commander? Lucille? You need to deploy now! We have a chance! The aeldari has launched an attack through the tunnels beneath the desert. Utterly stalled our assault. It's perfect! My Eyes are already down there! You can swoop in and save the day! They have nowhere to hide!'

He was ecstatic. And manic, perhaps bordering on unhinged,

but ecstatic nevertheless. Perhaps he saw a window, an opportunity to turn things around.

'No, you need to… Why would that matter?'

Esec's head tilted as he listened. I had no idea what she said, and struggled to read his expression with so much of his face covered.

'I swear to you, the aeldari aircraft is in those tunnels. Check the footage. Check it and get your Lightning and– It clearly isn't impossible! Because I just saw it! Cesh launched at least three attack runs, hurtling down those tunnels, and if he can do it then so can– How can you not believe me? Fine, let me get hold of one of those damn sergeants. What is his blasted name? You're still watching, right?'

He tapped some buttons on the side of his helm.

'Sergeant Xvier? This is Esec. Send scouts forward – our foe appears to have retreated.'

I wonder if they found his insincerity convincing. Probably not, but it didn't matter. Orders were orders. Within a minute a pair of Láech soldiers emerged from the rubble, creeping through the press of rock and entrails that now occupied the tunnel.

'Keep watching,' Esec said.

The pair had reached the smouldering wreck that was once the commissar's Hellhound. It seemed to mark a territorial border. The soldiers knew it, for they slowed, exchanging glances.

'Sergeant Xvier, it almost appears that your men are refusing to advance. I know this is not the case, because–'

The Eyes were sophisticated enough to draw a bead on both men. They looked terrified, brutal warriors reduced to frightened children. I do not judge them. Their glorious victory had been upturned, their comrades dispatched by an unseen foe. And now they were abandoned, trapped and surrounded by the sobs of the dying and the stench of the dead. Who could endure such and feel nothing? Fear is not cowardice, and bravery is not knowing no fear, but overcoming it. And when the order was given, those brave soldiers rose, whispered their prayers to the God-Emperor, and hurled themselves into the darkness.

And died.

At least it was quick – a storm of light, a blinding flash. Nothing left but smoke and ash.

'There,' Esec said, turning away from the screen. 'You see? Get in your Lightning and get down there! We can lure Cesh out with a few soldiers and then strike when the aeldari is distracted! This is our chance to fix everything!'

He glanced to me, eyes hidden by the helm, mouth drawn in a jagged smile.

'This is it!' he said. 'We are minutes from victory!'

The better part of an hour had passed before Shard was ready to launch.

Esec did not handle this delay well, alternating between loquacious and mute. Twice he was convinced the aeldari had retreated, and twice more soldiers were ordered to advance, their technicolour deaths confirming the xenos' presence.

Finally, confirmation of her launch was received, though when it was, Esec's face fell.

'A Valkyrie squadron? No, I am afraid that is unacceptable. I want speed, I want– If the aeldari can manage it, then– No. No… Well, the vox is coming through perfectly clear to me. I…'

He trailed off, fingers pressing against this control helm, seeking to restore the connection.

'Blasted thing,' he muttered. 'Why on earth is she flying a Valkyrie?'

I didn't reply because the answer seemed obvious: a Valkyrie was better suited to a tight engagement supporting troops in a confined space. Trying to fly a Lightning through that tunnel would be akin to aiming a bullet up the barrel of another's gun.

He must have known that. On some level. But he was fixated on the outcome, the image he sought to forge. Shard was supposed to best Cesh one on one, in a contest of speed and skill. A squadron of Valkyries advancing cautiously, attempting to pounce pack-like on a single foe, lacked a certain gravitas.

The Eyes shifted, their focus now the dead and dying. It made for rather grim viewing. At a glance, it seemed the Láech were sprawled in mud and filth, but in truth it was the remains of the fallen. The survivors were scattered, clustered around whatever cover they could muster, awaiting the order that would send them to their deaths, so Esec could confirm there was still a chance to craft his pict. Perhaps they prayed for a miracle. A saviour. An intervention by the God-Emperor.

They got Shard.

'There're entrails stuck to my cockpit. Where on Terra did they drip from? By the Throne this is disgusting.'

We still did not have a visual. Esec had directed one of his Eyes back down the tunnel. It had yet to reach the advancing Valkyries.

'She dawdles deliberately,' he said softly.

'Or perhaps she is cautious?'

'Why are you so keen to defend her? Whose side are you on?'

I could not think what to say. Technically, I supposed I should be aligned with the commissar. Except he was almost certainly dead. Did she know? Had Esec told her? I could not recall him mentioning it.

'Flight Commander Shard?' I said, engaging the vox.

'What?'

'Your brother Tobia. The commissar? It looks like… he's missing. Dead, perhaps.'

'*...I see.*'

'I just thought... I should probably–'

'*It's fine, Simlex. Thank you, but try not to fret. The man is a cockroach – he can survive anything. Esec, is the light ahead one of yours? I am inclined to shoot at it unless given a reason not to.*'

'It is one of mine. And what is taking so long?'

'*It's dark. And a tunnel. And there is barely space to fly two abreast. And this has every indication of being some form of trap. To give a few reasons.*'

'Could you at least accelerate above walking pace? My Eyes move faster than this?'

'*Yes, because they are small and expendable. And I am neither.*'

The vox fell silent, but at least we had Eyes on them. They were still some distance from the front line.

'Damn aces. Honestly, if I could insert Eyes into the cockpits of the planes instead of pilots then I could solve this sorry mess single-handed. The aeldari has probably departed due to her dallying. Shard?' he said, engaging the vox. 'We are going to have one final stab at flushing him out. Sergeant Xvier? This is Esec. Send another scout forward. Double pace.'

The reply made him stiffen. No one moved.

'I am not wasting an Eye!' Esec hissed. 'Listen to me, soldier – I speak with the authority of Colonel Surling! If your men are reluctant to move, I suggest you discipline them accordingly.'

I did not hear the response, but Esec seemed to settle, somewhat appeased. And it was not long before a figure stepped from the shadows. He was stripped to the waist, tattoos barely visible in the half-light. He carried no weapon.

It was Sergeant Xvier.

He stopped scant feet from the Hellhound, bowed his head, and crossed his arms, the gesture either the breaking of waves or sign of the aquila. His hands flashed across his face, foot arching back. Almost a dance, like an act of offering.

Esec shifted in his seat.

Xvier screamed a battle cry, beating his fists against his chest before racing forward, hurdling the tank's wreckage as he sprinted down the tunnel.

Five yards. Ten.

'I knew it,' Esec said. 'The damn thing–'

A spear of light lit the scene. And Xvier was gone.

'Now!'

The Valkyries accelerated, their walking pace soon a run. Then faster still, as they soared towards the defenders and the lights now flickering further down the tunnel. I could not find Cesh's silhouette amidst the dazzling display, even as the light seemingly raced to meet them.

'Fire.'

They unleashed everything in one apocalyptic salvo: multi-lasers spewing a barrage of crimson energy beams, heavy bolters spitting devastating volleys of explosive rounds, the passage erupting in light and fire, even before the missiles detonated and the screens were bleached white by the explosion.

'Dodge that, you básk!'

We could see nothing for a moment, for though the Eyes quickly adjusted to fluctuating light, the tunnel was now wreathed in smoke. But there were the Valkyries, still advancing, now almost level with the stricken Hellhound, weapons still trained down the tunnel's length.

Twin flashes of cyan light erupted from the darkness.

One Valkyrie was split open, collapsing into pieces. The second had its wing clipped, slamming into the tunnel wall and crumpling into a heap, turbofans still roaring in protest.

Only Shard remained.

She attacked, accelerating towards the hidden foe, weapons blazing. I kept expecting her to fall. Instead, the light seemed to retreat from her. She gave chase, until the Valkyrie was at full speed, but it made no difference. Her target pulled away, the light storm accelerating yet somehow fading, dispersing into the shadows.

Cesh's voice pierced the vox. *'No, commander. You do not get to die yet. But I would suggest you stop squandering your time on useless endeavours. Say goodbye to your loved ones. Make peace with your carrion-liege. Accept your fate.'*

Then the light was gone, and Shard chased only shadows.

CHAPTER TWENTY-FIVE

'Commander, it's impossible! The orks outnumber us fifty to one. We're outgunned!'

The voice boomed throughout the theatre, an officer screaming the warning over the vox. But the vid screen itself was occupied entirely by Lucille von Shard. She turned to us, an impressive feat, considering she was supposed to be strapped into her Lightning's seat. But there she was, staring right at the audience, which sadly included me.

'Outnumbered?' she said. *'That merely means we have more opportunities to slay in the God-Emperor's name! Outgunned? Perhaps, but who ever met an ork who could shoot worth a damn? Let their bullets blacken the sky, we will still burn it clear with the God-Emperor's light!'*

External cut. A formation of aircraft accelerating towards an unseen threat, the footage vaguely familiar. I think I obtained it early, when I was still figuring out how to capture the conflict. A waste of time, as it transpired. I should have followed Esec's method. Snap a few shots, stitch them together using archive footage, impose a suitable narrative, and call it a day. Of course, had I done that, it's likely we would not have devised a means of defeating the orks. Bacchus would have been conquered, all of us slaughtered or enslaved, and the pict I was enduring never completed.

I was starting to think that would have been the better outcome.

The planes accelerated. Presumably, for suddenly they had travelled hundreds of leagues. Either that, or a storm cloud had spontaneously materialised behind them. No effort was made to explain it. But here came the orks. They looked a little more authentic, though the footage was accompanied by stirring music rather than their belching engines or thunderous fire.

Cut to Shard again, once more without her pressure helm. It irked me more than it should. None of the pilots in the audience seemed perturbed by it. Then again, this hastily convened screening of *The 2208th* was not optional viewing. We had been crammed into a former briefing room now dressed as a cinema. A couple of burning braziers provided warmth, for the ceiling was cracked and the night air cold.

Esec had ensured the pict was being cast across whatever territory we still controlled. I kept expecting the aeldari to hack the Feed with another damning vid intended to demoralise us. But perhaps they judged having to sit through this travesty damaging enough.

Shard's face again. Assuming that was her face. I could not tell any more. The voice sounded like her. But perhaps that too was easy to simulate.

'Warriors of the Two Thousand Two Hundred-and-Eighth,' she thundered. *'No matter the odds, no matter the cost, the God-Emperor is with us! Pity those who survive this battle, for they will be deprived of a most glorious martyrdom and a guaranteed seat at His table!*

And if I fall first, rest assured there will be a round waiting for the rest of you!'

Cut to shots of the pilots laughing in their planes, their mortal fears soothed by this banal joke. I didn't recognise any of them. No reason I should, given they were players, their parts crafted purely for this pict. Because at this stage in the war, only three of us had been left, only one of whom could fly a plane. Alone, she had faced down an armada and a flying fortress the size of Edbar, her only support a one-armed mechanical and a crippled propagandist.

We saw little of that. I suppose the orks' machine would have offended someone's sensibilities. They were supposedly savages after all, their technology only obtained through looting the Imperium's aircraft. The average citizen would be rather unnerved to discover the beasts could construct airborne fortresses and teleportation devices.

But I recognised the footage. Ironically, Esec had painted over the flickering holo-images we'd employed in the final battle, the illusionary planes now rendered real, at least for the pict screen. Because that was the story he told – that the regiment had triumphed, not that it had already been wiped out by Imperial arrogance and a refusal to adapt. These counterfeit pilots laughed and exchanged witticisms, even as the hail of bullets hammered against their craft.

It sounded like rain. That's what Plient had said. And he was right, at least back then. These days I find the inverse holds true. Now, when I listen to rain, it sounds like bullets.

I rose, muttering apologies as I shuffled along my row. I could feel Esec's gaze shadow me, and made efforts to grasp at my stomach. Gastric distress – that was why I suffered. Not because of what he was making me relive.

As I departed, Shard's voice echoed through the theatre.

'Here they come! When they open fire, try and stay in the centre of their crosshairs. It's the only spot they never hit.'

Laughter. I wanted to scream at them. Why were they laughing? None of it was funny. Not then or now.

Perhaps it was under duress. Or perhaps they needed to believe that this was how it had been, the war a stirring jaunt with friends and comrades, a game where lives were bartered for glory and immortality. Only cowards and weaklings fell before their time. This was self-evident – the audience were still here, and surely none of them were weak or cowards.

Outside it was dark, a few stars piercing the chasm-like gaps in Edbar's crumbling infrastructure. There was still little sign of repair work. Rather, the citizens seemed to be adapting to the new environment. Small, squalid dwellings assembled from scrap were accumulating between the cracked walls. They would keep accumulating, as speculators sieved the remnants of the data-hub, seeking any valuable scraps they could salvage. The numbers would probably increase, until someone senior peered through a window and saw the slum accumulating on their doorstep. Then they would be removed. Or cleansed.

I leant my back to a warped railing, staring up into the stellar void and shivering, my robe insufficient against the night air. I heard distant laughter and cheers. No doubt another witticism had been uttered during an implausible firefight. I could not bear it, forcing myself on despite my aching leg. Anywhere else was better.

I did not pick the path leading to the crystal gardens. But I found myself walking that road, seeking solace in the flower-beds. But they were dead, unable to survive unaided in the harsh climate or, in the case of the crystal blooms, shattered, the shards missing. Stolen, perhaps, to barter for food or supplies. The same was probably true of the data-scraps once caught on the wind. They were gone now, sequestered onto the black market.

Footsteps.

I heard them running away from me. Was I so fearsome? Perhaps it was the robe, or the seer-skull hovering behind me. Or perhaps their work had concluded, for they had left their mark scrawled across a plastered image of Shard, one of the many posters that once occupied Edbar's walls. The new epithet was still wet.

Coward. Murderer. Bringer of Darkness.

I walked on, alone for the most part. Few seemed inclined to ascend to the hill's summit, and not without reason. For it was still there, the unexploded bomb imbedded in the grounds. It should have been removed by now, simply for the danger it posed. But someone would have to take on the task, and I could already see the various wings of our military abdicating responsibility. The Aeronautica's forte was depositing such weapons, not removing them. The Láech would no doubt consider it a problem for the sky-hogs, while Esec would regard such duties as beneath his notice.

I saw a flicker as I approached – a glint of red, too small and low for a star, bobbing a few feet above the ground. The glowing tip of a lho-stick.

Its owner was leaning against the unexploded bomb, barely visible in the darkness settled over Edbar. That is, until she inhaled, and for a moment the burning tip flared, etching her profile in its dying light.

Shard.

I assumed she had elected to ignore me, for surely my cane was audible on the path. So I did likewise, pretending to be intent on the shattered flowers. But I studied her from the edge of my vision, saw when she flicked the lho-stick into the darkness and drew another from her greatcoat's breast pocket, cupping her hands against the wind to light it.

It was then that she must have seen me. I knew because she froze just as the match was struck, its flame quickly swallowed by the cold.

She did not move. Neither did I, both of us feigning ignorance of the other's presence.

Another match flared. She lit the lho-stick, turning, her back bent against the bomb as she exhaled.

'I assume you don't partake?'

Her voice was quiet, her face turned away. But there was no one else she could be addressing.

'No.'

She nodded, exhaling a thick cloud of smoke. The lho-stick continued to burn.

I found I had nothing to say.

Then there was an uproar from the distant theatre. We both glanced to it, listening to the laughter and braying cheers. Esec seemingly knew his audience, or perhaps he merely knew how to ensure an audience followed its brief. I think I made a sound, something between a sigh and a snort. She looked at me, and almost managed a smile.

'Your pict is terrible.'

'It is more your pict than mine. And it's not terrible, it's an abomination.'

'Agreed on the latter. As for the former, as I recall it you were the one taking all the pictures.'

'Nice you remember that now.'

'Plient reminded me. And I concede I might have had a vague recollection of who you were, it just didn't seem worth the effort recalling the details. But, to my point, this is footage you captured, is it not?'

'Some of it.'

'So it's your pict. Yours and Esec's. A collaboration.'

'If I took your plane, set upon it with an arc welder and power hammer, bundled you into the cockpit, and shoved you from a clifftop, would it be your fault the plane crashed?'

'Definitely,' she said. 'For starters, how did I let you steal it? You can't punch worth a damn, and I've known rust-poxed servitors with superior grace and locomotion. In this hypothetical scenario did you poison my recaff or something?'

'It depends. Do you drink recaff in this hypothetical scenario?'

She smiled. Just a little.

'Besides,' I continued, 'I seem to recall you previously stole a plane by wandering into the hangar and getting in the cockpit. It hardly seems a challenge.'

'It's possible security was a trifle lax that night.'

'Yes. I was surprised to subsequently discover you were only following orders, albeit clandestine ones. You play the part of a rebel, but perhaps the truth is you are as dutiful a servant to the God-Emperor as any other enlisted officer.'

'Have you tried rebelling against the Imperium?' she said, nodding to the semi-visible stars. 'This city should serve as a warning. But look at who I am talking to. A man who thought he would be lauded for telling the citizens that war is terrible. I told you then it would be your ruin. Did you really think that pict would earn you anything but disgrace?'

'No.'

'Then why in the Throne's name did you make it? And why storm off when I pointed this out to you?'

'Because I set out to show the truth. I didn't know what that was when I started. But once I did, how could I go back? War is not the sanitised, glory-soaked lie they tell us. It is bloody and stupid. And people die, whether innocent or otherwise. All for nothing, for I hear Bacchus is still a warzone. Resources are brought in to battle the orks only to be scrapped, salvaged, and redeployed against our forces. My mistake was not submitting the piece. It was believing I could craft a pict that was anything other than an ugly, violent debacle that drags heroes and villains alike into the dirt to die.'

'I'm not sure that's the best logline for a recruitment pict.'

'I'm not sure I care.'

'I see. So now you're the rebel?'

'No, because however I curse and moan, I still play my part.'

'Ah. Then you're a hypocrite?'

'Aren't we all?' I agreed. 'Though with your brother... missing, I do not know whether I even have a role any more. Even the escort Esec once burdened me with is now in the medi-unit with a crushed ribcage. As far as I can tell, the commissar's Scions are all dead or incapacitated. I have no place left.'

'What about Esec's underling? You seem well suited to such a part.'

'That role appears taken.'

She chuckled, the sound quickly running into a rattling cough that she suppressed with another draw on the lho-stick. She then exhaled, flicking the butt into the darkness, where it burned like a tiny flare.

'Jealous, are we?' she asked.

'That he succeeded where I could not? Found a means to put you on a leash? Not really. More sad. And disappointed.'

The coldness in my voice pleased me.

'Básk you,' she spat. 'You and your whole sorry enterprise. You're all parasites looking down on us, acting like you're better. Cleverer. Because you get to sit behind a desk and pass judgement on those of us who actually fight and die. You didn't know what an ork was before you met me, and you know nothing now. Besides, even if I was Esec's champion bootlicker, there will soon be a vacancy. We both know that. My only regret is I won't witness the moment where you discard your mighty principles for a chance to ride his coattails.'

She spun on her heel and stormed off. I did not look after her, keeping my gaze on the smouldering butt of the lho-stick, until it finally went dark.

CHAPTER TWENTY-SIX

I retired soon after, but did not sleep despite stretching out in my bed. I could not close my eyes. They seemed fixed upon the bunk above. It was empty now, like all of them. I was the only one left, unless you counted the commissar's cargo. I should perhaps have checked on the psyker, ensured his life signs were stable. But I did not want to risk him speaking to me again. I could still recall his words.

Witness her fall. Mourn her death. Seek no more.

I was almost relieved when Iwazar's lenses lit up, its projector firing. It would be bad news, I knew that. But at least it would be news I could share with someone. At least it might take me from that bunk.

'Seekers of the God-Emperor's light. I fear it is time to impart some painful truths.'

The voice had that same tone, honeyed but laced with poison. And there he stood, manifesting before me. Assuming it was a he, for it was difficult to be sure given the diaphanous robe and androgynous face. But though angular, his features were close enough to human that one could almost forget what he really was, despite his tapered ears.

It was probably his eyes that were most telling. They were mournful and beautiful and cold as the void itself. Whenever his gaze chanced in my direction, I had a horrible sensation that he was staring straight at me.

He smiled. At least, his lips curled and teeth glinted.

The image then cut to the Láech breaching Edbar. I had seen some of the footage, but much was new. Notably the priest attempting to flee, only for a blade to be thrust into his back, the attackers howling in triumph as he fell, Cesh's voice narrating it all.

'The off-worlders? Supposed servants of the God-Emperor's light? They slaughter your people, murder your priests, and burn whatever is left.'

The image cut to Commissar Shard's manic grin as he rode the Hellhound into the ranks of the separatists, chainsword wailing as flames consumed living and dead alike. The playback slowed, the lens focusing on the commissar's face, his mouth torn open in glee, eyes shining as his blade ripped through the fleeing troops.

Cesh again, head hung low, as though overcome with sorrow, hair spilled over his shoulders. He conveyed an eternity of pain in that gesture, unimaginable hardship in the simple bowing of his head. Were he an actor, I would have recommended him to the finest playhouse on Terra.

He seemed to meet my gaze. And by extension the other viewers, for I had to presume his message was cast through Edbar's remaining vox-units and projectors. He hesitated, looking away, as though unwilling to admit to what would come next. I found myself leaning forward, drawn by his words. The words of a xenos. I had to remember that. You could tell from how he moved. Too graceful. Too self-assured.

'My people serve the Light of Truth. Just as your world once did, and just as your God-Emperor still does. That is why we did not interfere in your lives, content to leave you to your labours. Until they came. Until they sought to choke out the light with their lies.'

He paused to smooth his hair from his eyes, so once more it cascaded down his shoulders.

'Your ways are the ways of the God-Emperor. They have persisted, unchanged since He first arose from the desert and cast His light upon you. Yet outsiders now claim you are unworthy in His eyes? That they are His true followers, and you must surrender your world to them? No, you have not fallen from His light. Your only crime is hesitating when they demanded subservience, and that was only because you did not know if they truly served Him. Now you have your answer. They will kill you all. By neglect or violence – they care not which.'

The image cut to a plane flying Shard's colours. It was from the battle days earlier, where Cesh had slain a dozen foes whilst avoiding her attacks.

'And who is their figurehead? Who is Lucille von Shard?'

Her face replaced his own. Not her real face, instead one of Esec's enhanced picts. But slowly it shifted, the slash on her cheek widening to a raw scar, steely gaze now haunted, lines carved around her eyes as though by a blade. Her flowing mane reduced to a half-bob, the left side scorched short. Her smile was now a bitter, broken sneer.

'When I heard tales of her skill, I confess I feared facing her. But that was before I learned others fly in her stead, that the picts proclaiming her skill are lies. And the truth is plain to see. The greatest ace in the Imperium. Is that what they call her? Is that what she proclaims to be?'

Another shot of the skirmish. Were these all Esec's files? I could not tell, only that this angle revealed the truth: Cesh had had a dozen chances to end her. To carve her plane from the sky. She only lived because he had elected not to fire.

'Do I have your attention now, Lucille von Shard?'

Cesh materialised again, but now adorned for battle. His armour was sleek, as perfectly fitted as an insect's exoskeleton. It was a deep blue, and inscribed with markings that seemed to dance as I watched.

Beside him, another figure faded into view. His uniform was in tatters, the right side of his face blistered and torn. He was unconscious, his head hanging forward but still adorned with his peaked cap.

Commissar Shard.

'Your beloved brother Tobia. He was barely alive when I rescued him. But I thought I should, if only to demonstrate my honourable intentions.'

He glanced at the commissar, distaste flashing across his eyes.

'Frankly, I'd intended to hold him longer, but I'm not enjoying the smell. I could dispose of him, unless you'd prefer I return him to your family? With but one small condition.'

He met the viewers' gaze, face a mask of serenity, features chiselled in exquisite symmetry. But his eyes burned with a terrible cold, a malice born not of hate or fear, but absolute contempt.

'In three days, you must agree to face me. Alone, your honour at stake. In turn, I will provide details of where and how you can retrieve your brother. Rejoice for the opportunity I grant, for it is your chance to prove me wrong. To prove that you can match a foe of my calibre. Know that I have flown for centuries, dedicated decades to every aspect of war. There is no greater test. I will reveal the truth about you, and free Deighton from your tyranny!'

He bowed his head, sombre, the light fading.

I expected the transmission to end. Except a smirk suddenly spread across his face, teeth glinting bright and perfect.

'I feared I would not get through that,' he said, turning once more to look seemingly straight at me. *'It's just so hard to take you people seriously. Should I next declare war on an anthill? Do you know of anthills? It's difficult sometimes to assess what simplistic imagery will be accessible to you.'*

He took a step closer, squatting down until his face was level with mine.

'Your language is so limited, so lacking nuance. Do you have a term for that sense of regret for a necessary action? Not regret of the act, which is necessary, but rather the pleasure derived from it? Because it's unworthy of you, and it reflects your flaws. And a single drop of such sweet poison can twist your intentions. Erode your resolve. Because behind that spark of pleasure lurks a hunger for more. A hunger wholly detrimental to satisfaction but oh so satisfying to indulge. But you must do your duty. So you do your best not to feed the hunger, but find your victories hollow. In need of something extra to derive that same satisfaction. And you think you are still on the right side, because you still fear what you might become. But perhaps they all fear it at first. Perhaps that is the first step. Do you have a word for that?'

He was staring at me.

'If it helps, it might also refer to a ballad sung in malice to a loved one. Or a season's promise revoked. Or a child learning of their mortality.'

I found myself shaking my head.

'I thought not,' he sighed, rising and turning away. *'It's a miracle you have any language at all. I cannot see you, by the way, this is nothing like that. You're just predictable, even to one who has never walked the Path of the Seer. It's easy to know where you would sit. What you would think. How you would react. It has all been seen*

before. Still, I hope my little speech will provoke your ants' nest into activity. Incidentally, if you haven't heard of these insects, you should really make the effort. Fascinating creatures, each worth a dozen of you.'

He glanced over his shoulder at something I could not see, before turning to me one last time.

'One final thing. Please tell your muse not to fret. Despite the rhetoric, I have low expectations for our skirmish, as my people's seers have sadly spoiled the outcome. Just tell her to try her best, and I promise to make it quick.'

CHAPTER TWENTY-SEVEN

The next morning I arrived at Plient's workshop to find it sealed. I stopped outside, looking for a vox-relay but found none.

Should I knock?

My new Scion escort, who had taken duty the previous night, was quick to step in, hammering the butt of his weapon on the door, until I heard a commotion from within. A series of bolts clicked, before the door crept open a crack, Plient's face emerging.

'Ah,' he said, glancing from me to the Scion. 'This really isn't the best time, sir.'

'Plient? Did you see Cesh's vid? His challenge?'

'Everyone did, sir.'

'...Do you know where Shard is?'

'Tell him I'm not básking here.'

The voice echoed from the half-opened doorway. A pained look crossed Plient's eyes.

'I'm sorry, sir,' he said, looking once again at my unwanted

Scion bodyguard, 'but we can't be disturbed. You saw what he said. I must get *Mendax Matertera* in perfect order so the flight commander can meet the challenge. Plus, there are some adjustments that I still have to figure out–'

'Stop talking to him and get back in here! That's an order!'

'Sorry,' Plient said again. But before he could withdraw his head, the Scion seized his collar.

'Scribe Simlex is permitted access to whatever facilities are required to complete his duty. If you do not open this door–'

'No,' I said, placing my hand on his shoulder. 'No, he is quite right. The repairs are the priority. I will… I hope I will speak to you again soon.'

The Scion seemed to be glaring at me, though it was impossible to know through his helm. But after a moment he released his grip, Plient ducking and disappearing through the gap.

'Plient! Wait! One last thing?'

He hesitated, meeting my gaze.

'The message Cesh sent. How did it end?'

He frowned. 'You heard it, sir. He has the commissar and if we want to see him alive then the commander must face him in a one-on-one duel.'

'Nothing else?'

'No, why?'

'Nothing. I just… I thank you, Plient, for–'

He had already vanished, the iron door grinding shut, the lock clicking into place behind it.

Esec offered even less assistance. He permitted me entry to his barge, my escort securing a shuttle. From its viewport, I could not help but note that Edbar's remaining Hydra batteries and flak missile launchers were clustered beneath the barge.

I thought it hinted at paranoia, and meeting him only confirmed my suspicions. He appeared to be on some sort of stimm, given the pinprick pupils and constant clearing of his throat, but perhaps it was just the pressure. The studio was already festooned with images of Shard, her face occupying every screen. Many were speaking, though the audio had been deadened enough that their voices were whispers, at least to me. But Esec seemed remarkably focused on them. So much so that he did not see me enter, almost leaping out of his chair when I spoke.

'Kile! How in the God-Emperor's name did you get in here?'

'You granted me access.'

'Ah, yes. Yes, you can help me. Perhaps. You saw the message, I trust? Very bad, very bad form cutting in like that. And Colonel Surling! He is furious – apparently this whole operation is starting to reflect badly on him. The cheek! I made him! I mean, he was a colonel before, but who cares? There are loads of them. This was a war that went beyond the battlefield, a war for hearts and minds, and to assure both remain under our total control. Pioneer stuff.'

'What did Colonel Surling say?'

'Hmm?' He blinked, eyes closing sequentially.

'Colonel Surling?'

'Oh him. He's furious. Has half a mind to obliterate the xenos and commissar from orbit, except we have no idea where they are. So instead, he's ordered we smoke out this Cesh creature. If that fails, he wants Shard to face Cesh alone, so we can prove humanity's superiority. Won't work, of course.'

'Why not?'

He met my gaze, frowning, confused. When he spoke again it was as though he were addressing an infant.

'Because he's going to kill her.'

'But you've not seen her fly,' I heard myself say. 'Not really. Not at her best. She's an–'

'When was the last time she was at her best? Bacchus? She doesn't sleep any more, did you know that? Barely eats either. And her drinking, well… let's just say that has led her into trouble more than once. It's not unexpected. I knew this was falling apart, but I thought I could control the descent using other pilots. But that was stupid. Why risk it? Why not just construct everything here?'

He pointed to the myriad screens.

'We have so much footage of her. Half of what you shot on Bacchus has not even been used yet. I've done more than one vid of her just from splicing offcuts. But now I'm working on a fully functional facsimile. Look!'

On the mainscreen the image of Shard turned, quite jerkily, and faced us.

'Good day to you, Propagandist Esec. And to you, Scribe Simlex.'

The voice was as disjointed as the image, the tone swinging wildly and overlaid with an unpleasant synthetic quality.

I looked at the beaming Esec. His face fell a little.

'It's a process,' he said with a shrug. 'This is just a test run. But I think I can make her say almost anything in time. Then we just need a pilot to fly the actual plane. I was thinking Vagbon – similar build, seems talented, has almost recovered from her injury.'

'Why does her build matter?'

'It doesn't at first, but long term we might need a stand-in. And with a few surgical interventions and a hair transplant, I think we could achieve the look. Voice might be an issue, but she can just wave. Doesn't have to be Vagbon, of course – we could have a separate stand-in and pilot, but I think if both are the same person it lends a veneer of authenticity. What do you think?'

He glanced at me, as though seeking a colleague's opinion. I think he said something else, but it was hard to hear him over the blood pounding in my temple. My fist was clenched, seemingly of its own volition. But before I could do anything foolish, Lanlok stepped forward, intent on me. Whatever his other failings, he had a gift for anticipating violence. He offered a low growl of reproach. I suspected I would not be lucky enough to receive a second warning.

Esec was still babbling, a smile slowly forming, oblivious to my anger. It would have been so gratifying to just strike him there and then. To remind him what lay beyond the picts. But my Scion escort would no doubt intervene, or Lanlok would step in to restrain me, and perhaps remove a limb in the process.

And what would be achieved?

I took a deep breath, willing all that anger into a little searing ball of white-hot fury that I choked down. Just like all the others.

I forced myself to smile. 'Have you spoken to Shard?'

'Hmm? No, she's preparing herself or something. I confess I wasn't listening. It's better she's out of the way. We need to shift the focus for a time. Less on Lucille and more on vilifying any traitors. Treat this whole campaign as a warning as to what happens when one resists the Imperium.'

'Traitors? What happened to separatists?'

'That was then. Now they are traitors who consort with xenos and will be treated as such. Frankly, it's how it should have been dealt with from the beginning. I've always said that unyielding force is the swiftest and most compassionate way of resolving a conflict. Waste of time trying diplomacy.'

He sounded like he believed the words, though perhaps he was just an extraordinarily gifted liar. Or both. The best liars are able to convince even themselves that they speak the truth.

He coughed before returning to the screens. I would then have made my excuses, but I was already forgotten, his focus once more on the composite Shard. He seemed so proud of it, as if he had assembled facets into a diamond, not realising that all he held was broken glass.

I spent the rest of the day seeking a purpose. I stopped in the medi-unit to find Brice had passed on, but Selt was recovering, though he'd suffered two broken ribs and would be incapacitated for some time. But there was nothing I could do there, my presence a disruption. So instead I returned to the *Traderi*, where I could guard the cargo if nothing else. Assuming he hadn't expired, for I still could not bring myself to enter the commissar's chamber. The Feed was quiet, for what else was there to say? The day was set.

I could not put Cesh's message from my mind.

Had he really directed those final words to me alone? I was beyond questioning what was possible. My only doubt was whether I'd somehow dreamt it, or compelled Iwazar to manifest the spectre, my subconscious cribbing the nihilistic philosophy he spouted from some half-forgotten tome. I had long since blamed the device for being defective, but maybe Shard was right. Maybe I was the problem, the flickering images it summoned a manifestation of my own guilt and fear.

By the God-Emperor I was tired. It could simply be that – delusions brought on by sleep deprivation. I was approaching the point where I would give almost anything for a respite from existence. For the peace of nothingness.

I refrained from consuming more recaff, hoping that exhaustion might help me rest. Instead, I brewed a cup of the commissar's insipid tea. It was while standing there that I noticed a red light flashing on the control panel. I did not understand the vessel's systems and quirks, but I had resided there long enough to be familiar with its patterns.

A small red light. It was new – I was sure of that.

I pressed the adjacent switch, but the miniscreen displayed an error. It was gene-locked, and I lacked the appropriate heritage to access it.

Could Shard? Was it keyed solely to the commissar, or an immediate family member? Assuming they shared the same genealogy – sometimes I had my doubts. But what did it matter? She and Plient were holed up in his workshop, hatching some last-minute gambit to defeat Cesh.

I should have been with them. Perhaps it would have made a difference.

CHAPTER TWENTY-EIGHT

'Greetings, admiral. My apologies for contacting you again.'

Cesh stood beside the seated and slumped commissar, though there was a pace between them, and Cesh's nose was turned away from the unconscious figure.

'We have a developing situation. I take full blame, for I had not anticipated how unpleasant it is being in your kind's company for a sustained period. I had no idea you periodically vent foul-smelling gas from your digestive tract, or constantly secrete fluids from the skin. I might have thought it a deliberate insult, were Commissar Shard not unconscious. Honestly, if we had not made our pact yesterday, I would already have disposed of this waste of flesh. And he might die irrespective of my actions – I'm wondering if the smell is partially his wounds? They stopped bleeding, but the colour is quite unpleasant. A purplish grey. Is that a bad sign?'

Cesh glanced at the commissar, wrinkling his nose before returning his view to the lens.

'I will make you a new offer. Retrieve this thing in the next few

hours and it might still be alive. Or, if you'd prefer, I can provide coordinates from where you can collect the carcass. Stand by for further instructions.'

The mainscreen went dark. I turned to Esec.

'When did you receive this?' I asked.

'In the night. I was asleep,' he murmured, intent on the blank screen. Given the markings around his eyes, I suspect his sleep had been medicated.

'Who else received it?'

'I assumed everyone! I couldn't understand why there wasn't already a commotion, people hammering on the door. But they all seem to be carrying on as if nothing has changed. That's when I summoned you.'

'Cesh addressed an admiral. Did he mean you?'

'I don't know! He might have sent it to me in error.'

'Possibly. Or is this misdirection intended?'

'Why? For what purpose?'

He had a point. I lapsed into silence, my gaze falling to my hands. The nails were filthy. I could not recall when I had last cleaned them.

'Kile?'

I looked up. 'Yes?'

'We must do something! I can't go to Colonel Surling – he's written off this entire project as a waste of time. Suddenly all he cares about is the offensive in the north. I have few other allies. I hope I can count you amongst them. You know what it's like to be an outsider with these military sorts.'

'I am unsure what help I can provide.'

'What do I do with this? Do I tell Shard? Erase it and pretend nothing has happened? It wasn't meant for me. It's not my business.'

He looked hopeful. But brittle too.

'If it was sent to you in error,' I said, 'the follow-up instructions might be sent to the correct recipient. Or details could come out later, and you'd find yourself accused of being complicit in the death of Commissar Shard.'

He swore, slumping back in his command chair, Lanlok looming behind it. His gaze remained fixed upon the mainscreen, despite the fact it had long since grown dark.

Esec was rubbing his eyes. 'I can feel a migraine coming on.'

'If you message Colonel Surling, will he respond?'

'I doubt he will even read it.'

'Then do it. That way you cannot be blamed for failing to keep him abreast. Then we must tell Shard.'

He flinched. 'Should we, though? She's not at her best in the early hours.'

'He's her brother.'

'But she's working on something with that mechanical. They have been at it all night. Distracting her now might cost us the victory. That could even be Cesh's plan!'

'I thought you had counted her out of the fight?'

'That was before. Whatever is going on in there is big – they've already gone through two servitors! I'm waiting for an update on the third.'

'You are watching them?'

'Of course. I have Eyes everywhere.'

He smiled as he spoke. It looked horribly rehearsed. When I did not return the expression he sighed, rolling his eyes.

'Not like that. I'm not spying, just keeping up to date with her progress. And it's a good thing I did! I would have assumed she was drowning her sorrows, but I caught a glimpse through the window. They are putting something together. We might still have a chance.'

'Do you know what it is?'

'I thought you were opposed to snooping? And no, I have no idea. Their machines drown out their voices, and the windows provide limited visibility. But I don't think we should count out our commander just yet. If nothing else, we're in for a show.'

'We still need to tell her.'

'Let's at least wait for the next set of instructions. For all we know–'

'Admiral Esec. I don't believe you have had the pleasure.'

We stiffened, turning as one to the mainscreen.

Cesh. He stood in seeming darkness, though his armour held an iridescent glint and his face was lit by some unseen source. He tilted his head in lieu of bowing.

'Admiral?' Esec murmured. I could hardly hear him, but somehow his voice still carried through the vox. The aeldari frowned, though his smooth brow barely creased. He had the most expressive eyebrows, the barest arch conveying his confusion and disdain.

'Not an admiral, then?' he said. *'Flight commander, is it? Or colonel? Forgive me, I struggle to catalogue your petty hierarchical distinctions. Esteemed Enemy Esec – how's that?'*

'That is fine. Acceptable,' Esec replied, drawing himself up to his full height, until he was staring down his own nostrils. 'So then, Commander Cesh. Tell me–'

'Cesh. Not commander.'

'Not commander? Do you not hold–'

'I fear it would take the better part of a day to ground you in the fundamental concepts required to glean a rudimentary understanding of the tenets upon which my current and transient designation is determined. And, sadly, I have plans.'

He smiled. It was ever so cruel. Esec swallowed, shuffling in his seat.

'Well,' he said, clearing his throat. 'I do–'

'This is what will happen. You will send a single vessel to collect Commissar Shard. No attack vessels, please – one of those stubby landing craft would be acceptable. It will be airborne in five minutes flying directly west. Further instructions will be delivered then. The handover will be facilitated by your subordinate.'

He nodded to me.

'But he is not–'

'Have I erred again? Is the burly one your second?' Cesh said, glancing to Lanlok. *'He does stand to attention remarkably well, and I gather your people consider that a vital trait for junior officers. Oh dear, how embarrassing for me. Perhaps, in shame, I should end this conversation, flay the commissar alive, and inscribe a letter of apology on his still-bleeding hide. Would that–'*

'Wait!' I said. 'Please wait. I will do whatever is necessary. But I cannot pilot such a craft, and–'

'Why?'

'I never learned. I don't–'

'How sad. I suppose you can have a pilot of your choice, then. But be quick. Five minutes. Four now, actually, as I have already set the timer. I suppose I could start it over, though. Could, but won't.'

The mainscreen went dark. I stared at Esec. He was still intent on it, his expression almost identical to Lanlok's.

'Esec!'

He shook his head. 'No. No, no. She cannot fly the craft. There is–'

'Agreed.'

He sighed with relief. 'Oh, thank the God-Emperor! I just assumed… Well, never mind. It cannot be her. It's obviously a trap.'

'Obviously. But I owe the commissar, and we have but minutes. Can any of your Scions pilot an Aquila lander?'

* * *

It was cramped in the vessel. Especially with Iwazar. The device took up the majority of my lap, and if the craft came under fire it could prove disastrous, bouncing around inside the transport hold and inadvertently bludgeoning me in the process. Not that it mattered. If we were attacked we were dead anyway.

The interior was quite unlike the commissar's shuttle. No hidden nooks or crannies, no living quarters. I was in a small fore section, in one of five seats, the rest of the vessel reserved for cargo. Vid cartridges apparently, each capturing Shard's exploits. Future exploits, as it transpired. If we survived, I wondered if Esec would still dispatch them. Some might travel through the warp for years, perhaps being played long after she had fallen in battle. The echoes rippling out, worlds discovering her faux heroism long after she was dead and disgraced.

It was an odd thought. I found many of them were rising unbound. And my foot was tapping, unbidden. I willed it to stop, but it was difficult not to fidget. The vessel was stiflingly warm, and it felt almost as though the walls were pressing in. There was a viewscreen, but I could not access any external cams. My only contact with the pilot had been to authorise a course correction and increase in speed. Since then, I had waited.

It reminded me a little of the descent to Bacchus, where Plient flew the shuttle. It was only his skills that had kept us alive. And Shard's too. She had swept in at the last moment with a daring rescue and some barbed comments.

Not this time.

The vox hissed. *'Scribe Simlex? We are approaching the coordinates.'*

'What can you see?'

'Nothing so far, only the… Wait, I can see the xenos.'

'His craft?'

'No. He is just standing in the desert. Alone.'

'Is the commissar visible?'

'No.'

'Very well. Proceed to the designated coordinates.'

The vox crackled, the channel left open.

'Scribe Simlex?'

'Yes?'

'This craft is equipped with a heavy bolter. A defensive weapon primarily, but it would be enough to slay a lone aeldari.'

'Your sure? Have you fought them before?'

'No, sir. But I stand by my assessment. I await your orders.'

'Can you put him onscreen?'

'I will try, sir, but I am unfamiliar with the modifications to this vessel.'

I waited, intent on the blank screen, wondering if anything would materialise. I could feel us slowing, beginning the descent. Was a surprise attack worth chancing? Surely he was prepared? But, even if he wasn't, there was no sign of the commissar.

The screen lit up. Desert, and a sole figure clad in midnight-blue armour, seemingly unperturbed by the heat. He seemed to stare at me through the screen, waving with just his fingertips.

'Do I take the shot?'

And I found myself unsure. Perhaps this was our best chance, but was such an attack part of his plan? An excuse to justify some atrocity, or portray us as monsters? But surely we had to try? We couldn't presume any attempt to seize the initiative played into his plans, for that way lay madness.

What if it was an illusion? What if the commissar stood there, his appearance masked by xenos sorcery. What if we gunned him down?

I clicked the vox, realising that I could not recall the pilot's name.

'Scion?'

'Yes?'

'Land as requested. Do not take the shot.'

'Yes, sir.'

'We cannot risk the commissar's life.'

'Sir.'

I could hear disdain in his voice. Perhaps he was right, for as we descended I began to question my hesitation. Impose your plan upon them – that was what the commissar advised.

Then again, he was now their prisoner.

There was a jolt as we touched down. When the transport bay opened, I was struck by a wave of heat and the blinding light of the morning sun. There stood the Scion, ready to escort me, weapon drawn but lowered.

As he helped me from the shuttle, my cane affording minimal purchase on the sand, I wondered if he would take the shot if I ordered it. Scions were notorious for obeying orders unquestioningly. But I was his charge, not his commander. Still, Esec might have already given instructions to slay the xenos should the opportunity arise.

I would find out soon enough, I supposed, marching stiffly towards the xenos, my forearm shielding my eyes from the glaring sun, the Scion trailing in my wake.

Cesh held his hand up. I stopped.

'I am here for Commissar Shard,' I said.

He stared back at me, arching a perfect eyebrow.

'Where is the commissar?'

He said nothing. The Scion advanced suddenly, hellgun raised.

'Wait,' I said, and was surprised that he did so, though his weapon remained trained on the xenos. Something was wrong. It took me a moment to see it.

'You have no shadow,' I said.

'Is that right?' Cesh replied, glancing to his feet. 'How embarrassing.'

'You're not even here.'

'Or perhaps my kind don't cast a shadow?'

I nodded to the Scion. He fired, three las-bolts shearing through Cesh without leaving a mark.

'Ah, you have me.' He smiled. 'How perceptive you are, once-and-future-Propagandist Simlex.'

CHAPTER TWENTY-NINE

Cesh smiled. At least his image did. I could see no projector, unless perhaps it was beneath him. But the likeness was incredible, beyond anything Imperial technology could summon. He looked real, every single hair picked out in exquisite detail.

'Do you even have the commissar?' I asked.

'No. I imagine his remains are smeared somewhere inside those tunnels, along with those other humans he was anxious to incinerate. But I don't know for sure. Or care overly. He doesn't matter. Very few of your kind do.'

'So why the deception? Why summon me out here? You have lost your bargaining piece. Flight Commander Shard does not have to face you.'

'Yes she does. You think she can walk away now? With so many watching? No, her story is almost done. You must see this, Propagandist Simlex.'

I wanted to ask how he knew my name. And I'm sure he knew this, for he smiled again, this time at my defiance.

'Propagandist,' he continued, savouring the word. 'So odd to use that term as a title, without irony or shame. Do you humans have artists? Poets? Storytellers? Do you know these words? Of course you do. Such crude, laboured terms. All your language is like that – no precision, your lexicon wielded like a club to beat the opposition into submission. I sometimes wonder if your aggression is a product of your poor grasp of semantics.'

'The aggression is yours. You attacked us.'

'Your creed decrees that my species should be slain for the crime of existence. How is the aggression mine?'

'This is not your world!'

'You think it your world? Do you know how long this planet existed before your kind? Or how long it will persist after the Imperium fades? You think you're entitled to any of this? My people ruled this galaxy whilst yours were still eating their own excrement and cowering from the rumble of thunder.'

'Is that why you are here? To take this world from us?'

He laughed. It was soft, melodious and cruel.

'No. And if I desired to, there are easier ways. I could introduce something into the environment – perhaps an engineered flora or fauna that would spread disease or prolificate dangerous species. Perhaps I would gift it to the planetary governor for added irony, watching as it eroded their sanity, even as their world descended into an ork-infested quagmire.'

As he spoke, his grin stretched until it seemed to encompass his face. And with it, he no longer looked even slightly human.

'Bacchus,' I whispered. 'You did that?'

'Of course not. I merely provided a hypothetical scenario for how one might destabilise a planet. But that is not my goal here. My efforts are more focused.'

'Why are you doing this to her?'

'Who?'

'Dammit, you know who! This whole campaign has been about discrediting Flight Commander Shard! Dragging her down!'

'From your perspective perhaps. But you are confusing the means with the goal.'

'What goal?'

'The truth, propagandist. Only the truth. That is all I have ever sought. It's something we share. It was why you were cast down, because you wanted your citizens to know how the Imperium really fought its wars.'

I shook my head. 'You will not deceive me. Scion, let us return.'

I didn't hear the shot. Only the muffled thump as my guard fell. I spun, dropping to a knee and examining the body. There was no obvious wound, but he was quite still.

'I was not done,' Cesh said softly. 'And we have precious little time until reinforcements arrive.'

'I will not listen to you! You are a liar and deceiver!'

'What have I said that is a lie? What untruth have I spun? It was not I who tried to replace a fallen hero with a cheap facsimile. I did not attack Edbar, or slay its citizens, or slaughter Deighton's sacred beasts to fatten up my soldiers.'

'You told us you had the commissar! Gave your word as a warrior!'

'Ah, well you have me there. But that was lying to the liars, and necessary to get you here. But that poor, ignorant rabble that populates your worlds? Clinging to the fiction of a loving God-Emperor? They are owed the truth. You must see that.'

'There have been *missteps* during this campaign. But the Imperium seeks to liberate this world.'

'From whom? Its inhabitants?'

'I... It's not as simple–'

'Nothing is simple. Nothing is easy. There is no light and dark or good and evil. There is only truth and falsehood. And the truth is tomorrow I will face Shard and she will fall. It has been foreseen. But what follows, I do not think you have a word for it. Fluid? Unwritten?'

He frowned, dissatisfied at either choice.

I shook my head. 'I will not help you!'

'Perhaps you have already.'

I turned, following his gaze. Aircraft were approaching, still some distance hence. But closing in on us.

'I am bait,' I murmured.

'Oh please,' he said. 'You think anyone would value you enough? They merely hope to catch me off-guard. Already they have failed.'

He sighed, and for a moment he looked tired. Then his gaze met mine, and for the first time there was no disdain in his eyes. Only sadness and resignation. And when he spoke, his voice had no venom. He sounded earnest. Almost pleading.

'There will come a time when you are asked what happened. How she fell. And a great deal will rest on what you say. On whether you once again have the stomach to tell the truth. You are but a pebble, Kile Simlex, your life the brief flight from hand to pool. But when you strike the water, in that moment you leave ripples.'

He was fading now, the sand visible behind him, even as the fighters closed in. But behind them, the light too had shifted. They must have seen it as well, for they broke formation, attempting to turn to face the oncoming distortion.

Except it was coming from all sides, tightening like a noose. Meanwhile Cesh's image was almost gone, though his voice remained unchanged.

'When they ask you what happened, when you are called upon

to tell your tale? You must speak the truth, propagandist. To do otherwise would be to begin a path from which you cannot walk back. Make the right choice. The future of your Imperium may well depend upon it.'

Then he vanished, just as the sky was set ablaze. Perhaps I should have fled for the shuttle, though I suppose it might have made a more obvious target. But it did not matter, for I could not move. It was as though my feet, ruined leg and all, had merged with the sand, Iwazar hovering beside me, equally transfixed by the carnage unfolding above.

The Imperial fighters tried to disperse, but the enclosing light swept through them. There were flashes of cyan, and already planes were tumbling. I did not know our force's numbers on the onset. Twenty, perhaps? It was simpler to count them as they fell.

A quartet of Avengers tried to regroup, converging and unleashing their bolt cannons. I recalled the weapon from Bacchus, its weight of fire and deafening bark striking me as reminiscent of an ork firearm. Perhaps it was a better choice against the aeldari, its indiscriminate firepower piercing the veil of light that shrouded the xenos craft. But the sky was in chaos, Imperial fighters threaded between the hawk-like silhouettes. There were dozens of them, flickering in and out of reality as their forms fractured into bladed diamonds. With the Imperial formation broken, it was almost impossible to target the aeldari without risking a stray shot striking an ally.

Then a spear of cyan light took the lead Avenger. Another fell a moment later, the blast coming from the opposite direction, Cesh's craft seemingly crossing the sky in a heartbeat. I'd once thought our planes so agile, and I supposed they were compared to the orks' smog-spewing aircraft. But the aeldari seemed unrestrained by the limitations of the physical world. It was as if they were long-passed ghosts seeking vengeance against those who still lived and fought. And died, of course.

A craft in Shard's colours erupted in flames. I barely flinched, for I was accustomed to it now. Instead, I sought her amongst the carnage, though it was Iwazar who spotted the vessel. She had hung back, letting the first wave engage the foe. Seeking a moment.

When she attacked, it was with the fury of a falling star. She accelerated through light and fire, ignoring the carnage, straining for a target unseen amid the barrage of bladed diamonds.

She fired.

My heart leapt as her volley struck home. Not a glancing hit this time, the las-bolts piercing the xenos craft, the shimmering alter-images collapsing into a vessel even as it fell, spiralling towards the sand, engulfed in flames.

He had fallen. We had won.

But then why was the sky still ablaze?

The answer came to me a moment before they struck, before the riot of light and colour coalesced into five silhouettes. Because we did not face Cesh this time. Not alone. He too had brought reinforcements.

They fired as one. As they did, it struck me the aeldari never used bombs or missiles, bullets or shells. Their weapon was light itself, each searing bolt claiming an aircraft, perhaps in retribution for their fallen. Had they remained I suspect they could have finished us, but with that last volley they fled, the vessels scattering and accelerating in different directions, even our fastest planes unable to match them.

CHAPTER THIRTY

For once the light was out in Plient's workshop.

That, or the windows had been blackened from the inside. Either way, it was hardly a beacon. In fact, the passageway leading from the main hangars looked particularly uninviting. The area had been a hive of activity on our return, but once repairs were concluded it just seemed to shut down. I don't know if an order was issued, or the soldiers and workers simply bled away.

For what were they to do now?

There were no easy victories left, no outgunned separatists to eliminate. Only the aeldari, who fought like a toxic cloud, poisoning our war effort whilst seemingly immune to retaliation. They had killed barely a handful; I think more aces were lost defending Planetary Governor Dolos' château on Bacchus. Nevertheless, their forces undermined us at every turn, redirecting our attacks against us.

Why?

However frustrating and bleak it became, their actions amounted to nothing. Not in the grand scheme. The war was being waged across continents. Even if our forces were wiped out, the losses were barely a blip. Logistically insignificant set against the war effort.

Shard had to be the key, despite what Cesh had said. She mattered to them, or at least her death did. Perhaps she had a part to play in some future conflict, or her legacy would inspire a crusade or similar. That made the most sense to me, for they did not just seek her death. They wanted her cast down, debased in the eyes of the citizens.

I still stared at Plient's door, listening but hearing little within. But he had left me a message, an invitation to join him for dinner. It had been years since I had received one. In fact, my last formal invite had been to Governor Dolos' ball, a quite exclusive event where I had almost suffocated under the weight of the enforced dress code. Shard had been my dance partner that night. Or possibly I hers – I could not quite recall any more.

I knocked. Quietly, for it felt wrong to disrupt the peace. The second rapping echoed along the passageway, breaking the all-consuming silence and quite clearly marking my location. I had no escort this time, and there was no one to protect me save Iwazar. I was relieved when the door swung open.

'Welcome, sir,' Plient said, beckoning me in. He had a welder's mask atop his head, and his undershirt was stained. His eyes were sunken, but his smile was warm, if a little thin.

'I'm not sure you should call me that,' I said. 'I think you outrank me now.'

'Too late to change old habits,' he replied as I entered. 'No guard this time?'

'No. I wonder if it was him who flew me. I'm ashamed to say I did not take the man's name before he died.'

'If I'd known, sir, I'd have ensured an escort. Edbar is not safe after dark.'

'It's fine. I had Iwazar.'

'True enough,' he said, smiling at the seer-skull as he led me inside. 'I'm sorry we couldn't speak the other day, sir. The flight commander and I were working on something not entirely above board. Esec cannot know.'

'I understand,' I said, crossing the threshold. I was surprised to find the workshop looking remarkably clear. Plient usually had half a dozen devices semi-dismantled, but on this occasion the station was swept and clean, arc welders stowed and secured in their allocated spots on the wall. *Mendax Matertera* was under cover, though given the lubricant stains beneath it Plient must have only recently completed his labours.

'You have finished your work?' I asked, turning to him.

'Almost.'

'And you think your plan will be successful?'

He smiled, though a sadness lingered in his eyes.

'Not my place, sir,' he said. 'I can only do my bit. But isn't that always the case? We only have oversight over our own efforts. All we can do is hope they make a difference when the time comes.'

'Do you think she can win, Plient?' I asked softly after a moment.

'Yes, sir,' he said with utter conviction. 'She will win, providing the rest of us don't fail her.'

As he spoke, his gaze shifted to the covered vessel, concern creeping into his gaze.

'You haven't failed her, Plient.'

'Not yet, sir.'

'So, what is my part?'

'Sir?'

'I assume that was why you requested my presence.'

'Not exactly, sir, I... Perhaps we should wait. I'll explain soon enough.'

He lowered himself onto a stool, elbows resting on the worktop, chin cradled.

'You look tired, Plient.'

'With respect, sir, you look as though you haven't slept for months. I've just had a tough few days and late nights. But I'll rest soon.'

I nodded, lowering myself to the stool opposite.

'I used to sleep so easily,' I said. 'I never realised. It was like breathing, it just happened. But now there is no respite, I awake more exhausted every day. Sometimes I'd give anything for a few moments of blessed oblivion. Do you know what that's like?'

'I'm not sure I do, sir,' he said, raising his head. 'But she does.'

Footsteps. The clink of an officer's boot on railings. I would have said I recognised her gait, but in truth there was something off about it. I heard her curse and stumble, my gaze meeting Plient's.

'Drunk already?' I said.

'Don't, sir. Not tonight.'

'Fine,' I said as he rose and opened the door.

She stomped in. Or tried to, her right leg marching on, the left hobbling after. She was still clad in her flight suit, the stench of promethium accompanying her.

When she saw me she frowned. 'What is he doing here?'

'Good evening to you too,' I said. 'Have you now taken to mocking my limp?'

'Plient, this is important work,' she continued, ignoring me. 'We cannot let–'

'It's done, sir.'

'Done?'

He nodded.

'You're sure? Because the first two attempts did not—'

'As sure as I ever will be, sir. There will need to be a couple of last-minute adjustments, but we are ready.'

'Oh. Then why did you drag me all the way over here?'

'Dinner, sir.'

'Excuse me?'

'I prepared us some food,' he replied, dragging out a rattling carriage, upon which was assembled a motley collection of field rations, vacuum-sealed produce, and reconstituted meats, accompanied by a bottle of amasec.

We both stared at it. Shard spoke first.

'Plient, you know I eat in the officers' mess hall.'

'Yes, sir.'

'And propagandists don't really require food, as they subsist solely on the labours of others. Besides, this can hardly be called a meal. If it was served in the mess hall, the chief would be lynched. Or possibly end up in the firepit, depending on the dispositions of those present. And this amasec is—'

'It's the best I could do, sir!' he snapped, rounding on her. 'We're at war! And this is a dust ball of a planet with little to offer! And tomorrow... Tomorrow will be a difficult day and we might not all... We might not meet up again. We didn't last time. And I never got to say goodbye.'

He bowed his head.

'I do a lot for you, sir. I don't ask much. For once, can we just sit and eat and pretend things were how they used to be? Just once. Just for tonight.'

His voice barely broke. But we both heard it. I did not know where to look, my gaze settling on Shard.

She sighed. 'All right, Plient. We will break bread.'

'You will?'

'Well, no, because I don't think there is any bread here, except possibly the mouldy sort used to pad out the corpse-starch. I assume that's what these biscuits are baked from? But I agree to share this rather uninspired repast with you and the propagandist. Assuming he can stomach it.'

We ate in silence at first, the food laid out on a workstation, stools clustered around. Plient chewed steadily, grazing, while Shard inspected the dishes, checking the biscuits for larval eggs, her gaze constantly flicking to the amasec. I ate sparingly. I had little appetite, but did not want to offend Plient.

Despite his wishes, it was not like old times. Assuming they were ever real, for my recollection of Bacchus remained a horror show, a protracted descent into the filth from which none emerged untainted. Maybe there are never really good times, we just survive long enough to forget the bad, or the present deteriorates sufficiently that the old times seem better by comparison.

Perhaps that was what had happened to Plient, for he was smiling, despite a shimmer in his eyes.

'This is nice,' he said.

Shard and I exchanged glances.

'What is?' she asked. 'I assume you are not referring to the food. Or company. Or present circumstances. Or the political structure that–'

'Can it just be nice?'

She shrugged and swallowed another biscuit.

He sighed, and I tried to think of something to say. A question to ask. A topic to share. Anything.

'What have you been up to since Bacchus, sir?'

Plient was looking at me. I smiled sadly at him. 'Precious little.'

'C'mon, sir, you can give a little more than that.'

'I have been locked in a cubicle deep in a data-store, classifying clips of footage that will probably be stowed and never used. That has occupied the majority of the last few years.'

'...I'm sorry to hear that, sir.'

'Don't be,' Shard said, spraying crumbs. 'It's his own fault. I warned him.'

'Yes, you did,' I agreed. 'And yes, it was my fault.'

Her chewing slowed, just for a second. Then she resumed eating.

'What happened, sir?'

'I'll tell you,' Shard said. 'Whilst we were celebrating victory on Orbital Station Salus, our propagandist informed me that he intended to confront his superiors with the truth about what we faced – monstrous orks, squalid conditions, corrupt nobles and incompetent commanders. When I pointed out that this was a stupid idea, he took offence. Even used some quite appalling language.'

'That I did. And once again I am sorry.'

'Don't be. I don't care. Pity though, we were having an almost not awful time before that. You were acceptable company for once. But you just couldn't handle someone pointing out the flaw in your artistic vision. Had to run away.'

'That isn't why I stormed off.'

She was reaching for another morsel. But her hand slowed.

'Oh?' she said with a wicked smile. 'Don't tell me it was from what happened earlier? Were you so ashamed?'

'No. Not of a momentary indiscretion.'

'Give yourself some credit, propagandist – our indiscretion lasted a little longer than a moment.'

Plient frowned, glancing between us. 'I don't understand. What happened?'

'Yes, Kile dearest,' Shard said, still smiling. 'Why don't you tell Plient what happened.'

I grimaced. 'Shard and I talked. Shared some... intimate moments. Then I told her everything. I knew the risk, but it seemed the right thing to do. I thought... I thought she might be impressed. Proud, even, that I was choosing to take a stand. But she just laughed at me, said I was a fool.'

'And I was right,' she said. 'Nobody wants the truth. Wars should be righteous and glorious. Heroes should be paragons of nobility and villains craven wretches. Discovering they are just as broken and miserable as everyone else doesn't humanise them. It weakens them.'

'Perhaps you are right. I just wish you were not.'

'No arguments from me,' she replied, wiping her plate with a chunk of biscuit. 'Are we going to open the amasec?'

'In a minute, sir,' said Plient. 'I thought maybe a toast?'

'Not sure what we have to drink *to*,' she said as he poured three glasses. 'But as long as we get to drink, I don't care.'

Plient passed a receptacle to me. I no longer drank. Not since Bacchus. But at least the pale liquid lacked the sickly aroma of that planet's tainted wine. I resolved to choke it down. For Plient, if nothing else.

He raised a glass. 'To friends old and new.'

Shard rolled her eyes, but clinked the glass. As did I. And I confess the liquid was not unpleasant: sweet, with a lingering but not distasteful bitterness.

'Not bad,' Shard muttered begrudgingly.

'Now you, sir.'

'What?'

'Your toast.'

She stared at him. Then me. Then shrugged, as if it wasn't worth the effort to argue.

She raised the glass. 'May death come swiftly to our enemies.'

We took another sip. Plient then glanced at me. He didn't

have to say anything, for I knew it was my turn. I just did not know what to say. I glanced to Shard, but she was smiling, glass raised, eyebrows arched, enjoying my discomfort.

'To... the truth,' I said, but it sounded feeble even to me. Plient raised his glass, whilst Shard shook her head before draining her own.

'The truth?' she said. 'So, after everything I told you, you learnt nothing?'

'You were right. The Imperium does not value the truth. But I still do.'

'That might be a little much, sir,' Plient said, collecting the glasses. 'I'm sorry for what happened to you, but the God-Emperor is the embodiment of the truth. Even if His followers sometimes fall a little short of His example.'

'You are right, of course. Forgive me,' I said as he tidied our plates. He smiled, carrying the food containers to the wash-unit.

But Shard glared at me. 'Truth?' she said, arching an eyebrow. 'That didn't last long.'

'I did not wish to upset him.'

'So, you are willing to lie if it spares some gullible sap's feelings?'

'I see no benefit in hurting him.'

'Should I have done likewise?' she asked. 'When you told me of your plans and concerns, should I have pretended to be impressed? Told you they would listen, that your actions would help reform the Imperium into something better?'

'No. Though you probably didn't need to refer to me as an entitled moron either.'

She smiled. So did I, my gaze shifting to Plient. He was cleaning the crockery, humming some old song to himself. I could not read his expression. There was something behind his eyes I had not seen before. It almost seemed like he wanted to say something. But he met my gaze and smiled, before shaking his head. Just once.

Shard too was watching him.

'What now, Plient?' she said. 'Do you have dessert planned? A show? If you like I could beat up the propagandist again.'

'I'd rather you didn't, sir,' he replied. 'In truth, I need to ask you both to leave. I must make some final adjustments before tomorrow.'

Shard frowned. 'I thought you said everything was ready?'

'It is. Or will be. I just need to complete some final checks. For my own peace of mind, if nothing else. Don't fret, sir, I won't let you down. I swear on my mother's life.'

'I know you won't,' she said. 'But perhaps I should stay and supervise?'

I cleared my throat. 'I can assist too.'

As one they rounded on me.

'Thank you, sir, but I don't think that–'

'–something you can help with, even–'

'–likely to be able to–'

'–might get wind of the plan and–'

'–surveillance is too–'

I pulled my seat back, rising. 'I understand. I wish you both the best. Thank you for your hospitality.'

I tried to move away, but Plient had rounded the table, heading me off.

'Sorry, sir, I don't mean to chase you out. It's just this is an all-or-nothing plan, and if the enemy were to uncover... It's not that I don't trust you, sir. But Esec might be spying on you, or have planted some recording device that–'

'I understand. Goodnight.'

I turned away, but he caught hold of my arm.

'Sir? It's been an honour to know you.'

He extended his flesh-and-blood hand. I took it, confused. Even more so when he pulled me into an embrace tight enough to restrict my air supply. I was lucky he kept his augmetic limb by his side, or my ribs might have cracked. It lasted a moment longer before he pulled away, embarrassed but smiling.

'Honestly,' Shard said, rolling her eyes. 'You don't need to feel bad about kicking him out. He's not military.'

'Yes, sir. And you must go too.'

'Excuse me?'

'With respect, sir, you won't help. You will drink and rant and interfere at some point and distract me because you are bored. I need to concentrate.'

He handed her the half-empty bottle of amasec.

'All that is true,' she said, tucking the bottle into her jacket. 'I suppose I should ensure the propagandist isn't slaughtered on the way home. There are damaged people roaming those streets, many of their minds broken from the horror of having to endure one of Simlex's vids.'

She rose, glancing to Plient. 'I will see you in the morn. We have a duel to win, after all.'

'Yes, sir,' he said. 'Goodnight.'

CHAPTER THIRTY-ONE

'Do you get recognised?'

'Of course,' she replied. 'The regiment knows the name Lucille von Shard better than most of the commanding officers.'

'I meant by them,' I said, nodding to a group clustered beneath a fallen arch. They had a fire going, and I wondered what exactly they were burning. Or cooking for that matter – I smelt flesh sizzling, and the options for meat were limited unless one made some drastic dietary decisions.

'I don't think so,' she said. 'Maybe they'd recognise the woman in the posters.'

She gestured to a walkway. Her face, cleaned and preened, still adorned the wall, but a fine layer of dust had stripped its sheen. A crude insult had been scrawled across it, along with a rather sordid illustration.

'They seem to have fallen out of love with you.'

'They never loved me. They loved Lucille von Shard, the fighter ace who appeared on their vid screens. And I wonder how many of them even loved her.'

'They overthrew Edbar's rulers in your name.'

'That's what Esec says.'

'You think he's lying?'

'The man is a propagandist. Of course he's lying.'

'Then why follow him? I have never seen you talk back to him, or insult him. Surely you are the asset, and he simply holds the cam? You could dismiss him at any point.'

'And instate you in his place?'

'That is not what I said.'

She didn't reply, instead reaching into her lapel and withdrawing the lho case. She tucked a stick into the corner of her mouth, fumbling for matches.

'Blasted thing,' she said, looking in the direction of the vagrants. 'Should I go ask if I can use their fire? Or do you think they'll eat me?'

She met my gaze and sighed.

'What do you want from me? I made a mistake and Esec took advantage of it. I now find myself in a position where I must remain aligned with him. It doesn't matter any more. Not after tomorrow.'

'Nothing is certain about–'

'Oh come on, Simlex. Plient's not here. There is no need to mollycoddle him. We both know what the duel will bring.'

She must have found her matches, for she lit up, taking a long drag before exhaling.

'But I…? You and Plient have a plan.'

'We have a gambit. Nothing more. And I'm not sure how successful it will be against a foe who can allegedly see the future.'

She must have caught something in my expression.

'This is how it is,' she said. 'Aces don't get old. We don't last long enough. Because even if you're lucky, someone else will be luckier, and even if you're good, someone else will be better. And I can barely see my target, much less hit it.'

'You slew one of his squad yesterday! Surely that–'

'Luck. Nothing more. I squeezed the trigger and hoped. That's all I can do.'

'At least tell me your plan. Perhaps I can–'

'No. It's clear that someone on this base is compromised, and given that we face the aeldari, they might not even be aware of it. Better we keep quiet, lest something slip. Who knows, maybe it is all bluff. Maybe the little surprise Plient has cooked up will win the day.'

'Overcoming the odds does sound like the sort of thing Flight Commander Shard would do.'

'Precisely.' She nodded, exhaling. But she would not meet my gaze, her own drawn to the cracked roof and stars beyond.

'You do want to win, don't you?' I asked.

'What possible difference would that make?'

Her eyes were cold. Hollow. Like everything inside was used up. I knew the look, I had seen it many times, staring back from every polished surface.

I turned away, focusing on the architecture. Ahead lay the crystalline garden where we had had our first reunion. Abandoned now, the beds stripped bare, perhaps bartered for food or shelter.

I could feel my eyes welling.

'Sorry about the smoke,' she said, tapping her lho-stick against the railing. 'Damn things sting the eyes.'

'I'm fine. But thank you.'

She shrugged, taking one last draw before flicking the butt into the darkness, the pinprick of red swallowed by the gloom.

'I suppose we should retire.'

'Yes. You should get some sleep before tomorrow.'

'Ha! If only.' She grinned. 'Do you know how long it has been since I slept well?'

'Bacchus?

She nodded. 'Yes.'

'I dream of it. Every night. The darkness. The storm. I see us flying towards it. I know there is danger, but there is nothing I can do. I think the war, what I saw… It broke something. Broke me. And I don't think I can be fixed.'

I spoke quietly. I think it was the first time I had admitted it to anyone. She stared back, expression inscrutable.

'It was the orks,' she said.

'Hmm?'

'The nightmares? It's because of that ork weapon that struck us, the one that threw us halfway across the swamp. I figured it out – warp travel.'

'Warp travel?'

'Think about it. The warp allows craft to cross light years in a matter of weeks. Why could it not be used to move a few miles in a matter of seconds? The orks weaponised it somehow. When it struck us, we were thrown through the warp. Just for a moment. And you know what they say about the warp, how it can adversely impact the mind and soul? Strange dreams, unutterable terrors? They are commonplace. That's what happened.'

She spoke quickly, the words bursting forth like an undammed river. I rarely saw her so animated, or so brimming with conviction. She was determined to be right.

'It's not the war,' she finished. 'Nothing as mundane as that. It's a sickness, inflicted by xenos tech and warp exposure. That's why you keep seeing them dying over and over. That's why you sometimes feel the urge to join them, just to escape from it.'

'I don't recall telling you that part.'

She hesitated. Then turned away, rummaging in her lapel.

'Well, it was obvious,' she muttered. 'I could see it on your face. Have you looked in a mirror recently?'

'I try not to.'

She made a sound. Perhaps it was a chuckle. I thought it was directed at me, but as I turned I could see her glaring at her reflection in an adjacent window's cracked glass. She said something I didn't catch and spat before taking another drag.

'When did you start smoking lho-sticks?'

'Don't start. You sound like my brother.'

'The commissar?'

'No. Rile.'

'I remember the name. But I do not think I ever met the man.'

'I used to think he was one of the better ones. But this is all his fault. And mine, I suppose. And yours for setting this whole sorry thing in motion. Plenty of blame to throw around.'

'If it helps, I wish I'd never made the damn pict.'

'That's a stupid wish. You should wish that you'd made a better pict. One successful enough for you, Plient, and I to retire and spend our dotage relaxing on some garden world, where the water is warm, and the drinks are the same colour as the sunset.'

'That would indeed be a better wish.'

'Or taller. You could wish to be taller.'

'Noted.'

'Or perhaps you could do something about your voice? Anything less nasal would be an improvement.'

'Perhaps I should just wish to be a completely different person? Start over from scratch?'

She inhaled, considering this. 'Yes. That would probably be my first choice. Ah well, too late now.'

'I'm sorry about the commissar,' I said.

'He'll turn up. He's survived worse.'

'I heard the tunnel partially collapsed. The Láech have withdrawn.'

'Still.'

She had almost finished the lho-stick. It was time to leave. But I did not wish to go back to the *Traderi*. Not to lie in the darkness alone. Perhaps she sensed this. Or perhaps she thought she owed me something. I don't know exactly. But as she inhaled, she looked at me, as though weighing a decision. Then she exhaled slowly before meeting my gaze.

'You really want to know what happened?'

I knew better than to ask what she meant, or offer any other question. I simply nodded.

'Fine,' she said, stubbing out the lho-stick on a railing. 'But you'll need to bring that skull-thing of yours. I have something to show you. I think you'll enjoy it.'

'Should I fear the worst?'

'No. Perhaps it will amuse you. It would certainly amuse me if it had happened to someone else.'

CHAPTER THIRTY-TWO

The first thing I noticed was the smell.

It wasn't the worst odour I'd encountered. Nothing like Bacchus' putrid swamps, or even the cramped *Traderi* during warp transit, when it was impossible to escape the scent of unwashed bodies. This was the smell of neglect. Dirty clothes, empty bottles, stale lho smoke, and the ever-present stench of promethium fumes.

Shard stumbled through the doorway, cursing as she tripped on a discarded flight suit. A bottle lay beside it. She kicked it aside, the receptacle clattering across the floor before coming to rest beside an unmade bed laden with discarded clothes and unwashed dishes.

'Excuse the mess,' she murmured. 'I don't entertain.'

'I would have thought your rank would permit a housekeeper?'

'It didn't work out. Doesn't matter now.'

She stooped down, rummaging through a stack of stained clothes. I looked away, my gaze coming to rest on an iron perch in the corner of the room.

'You still have your raptaw?'

'No. It didn't survive Bacchus. Haven't been inclined to replace it.'

'I thought von Shards always kept a hunting hawk?'

'Then I guess I'm not much of a von Shard,' she replied, tossing aside a blanket. Beside it, on the floor by her knee, I spotted a sheathed blade. The pommel was distinct enough. It was her father's sword. She had once carried it everywhere. Now it lay discarded and forgotten.

'Where did I put the blasted thing?'

'What are you looking for?'

'Data-slug. I could have sworn… Ah, here we are!'

She tossed something aside, retrieving a sealed strongbox.

'That looks rather robust,' I said as her thumb brushed the key lock.

'It was a gift. As were the contents.'

The box clicked open. She reached in, withdrawing a small data-slug.

'Would you like to do the honours?' she said, tossing it to me.

I caught it, turning it over in my hands. It appeared standard, the kind used by propagandists across the Imperium. Not exactly untraceable, but common enough that it could originate from anywhere.

'Iwazar,' I said, coaxing it closer. 'Begin playback. Mod–'

'Wait!'

I turned to find her raising the amasec to her lips, taking a long swig. I waited as she drank, the contents of the bottle slowly but steadily receding. When it was empty, she tossed it aside, though it failed to shatter in dramatic fashion, its fall cushioned by the room's detritus.

'All right,' she said, nodding. 'Go ahead.'

I inserted the data-slug into Iwazar, its engines whirling as it accessed the contents. Its projector flared.

Shard. Her image was clear enough, as was the bar upon which she was propped. Behind her I could make out faint figures, and the bustle of what appeared to be a taverna. She was listening to someone offscreen, I could see from the way her head tilted. But I could hear nothing except when she spoke, the other voice muted.

'Of course, they found it,' she said, frowning at the unheard response. *'Well, I presume they destroyed it. Why are you worried anyway?'*

The response was inaudible. Pict-Shard rolled her eyes.

'You think Rile would care about some dodgy pict-cam? Have you seen what my brother faces? It's nothing you could put on a pict screen. There is no way of presenting those things in a positive light. They are an existential threat to our very existence. I don't think they even hate us. They just want to feed.'

She knocked back a drink, while the unseen viewer muttered something in response.

'Because one of them smashed through the cockpit and tried to eat me! You see this scar? That's from the acid it spewed over the navigator. One drop. Stung like hell. Still stings, actually.'

A muffled question. Shard shot the enquirer a look.

'Then smooth it out like you do my other flaws. Or leave it in. Who cares? We're all dead anyway, one way or another. Our efforts may slow or speed the demise, but our end is written from the moment of birth. The rest is filler.'

I glanced to the real Shard. She was sitting on the floor beside me, knees drawn to her chest. Somehow, she had secured another bottle of amasec.

'Esec?' I asked.

She nodded, though her head hung low. I looked back to the image, to find the pict-Shard knocking back another shot. Esec must have said something to her for she stiffened, slamming the glass down.

'I will sit here and drink until I am damn well ready to leave. I don't care what you have planned tomorrow. Básking propagandists. You are parasites – you don't get it.'

She took another shot. I had never seen her drink like that.

'It was just darkness,' she said. *'Darkness and mouths. And I couldn't help but think that our masters would kill for servants like that, soldiers willing to hurl themselves to their deaths without thought. That's how the little ones got us. Just jammed themselves into intakes and engines until the planes stalled and fell. That's the real terror. Not the giant monsters swatting us from the sky. It's how unified they are, in a way we never can be.'*

She paused only to swallow another shot. Her voice was starting to slur.

'I watched a world die. When we reached the moon and my brother's precious cargo was delivered, I sat in the cockpit and watched the skies burn and seas bleed. And you know what I felt?'

She glanced to the cam, her gaze fixed just above it, presumably meeting Esec's gaze. I suspected she had not known she was being recorded.

'Nothing. I felt nothing. How many billions died? It should have meant something, even in an abstract sense. But it's just another world. There are millions more. Billions more. And none of them matter either. Nothing does. It will all be swallowed in the end. Or we will just murder each other first. Either way is fine. All the ways are fine. All is the same. All dead.'

I could not tell if she was still addressing Esec. Her eyes were glazed, but she rallied, shaking her head, straightening her back, and ingesting another shot.

'What were you drinking?' I asked.

'I have no idea. I don't remember any of this. It had been a difficult day.'

'Do you know what he said to me? My own dearest brother? After

he had coerced me into flying that suicide mission? After I had overcome a maelstrom of multi-limbed monstrosities? Snatched him from the jaws of a monster large enough to swallow a battle tank? Do you know what he said?'

She stared at the spot above the cam. Esec must have murmured something because she shook her head so forcibly I thought it might detach.

'He told me to keep my mouth shut, else I might have an unfortunate encounter with his precious inquisitor. Básk you, Rile. I save you and you talk down to me. Keep your head down, Lucille, be a good soldier, Lucille. Let your betters deal with the important things and don't ask questions. You just keep fighting and bleeding until one day you can't. Do you think I'm stupid, Rile? That I don't know what you did. You and your little device. You brought it here, you and your master. It's your fault.'

The slur was worse now, some words almost unintelligible. Her gaze had drifted to the bar, perhaps assuming another drink had materialised. I heard the muffled sound of Esec's voice, but she cut him off.

'I. Don't. Care. Básk Rile. And básk his master too. Damn inquisitors, judging others' righteousness when they are the biggest hypocrites of all. Them and the priests. Actually, the priests are worse. At least the inquisitors have a goal beyond their own self-gratification.'

A hand reached out from behind the lens, the owner trying to place it on her shoulder. She batted it aside.

'I don't care! Let them hear the truth. The Ecclesiarchy are crooks and liars, and I know this because my brother is one of them, and he's as fat and content as a tick suckling on a grox. And whilst he pays lip service to the God-Emperor, I've noticed a curious phenomenon. Serving the God-Emperor's will always seems to involve an outcome beneficial to my brother. Have you noticed that? All the priests, all the colonels, all the adepts of the Administratum? They

all serve His will by means of doing whatever it is that suits their own interests.'

She sighed, her gaze falling to the bar.

'Not that the common citizens are any better. Dull people with pathetic lives. None of them think properly. Half the time they toss grains in the air, watch where they fall, and proclaim the outcome is some divine message from the God-Emperor concerning the harvest. Do you know how many wars I have witnessed where both sides claimed the God-Emperor was with them? Humanity eviscerating each other, each life they take gifted to Him, just as each casualty they suffer is also a gift to Him. Do you think that counts double? Maybe that's why He seems reluctant to step in? Ups His tally I guess, while we murder each other for little discernible benefit.'

Esec muttered something. But this time Shard broke into a belly laugh, leaning back in her chair and shrieking.

'You idiot! Do you think He cares about anyone? Do you know how many soldiers I have seen pray before a battle? For His aid, His protection, His strength? That He will judge them worthy to return home? And do you know what happened to those brave fools? They died. They all die in the end. Because He doesn't care enough to protect them. Or because He can't.'

Esec murmured. Beside me, the real Shard turned away, burying her face in a bottle.

'Oh, we've all heard the miracles. The Living Saint who overcame the darkness, the Lord Regent returning from death's clutches to rule in his father's name. But do you know who has never prayed? Me. Never once. Not since I was a child, when I asked Him to let me go with her and sail the void. He never answered. But I'm still here, whilst more pious pilots stain the ground below. What does that tell you? Either He loves a bastard, or His favour is worth nothing.'

Another hand on her shoulder. This time she batted it off, rounding on Esec, her face just remaining in frame.

'Básk off, you parasite! I don't have to do what you damn well say. I am Lucille von básking Shard and I deny you all. Básk you. Básk the bastards who run the Imperium, and básk the Imperium itself.'

She reached for her drink, paused, and turned back one last time.

'You know what? While I'm at it? Básk the God-Emperor. Him and His básking Throne. Because maybe if He got off His backside once in a while, things wouldn't have gone so much to shit.'

The recording cut out.

We sat a moment in silence, my mouth hanging open, Shard's clamped around a bottle that I assume was long since drained.

'Básk the God-Emperor?' I echoed. It was hard to even utter the words.

'It was that last drink,' she said. 'If I'd have knocked it back that would have tipped me over. I would have run outside, voided the contents of my stomach, and staggered home. Stupid!'

'Yes. The lesson here is clearly the dangers of not drinking enough.'

I was surprised by the steadiness of my voice. Saddened too, for it showed just how numbed I was to all this. Once, not long ago, I'd have been terrified by the mere existence of such a recording, let alone being in the same room as it.

'And this is how Esec–'

'Oh, he was thrilled to have this. Of course, I didn't remember any of it, didn't believe it was real. Not until he sent me that data-slug. Not the original, of course, he still has that. And probably hundreds of backups. So, I fly the missions the way Esec likes, and that footage remains suppressed. If I don't, then you can guess what will happen.'

In truth, I wasn't sure exactly what would happen. Execution seemed the obvious answer. But perhaps there were worse fates for a hero turned heretic, a protracted and painful passing.

Heretic. I suppose that was what she was, technically. I'd never met one before.

'This recording is why you summoned me to this world?'

'That again?' she said. 'How many times – I never summoned you! You've seen how much fake footage of me is rolling around. Maybe it was Esec. Or Plient, actually – poor fellow has been struggling.'

'Esec has no motive. And Plient lacks the skills.'

'You underestimate him. That boy can do anything with machines. He can even… Well, he could be responsible. Or someone else. Either way, it no longer matters.'

'Perhaps. Though if I could–'

'No. You can't,' she replied. 'Whatever it is, you can't. It can't be put back. Esec has copies everywhere. But it doesn't matter any more, that's the beautiful thing. Because soon he'll have no power over me at all. Not after tomorrow.'

Despite the drink her voice was perfectly clear. She smiled, the expression almost warm. But her eyes were downcast. Resigned.

I could not look at her, turning away.

She sighed. 'Anyway, I should probably try and get that sleep. Lucille von Shard must look her best tomorrow. Can't disappoint the crowds.'

'You do have a plan, though?'

'Oh yes. I have a little trick up my sleeve. Perhaps it will be enough to fool the aeldari. You needn't worry, Simlex, either way your job is done.'

'I fear I have done little.'

'You got punched in the face. I enjoyed that.'

'Glad to have helped.'

'And… and I'm glad we got to speak before… before anything could happen. I mean, an idiot like you is always at risk of dying on his walk home. But if that happens, at least issues between us are settled.'

I nodded, not trusting myself to speak.

'By the Throne you're soft,' she said, motioning me to rise. 'C'mon, you need to go, and I need to prepare. The aeldari will no doubt want an early confrontation.'

'Will I… Will we speak before the launch?' I said as I rose, and she escorted me towards the door.

'Probably not. I need to focus. Perhaps I'll try praying. He must owe me a favour, right?'

She caught my expression and sighed again.

'How about we meet for a drink afterward? Toast my victory.'

I forced a smile. 'I look forward to it.'

'Good,' she said, smiling back. 'I hope you get some sleep, propagandist. Goodnight.'

The door closed.

I stood there a moment, unsure where to go. Part of me wanted to hammer on the door, to convince her there was another way. But I had no idea what it was. So, I walked away, down the stairway, ignoring the dregs huddling in the rubble. It was freezing with the sun down and the outer wall breached, but I barely felt it.

As I continued towards the hangar, I passed Plient's workshop. The lights were on again, and I could hear the thrum of an arc welder. I slowed, debated knocking. But he was busy, as was she, and I could offer little help to either. My options exhausted, I did the only thing I could. I tucked my cane beneath my arm and, leg trembling, lowered myself to a knee. I crossed my arms in the shape of the aquila, and I prayed to Him. I prayed she would best Cesh. And I prayed the aeldari would be defeated. Most of all, I prayed for a way out, a means to escape her fate.

I prayed to the God-Emperor for deliverance. And He offered only silence.

CHAPTER THIRTY-THREE

There was no vid message from Cesh on that final day. Simply a time and coordinates. I didn't see why we had to follow them. But according to Esec, Colonel Surling was insistent.

'It's become a point of pride for him,' Esec explained. 'After everything that has happened, he wants the aeldari bested in single combat. Though, if that fails, we have reserves awaiting in orbit. If the battle does not go her way, they will descend on the aeldari and wipe him out.'

I nodded, intent on the screen. It seemed futile to point out Cesh's speed, or ability to conceal his craft. Could reinforcements really make a difference? Still, I hadn't quite given up hope. Plient had put something together. Perhaps a holo-projector, like we had employed against the orks? Somehow, I could not see Cesh being so easily deceived. Maybe it was something else, a relic weapon that could bypass the aeldari's defences.

We continued across the desert, escorted by squadrons of

Valkyries. The sands soon gave way to the glass. The last time I had crossed the plain was when we hunted the mamutida. So much had changed.

'Commander Shard? Are you there?'

'I will be.'

She remained cryptic, eager to engage but reluctant to tell us when. Surprise, apparently; that was the key to whatever she had planned. So, we were reduced to spectators. Esec's fleet of Eyes emerged from the barge across the gleaming plains, anxious to capture every moment of the duel. I confess that I would once have been excited at the thought of recording such a battle for posterity. But I kept seeing her face. The smile without its edge. Eyes hollowed. Broken.

She looked as though she'd already lost.

'You think she can do it?' Esec asked.

'Of course.'

'I suppose we'll know soon either way.'

We slowed, the Valkyries shifting to hover and deploying around the barge. Cesh had assured our safety, but none of our leaders trusted a xenos. Somewhat ironic, considering our reinforcements awaited in near orbit.

When the hour finally struck, the skies were empty.

'Coward,' Esec muttered. 'Dragged us out here for nothing.'

Perhaps he was right. Perhaps pretence of a duel was another ruse, allowing Cesh to strike elsewhere. With that thought came the faintest flicker of hope. But then the sky began to bleed colour, a swarm of winged shapes coalescing into a predatory craft, its form mirrored in the glass below.

It was my first time seeing it so clearly, unmasked by the aeldari's deceptions. So different from the Imperial vessels, its hull sleek and curved, wings tapering to bladed points. It looked almost fragile, as though it might shatter under such velocities.

But it accelerated again, the silhouette stretching into myriad alter-images, until it was lost amidst a swarm of knives.

Cesh's voice pierced the vox.

'Greetings, servants of the Carrion Throne. I see you have your cams deployed to capture this moment. I'm not sure why – perhaps you think your hero requires an appropriate epitaph? Assuming "hero" is the right word, for I cannot help but note that Flight Commander Shard is absent. Is she unwell? Or suffering engine troubles? Surely she is not afraid?'

He circled us as he spoke, vulture-like, as though awaiting our demise.

'How disappointed you must feel. How betrayed. I suppose I could still stretch my wings, perhaps slay your escort. But I think I'll spare you. Someone needs to break the news to your citizens that their hero would rather cower than–'

I caught it on the far monitor. Something was descending from on high, blazing like a comet. Esec was already barking orders, his Eyes focusing on the descending vessel. But I knew the craft even before he had visuals.

Mendax Matertera.

Not some lesser vessel draped in her colours. The real thing, the Lightning that once defeated an armada single-handed. But it had changed much since I'd last seen it. Plient had been busy, and through his labours the Lightning almost resembled an ork vessel, so festooned was it with bolted-on weapons. An array of missiles bristled from its wings, both over and undersides, along with additional autocannons liberated from the Astra Militarum, their ammo feeds flapping as the craft hurtled towards the circling Cesh. The tech-priests would have declared it heretical, and given the way it was wobbling I doubted the additional payload did much to improve its speed or manoeuvrability. But neither mattered much if one was diving from the void itself. She had already reached terminal velocity.

I expected her to say something, to offer a challenge over the vox. But it seemed that time was done. Cesh certainly felt no need for words, his craft pivoting at an impossible angle before hurtling to meet her, his silhouette fracturing into a score of images, until it appeared she faced a squadron of spectral foes.

The autocannons fired. I counted four in total, unleashing a collective volley comprising hundreds of rounds. The spectral squadron weaved through the firepower as they closed, the barrage leaving them untouched.

Perhaps that was the intent, the volley's purpose to force Cesh to reposition, leaving him exposed. If it was just the first gambit, then what followed was perhaps the final.

She launched the missiles. All of them.

Those beneath the wings were wired into hard points, the same that once held my seer-skull, the device discarded to increase her firepower. How the missiles mounted above the wings were launched I do not know, but they fired as one. They were not precision weapons, for I doubted there was a targeting system. Half the challenge must have been aligning them so they didn't simply collide and detonate. Instead, they spread slightly, almost forming a squadron of their own.

At that speed, it was seconds before impact.

I don't know the payload, but it was not an implosive charge, for the sky was at once an inferno, Cesh's spectral squadron of flickering alter-images hurtling into the flaming maelstrom, even as Shard pulled away. There was a sluggishness to her manoeuvre, the craft less responsive due to the additional weight.

She was still turning when Cesh's vessel burst from the inferno: a bladed silhouette against a newly born sun, his craft as solid and substantial as any Imperial vessel. Somehow, the barrage had removed his greatest advantage, if only for a moment. I felt the agony of hope, that perhaps my prayer would be answered, that she could do it. But he was accelerating towards her, *Mendax Matertera* struggling to reposition.

He fired.

Twin beans of cyan light erupted from beneath his wings. They struck *Mendax Matertera* as one, dead centre.

And the vessel exploded.

Perhaps it was the modifications that made the blast so violent, or simply the power of the xenos weaponry. The plane was at once erased, supplanted by an expanding ball of flame and metal. I kept waiting for the ejector seat, for Vagbon had survived her encounter in such a manner. I waited even as a wing tumbled from the conflagration, waited even as it plunged like a stone towards the glass plain.

Beside me, Esec sighed. 'Well, it was fun while it lasted.'

The burning remnants of *Mendax Matertera* struck the plain like a falling comet, the glass shattering on impact. All that remained was an inferno.

Silence followed, broken by Cesh's voice.

'My sincere apologies. That was just sad. I honestly thought she would avoid the attack, that we would duel a little longer. Had I realised her skills were so pitiful I might have extended the engagement a little, perhaps given her a moment to shine before I ended it. Forgive me, I should have known better.'

'Kill him!' Esec roared through his vox. 'Send them in! Wipe the damn–'

'I will leave you to your grief, and I look forward to your propagandists telling the tale of Flight Commander Shard's final battle.'

His vessel suddenly erupted in colour, its silhouette breaking into bladed diamonds. It seemed he had suffered no real damage, only disengaging his protective glamour as a lure or feint. Before our reinforcements could descend, he had already accelerated away.

On the mainscreen, what remained of *Mendax Matertera* continued to burn.

CHAPTER THIRTY-FOUR

I drank.

Perhaps not the most mature reaction, but given the options it seemed appropriate. Of course, there were few places one could procure alcohol, at least places I knew. But Shard's quarters were unlocked. Presumably she never expected to return.

It didn't take long to find something – a half-finished bottle tumbled behind the bed and forgotten. I sat upon the stale bedding, forced it down one bitter mouthful at a time. It didn't help. It didn't have to. But it gave me something to do, other than think. And regret.

No tears. I'd shed a few while she was alive. But now I just felt numb. Numb, and cold. And empty.

I'd drained about half of it when a thought came unbidden: maybe it was better this way. Maybe this was the best she could hope for, a quick death in battle and whatever peace awaited after. She may have fallen, but she did her duty to the end, even against a foe she knew she could not best. She would never be cast as a heretic now, never bring shame to her siblings. However she had lived, she died a hero.

For the best. I knew then I should leave, stopping long enough only to retrieve the incriminating data-slug. At some point someone would go through her possessions, if only to free up the room. I thought it better that the recording went undiscovered.

I stumbled as I emerged from her room, my cane sliding across the walkway. Perhaps I was more inebriated than I'd realised, though my thoughts felt remarkably clear. I saw her face as I walked, not in my mind's eye, but on the defaced posters that still clung to some of the walls.

Coward. Murderer. Betrayer.

The last I found especially galling, betrayal apparently synonymous with failure. It made no sense, but why should it? They had been told Shard was invincible, the God-Emperor's vengeance made manifest. Someone had to be blamed for that lie. Who better than her?

I rounded a corner and saw a figure lying sprawled ahead. I assumed it to be another vagrant, but as I approached, it became clear they were dead, a pool of blood congealed around their face. It appeared their throat had been slit, the corpse ransacked.

It was just the beginning. Edbar's order and infrastructure had been shattered, and no effort made to repair it, our factions too preoccupied pressing their own advancement. Once its citizens died from war, but now our peace was killing them, the destitute already turning on one another for scraps. How long until they decided to band together against their greater foe?

I continued, cane audible as it clicked along the path, Iwazar trailing behind. I must have looked an easy target, and wondered if someone would take the chance. A dagger in the back was not the ending I would have chosen, but it had a certain poetic symmetry given the day's events. Iwazar could even capture my final moments. It would no doubt be a poignant shot – the propagandist bleeding to death in the cold outside his former muse's abandoned dwelling. A shame no one would care to see it.

Above me, Esec's barge still dominated the skyline, a shadow against the star-strewn void. He had been silent the majority of the return flight, not even bothering to retrieve the wreckage of *Mendax Matertera*. But I had seen him gathering old files, comparing them to the brief footage of that final battle. Perhaps he sought to craft a fitting send-off, or hoped there was sufficient material for one final pict. The 'Death of Lucille von Shard' had a certain punchiness to it, assuming there was some way to present her demise as a glorious victory instead of an ignominious end.

Was she a hero?

I could not decide, could not even judge the criteria. Was heroism about intent or outcome? She had bested the Green Storm almost single-handed, and probably prevented the orks rampaging across the subsector. How many lives did that save? Billions?

But Bacchus was still at war, with no end in sight. Perhaps she had merely delayed the inevitable, postponed the deaths that would surely follow. And, for all her efforts, she had fallen, her death casting a malaise over our forces. But at least she had tried. Fought until the end. Death before dishonour.

Was that enough? I had no idea.

Ahead lay the turnoff to Plient's workshop. I could see light bleeding around the doorframe. He must have heard by now. Everyone had, for footage had already leaked. Perhaps Esec had done it deliberately, or someone else was quick with a pict-cam. Plient would have been waiting, watching for any sign, hoping for good news.

I knew I should go to him, offer whatever comfort I could. But

I could not face him, and knew of no way to relieve his suffering. So I turned from the path, continuing towards the commissar's hangar and the docked *Traderi*. I still had a bunk, for now, though presumably at some point someone would seek to retrieve the vessel. His family perhaps, or the Officio Prefectus itself.

Would I be returned to my cubicle? It seemed unlikely anyone would take the time and trouble to ship me halfway across Subsector Yossarian. More likely I would join the indentured workers on the ruined streets of Edbar, until someone had the bright idea of slitting my throat and looting my corpse. Or perhaps I would be radicalised, end up joining a future uprising against the Imperium. And no doubt be gunned down in the streets.

Perhaps the *Traderi* would remain. The commissar may have secured the hangar indefinitely, for I doubted paperwork was being properly filed in the dust-strewn ruins. I could linger like an old wound, subsisting off the rations stowed within the ship's many nooks and crannies. Years from now, children would whisper not to go near the abandoned hangar, where the crazed old man lived and made fanciful claims about how he once toured the galaxy.

Of course, I could speak the truth.

Would she like that? A pict showing her navigating the mad contradictions of the Imperium's war machine. How it broke her, until in a weak moment she cast aspersions against the God-Emperor Himself. I still had the data-slug, after all. They would kill me, for whatever that mattered, but it was certainly a tale worth telling. And I was rather untroubled by a prospective, hypothetical death. My more immediate concern was that the hangar door was ajar.

I slowed, frowning, trying to recall who had access. The commissar had claimed he had restricted it to our crew, and none of them were alive to my knowledge. Esec's Scions had been unable to enter, but they had not actively attempted to breach the security. I pushed the door with my cane, the hinges creaking. On close inspection it was clear the lock had been overridden, the panel hanging loose from dangling wires.

Someone had bypassed it.

Beyond lay darkness, the hangar's lumens apparently non-functional. I could make out the *Traderi*, the ship's internal illumination bleeding through the windows and observation dome. Everything else was swathed in shadow, the blackness so all-consuming that I had made it halfway to the *Traderi* before I spotted the other vessel.

It was black. Completely black, as though carved from a chunk of obsidian. It was a similar length to the *Traderi* but narrowed, what little I could discern of its shape reminiscent of a knife with thrusters. Its weapons looked Imperial – lascannons and a rack of underslung missiles – but the overall design was unfamiliar, partly because it blended so seamlessly with the shadows.

A gunship? If so, it was a small one.

I had drunk too much, my judgement sufficiently impaired that it only then dawned on me how precarious my current situation was. I was alone, unguarded, and someone had breached the commissar's sanctuary.

I turned, beginning a stumbling retreat, gambling that Esec might offer sanctuary on his barge. But the doorway was blocked suddenly by a figure stepping from the shadows. Tall. Humanoid.

'Who goes there?' I said, voice shrill, even as Iwazar glided silently in front of me, my last and only line of defence.

The figure did not reply. Not immediately. Instead he took a step closer, his broad shoulders eclipsing what little light escaped through the doorway. He wore black, his armour vaguely reminiscent of the Scions', but slimmed down and partly concealed by a greatcoat.

As he drew closer, the light from the *Traderi* revealed his face.

His hair was dark, as were his eyes, and his jaw square. In fact, he would not have looked out of place as one of the pilots in Esec's picts. Except for his eyes. There was strength there, but also an indifference. An emptiness.

'I'm warning you!' I said, though of what I am uncertain. But he slowed, raising his hands to show he held no weapon.

'I do not wish to harm you, Propagandist Simlex. Not unless I have to.'

His voice was deep. Calm. And just as measured as his movements.

'That is no longer my title,' I said, taking a step back. 'And how do you know of me? Who are you?'

He did not reply; instead his hand slid into a fold in his greatcoat, withdrawing a small token. An amulet, in the shape of a stylised column adorned with a skull. In the darkness, and my drunken state, it took me a moment to recognise it.

And suddenly I felt very cold.

'You're an inquisitor,' I managed.

'Not quite. Merely in service to one,' he said, tucking it back into his coat. 'My remit involves dealing with xenos threats. Beings that, as I understand it, you are acquainted with?'

'I... I have had encounters. But I am not... I don't...'

I was stammering, retreating even as he advanced. I had faced orks and aeldari attacks, but neither held as much terror as that one man and his cold, dead eyes. For the xenos would only kill me. The Inquisition could do so much worse.

He slowed a few feet from me, offering a smile which provided zero reassurance.

'My name is Rile von Shard. And I have questions.'

CHAPTER THIRTY-FIVE

'Von Shard?'

'For my sins,' he replied with a modest bow. 'Though I see little of my family, my duties requiring me to operate in the shadows. But I fear the situation may now require intervention.'

I could not speak. It was not fear exactly, more a sudden awareness of every word I'd ever uttered, every thought that had merely crossed my mind. What if he had recording equipment in Shard's quarters? What had I said? Or not said, or failed to report? That conversation alone would be sufficient justification for an execution. Or worse, interrogation.

He stepped closer, pace measured, no threat apparent or weapon drawn. Even his face was pleasant enough, providing you didn't dwell on the void behind his eyes.

'You seem nervous, propagandist.'

'I am only a scribe, my lord. I lost that rank.'

'Ah. You see? Already I am learning,' he said. 'Scribe. The title does not suit you.'

'It was not by choice, but, my lord, I... I don't know what you have heard, but your siblings, Commissar Tobia von Shard and... Lucille. They are dead.'

He did not seem to react. As though he knew.

'Thank you,' he said. 'But I would prefer to discuss the matter aboard the *Traderi*. Please, after you.'

He gestured to the descended transport pod. Perhaps shared ancestry allowed him to access the gene-lock, or he had simply disabled it in a similar manner to the door. Either way, from the ease with which he operated the controls, it seemed this was not his first time on the shuttle, a suspicion confirmed when we entered the communal area and I saw the figure draped across the table, swathed in bloodstained gauze and scorched rags that might once have been a uniform.

My heart leapt as I entered, for the diagnosticator attached to the figure's forearm indicated they lived.

'By the God-Emperor, is that her? Did she–'

Then I saw the peaked cap nestled upon his head. Unlike every other inch of him, it was pristine.

'Commissar Shard,' I said.

'Indeed. I had to drag him out of the tunnels,' Rile said. 'Thank the God-Emperor for his refractor field. I think it was the only thing that saved him from whatever transpired down there. It's a mess, I can tell you.'

'How did you find him?'

'Tracking implant. Still took me an age. I think he'd crawled or staggered deeper underground. Left behind the remains of a couple of aeldari rangers. But he lost too much blood, and was unconscious when I found him. And I am uncertain if that will change.'

'Why is he wearing a hat?'

'My brother takes pride in his uniform. He would prefer it this way.'

'Perhaps we should move him to his bed.'

'I wish I could. I would like to sit and would prefer the table not to reek of my brother's scorched flesh. But his room is an area of the ship I cannot access. There is a separate code.'

'I know it.'

'...I see,' he said, frowning as he reappraised me. 'I did not know the two of you were so close. Forgive me, I would have braced you better for the sight of his injuries.'

'We are not close in that manner. There was an incident that required me to access...'

I trailed off, remembering suddenly why I had been required to enter the room, and the presence of the cargo, assuming he still lived. And it struck me an imprisoned psyker was the sort of thing that would raise an Inquisitorial agent's suspicions. But it was too late, for Rile had already bent down, scooping the commissar and diagnosticator in his arms without apparent effort, before turning towards his chambers.

He glanced over his shoulder. 'If you would be so kind?'

I wavered. I could input it incorrectly, tell him I could not recall it? But then he might decide to assist me in extracting the buried information. And I doubted my ability to endure interrogation.

So I nodded, squeezing past him and inputting the code. The chamber slid open, and he stepped through while I followed. Mercifully, the psyker's hidden chamber was sealed, and without it the room was unsurprisingly spartan. There were no ornaments or trophies, besides a passage of scripture and hanging pendant. But, as the commissar was lowered onto the bed, I noticed a small pict frame on the table beside it. Two young men, one of whom might have been the commissar, were pictured. They weren't smiling, but they didn't look unhappy.

Then the diagnosticator was placed before it, blocking my view. Acolyte Shard stepped back, sighing.

'Ideally, he'd see a physician. But I'm not confident anyone on this world can be trusted.'

He was looking right at me.

'Perhaps one of the Láech medics?' I said. 'He seemed to have an affinity with them.'

'I will consider it. After our conversation.'

He then stood, leaving the commissar to his convalescence, and returned to the communal area. I followed, for what else was there to do? He was at the recaff machine when I entered, opening the hidden cupboard where the commissar kept his tea.

'Sit down,' he said. 'I will prepare a beverage. You look as though you need to sober up.'

He was mistaken on this last part. His presence was having a remarkably sobering effect. Anyone could appear threatening with a big enough weapon or loud enough battle cry, but he could accomplish it simply by stirring tea.

The ritual concluded, he made for the table, selecting the seat opposite and placing the cups down, his gaze unwavering.

'Scribe Simlex,' he began, before a frown suddenly stole across his face. 'Oh, my apologies. This is embarrassing.'

'What is, my lord?'

'I left my implements on my ship.'

'Implements?'

'My interrogation tools. Still, not to worry. I think I can make do with what we have here. There are still knives in that drawer, correct?'

'I don't–'

'And the recaff machine can provide scalding water. I have my plasma pistol if I want to get creative. Yes, there is enough to work with. Especially if you cooperate, Scribe Simlex. I assume you intend to cooperate?'

He smiled again. I nodded.

'Good. Because I know a little of you, Simlex. You have put some work my way before. And I know you are a man who respects the truth. Is that correct?'

'I... It was.'

'Was?'

'I no longer know if there is a truth.'

Ah,' he said, smiling softly. 'Well, rest assured that there is a truth. Beyond the lies, obfuscations and self-deceptions, there is a cold, hard truth to this galaxy. About what it is, and what it could be. But this truth is hidden.'

He leant forward, until his face was inches from mine.

'My duty is to ensure it remains so.'

CHAPTER THIRTY-SIX

Dawn crept through the hangar's armaglass window.

I sat just outside the *Traderi*, my back to it, watching the light invade Edbar's passageways. I could see no guards, or sign of the Eyes. There had been no more vids either, though Esec had to be working on something. Perhaps he had forgotten me, or no longer had the resources for surveillance.

Behind me, I heard the tread of Acolyte Rile von Shard, his footsteps heavy, perhaps deliberately so. But I did not look round to see what he was doing. He had been clear on that.

The interrogation had been little of the sort. There was no need for blade or fire to coerce me, because I had told him everything. Almost everything, at least. Frankly, it was a relief to unburden myself. I told him how I travelled to Deighton at Commissar Shard's request, after he intercepted a message allegedly from Flight Commander Lucille von Shard, of which she had subsequently denied all knowledge. I told him that there had barely been time to investigate before the aeldari attacks had commenced, though files provided by Plient suggested their campaign began much earlier.

When he asked how the aeldari first made contact, I found myself unsure. I told him of the messages, the vids. Even how I was assigned to retrieve the commissar, only to find that too was a ruse, a trap intended to demoralise our forces. All as part of some convoluted plan that made little sense to me.

But was that the first time?

Cesh had mentioned Bacchus. Another lie perhaps, crafted to present their forces as a shadowy threat capable of manipulations that could doom a planet. But there had been whispers that aeldari had attended some of Planetary Governor Dolo's infamous balls. And the paintings she'd produced, the strange, angular figures that did not quite appear human. When I mentioned Dolos' name, Rile stiffened just a fraction. It was only then that I remembered he was the one who had detained the governor. At least, that was what his sister had told me.

I kept only two confidences during the interrogation: Shard's incriminating rant and the commissar's secret cargo. I doubt I could have kept either if pressed, but my interrogator appeared content with the answers he received. When the conversation was concluded, I had been instructed to stare from the window and await his next order. An hour had passed since then, and though I heard his movements, I kept my gaze fixed ahead.

Even when I heard footsteps approaching behind me.

'Hold out your hand.'

I turned to find him standing behind me, motioning for me to raise my hand.

'This will only take a moment,' he said.

I extended my arm, palm upright.

'Keep it steady,' he continued, retrieving a device from his greatcoat. It was an odd thing, an irregular shape festooned with unknown runescript, the light folding around it at ugly angles, causing it to shift in and out of focus. It shimmered as he lifted it, leaving a faint trail of ghostly afterimages. Like the aeldari.

'You need to keep very still,' he warned, placing it in my palm. It was unpleasantly warm, but not as unpleasant as the way Rile was staring at me.

'How is it?' he asked. 'Any pain?'

'No,' I said, ignoring the slight discomfort.

'Hmm. Then I suppose we will have to assume you are untainted, at least for now.'

He did not sound wholly convinced.

'Untainted?' I said as he retrieved the device. 'By what?'

'The aeldari. This device resonates with warp taint. If one of their witches had you in their thrall then your reaction to touching it would have been more severe. As would mine.'

'You think that is what happened? Someone here has been possessed by their sorcery?'

'Not possessed exactly. More *influenced*. Clouded. The aeldari portray themselves as infallible, but even their sorcery is ill-suited to manipulating data transmissions. But orchestrating someone to do it on their behalf? Someone slow of mind or weak of will? That is entirely possible.'

'So, if not me…?'

'Esec? His entourage? Some grunt or data-scribe toiling in the background? Who knows.'

He shrugged and spread his hands, before turning back towards his ship. Shadows still clung to its bladed hull, in stark contrast to the familiar blockiness of the *Traderi*.

'Keep up, scribe.'

I blinked. 'You wish that I accompany you?'

'For now, until I decide what to do with you. But leave the

seer-skull behind – we have business that I would prefer to keep undocumented.'

'Where are we going?'

'To pay my respects.'

CHAPTER THIRTY-SEVEN

Rile's vessel, the *Aenigma*, showed little evidence of habitation. I saw no sign of accommodation or communal areas, though I suppose both could have been hidden in the bowels of the ship. The transport pod ascended directly to the bridge, where everything was cast in black, just like the craft's exterior. There at least it made some sense, but internally it just presented a tripping hazard.

Rile entered first, making for the pilot's seat. Another figure lounged beside it, their feet on the console.

'Are we finally to depart this wretched world?' they asked. The voice sounded male, though it was hard to tell.

'Not yet,' Rile replied, flicking a switch. I heard the rumble, then felt it, as the craft eased skywards.

'But you have the cargo. I saw you secure it. That is the end of our mission.'

'First I must retrieve a body.'

'Any in particular?'

Rile glared at him. The co-pilot looked away.

'Fine. But then we leave. You already had one unsanctioned detour rescuing that brother of yours.'

'We have the cargo and there is no urgency to our current assignment. Atenbach would not object.'

'That's a bold assumption.'

We were ascending now, the hangar's skydoor unfolding above. Through the cockpit, I could see the early light bleeding from the horizon.

'I'm not comfortable with this dereliction of duty,' the co-pilot continued. His voice was smooth, with an accent unknown to me. But I thought there was a hint of insincerity in his tone.

'I'm not sure you understand the word *duty*.'

'Touché.'

'Is Falon behaving?'

'No. Not since the cargo was brought on board. Can't you hear him?'

'No.'

'Then try listening properly. It's there, beneath the grunting of the engines.'

Rile tilted his head, and I too found myself listening along, but the ship was seething with clunking mechanisms and ignitions. It was hard to separate the–

A moan reverberated through the ship, the floor shuddering beneath my feet.

Rile swore, before glancing to his co-pilot, who still had his feet on the console. That was all I could see of him, my view obscured by his highbacked chair and the hooded cloak pulled over his head.

'Did you try calming him?' Rile asked. 'Reciting the tenets? Repeating the oath?'

'Regrettably my presence only seems to agitate him further. Cannot fathom why.'

Another rumble. Or perhaps a growl. The hairs on my neck certainly thought the latter.

Rile swore again, unstrapping himself from the cockpit. I had to press against the hull to provide sufficient space for him to pass. As he did so, he glared at me, gave an awkward smile, and continued to the exit. The door slid shut behind him.

'You should sit down.'

The voice came from the co-pilot. I turned to find his fingers dancing across the controls, his feet now planted firmly beneath him.

'I'm serious,' he continued, not looking round. 'This vessel provides a smoother ride than the average Imperial craft, but if I am required to take evasive actions you may find yourself smeared against the cockpit. And I'd rather not have my visibility obscured.'

I reached for one of the collapsible seats at the bridge's rear.

'No. Come sit up front with me. Rile will be down there some time. Our colleague is not easy to pacify.'

He still had not looked round.

I made my way to the front of the craft, easing into the pilot's seat, mindful not to touch the myriad controls laid out before me.

'Good. Now strap yourself in.'

I secured the restraining belt, studying the co-pilot from the corner of my eye. He seemed to be clad in form-fitting armour, but it was hard to tell with the cloak draped over his shoulders. Its hood concealed his face, only his mouth and chin pointing from beneath.

'There. Little more comfortable?'

'Yes. Thank you. But I am not–'

'Rile was remiss by not introducing us. I'm Uli.'

'Simlex.'

'I know. Your name came up during the briefing. I gather you are facing those damnable aeldari?'

'Yes.'

'Any idea what fiendish scheme they are up to this time?'

'No. I thought it was to discredit Flight Commander Shard. But I'm not sure why.'

I trailed off. It was all too much. Yet did it even matter? It centred around one data-fortress on a forgotten world. Ultimately the Imperium could simply bombard it from orbit, erase it from existence if they chose. Cesh's campaign would do little to slow the offensive. So what did he seek?

'Feeling overwhelmed?'

I looked to Uli, though his own gaze was fixed ahead.

'I fear so. I have been shuffled through events, second-guessing every step, because I don't have time to stop and think. Or the information to make the right decision.'

'That's the aeldari way,' he said. 'Everything is artifice, each word and idea intended to conceal as much as it reveals. It isn't that they lack power or skill, for they have both in abundance. But it's how they employ them. Humans envision war as two armies lining up for battle, victory awarded to whoever endures long enough to grind their foe into the dust. For aeldari, a battle should be won before the first shot is fired, before war is even declared. Did you know their warhosts are led as often by witches as by warriors? Though to an outsider the difference might seem superficial.'

I shook my head. He continued.

'That is the key to their victories. Humans understand the broad concepts – attacking a supply line, launching a night raid, targeting civilians to undermine morale. All tried-and-tested tactics. But take it a step further. Obliterate the harvest before it can even be converted to supplies. Launch the night raid before your opponent's recruits have even completed basic training.'

His voice had an edge, absent moments ago.

'And as for the civilians? Why slaughter a soldier's lover or child when you could murder their parents prior to conception? Imagine if humans had the means to secure such victories? Imagine the atrocities they would justify if they had such skilled seers to guide them.'

Humans. The word had a harshness in his mouth.

'You think aeldari seers are that reliable?' I said, holding my voice steady, watching him from the corner of my eye.

He smiled, then turned, the hood falling partially away. His skin was pale, his features impossibly sharp, brows arched, ears tapering to delicate points. And his eyes dark, soulless pits.

He was aeldari.

I would have jumped from my seat, but before I could move, he flicked a switch, and suddenly my flight harness was squeezing the life from me. I thrashed, suffocating. He laughed.

'Poor trusting Kile. You should have known that our kind are everywhere, orchestrating your life from conception to death. And you will die in that chair, ignominiously, for reasons you will never even fathom. Would it grant you solace to know your death will save many of your fellows? It's a lie admittedly, but perhaps it would ease the pain of your final moments.'

I tried kicking out for the controls, gambling I might hit something that would at least distract him. But he blocked me effortlessly; I didn't even see his hand move. It was suddenly just there, grasping my ankle. He squeezed, and I felt the bones creak. I tried to scream, but had no breath, the edges of my vision bleeding into darkness.

It was impossible. I could see that now. They were everywhere, able to infiltrate even a ship in service to an inquisitor. Rile must have been deceived. Or was he a traitor? Had he already been bought–

His voice echoed from the stairway. 'Uli? Are you behaving yourself?'

Uli tutted, glancing to me and rolling his eyes, as though I shared his disappointment at the intervention. His finger flicked a switch, and the pressure eased. I gasped, sagging in my seat, before seizing the restraint and tearing it clear. I considered striking him, but what would be the point? He was too fast, and no doubt too well prepared.

Instead, I scuttled back towards the door. He watched me go ruefully, before returning his focus to the controls, as though nothing had happened. Behind me, Rile emerged from the doorway. He met my gaze and sighed.

'My apologies. He wouldn't have really hurt you.'

He patted my shoulder before pushing past and taking his place in the cockpit. I folded myself into one of the chairs, watching them, my hands trembling.

An aeldari. A xenos.

I had been raised to hate and fear their kind. It was a foundation of the Imperial Creed. Suffer not the witch, the xenos, or the heretic to live. Yet here, Rile, an agent of the Inquisition, was seemingly allied with such a creature.

Was it all a lie? Everything I had been taught? Or had Rile deceived me, betrayed the Imperium to side with our foes?

'Did you calm Falon?' Uli asked.

'Yes. I've placed him in stasis. But I'm not sure the conditioning is holding. He needs re-indoctrination.'

'All the more reason to depart swiftly.'

'Soon. My sister was shot down.'

'So? Surely someone else can scrape the corpse off the seat and toss it into whatever sarcophagus you people deem appropriate. Or do you eat your dead? I can never remember.'

Rile ignored him, which seemed to irritate Uli. He turned to face me, smiling brightly, as though I were his co-conspirator.

'It's sweet really,' he said. 'You see, Rile here feels responsible.

He and his sister had a little assignment together a while ago and... Well, he thought there was something off with her. Did nothing, of course, wedded to his duty this one. Blames himself. As would I, assuming I cared either way.'

'That's enough, Uli.'

'But what about you?' the aeldari continued, looking me over. 'How are you mixed up in all this?'

'I suspect you know better than I,' I said.

'Ha! Not as stupid as you look.' He smiled. 'Of course I know. Or at least I could know, were I inclined to give it much thought. But I didn't lie when I said your name had come up before. With the woman. What was her name?'

'Flight Commander Lucille von Shard.'

'No, not that one. The lumpen aristocrat from Bacchus. Bulus? Dolos? The woman that smells like swamp water.'

I felt cold suddenly, despite the daylight blazing through the cockpit.

'You mean Planetary Governor Dolos?'

'That's the one!' he said, grinning. 'She was an interesting subject for interrogation. Mad, of course, but all the interesting ones are. She blamed you for all sorts of things. Not just you – there was enough blame to go around. But she never could wrap her head round the idea that, just maybe, accepting a gift from a glamorous alien with an enigmatic smile might not have been the shrewdest of choices. Even when Atenbach decided to–'

'Enough.'

Rile's gaze was fixed ahead. He did not raise his voice so much as steel it. Uli rolled his eyes again.

'Sorry,' the aeldari said. 'I forget how you humans love your secrets. Forget I spoke, propagandist. Rile is, of course, correct. It's better if you don't know the truth.'

He turned back to the viewscreen. Ahead, a thin plume of smoke was visible on the horizon.

The remains of *Mendax Matertera* were little more than a black smear upon the glass plain. Both wings were missing, though one had landed a few dozen yards away, the other presumably vaporised during the attack. Smoke still wreathed the wreckage. I wondered how long it had burned.

'You people don't collect your dead?' Uli asked, scanning the horizon.

Rile snorted. 'Depends. I imagine they did not wish to squander the promethium required to drag back the wreckage.'

'My people have fought wars just to retrieve a handful of our fallen.'

'Well, my people value a tank of fuel over sentiment. And there is nothing to be salvaged from this wreck.'

He was right. It was just blackened and blasted metal now. In fact, it was impossible to tell whether it was really her craft. Once more I felt that horrible flicker of hope. Perhaps this was not her vessel. Perhaps it had been switched–

'You sure it's her?' Uli asked.

'Yes. The tracker confirms it,' Rile said, glancing up from a handheld scanner.

He met my gaze and shrugged.

'Do all your siblings have tracking devices implanted?' I asked.

'No. Only the ones I have access to. I'd like to say it was difficult, but to be honest I just waited for her to drink herself into oblivion and tagged her foot. Told her she'd stumbled on something the next morning. She never questioned it.'

He rummaged through the blackened metal, retrieving a small disc that still glinted silver beneath the grime.

'Shame,' he said, slipping it into a pouch. 'Real shame how all this turned out.'

He seemed lost in thought, gaze fixed upon the twisted remnants of the cockpit. I had dreaded seeing it, seeing her. But there was no body. Not really. The heat had rendered the pilot to little more than ash. I had held some vague notion of us retrieving her remains, perhaps laying them to rest in whatever vaults the von Shards used for their departed. But to do so now would require a brush and bag.

Rile hadn't moved. He was still staring at the smoking ruins. But Uli was twitchy, his gaze flickering over his shoulder, intent on something in the sky.

'We should leave.'

'I need a moment.'

'It's not safe here. If Cesh launches an attack–'

Uli paused suddenly, frowning, before reaching beneath his coat. He withdrew a curious compact device that unfolded in his hands, extending into a long-barrelled rifle. I had never seen a weapon like it, every part smooth, without ridge or rivet. It looked like it had been grown rather than assembled.

He raised it skyward, aligning the sight.

'Aircraft?' Rile asked, still intent on the wreck.

'No. Too small.'

I believe he squeezed the trigger, though the only sound was a faint hiss. He then collapsed the rifle, folding it back into his cloak, before turning to Rile.

'We are exposed out here. Neither of us want our face caught on vid.'

'I suspect that would be worse for you than I.'

'Which is why I am getting back on board. If I see an aircraft, I am taking off. You may do as you will.'

'No, you won't. And I will be but a moment.'

Uli sighed, turning to me. I expected that mocking smile, or some barbed comment. But it was so much worse.

'I'm sorry,' he said, seemingly sincere. 'This must be hard for you. Losing someone you love like that.'

He lifted his hand to pat my shoulder, then perhaps thought better of it, nose wrinkling in repressed disgust.

'I did not love her!'

'Oh?' he said, frowning, though his brow remained unlined.

'She was vile! And a liar! Because of her I lost everything. I was… I never–'

Pity. I think that was his expression, though the distaste lingered.

'Of course you didn't,' he said. 'What artist loves their muse?'

Then he bowed, before making his way back towards the ship. Rile did not move, his gaze still levelled at the ruined cockpit.

'I thought there would be something,' he said. 'A body. A clue.'

'Perhaps there will be something in her quarters? She did not take her father's sword with her. That's unusual. Perhaps–'

'Father's sword? What do you mean?'

'I… She told me she carried her father's blade? As the mark of a true von Shard? I saw her slay an ork warrior with the weapon.'

'Ah. Perhaps it was one of his lesser blades.'

'She lied again. Didn't she?'

'Honestly? I don't know. I sometimes think it is all artifice. The face we present is one crafted to our audience, whether to win their love or invoke their fear. Perhaps she just understood this better than most. Or perhaps she really believed it was her father's. Maybe that was what they told her.'

'But you know better?'

'I think I do, though I too could be deceived. We can only work with what we have.'

He sighed, face softening a shade.

'She was never a natural duellist,' he continued. 'Not like Tobia or Sinest. But she put in so many hours, so much training. Just to become competent with a blade.'

'Is that where she got her scar? Duelling?'

'No. At least, not how you mean. The scar was–'

There was a crash behind us, like a thousand glasses shattering. I turned to find the smoking remnants of one of Esec's Eyes. At least, that's what I think it was, for it was now in pieces, the plain beneath cracked but intact.

Rile glanced at it, before raising his gaze skywards.

'Hmm. Uli has remarkable aim. And he was right, we are exposed.'

I prodded the smouldering remnants with my cane. Odd. The outer casing had shattered, but what lay within was not what I expected at all. It resembled a flat metal disc, beneath which was mounted a curious array of smashed machineries. They seemed to have connected with the outer structure, but the latter was more like a frame than an actual interface. Ablative armour perhaps? But why would one armour an agricultural unit? And why was so much of the interior apparently just empty space? It was as though the outer frame had been built over an existing device. But in its shattered condition, it was difficult to be sure.

I frowned. How had it navigated so far from Edbar? There was no way Esec could operate it at such distance. Perhaps it had locked on a target and become estranged, venturing deeper into the desert? Or perhaps it had been left out here deliberately as an early-warning system.

'I would leave it be, were I you,' Rile warned. 'You do not wish to be caught handling that tech.'

'It's not Imperial, is it?'

'No. The exterior might be – the Opus Machina symbol is a good touch. But no, what lies within is not. In fact... bear with me.'

He retrieved a device from his greatcoat. It looked a little like an auspex. He wafted it over the wreckage, intent on the display.

'Hmm. Nano-crystalline alloy, with some iridium. Most likely–'

He paused, frowning and glaring at the device, before his gaze slowly slid back to the wreckage of *Mendax Matertera*.

'Propagandist Simlex?'

'Yes?'

'Did my sister suffer any serious injuries recently?'

'No. Not to my knowledge. Why?'

He reached into the ruined cockpit, retrieving a fragment of something small and metallic.

'Wrong alloy for an aircraft,' he said. 'Bespoke. I've known augmetic limbs to be constructed from such a compound. You are certain she had suffered no injury? Lost a leg or–'

'Arm,' I murmured, examining the metallic shard. It was blackened, almost unrecognisable, but I recognised it. And, despite the flames and smoke, I could faintly make out the von Shard crest emblazoned on the plating.

It was the arm that had once belonged to Flight Sergeant Plient.

CHAPTER THIRTY-EIGHT

Plient's workshop was sealed.

'No gene-lock,' Rile said, examining the mechanism. 'Looks like a basic keyed layout. If you want to breach it, I have some bio-acid that will melt through–'

'No. Plient would be horrified.'

'Should that be the priority? Given what has happened?'

'We don't know anything for sure. Perhaps he used spare parts from his limb to make repairs.'

'Fine,' he said. 'But breaking and entering is more Uli's speciality. And since he has elected to remain on the *Aenigma*, this might take a moment. Keep an eye out.'

He bent close to the doorway, something glinting in his hand.

I stood with my back to him, trying to hide him in my shadow while Iwazar monitored the passageway. Not that anyone was watching. The external lumens were dark, the only light spilling from the workshop. Plient must have had a backup generator.

Of course he did; he had that sort of mind. He saw the world as problems to be fixed. Barriers to be overcome.

Rile twisted his wrist and something clicked. There was a sharp flash, and the mechanism gave. As the door swung open Iwazar zoomed ahead, scanning the interior.

Spotless.

I had forgotten, but Plient had swept it clean the last time I was here. There were the dishes, stacked and dried. He'd been quiet that night, his smile haunted. I'd thought it was because he feared for her life.

'Plient!' I bellowed, knowing there would be no answer. Because there was nothing there any more. It had all been tidied away. No mess left to clean up, tools mounted on their allocated spots on the walls, Iwazar for some reason fixated on the arc welder. The room felt almost spacious with *Mendax Matertera* absent. The plane had been genuine. Just not the pilot.

No, surely not. She wouldn't have sent him in her place.

But she'd told me that she couldn't beat Cesh. Several times. I had thought her so brave, so noble in the face of death. But it had been another lie, because she must have known by then that Plient would be flying in her stead. Dying in her stead. I was a fool not to see it.

I sagged, fumbling for a stool, my ruined leg suddenly betraying me.

'Blasted tracker,' Rile said. 'She must have realised I'd tagged her. Cut it out of her foot and stashed it on the plane.'

'She was limping. The last night I saw her.'

'I underestimated her. She probably left when everyone was distracted by the duel. Perhaps stole a plane, though there aren't many hospitable destinations round here. Not for a deserter.'

'Will you go after her?'

'How? Without the tracker I have no idea where she is. And I have neither the time nor resources to scour this planet.'

'But what of the xenos threat? The aeldari? Esec's Eyes?'

He just stared at me with that empty gaze.

'I will relay my findings to my superiors,' he said. 'They may elect to take action at some point.'

'Are any of your superiors aeldari?'

For a moment, anger flickered across his eyes. In my frustration I had forgotten his rank, what he was no doubt capable of. He could have shot me there and walked away without any repercussions. Most likely, he could have shot me in front of high command and still got away with it if he produced proof of his authority.

But he did not reach for his pistol. Instead he sighed, leaning back against the worktop, arms folded.

'This is a skirmish on a backwater world. There are greater priorities.'

'Not to those of us caught in it.'

'Perhaps. But tell me, have you recently been consumed by twelve-foot-tall, six-limbed semi-sentient bioweapons?'

'No.'

'Have eldritch terrors erupted from a shadowy realm and feasted upon your soul?'

'No.'

'Have things long dead arisen from beneath to enslave and eradicate humanity?

'No.'

'No. And that is because my master and I prioritise the greater threats. Do you think I enjoy sharing a cockpit with a creature like Uli? I do so because of his knowledge and capabilities, not because I do not consider him a threat. We are allies of convenience because we both know far worse things haunt the void. It was for that reason I came to this world, to collect something of vital importance for my master. I have subsequently tarried to rescue my brother and mourn my sister. But I cannot afford to squander any more time. Once the sun has set, I shall use the darkness to slip away.'

'And what will become of me?'

'I should probably kill you. It would be cleaner. But I don't know if I have the stomach for it. Someone needs to keep an eye on Tobia until he recovers. He is family after all.'

His gaze swept the workstations before settling on Iwazar. The seer-skull was still intent on the wall-mounted arc welder. I kept waiting for him to say something. Instead he rose wearily, straightened his greatcoat, and strode towards the door.

When he reached it, he paused, glancing over his shoulder.

'For what it is worth, I liked your pict. The original. The scenery was breathtaking.'

The door then closed behind him, and I was alone. Except for Iwazar, though the seer-skull was still preoccupied with Plient's carefully stowed tools. I willed it to return, even vocalising the command, but it dithered, looking from me to the implements. Its engine made that whining sound again.

I approached, studying the section of wall that so fascinated it. There were markings on the metal sheeting, just behind the arc welder. It looked as though something had been cut away and then replaced.

I retrieved one of Plient's spanners, wedging it into the gap, peeling back the outer plating. There was a hidden compartment. It must have predated his presence. Perhaps one of the indentured workers had stashed supplies there, or items to sell on the black market, all under the eyes of their overseers. I couldn't know for sure, because all it held in that moment was a grinning, blackened skull.

Kikazar.

Plient must have removed it from *Mendax Matertera* before that last flight. He'd attempted to clean it up, but its eyes were dead, systems non-responsive. It had died slowly, I remembered. The orks had co-opted it, used it to relay their demands. Something in the device had been unable to cope afterwards. It almost felt like it had chosen this end.

Iwazar would not stop fussing, clicking uncertainly at its departed sibling. It kept drifting in front of me, blocking my view.

'Enough!' I snapped, rounding on it. The seer-skull retreated, ducking behind a workstation. I felt bad, then stupid. It was supposed to serve me, to make my life easier, but our connection was sloppy and my attempts to call it to heel unsuccessful. It too had been damaged on Bacchus. Broken by the war. But, unlike its sibling, Iwazar still functioned.

I turned back to the hole in the wall. Why had Plient stashed Kikazar there? He would have removed it from the aircraft to provide space for additional ordnance. But why hide it? Who would steal a broken piece of junk like that?

Was it left for me?

I retrieved the device, placing it upon the worktop. It was so streamlined compared to the now lumbering Iwazar. It looked almost poised to arise, except the lenses were dull, dormant. Dead.

But something jutted from beneath the input panel. A data-slug.

I extracted it, turning it over in my hand. It looked new, unmarked by the film of corrosion that marred Kikazar's other components. Beside me, Iwazar's engine whirred as it prodded its sibling, perhaps hoping to raise it. It then turned to me, meeting my gaze with its unblinking lenses. Slowly, it shifted its focus to the data-slug nestled in my hand.

'Fine,' I said, inserting the drive into its data-port. The seer-skull paused, accessing the files. Then its lenses flashed, the holo-projector flaring. Shard, Plient, aircraft – a cascade of images tumbled from its memory.

Until suddenly it was just his face.

It was a terrible shot. Whatever cam he had used was poorly placed, angled so I was staring up his nostrils. But the sight of him still brought a lump to my throat.

'Hello, sir,' he said with a tired smile. *'Glad I managed to chase you off. Otherwise, I wouldn't have been able to record this. Not if tomorrow goes as expected.'*

He paused, glancing over his shoulder at an indistinct shape. It might have been *Mendax Matertera*.

'I always wanted to fly it. Never told her. Or anyone. But I guess that's the advantage of knowing your time is up – it's not worth getting embarrassed any more. Or scared, because I know what's coming. I hope I've done enough, earned my place at the God-Emperor's table. But I shouldn't worry about that either. It's not my decision. Or my place. I have my duty.'

He smiled. Warmer this time. But his eyes darkened and the expression faded.

'I am sorry, sir. I'm sorry we left you out of the plan. It's not that I don't trust you, but the commander… She doesn't trust anyone any more. Not since Esec. He… he faked some footage of her, sir – made it look as though she said some awful things. I'd hoped you'd have been able to expose him. And maybe you still will. Perhaps, now she has defeated Cesh, it will be easier.'

He sighed.

'She did beat him, right? Of course she did, I'm being stupid. She just needed an opening you see, a feint to lure him into an attack run so she could strike from another angle in a separate craft. It's a good plan, sir, a really good one. But I couldn't quite do my part.

Not enough time. Or talent. But there's never going to be enough time, I realise that now. And I will not fail her. Someone must fly Mendax Matertera. Someone needs to be a decoy. Might not be the most honourable plan, but that's now how the aeldari do battle. I hate to say it, sir, but I almost miss the orks.'

He grinned, but it faded into a frown.

'Maybe I just miss those times, sir. I think sometimes that I keep the good memories and lose the bad. I suppose that's a blessing. But I don't think it's the same for her. The bad stuff just lingers. She has nightmares. Passes out whilst I'm working, sleeps for a time. But the screams, sir. No matter how loud I turn up the machines, I can still hear her screaming. I can still hear it now.'

He turned from the cam, perhaps distracted by something outside.

'I need a favour, sir. I know it is unfair to ask like this, but I couldn't tell you or you'd have tried to stop me. And I've made peace with my decision. But she needs help. Because I won't be there for her any more. And someone needs to be. So I ask you, as my friend, please keep her safe. Protect her from herself. Please, Kile.'

He smiled, shaking his head.

'Still sounds odd using your given name, sir. My only other request is that… Well, I've left some letters. For my mum and siblings. And my nieces and nephews. If you could ensure they… I wouldn't want them not to know, sir, or to wonder how it happened. Please tell them I did my duty. That's all any of us can do. Pray, and give what we can to the God-Emperor.'

He hesitated, then slowly crossed his arms, in the sign of the aquila. I could not bring myself to return it.

The image faded. And he was gone.

CHAPTER THIRTY-NINE

Protect her.

I almost laughed. What was I supposed to protect her with? A glitching seer-skull? A withered limb? My non-existent influence as a former propagandist turned lowly scribe?

My anger bubbled, swelling into righteous fury. How dare he place this burden on me? One I could not possibly fulfil, even if I so desired it. Already I had failed him in his dying request. Bastard.

Except he wasn't. He was instead the bravest and best man I had ever known. He gave his life not knowing if it would make a difference, and even his last request was about helping others, not himself. He died because he saw no other way of fulfilling his duty.

And I realised my anger wasn't about him. Or even her in that moment. It was simply a means to cope with the horror of what had happened. We are taught from a young age to hate our enemies, that our wrath is a weapon to be unleashed. But perhaps in truth it is a balm, soothing, keeping us warm and preventing darker, colder emotions from finding purchase. Fear. Guilt. Sorrow – all burned away by blessed, righteous fury.

Anger keeps us going. And with that realisation I felt mine fade a little, leaving behind an emptiness.

I slid to my haunches, and then the floor.

How long I sat there I do not know. But it was Esec who shook me from my malaise. Or rather, his voice erupting from Iwazar. The seer-skull had been slinking about my feet, but suddenly it rose, the holo-projector throwing up an image of a Lightning with a familiar design on its wings.

'On this dark day, we look to the God-Emperor to accept Flight Commander Lucille von Shard into His embrace. For, though she fell in battle, we know this to be part of His plan, that one more angel will now accompany His forces on the blessed day. But we need not wait until then, for through her death a million others will be inspired to fight in her stead. None braver than Flight Sergeant Keeri Vagbon.'

The image shifted. The craft was the same, but no longer had the black griffin motif. It had been replaced by a blazing orb. Perhaps a sun, or symbolic explosion? I knew not.

'The capricious aeldari may have fled after the damage Flight Commander Shard inflicted upon them. But they cannot keep running forever. Soon they will be hunted to–'

'Enough.'

Iwazar ignored the command, the image swelling until it swallowed the room, Esec's voice now deafening.

'–no matter who opposes us, the God-Emperor's forces cannot be stayed. If victory demands we drown them in our blood, then so be it! For His gaze is upon us, and any who are not loyal to–'

'Enough!' I snapped, rounding on the device. 'Cease playback or I will set the arc welder to you!'

I grabbed the implement from the wall. I had never wielded

one before, but the controls were simple enough. A spark erupted at its tip, and I felt the hairs on my arms stand. I advanced on Iwazar, who retreated, but refused to cease, Esec's incessant tones clawing at my ears.

'*–forget the deceptions they feed us. For the aeldari are liars first and foremost, their every word a distortion of the God-Emperor's Truth. Through magics most foul, they try and steer us from the right path. For that is their only hope – to drive us into damnation, for–*'

I lunged closer, but it pulled away, hovering high above me.

'*–do we just sit here? Do nothing, whilst their lies destroy our great works–*'

There was a flash of light. Blinding. I staggered, losing my grip. Mercifully, the arc welder's spark faded before it struck the ground, but I still felt a shudder run through me.

'*State your name.*'

'*Lucille von Shard.*'

There she sat. Not the woman I'd met, for in the image she was barely more than a child. Unscarred as yet, at least physically, though her eyes told a different story.

The image flickered, Plient's face materialising momentarily.

'*Protect her from herself.*'

'Protect her?' I said, laughing. 'What is left to protect? She was broken long before we met. It's what they do – they break us and mould us into whatever is needed. Keep us angry and ignorant. There is no fixing that, and if there was, I am not the one to do it. Not now. Probably not ever.'

Iwazar merely stared back, lenses glinting.

It is difficult to outstare a seer-skull. I threw up my hands. 'What do you want from me?'

It did not reply. How could it?

'I don't know where she is! And I cannot traipse around Edbar on a ruined leg, assuming she is still even here. Besides, finding her will just place her in jeopardy. Better she vanishes. Esec will document her demise, frame it as though she's a fallen hero. He'll probably claim she slew ten aeldari craft, dying only due to treachery or impossible odds. On that basis, it would seem I've accomplished the mission. She died a hero – that is what the history books will say. The commissar will be delighted, assuming he ever wakes up.'

Its dead eyes betrayed nothing. Neither did its fixed grin. But I saw my reflection in the chrome casing. The lined face, gaunt cheeks, hollowed eyes.

How long until I too was nothing but bones?

Perhaps I would endure for years, slowly diminishing, until all that lingered was an infirm echo of the person I used to be. Or perhaps my end would be short and sudden. A bullet in the gut, or knife in the back. Or something more benign – an infection or accident. And what then? Would the God-Emperor favour me with a place at His table? It seemed unlikely.

Plient was right when he said there was no more time. There was only the present. He had asked that I protect her, but I felt she should be punished, face justice for her cowardice. I did not know which impulse to follow, but neither would be possible. Not unless I found her.

Iwazar still stared at me. Slowly, its gaze shifted to the arc welder still at my feet.

'I am sorry,' I said. 'You cannot help what you have become. War broke us all. Breaks us still. But if I am to do this, I need your eyes.'

I reached for it. It had been years since I'd fully synced with the device, our unions mere snatches and stolen moments. I thought it would be stilted, or painful, or that I would be overwhelmed by memories encoded in its data-store. And I did glimpse them – scattered vids of swamps, and death. Her face, and so many more long lost.

But I pushed through them, and the pain fell away. That dull throbbing in my leg was gone. Even the sting of losing Plient. It faded, becoming little more than information retained.

Through Iwazar, I ascended, examining the room with lenses untainted by human frailty. There was so much more to see: the residual heat of the arc welder, a welcoming glow slowly disappearing into the floor's rockcrete slabs. The myriad colours resplendent in an oily stain. And my own body, seated now, eyes staring vacantly.

It looked old and sad.

Iwazar slid through the access port, the passageways and corridors of Edbar falling away, as it emerged into the world beyond.

It was beautiful. Blue, crystal-clear skies, unmarred by cloud or mist. The waning sun still blazing, its light blinding to human eyes but radiant to Iwazar. Cleansing. For a moment I basked in it.

But something irritated me, like dust in the eye. Little sparks flickering in the sky, like embers thrown from a fire. Once I noticed them I soon realised they were everywhere, scurrying back and forth, but focused most closely about Esec's barge.

The Eyes.

Through Iwazar they looked different, swarming like insects, each a blazing firefly, though there was something unsettling about their energy output. It looked wrong, alien. But what struck me most was the coordination. There should have been collisions, or at the very least close calls. Even if each had a human operator, there would still have been incidents. Errors. But they functioned seamlessly, as though guided by collective consciousness. It seemed impossible they could be governed by pre-programmed commands. Perhaps there was a mechanism that detected collisions, but following that should have seen them circling, or trapped in recursive loops.

It was as if they could communicate. Cooperate.

Think.

I drifted closer, drawn by the activity. It was simple enough to follow one through an access port, though when a second fell in behind me I almost panicked, thinking I might be crushed between them. But instead we advanced down a narrow passage, twisting through openings, until suddenly I was met with a vast chamber, and all around were Eyes.

Most were embedded in housing points in the walls and ceilings. But some, perhaps damaged or worn, were being dismantled. No human or servitor was involved, the entire process automated. I watched as one was extracted from its damaged shell, the disc within darting free, like a moth escaping a cocoon. It moved so much faster and freer, zipping to a second location, only to be encased in another external frame by a multi-limbed machine.

This was not human tech. I knew enough to recognise that.

A larger device, a horizontal disc with antennae and sensors protruding from its centre, suddenly drifted over to Iwazar. It seemed to be examining the seer-skull, its lenses clicking uncertainly. Perhaps there was a system for dealing with potential infiltrators, and while Iwazar was not entirely without defences, I thought it best to depart, fleeing as a score of Eyes trailed in my wake, each soaring out over the desert, intent upon its individual assignment.

I rose higher, until the barge receded beneath me. From above, it was so much easier to get a sense of Edbar's current state. Through shattered roofs and cracked walls, I could see its citizens huddling in whatever shelter they could find. I watched a young woman scuttle beneath a twisted frame that might once have led to a dwelling, a knapsack thrown over her shoulder, stuffed with scraps of parchment. A score more people sheltered in the cloister of what might once have been a church. Through the cracks in its vaulted ceiling, I saw them pray at an altar, where an effigy that I took to be the God-Emperor rode upon a six-limbed mamutida.

At the building's rear a smaller firepit had been dug, perhaps inspired by the Láech's efforts. Greying meat had already been speared on skewers. I could only assume it was mamutida flesh, though whether the congregation were aware of this was another question. Perhaps they asked forgiveness, their hunger compelling them to commit such sacrilege. Perhaps the meat was stolen, or bartered, and they had no idea of the profane nature of their meal.

I moved on, Iwazar skirting through passages and over rooftops. I saw scribes toiling, their labours now stacked in neat rows while the data-stores were still awaiting repair. And I saw indentured workers stealing the reams of parchment when the scribes' backs were turned. Curiosity compelled me to follow one, half expecting to stumble across an illicit market, where data was bought and sold. I was ashamed to be mistaken, instead finding the parchment added to a fuel store. It seemed a family had found a bolthole a little way off from the crystal gardens. They were sheltering from Deighton's setting sun, two children laughing as they scribbled on the back of the scraps they would no doubt burn at dusk, the tithes consumed to keep them warm another night.

I continued onwards, gaze now falling to the crystal gardens themselves. They were even more depressing in daylight. Perhaps it was the bloodstained flowers, or the marks indicating that whoever had been injured there had subsequently been dragged away. I remembered Rosln's words on the inevitability of cannibalism, and wondered whether the pious would consider the greater sin to be consuming the meat of the mamutida, or that of their fellow citizens. Because, unless supplies were brought in soon, that seemed to be the choice they faced. That, or stealing rations from the Láech. I had seen few of their soldiers, most still focused on the subterranean war, though now they acted as guards, clustered in the dark tunnels, fearful the light might return. Did they know of the disquiet on the surface? It struck me that it would not be difficult to collapse the tunnels' entrance, trap them underground.

I tried to move on, but Iwazar loitered, its gaze drawn by something jutting from the garden's crest.

The bomb was still there.

Madness. There were a dozen machines that could have removed it, or at least orchestrated a controlled denotation. But it remained wedged in the ground, caught in a perpetual state of potential destruction. How long would it be before some misguided soul built an altar around it? Declared it an artefact. Future generations might worship it, claiming the explosion had been stayed by His hand. Or perhaps they would decide that He had left it there in warning, a declaration that He would annihilate the data-fortress if Edbar were to return to wickedness.

Then again, it could just detonate. Suddenly and without warning. And that would no doubt be seen as His will too, for it was all His will, irrespective of the outcome.

I would have moved on, except, under its foreboding shadow, I saw a slumped figure, a hood pulled over her face.

And a bottle resting in her hand.

CHAPTER FORTY

The slumped figure was still there when I finally ascended the ruined garden. Doubt crept in as I drew closer. Surely she would have fled? Stolen a plane and set off to anywhere that wasn't here. One of the Lightnings could even take her into orbit, though where she went from there was another question entirely. She'd once mused about launching a plane into the void and just accelerating into the darkness. Perhaps not the most heroic end, but at least it was one of her choosing.

But the woman sitting in the shadows did not rise upon my approach, keeping her head low, her face concealed by the hood.

'Shard?'

She did not react.

I bent lower, grimacing as my leg spasmed in protest. Pale skin. Too pale, even compared to the Láech. This was ghost-like, a spectre clad in rags. But there were no telltale red curls cascading about her face, which remained turned away and hidden.

'Shard?'

'You're mistaken, sir,' the woman said.

The voice was rough, a low rumble. But she was no actor – the picts proved that well enough. I reached for her chin, to turn her face to me, but her hand shot out, seizing my wrist and twisting. I grunted in pain, but the movement had dislodged the hood.

A half-familiar face stared back at me.

The right side of it was as I knew, but the scar on her left cheek was now concealed by a score more. And there was no hair to conceal the injury, for her head was close-cropped, bald besides a thin layer of stubble.

I recoiled even as she released me, unable to take my gaze from the damage she had done to herself.

'Told you,' she grunted. 'I ain't one of them sky-hogs. Now leave me be.'

'No.'

'I ain't askin' again.'

'Doesn't matter.'

'I'm not her.'

'You certainly don't look much like her,' I conceded. 'You cut off your hair, discarded your uniform, and disguised your face. But even with all that, even with your feeble attempt at an accent, you can't change your eyes. Or your expression.'

'Prove it.'

'Iwazar? Confirm identity.'

Its holo-projector flared, imposing Shard's face onto the scarred woman. It was not as fast as I'd assumed, perhaps confused by all the counterfeit images generated by Esec. But it finally found some footage from Bacchus, layering it over her. I heard a pip in my ear.

She must have heard it too, because she turned away, pulling the hood tight. 'Your machine hardly looks dependable.'

'No. It is an ugly and broken thing. But it does its job, and I know you too well.'

'You don't know me at all.'

'I admit I'm surprised to find you here. I would have thought you'd have stolen a plane and departed.'

I reached into my robes, withdrawing a carton of lho-sticks I had liberated en route, offering it to her.

She stared at it, then sighed and took one, striking a match and lighting it with shaking hands.

'Why are you still here?' I asked as she exhaled.

'Maybe I wanted to see Lucille von Shard's funeral. Listen to the weeping and wailing. Of course, for that they'd have to bother collecting the corpse. I suppose I should be pleased that no one cared enough. It makes the deception far easier.'

I had felt sorry for her. But her tone, the way she dismissed Plient like that. Suddenly I wanted to reach out and throttle her. Something must have carried to my face, for she rolled her eyes.

'Please. As if you could take me.'

'I'm pretty sure I could in the current circumstances. Coward.'

'Coward?' She laughed, the sound grating but genuine. 'I've endured horrors you could not fathom. Whatever my flaws, I am no coward.'

'Then why did you refuse to face Cesh?'

'Did you want me to die?' she asked. 'Are you so bitter and resentful that you pray for my fall? I suppose it would make a great pict. Every story needs an ending, right? The arrogant von Shard, convinced of her superiority, finally meets her match?'

'Isn't dying with honour better than living in shame?'

'Hard to say. Few have done both.'

'You didn't know the outcome. Not for sure. You might have won.'

'Oh please. I tried. I tried more than once, but it was like fighting a shadow. I'm good. Once I might have been the best, at least for a human. But Cesh might as well be a sorcerer. If we had fought, he would have won. Why throw my life away for nothing?'

'Better than letting–'

'Because I have seen what happens,' she continued, a gleam in her eye. 'Did my death galvanise our forces? Compel them to strive even harder in the God-Emperor's name? Of course not. The aces are no doubt clambering to replace me, and Esec already seeks a new lead. He doesn't need me. Nobody does. He can just stick someone new in the plane and keep churning out the picts. Call them Lucille von Shard if he likes, and if he does, I hope she brings him power and prosperity. Because being her has been utter misery.'

'So you don't care who dies in your place?'

'Why should I? The aces know their duty. And they will all die anyway. Do you know what our average life expectancy is? I've known wars where new pilots barely lasted twenty minutes, and anyone who survived more than three missions was considered a battle-worn veteran. Do you know why I never bother learning the names of new recruits? Because they don't live long enough to make it worthwhile. Only the bastards and monsters endure, and I have no desire to speak to them at all.'

'And Plient?'

'Plient will be fine if he obeys his orders and keeps his mouth shut.'

I heard the words, saw the dismissive look in her eye. She apparently misread my confusion.

'I ordered Plient to keep quiet. So long as he does so, he will be fine. Wing Commander Prospherous will see he's taken care of – let him retire honourably or something. The old man might have lost patience with me, but he's always had a soft spot for Plient. Everyone does. It's infuriating.'

She didn't know.

'What did Plient do that must be kept quiet?' I asked.

'He installed the servitor pilot,' she replied, frowning at the question.

'A servitor flew *Mendax Matertera*?'

'You think it flew itself? How would that work? No, it was Plient's genius. Though it was my idea, stolen from Esec and his stupid Eyes.'

'And Plient set it up. Accomplished something that, to my knowledge, has never been attempted before?'

'Yes. Why is that so hard to believe?'

'And he was happy with the deception? Helping you fake your own death?'

'Not exactly. I told him *Mendax Matertera* was to act as a decoy, so I could launch a surprise attack. Why are you looking at me like that?'

'Iwazar,' I whispered. 'Play back Plient's message.'

I couldn't watch it again. Instead, I watched her. Watched as she shifted from amused to puzzled. Dismayed, then horrified as realisation slowly dawned. And to my shame, I basked in it. Basked in her pain, as that smug self-satisfaction died in her eyes. When Plient said he would not fail her, and she gave the faintest sob, I could not help but smile. Because it was all on her. She had done this. Her desperation had become his, driven him into trading his life to give her a chance.

And she had squandered it.

I waited until it was over before I spoke.

'You said it made no difference whether you flew? Well, it might not have made a difference to many, but it would have made a difference to Plient.'

She said nothing. Just stared at the spot where his face had been. Quite still and silent.

'Shard?'

Nothing.

And I found my anger was gone. And I missed it almost as much as I missed Plient, because without it I felt only emptiness, a hollow within that once burned with a quiet fury. I think I had carried it since Bacchus, and it sustained me during my seclusion. But now it had faded, and I carried only a void.

I looked to her, but her eyes were empty. I touched her shoulder and she looked to my fingers, frowning slightly, as though she had forgotten me. Slowly, her gaze slid to her holster. It was empty.

'Shard?'

Nothing. No answer.

'We cannot sit out here,' I murmured. 'Edbar is getting dark, and I don't think it's safe any more. Plient's workshop is closest. We need to… I need to…'

I trailed off. There were no words, my voice swallowed by the gathering gloom as the sun slowly dipped from the sky, and we were left in darkness.

CHAPTER FORTY-ONE

The Eyes were everywhere.

They roamed freely, patrolling the streets. Having seen the bowels of Esec's barge, it was now clear to me how little they resembled Imperial tech. There was no means by which a propagandist could coordinate such a fleet. They had to possess their own Abominable Intelligence.

But Esec was the driving force. Even with so many Eyes, there were limited screens in his studio. He could not watch everything, and I had seen no evidence the devices made assessments of the footage they gathered. Perhaps their presence was for show more than anything else, to intimidate potential dissidents.

Still, we crept, slinking through the shadows, my pace slowed by my injury, Shard trailing behind like a shadow. She still had not spoken.

I tried not to look at her face. The wounds were raw, as though carved by a dulled blade. Perhaps that served us, assuming the Eyes were able to recognise certain faces. Then again, why would

Esec look for her? I would be the more likely candidate, depending on whether he still considered me of use.

We shunned the light, but we were not alone. The refugees of Edbar's fall also lurked in the dark. I caught eyes darting our way, and through Iwazar even the occasional glint of a blade. We should have been an easy target, given I was lame and she scarred. But they paid little heed, perhaps assuming we were two more souls cast down in Edbar's liberation. And those gathering in the dark did not seem concerned with finding prey or looting bodies. There was purpose to their movements. Something was going to happen, and it was better we were off the streets before it did.

We navigated past the main hangars, where the Scions clad in Esec's borrowed colours had mobilised, at least three squads waiting in reserve. Their ochre armour was garish against the greyed architecture, but no doubt proof against whatever weapons the citizens of Edbar could muster.

I glanced over my shoulder. Shard was crouching behind me, tucked tight against the rubble. Silent.

'We are too exposed this way,' I whispered. 'We should go back a few blocks, take the long way round.'

Her gaze was fixed upon nothing, and for a moment I was unsure she had heard me. But she slowly raised her head, turning and pointing to a crack running through the adjacent building. It looked barely thick enough for a human to transverse, and beyond there was only darkness.

'I cannot see the way.'

She just stared back at me.

'Have you walked that path before?'

No response. I could have addressed an empty room.

'Fine,' I said. 'Lead on.'

She hesitated, before slowly turning to the crack. It looked too tight to traverse, but she slid through easily, for there was nothing to her beneath the robe. I followed, Iwazar lurking behind, its sensors etching the walls in crimson light. It did little to lighten my fears. I had to inch sideways, some part of me forever scraping against jutting rockcrete. I was convinced it was narrowing.

'Shard... This is a bad idea. It would only take a tremor for it to crush us.'

She gave no response. In fact, I could barely see her in front of me.

'Don't you care if we get buried alive? If you have a death wish, there are quicker ways.'

Nothing. I could not see her at all now. She must have pulled ahead. Perhaps that had been her plan all along, to find an opening and escape. I tried to move faster, clawing my way forward, but my haste impeded my speed – my robes snagged on rockcrete, a shard of it stabbing into my shoulder, causing me to stumble and offer a silent scream.

But, by Iwazar's crimson glow, I could see something ahead. The gap widening a fraction, its grip loosening. I emerged on the far side, bursting forth and glancing desperately around me, hoping to catch a glimpse of the fleeing Shard.

But she stood beside me, back slumped against the rockcrete. Ahead, barely a dozen yards from us, was the glow of Plient's workshop. I must have left the lumens on.

I turned to her, expecting the vacant stare, but she was intent on something. I followed her gaze to the shadows but saw nothing, only the smooth rockcrete.

Beside me, Iwazar gave a faint hiss.

I synced with it, peering through its eye. And something shifted – a flicker of light, like the moon emerging from behind a cloud. And the scene no longer looked right. I could not say what changed. But one moment the crumbling ruins almost, but not quite, resembled a crouched figure, and the next moment there was a crouched figure who almost resembled the ruins.

'Iwazar,' I whispered, the device rising above me. 'Full wide shot on my–'

'Wait. By Vect, this is embarrassing.'

I knew the accent by now, or perhaps the lack of one, the pronunciation unnaturally flawless, bestowing the words with a lyrical harmony laced with disdain.

Uli.

He stepped forward, cloak falling away, its textured pattern of crumbling rockcrete shifting to a stormy grey.

'Spotted by *mon-keigh*,' he said, incredulous. 'This is the problem with fighting your kind. Most of you are so inadequate that one becomes complacent. You drag us down to your level.'

'You followed me?'

'A little. But I thought it easier to await your return. You are rather predictable.'

'Rile said you refused to leave the ship, for fear of being spotted.'

'Ah. Rile lies. A lot. Part of his job, I suppose, although he also has a gift for it. A charm, perhaps – is that the right word?'

'It's certainly a word.'

'But you are right – I would have preferred to remain on the *Aenigma*. However, I owe my colleague a debt, and amongst civilised beings, that is taken seriously. He wanted his sister recaptured. Frankly, having now met her, I have no idea why. But that is the deal.'

He looked from her to me, his smile widening. 'Unless you intend to stop me?'

His expression indicated he very much hoped I would.

I shook my head. 'I doubt I could stop you. On the other hand, were I to scream loud enough, a score of Imperial soldiers would soon be closing on this location. I wonder how many Scions it would take to kill you. Five? Ten? Because there are more than that.'

'Indeed?' he replied, arching a perfect eyebrow. 'Because I was led to believe the flight commander was dead. Her turning up now might invite some awkward questions.'

'Let them ask their questions. I am not a xenos and have committed no crime.'

'And you would let them detain her? Pass sentence for dereliction of duty?'

'I haven't decided yet,' I said after a moment's pause. 'But I would rather turn us both in than let you take her.'

Suddenly he stood right before me, and I felt the cold kiss of a blade pressed to my throat. I never even saw him move.

'What if I sever your vocal cords before you have a chance to summon aid?'

'Iwazar will scream on my behalf. And it has a louder voice than I.'

He shot a look at the seer-skull, perhaps assessing whether he could silence us both.

Then he sighed, stepped back, and sheathed the blade. 'Perhaps we should postpone this debate until we are somewhere a little less exposed?'

CHAPTER FORTY-TWO

Shard slowed as we entered the workshop, blank gaze surveying the silent machines, Uli darting in behind her, sealing the door. He seemed possessed by a manic energy. Perhaps it was a trait shared by his species, or perhaps he knew something we didn't. Either way, he was incapable of sitting still, loitering against the darkened windows or fussing over some vox-like device located on his wrist. I assumed he had already contacted Rile and he was coming for her.

There was little I could do about it. Shard was now slumped in the corner, legs splayed out, head lolling, looking as though she might never rise again. I could not move her, not alone. And there was no way I could overpower Uli. I was somewhat surprised he had not killed me yet.

'May I ask you a question?' I said.

He frowned, looking at me from the window. 'Are you not prohibited from addressing my kind?'

'Yes. But I would still like to ask.'

He shrugged.

'What does Cesh want?'

'How should I know?' he said. 'You think I know all my people's motivations? We are no more united than your kind. We just do not pretend otherwise.'

'Then what do *you* want?'

'Revenge.' He smiled. 'But it's a long, slow process to achieve it. Still, my people live long lives. We are patient. Some of us anyway.'

'And that is why you work for an inquisitor?'

'With. I collaborate *with* an inquisitor. And whilst Atenbach might be a doddering old man, he at least has a sense of priorities. Your kind are waning, your empire crumbling. But there are terrible things lurking in the void and beyond the veil, and my people lack the numbers to fight them without aid. Sadly, your society is founded on the principles of xenophobia and violent ignorance, and you are so indoctrinated that few of you are capable of grasping the bigger picture.'

He was intent on me now, head tilted, eyes narrowed. Focused. It was not pleasant to be under his scrutiny. I felt like a noisome rat who on succeeding in getting a slumbering feline's attention was starting to regret it.

'May I ask a question in return?' he said.

'I suppose that's fair.'

'What did Cesh tell you?'

I tensed, and he gave a predatory smile.

'So, you did meet him. I wonder if I should detain you for that. I am an agent of an inquisitor after all, working on behalf of the Imperium. And your people are not supposed to traffic with xenos.'

I turned away, my gaze finding Shard. She was curled up in the corner beside the fuselage of the recon plane. If she heard the exchange, she gave no sign.

'Did he offer some sage advice?' Uli continued, lounging against the workstation and watching intently. 'Or was it a threat? No? No, it was advice then. That must place you in a bind. Do you follow the guidance of a xenos... Or go against it, but always wonder whether that was his intent, and you fell prey to the manipulation. If it helps, aeldari always lie to humans. Every statement they make is untrue.'

'Thank you for that paradox.'

He gave a mocking smile. He had so many smiles, so many nuances of expression. But all were bright, and most were reminiscent of a beast baring its fangs. He opened his mouth to reply but hesitated, tilting his head. Listening.

'And upon that startling revelation this conversation is concluded – our final guest has arrived.'

I followed his gaze to the door.

Nothing happened.

'I have exceptional hearing. Wait just a moment and–'

It slid open. Rile entered, one eye over his shoulder.

'It's getting worse out there,' he said. 'We should be gone. Where is she?'

Uli jerked his thumb to the corner. Rile turned, stiffening as he caught sight of Shard's face. He advanced upon her, then bent down, hamstrings resting on his calves.

'Lucille?'

She did not respond. Did not even register his presence.

He frowned, glancing at Uli, who offered no comment, before turning his gaze on me.

'What happened to her?'

'I don't know. I think it's self-inflicted. Perhaps to disguise her appearance?'

'Why won't she speak?'

'...She lost someone.'

'Hmm,' he grunted, not fully convinced. I could understand why, given her character. It was easier to assume she was victim of a narcotic or witchcraft. I might have thought so too, if I had not witnessed her disintegrate before me.

Rile rose, turning to Uli.

'We will take her. It's dark enough now for the *Aenigma* to slip away. Then I can–'

'No.'

He frowned, turning his gaze upon me.

'You cannot just take her,' I said. 'Not yet. She has committed… She needs to be… There must be consequences. Plient is dead, and…'

I trailed off, withering beneath his stare. He did not look angry, not yet. Puzzled was closer.

'Scribe Simlex,' he said, 'I am grateful you found my sister, and at some point I will find a means of repaying you. But she is leaving. Now. That is all.'

'And what will happen to her?' I asked. 'Do you intend to nurse her back to health? Offer her a new life?'

'She will be taken care of.'

His tone was neutral, though behind his back Uli was miming a noose being strung about his neck, pulling it taut with one hand even as his eyes rolled back in his head.

Rile's head snapped round, perhaps following my gaze, to find the aeldari nodding along sagely, arms folded as he reclined against a worktop.

'Rile is right,' Uli purred, without a hint of insincerity. 'You should return the flight commander to her family. They have her best interests at heart.'

'This does not concern you,' Rile warned, glaring at him before turning back to me. 'Simlex, you are smart enough to know you cannot stop me. I owe you for finding her and would prefer to leave you alive and unharmed. But I will do what is necessary.'

'I concede you could kill me. But you might wish to consider the consequences. I have captured your likeness. Both of you. And, thanks to Esec's work on the Feed, it would not be difficult to transmit those picts across half the continent. You do not seem to want your presence here known. I could change that.'

He stared at me, perhaps debating whether I was bluffing. I wasn't sure myself. I did have his likeness, but whether I could access Esec's Feed was a separate question.

'Very well, propagandist, what do you suggest?' Rile asked, gesturing to the crumpled Shard. 'We leave the matter to whatever authority is left on this planet? Allow my catatonic sister to be court-martialled and executed?'

I hesitated, my gaze shifting between them.

'I don't—'

'Oh, just shoot him and be done,' Uli said. 'Or leave her, I don't care. But we have dallied too long.'

'He's right,' Rile said, taking a step towards me. He had yet to draw a weapon, though I doubted he needed one to kill me. Perhaps sensing his intent, Iwazar rushed to my side, offering a warning hiss. 'Last chance.'

'You don't understand. The aeldari told me I had to tell the truth. But what if that is the manipulation? What if I keep quiet about her fate and cause irreparable harm? I don't know... I don't know what is right.'

Rile slowed, sighing. 'Do you know what Tobia would say?'

'He would say I should impose my will upon the aeldari. Were he not currently comatose.'

'He is right, though. To beat them one must—'

'They can't be beaten.'

Her voice was barely a whisper. But we turned as one to see

Shard still huddled by the bisected recon plane. Her gaze upon the floor.

Rile stepped closer. 'Lucille, they–'

'We cannot win. It is like punching air. Or locking blades with starlight. They move too fast. Disappear at will. You didn't see them in the tunnels beneath Edbar. One plane held an army in a space where no human pilot could manoeuvre. I thought I was the best. Once,' she murmured. 'But I never had a chance. These aren't orks you can outthink, or traitors who can be outfought. They know the outcome before they engage. We have no hope against them.'

She raised her head, meeting Rile's gaze, her eyes empty, her fires long smothered by despair.

'By Isha, you humans are pathetic,' Uli said, still leaning against the counter, and currently inspecting his fingernails. Rile turned, glaring at him, but the aeldari shrugged.

'What?' he said. 'Cesh has won without even trying. Look what he did to one of your best and brightest. Vanish at will? Manoeuvre through impossible spaces? Do you hear yourself?'

'I saw it myself,' I said. 'In the tunnels beneath Edbar, Cesh held back an–'

'Did you?' Uli asked. 'Or did you see concealed weapons platforms taking out a score of your troops? Honestly, primitive as you are, you have cobbled together passable weaponry, lascannons and multi-lasers and so on. You think my people struggle to put on a light show? I would wager you could never have caught Cesh in those tunnels, because he was never there. You were chasing shadows. And as for disappearing? It's nothing more than a holofield. Like your little picts, the image of the aircraft is broken and distorted and replicated. It doesn't vanish, you just cannot get a fix upon its real location.'

He stared at Shard. She stared back, though I could not read her face.

'You weren't there,' she said. 'Why should I believe you?'

'Why do you believe Cesh?'

'He has a point,' Rile said. 'I have some familiarity with the aeldari methods and technology. Holofields are their standard defence, but there are means to circumvent them. Or mitigate them, at least.'

Shard turned to him. 'Do you have such a solution concealed in your greatcoat?'

'No.'

'Then he remains untouchable,' she said, glaring at her brother. 'Whether sorcery or science, if I cannot see where he is, I cannot hit him. He might as well be invisible.'

A slight edge had crept back into her voice.

'Well, not invisible,' I said. 'There is a flicker amidst the distortion. Little more than a silhouette, but–'

She rounded on me. 'Are you a fighter ace? You think your vision as acute as mine? It is impossible.'

There was more than an edge now.

'I was on the ground when Cesh struck,' I said. 'Twice in fact. I could see the whole battlefield. I saw him… Or perhaps Iwazar did.'

As one, we turned to the seer-skull.

'That?' she said, incredulous. 'You expect me to believe a barely functional rust bucket was able to see through the deception?'

'After Plient repaired it? Yes.'

At the mention of his name, she stiffened. Retreated, the light dying in her eyes. She was fading, but I remembered what Plient had said, right after the fighting pit when she struck me down.

Sometimes she needed a target.

'Iwazar, play back Cesh's second attack. Start at the midpoint.'

An image materialised of Deighton's sky, awash with light and explosions. I watched the colours cascade, flowing like oil on water. All were intent on the spectacle, even Shard rising to her feet.

And there it was.

'Freeze playback,' I murmured, pointing to the hololith. 'See? There.'

Rile and Shard exchanged glances.

'What are you talking about?'

'It's there!' I said, pointing to the silhouette. 'That grey shape? The pointed nose? You can even see the beginnings of a weapon discharge!'

Shard rolled her eyes, turning away. Rile looked to me, concern flashing across his face.

'I see nothing,' he said.

'But it's there!' I repeated, looking at Uli, who was still examining his nails.

'Hmm?' He frowned, raising his head. 'I'm afraid I must agree with the siblings. I see nothing. Though, based on the convergence of colours, you have picked roughly the right spot.'

'But I can see it.'

'Can you?' Uli said. 'Or is your connection to this device more complex than you realised?'

I followed his gaze to Iwazar, patiently awaiting its next command. None of them could see it. Maybe that was a limitation of the projector. Maybe it could not accurately reproduce the image captured, even if it could see it.

'Continue playback. Half-speed.'

The battle rolled on, the sky a storm of light and flame.

'Freeze. There!' I said, glancing to each in turn.

All three shook their heads. But I saw Shard was staring at the image, squinting as she studied the display.

'Where the magenta meets the cyan?' she asked.

'No. Lower. This ripple.'

'Show me another.'

The vid spun forward, ceasing only when the ship rematerialised.

'There?' she asked again, pointing before I could speak.

'Almost.' I moved her finger a shade. 'Here.'

She stared a moment more then turned, making for the shell of the recon plane, peeling open the hull and withdrawing the canister within. She staggered slightly under the weight, but tore it open, unveiling reams of film.

'Here,' she demanded. 'Where is it?'

I looked at the film. 'I didn't capture that image. I can't–'

'Then get this thing' – she nodded to Iwazar – 'to project it on top. Extrapolate.'

'I don't think–'

But I saw her face. Scarred, harrowed, eyes sunken. She was barely holding it together, on the cusp of falling apart. But something smouldered in her eyes. Not fire, but perhaps the embers, or the first spark of a blaze.

Because she just might have found a way to hit back.

CHAPTER FORTY-THREE

Reels of film lay spread about the workshop, Shard at its centre like a spider in a web, Iwazar beside her. She kept stuffing handfuls into the device, to be promptly spat out again. It could not amend the film, for the pict-cam on the recon plane had been unable to fully register Cesh's aircraft. But there was an impression there, a hint through which it could extrapolate the vessel's flight.

Maybe.

It was impossible to know for sure, but the seer-skull layered holo-images over the film, and with my assistance Shard marked in the aircraft with a length of charcoal, before cutting out the individual frames and laying them around her, as though conducting a bizarre ritual. At first I'd been hopeful, imagining that she'd found some pattern to the movements. But increasingly her work seemed that of a madwoman, the ritual's purpose only to stave off another breakdown.

I was not the only one who thought it, even if I refused to voice it.

'It would seem the sun has set,' Uli murmured, peering through the darkened window. 'Yet I find myself here.'

'We are secure enough,' Rile replied, not looking up. 'A few minutes more matters little.'

'You said that three and a half hours ago. Back when picture time was a novelty. But I am no longer amused. I grow bored. And my people do not do well with boredom.'

'Would you prefer to wait outside? Or in our ship?'

'Would that I could fly the damn thing without you disengaging the gene-lock,' he muttered. 'It's almost as though Atenbach does not trust me.'

'Your first meeting was an attempt to assassinate him.'

'Details,' Uli said, peering through the gloom. 'Though I must say, it seems to be getting more exciting out there. You humans do so love fire. Only discovered it a few mega-annum ago, and you just cannot move on.'

'Are they digging firepits?' I asked.

'No. More that they are gathering to discuss something. There are lots of torches. And a rather impassioned speech, even if the orator is dressed like a beggar.'

He reached into his cloak, his rifle unfolding as it cleared the fabric. Seeing it that close, I'm not sure that was the correct term for what happened. It was almost as though the barrel grew from its stock, like a claw being unsheathed. The whole thing had an unsettling organic quality.

'What are you doing?' I said as he took aim.

'Merely aligning the sight so I could read this man's lips and determine... Oh dear.'

'What?'

'We're done,' he said, turning to Rile, his weapon collapsing back into his cloak. 'The impromptu rally is about to become an incident. And, given your people's predisposition towards murdering mine, I'd prefer to be long gone before the shooting starts.'

Rile shifted his gaze to the window. 'What's happening?'

'Apparently whoever was charged with overseeing this little conquest has not been doing a good job. Something about slaying the sacred mamutida? Blotting out the Light of Truth? It doesn't matter, war is returning.'

'We could secure this facility. Lock down until–'

'There are tanks parked out there. How secure will it be once they start firing?'

'You think going out there now is better? When–'

'Bastard! That sneaky, pointy-eared bastard!'

Shard spat the words, the charcoal scrabbling across the parchment before being tossed aside. Her head snapped up, eyes aflame.

'He's doing the same damn manoeuvres over and over. Feint, redeploy, attack, repeat. I could do that if I had a plane that could pivot on a needle. See? There! He swoops in, banks, rolls under, pops out and takes the shot. Then just falls away and does it again. Rinse and repeat. Doesn't even respect us enough to vary his game! Look!'

She gestured to the parchment, now inscribed with crude sketches of planes. Rile hesitated, glancing from her to me.

'Be that as it may, I don't think–'

'But I can beat him! Don't you see it? It's not just random colours and light. There is a pattern, tied to his acceleration! Magenta, cyan, scarlet. There! Right before the yellow! Right before the damn yellow! That's when he strikes, when the shades are like sunset, when the deceleration makes the shot just a little easier. I see it now! I can beat him!'

She thrust the scrawling into our collective faces, triumphant, her fingers stained black by her labour. Her eyes were wide and bright, and she seemed to have forgotten how to blink.

Silence. Uli was the one who broke it.

'Right. Well, she has clearly gone insane, so I am going to leave and hopefully not die. Rile, if you subsequently make it back to the *Aenigma*, we can proceed from there.'

'I'm not insane! I found the–'

She trailed off, frowning at Uli, as though seeing him for the first time.

'Why is there a xenos here?'

'Uli,' Rile replied. 'You remember him? You met following the mission you flew on Shohi?'

'I remember the mission you coerced me into flying on Shohi,' she said softly, her eyes hard. 'Things took a turn after that.'

'I know. And I am sorry. I should have made greater effort with the debrief. And I should have followed up on Esec. That damn drone he tried to smuggle onto the ship. I knew then that there was something odd about–'

'I don't care about that! I need to face Cesh! Don't you get it? Last time… Plient died. Cesh killed him. I can't let him get away with it! I can't just let him die for nothing.'

Her voice almost broke, only held together with bile, anger sustaining her. It kept it simple, kept her from confronting what she had done.

Rile took a step towards her, arm outstretched. 'Lucille. I… You can't face anyone in this state. When did you last sleep?'

'Or wash?' Uli added.

'Be silent!' Rile thundered, glaring at him before turning back to Shard, his voice once more calm as the void.

'Sister, I promise that you can have a chance at revenge. But not yet. You're too close to see it. You must trust me.'

She gave a spluttering laugh, bordering on hysteria. 'Trust you? When have you ever trusted me, even when you turn up with half a story begging me for help?'

'That is not the topic under discussion,' Rile warned, glancing briefly to me. 'Come now, you know I speak the truth. You're not ready. Perhaps tomorrow. Perhaps longer. But not now.'

She glared at him, lip twisted in a snarl. At some point her rant had opened one of her scars, because blood was oozing down her cheek.

Then she sighed. Sagged, her head bowing, her gaze resting on the floor.

'I know,' she said. 'I'm sorry. I just... I failed. I let everyone down. I...'

She trailed off, shoulders slumped, voice breaking even as the parchment tumbled from her hand.

She looked so small. So thin and faded.

'It will be all right. We can fix it,' Rile said, stepping closer, offering his arms. She hesitated, then stepped into his embrace, pressing her face into his chest as he held her. Then she brought her leg back, and savagely drove her knee into his groin.

He gave a choked cry and folded slightly, though to his credit he remained on his feet. But the distraction was sufficient for her to snatch his plasma pistol from the folds of his greatcoat.

'I'm not asking,' she warned, levelling the weapon at each of us in turn. 'I will face Cesh. Now.'

'And how do you expect to do that?' Rile asked, still hunched from the blow.

She hesitated, glancing between us before her gaze settled on me. 'You. Simlex. Open the Feed. I will challenge him right now.'

'I cannot simply open the Feed,' I replied. 'Besides, why would he answer your challenge? What does he have to gain?'

'I don't care,' she said, aiming the pistol at me. 'Do it.'

'I cannot. Esec controls everything.'

'Do it or I end you.'

'I don't believe you,' I said, looking to Rile for support. His expression was less reassuring than I might have hoped. But she didn't fire, gaze shifting to other targets, skirting past Rile, lingering on Uli, before finally she aimed the pistol at her temple.

'Do it or I'll fire.'

If nothing else, it was a bold negotiating strategy. Uli looked almost impressed, but Rile shook his head.

'Come now, none of us believe–'

But I did. Even as he tried to placate her, I could see it in her eyes. Whether it had been her intention or not, part of her wanted to do it. Right then, just to end it all. Anger kept her moving, and moving kept her from thinking too much, but she had to keep going, never stopping too long to let the truth catch up with her.

I could see it. Even as Rile tried to talk her down, I could see the resolve in her eyes. It would be so quick an end. So clean. She would barely feel it, and then feel nothing at all. That was the appeal.

'I will try,' I said, though in truth I had no idea what to do. Esec was the one who held the connection to the Feed. My only hope was to contact him. Silently, I sent a ping through the vox.

'Stop stalling!' Shard warned, the pistol still levelled.

'I'm not stalling. It is not something I can simply conjure for you. All communications go through Esec. Besides, even if Cesh is listening, what will you say?'

'I will challenge him.'

'And when he declines? Why would he fight on your terms? What could you possibly say to draw him out?'

She hesitated, gaze flicking between Rile and I.

'I...'

Rile surged forward, lunged for the pistol. But he had not fully recovered and was a step too slow. Her knee came up again, striking him on the chin. She leapt back, priming the pistol and disengaging the safety. I heard the weapon hum into life, the cooling coils emitting a faint glow.

'Try it again!' she snapped, glaring at her brother. 'One more time! You think I won't? You think I have anything else to live for?'

He rose slowly, backing away, looking to me. 'Get her the damn signal.'

'I'm trying. It's not as though–'

'Simlex? What on Terra is it now?'

Esec's voice. Never before had it filled me with such relief.

'Esec,' I replied, 'we need to broadcast a message through the Feed. As far and wide as possible.'

'I will do nothing of the sort. Not until Vagbon is ready. We are moving forward with a new–'

'Shard is alive.'

'Simlex, I appreciate the attempt. But it is too–'

'She is alive and standing in front of me and wants to challenge Cesh. I'm sending you a pict.'

'...By the Throne, what happened to her face?'

'War happened. Can you send it or not?'

'I'm not sure about this. She's hardly stable and she looks like–'

'You said yourself this planet is a washout. How could it make things worse? Besides, look at her. The blood! The scars! Her miraculous return! Forget the little vids. This could be the climax of a real theatrical pict. Maybe the greatest of all time. This is your chance! This is the ugly face of war, a hero bloodied but unbowed. If you can connect me to the damn Feed, we can show Deighton that the aeldari are liars and the Imperium is not so easily bested!'

'Stand by. I need to confirm something.'

I heard a click, and muffled voices. Shard was still holding herself hostage while Rile, who was on his feet again, was intent on the window.

'He will track our location,' he murmured. 'Try and take control of the operation.'

'Probably,' Uli said. He was bent over a workstation, a roll of parchment laid across it, a stick of charcoal scratching its surface.

'Esec?' I said. 'Are you still there? We don't have much time. She's a flight risk and I can't hold her. If I can't send something soon, she's going to–'

'All right! I have opened the Feed. Whatever you transmit will be sent.'

'We have a connection,' I said as Iwazar drew in beside me. 'Whatever you want to say, you had best–'

'Cesh! You básking grox-herding piece of shit!' she spat. 'Guess what? I'm still alive despite your efforts. It seems your little prophecy didn't work out so well, because you failed to finish the job. I'm still here. I suppose your lofty predictions and promises aren't worth a damn. Either that, or you are just a liar.'

She grinned, then winced as the expression pulled on her scars. Uli, meanwhile, had finished his scrawlings, tearing off a scrap of parchment. He approached, holding it up behind Iwazar.

'Might help get his attention,' he mouthed.

Shard squinted at the paper, and I followed her gaze. But it was nonsense. At least, that was what it resembled, for though the alphabet was Low Gothic, the hodgepodge of letters related to no words I knew. Either it was phonetic, or Uli's gift for tongues did not extend to his cartographer's quill.

Shard glared from script to Uli. Then shrugged. And spoke.

It was unlike any language I had heard. Like ill-tuned birdsong, or a virtuoso garrotted with his strings. As she spoke, Uli winced, screwing his eyes shut and turning away, as though hoping to shield himself from the sound. At its conclusion Shard lapsed into silence, before glaring into the lenses one last time.

'One hour and I will be in the air. Face me if you dare. Best me if you can. Or remain in hiding and prove yourself a liar and a coward. You didn't finish the job, Cesh. What does your prophecy say about that?'

I cut the feed. Beside me, Uli appeared to be picking something from his ears.

'That was simply horrible,' he said. 'I've never heard someone vivisect my people's tongue so brazenly. I once faced the corrupted Astartes dedicated to She Who Thirsts, and the cacophony they unleashed was less bothersome to my ears.'

'What did you have her say?'

'Oh, some insults. Home truths. Nothing I could translate easily. I just hope he understood her mangled delivery.'

'Well, sister, what now?'

Rile stood, hands spread. Shard, who still held his pistol, looked to the weapon as if for the first time. She powered it down, before returning it to him.

'Simple. We find a Lightning, launch the attack run, and I finally silence that smug xenos.'

'Just like that?'

'Why not? It's hardly–'

Something hammered against the door.

We turned as one. It was shaking in its frame, despite Plient's efforts to secure it. Whoever was striking it either had an assault ram or–

I heard a familiar grunt, right before an ogryn-like force slammed into the metal. Lanlok. But he was not alone. The second voice was clearly human, and accustomed to giving commands.

'By the authority of Colonel Surling as enacted by his nominee Propagandist Emulle Esec, you are hereby ordered to open this door.'

CHAPTER FORTY-FOUR

Rile swore, gaze sweeping the room. 'Is there an alternative exit?'

Shard shook her head. 'The hangar door opens, but presumably they're guarding that as well.'

She approached a panel, fingers tapping a sequence. A screen unfurled, but when she tried to access it, nothing displayed.

'They've taken out the cams. Can't even get numbers.'

'Are you all insane?' Uli asked, gesturing to the window. 'There is an easy way out. Look, nobody is even down there. At least, nobody in uniform – there do seem to be a few locals out and about.'

I followed his gaze. 'It's a fifty-foot drop.'

'So? One simply leaps to that outcrop, slides down, vaults over those broken railings, shimmies between those sections of shattered turret, and lightly drops the last twenty feet.'

He looked at me. Then threw up his hands.

'Ah. Yes. Forgive me. I forgot how limited you all are. Apologies. Well, I have a revised plan. I will go out the window as previously outlined, and Rile, if you survive, I will see you at the ship. If you don't... Then hopefully I can operate the gene-lock by carving something from your corpse.'

He nodded to Shard and me. 'Lovely meeting you both, presumably for the last time.'

Then he fired a pistol. I didn't see a flash, only the window shattering moments before he leapt through the glass, effortlessly negotiating the almost sheer drop. In my zenith I attended circuses, saw gene-enhanced performers pull off some acrobatically exceptional feats, but none had moved like him. It was as though momentum and gravity were little more than a series of guidelines, negotiated and navigated as easily as the building's exterior. By the time he had got to the final drop, his cloak was already bound about him, his outline fading long before he reached the street below.

Behind us, another blow struck the door, its hinges groaning in protest.

I looked to Rile. 'Can you not talk them down? You are an agent of the Inquisition – that must count for something?'

'An agent who is not supposed to be here. To reveal my presence would be to invite some awkward questions.'

Shard snorted. 'What did you steal?'

'Not the pertinent question. Besides, were I in charge of the retrieval squad, I would simply brand any opposition as liars and traitors and open fire. Apologies can be issued later, and compensation paid.'

'We can't fight them.'

'No.'

Another thud. It felt as though the whole room shook. Plient may have reinforced the door, but once an ogryn sets his sights on something, it is exceedingly difficult to stay him.

'Window then,' Rile said, turning away and reaching into

his greatcoat. He withdrew a small, pistol-like device tipped with a bladed hook. A grapnel launcher. There was a hiss of compressed air as it fired, a length of cable launching into the night. It must have found purchase because the cable went taut, angling down towards a distant hab-block, though it was difficult to see through the smoke. Uli was right – fires were breaking out, their fumes clouding our view.

Rile inspected Plient's tools, finally selecting an arc welder and canister. He flicked the switch on the former, and set to work on the recon plane's fuselage, cutting clear three metal struts, their tips still glowing from the arc welder's touch. He handed two to Shard and me, before appraising the canister, holding it to his ear and tapping the metal. Apparently satisfied, he approached the shuddering door, placing the canister and arc welder on the ground in front of it, the glowing tip of the latter inches from the metal container. Already the exterior was starting to bubble.

'We don't have long,' he said, approaching the window. 'Wait until I am across before following. The cable won't hold more than one of us at a time.'

He hooked the strut over the cable, and hurled himself from the window. We watched him sail across the gap, knees tucked, greatcoat flapping behind him.

Shard glanced at me. 'You next?'

'No. Plient must be avenged. And I will probably fall anyway.'

'Try not to.'

She did as her brother had done, hooking the strut over the cable and pushing off. Her passage was a little less nimble, her legs kicking as she hurtled through the air. She narrowly avoided catching herself on an antenna jutting from one of the roofs, before colliding with the distant wall in which the grapnel was lodged, crumpling as she dropped from my sight.

I placed down my cane, examining the strut Rile had handed me. The tips still glowed, and it was warm to the touch. As I hooked it over the cable, Iwazar drew up beside me. It seemed almost excited. Perhaps I would be too if I had an anti-grav unit.

Behind me, Lanlok struck the door once more, the metal creaking in protest. Though I confess I was more concerned by the hissing emanating from the canister.

I kicked off. Slower than the others, for I had only one leg to launch from, relying on gravity to carry me forward. The bar was deceptively hot, and I found little strength in my fingers. Too late, I realised I should have used my cane, the narrower grip easier to maintain.

I was about halfway across when I heard the first shot, though I could not tell from where it originated, my gaze fixed ahead. But I felt the blast as the canister detonated, the sound carrying a fraction later. Rile, to his credit, had accurately estimated the force of his improvised bomb and secured the grapnel line accordingly. But the cable still thrashed serpent-like in the wake of the explosion, and the torn strut slid from my grip.

I fell, tumbling arse-over-head, the world spinning even as it hurtled closer. It was a sad way to die, though somewhat appropriate – a metaphorical fall culminating in a literal one. And the glimpses of the world below, the blood and smoke, the screams and flames, suggested that survival would have been improbable anyway.

But fate had other plans. As did Iwazar. The seer-skull, following doggedly, somehow slipped beneath me as I tumbled. It rammed into my back, pushing upwards even as its micro appendages scrabbled for purchase, raking my flesh. I might have screamed, had the impact not driven the air from my lungs. There was no way its anti-grav unit should have held me. But my previous and failed attempts to stabilise it had involved incorporating additional generators, and Plient's subsequent repairs resulted in surprising lift. Not enough to carry me, but sufficient to slow my fall, direct it.

I could hear the cries below, and saw a flash of faces, right before I struck the crowd.

Or part of it anyway, for the street was apparently at war. Perhaps the sudden appearance of so many Scions had incited the uprising, or perhaps it was already underway when they moved to apprehend Shard. Regardless, I tumbled through the press of bodies. A sharp pain thudded into my ribs, even as something heavy and wet fell across my face. It stunk like offal, a mass of pulverised meat bound in scraps of bloodied cloth. I crawled through it, the mess of blood and limbs. I could see nothing through the dark and smoke except the occasional flash of gunfire.

A hand seized my collar.

I fought, in vain, even as I was hauled upright and found myself face to face with Rile. His brow was cut and bruised, the plasma pistol bright in his other hand, coils glowing like a miniature sun.

'Move!' he snapped. And I tried, I really did, but I had no strength or breath to sustain me. I fell and he swore, hauling me upright and throwing my weight over his shoulders. He ran, managing a surprising turn of speed, despite favouring his right leg. I managed to raise my head sufficiently to see a vast shadow advancing through the smoke, crushing rubble and flesh beneath its rumbling tracks.

A Rogal Dorn battle tank.

Evidently, the Láech had decided to intervene in the dispute. Though, given the ordnance they brought to bear, it seemed their intervention would be rather indiscriminate. The turret swivelled as the tank aimed its main cannon. It did not appear a sophisticated weapon, but its presence probably explained the shattered mounds of flesh that had broken my fall.

'Tank,' I murmured.

I don't know if he heard me. More likely it was his own battlefield awareness, for suddenly he hurled us sideways, rolling through a doorway into one of the surrounding buildings. I tumbled from his shoulders as he took cover from the blast.

Then all was white and silent.

Sound returned first – a hissing whine. I coughed, spitting dust. The air was choked with it, the pulverised remnants of rubble and corpses. Rile was barely visible, little more than a shadow in the haze until he stepped close, face emerging from the dust storm. I was unsurprised to see he now wore a rebreather and photo-goggles.

'You need to move,' he said, voice muffled. 'I cannot carry you further. We must get off the streets.'

I coughed again. 'Where's Shard?'

'Present.'

Her choked voice came from behind me, deeper into the rubble. I dragged myself upright, using the wall for support as I sought her out. She, like everything, was stained grey by the dust.

'What happened whilst I was… incapacitated?' she said. 'I thought Edbar was under our control?'

'Taking and holding are two different things,' Rile said, peering through a crack in the wall. 'We can't stay here, they could send squads building to building. But stepping onto the street is suicide.'

'I might be able to find a path,' I said. 'Give me a moment.'

I reached out, seeking the panicked flicker lurking at the edge of my consciousness, syncing with it.

Iwazar. It was somewhere dark, cowering in the rubble. No, higher, perhaps lurking on one of the upper floors. I felt its reluctance to emerge, a sentiment I frankly shared, our connection slipping through my fingers.

'We have no time for this,' Rile muttered, turning to Shard. 'Standard protocol would dictate infantry is sent in to–'

'Give him a minute.'

I reached out again, soothing the seer-skull's panic, coaxing it from the shadows, its lenses struggling to pierce the dust cloud.

'The Rogal Dorn tank,' I said. 'It's advancing. I think… Throne, what are they?'

Figures had swarmed over it, black shapes clambering onto the rumbling machine, or hurling themselves from the upper windows to land on its armoured hull. I thought them xenos beasts at first, until Iwazar adjusted its lenses, and I caught the flap of their robes and a strangled battle cry.

For the God-Emperor!

'The indentured workers are assaulting it,' I reported. 'But they cannot breach the armour, there is no… Ah, I think they are using something on the vision ports. Some chemical? Trying to blind it. No one seems to be emerging to stop them.'

'First rule of armoured divisions – if someone is on your tank, don't open the door and let them in,' Rile said. 'What I do not understand is why there is no infantry support.'

'There are further threats behind,' I said. 'Iwazar cannot see clearly through the smoke. Stand by. There is… I think the tank's support ran into Esec's reinforcements.'

'And they too are at war?'

'Everyone is, I think.'

And I could not blame them. It was easy to see the absurdity of it through Iwazar's cold, analytical lenses. But it was different when you were wading through the bodies, the smoke blinding you. Every shadow might be a threat, former allies now potential traitors. The victors would no doubt praise the

God-Emperor, condemning their foes as the heretics despite their shared battle cry.

The insurgents were still swarming the tank, which appeared to be retreating, or at least attempting to dislodge them. It had seemed an unstoppable behemoth moments before, and in the open desert it would have annihilated the attackers. But they were too close too quickly, and it could not bring its weapons to bear.

Iwazar's sensors twitched as one of the insurgents clamped something on the side of the tank.

Grenade. But it did not appear to be of Imperial design, resembling an almost circular disc. The attacker attached it to the hull, presumably via magnetic adhesion, before diving clear.

It seemed such a small thing against the armoured war machine.

Then there was a flash. I cannot really describe it through human eyes, but to Iwazar it was a pulse of blinding light, a burst of electromagnetic energy that momentarily consumed its sensors. I felt the seer-skull falter, wobbling and barely clinging to the sky as it sought to maintain its vigil. But the tank ground suddenly to a halt. I saw no damage to it, the detonation barely leaving a mark upon the hull. But one of its tracks no longer appeared operational, and its lumens had gone dark.

'They have disabled the tank,' I told them.

'How?'

I heard the confusion in Rile's voice.

'I don't know. A grenade.'

'A single grenade blew up a Rogal Dorn?'

'No. Disabled it. Partially at least. One track is functional. There is no visible damage. Just a pulse of energy. I think the offensive has ground to a halt.'

'Simlex?'

Shard's voice. I felt her hand on my distant shoulder. My body seemed far away, an unnecessary burden.

'Simlex, come back. This is our opening.'

I nodded, releasing my hold on the seer-skull. It retreated, clinging close to the rubble, seeking a path to me now the immediate danger had passed. But there was no time to wait. As we pressed deeper into the ruins, through the smoke and dust, I found myself wondering how a lowly worker had acquired a weapon capable of disabling such a formidable war machine. Then again, how had said workers overthrown the rulers of Edbar? Their success had been attributed to Esec's propaganda efforts, as though faith and inspiration were sufficient on their own. But such action required tactics, planning. Armaments.

Perhaps the Imperium's forces had been too busy celebrating their victory and congratulating Esec to question whether an outside force had instigated the uprising.

CHAPTER FORTY-FIVE

Rile led us through the smoke and rubble, his photo-goggles granting him at least some visibility. But it was slow going, for the air choked us and only Rile had a rebreather, Shard and I settling for scraps of torn cloth. Still, I would not have been able to move faster, not without my cane, forced instead to seek out handholds I could use for support.

Intermittently, Rile motioned us to halt, scanning the area on a handheld auspex before requesting I take a look through Iwazar's eye. Even from the seer-skull's vantage point high above there was little to see – dust and rubble sanitising the crimson of the corpses, the heat of their bodies already fading. But it seemed the insurgents had fortified an interpass a hundred yards north, blockading it with heavy haulage vehicles. The Láech could provide only a token defence, for their numbers on the surface were limited, the majority of their forces deployed below ground. Perhaps the insurgents had found a way of sealing them there, but the Láech still possessed superior firepower thanks to their armoured vehicles. Their own tanks were concentrated a few hundred yards south, the space between an impassable kill-zone. It was a stalemate. For now.

We kept moving, slipping through a data-vault that was long since stripped clean, the security mechanisms and gates warped and broken. They must have fallen during the initial attack. I could not help but wonder how that campaign had seemed from within Edbar. Were the workers engaged in guerrilla warfare for weeks, their solitary goal securing a means of breaching the walls? Or were they already on the cusp of victory and ready to assume control when we struck, those planes familiar from the propaganda reels suddenly darkening the skies as their supposed liberators began reducing their home to rubble and ruin.

Rile stopped by the data-vault door, now hanging from its hinges. Beyond lay a dimly lit and narrow corridor.

'This should take us within a few dozen yards of the hangar.'

Shard nodded. 'Good. Once there I need to get to a Lightning. Ideally one with the right markings, but I can settle. You two–'

'Not that hangar. We are headed for the *Aenigma*.'

'No, we are not. There–'

'I have indulged you enough, sister,' he warned, turning on her. 'This is no longer some petty war. I am certain now that xenos tech is involved, and this uprising is too well coordinated. I need to report it to my superiors, and for that we need to get off-planet.'

'So you intend to run?'

'Yes.'

'This is the valiant Inquisition?' she sneered. 'Tucking their tails? I thought your sort deemed no heresy too small, no crime worth overlooking?'

'Some do and they are fools. This is a small city on a tiny world. Whether it thrives or dies means nothing. But if it represents a bigger conspiracy, if it's the symptom of a rot seeping into the Imperium, then that must be investigated. And that means we must survive long enough to raise the alarm.'

His voice was cold, detached, his face hidden by the goggles and rebreather. I looked to Shard, expecting to see her eyes blazing. But she hesitated, then nodded, shoulders slumping.

'Fine,' she said. 'I will follow your judgement. Lead on.'

He hesitated. 'You seem too agreeable.'

'Would you prefer I argued?'

'No. But do not expect me to be taken by surprise twice. I would prefer not to strike you, sister. But my preference means little when weighed against my duty. Simlex, can you see if the path is clear?'

'No. Iwazar's view is blocked – there is a section of undamaged roof I cannot see through. I can find another path, but I do not know how long it will take.'

'We must chance it.'

'There is something else. Esec is trying to reach me through Iwazar's vox.'

'Or perhaps attempting to track us. Do not respond.'

He set off once more, pistol drawn though its coils were dormant, providing no telltale glow to reveal our position. Shard followed, clutching a laspistol she had retrieved from a corpse during the initial chaos.

We reached the passage's end to find the doorway remarkably undamaged. Rile adjusted his wrist guard, engaging some auspex or scanner. He cursed under his breath.

'Can't make out much, too much dust and smoke. But there are life signs up ahead. They seem to block the path to our destination.'

'Any possibility they're our reinforcements?' Shard asked.

'I have no friends on this world. You?'

'I have no friends. What about you, Simlex?'

'What?'

'Can you use the skull-thing to look ahead?'

'I will try,' I said, reaching out to Iwazar. It was dark where the seer-skull lurked, even by the standards of its own sensors. It had found a shaft, perhaps providing power or ventilation, and was negotiating a path through, its internal guidance indicating the hangar lay ahead.

'Iwazar is close. I think I might–'

There was a flash behind it, a flickering light. I felt Iwazar whirling in alarm, its sensors unnerved. There was something wrong about whatever approached. It spun, and I saw two of Esec's Eyes trailing after it, even as the seer-skull began to panic.

'No!' I said, trying to keep hold of it, but Iwazar would not listen. Panicked, it fled, accelerating down the shaft before bursting through a vent.

Something struck it.

I felt the shock a moment before I lost my connection with the device, my body stiffening. I fell, but Shard caught me, though my weight almost threw her off balance.

'What happened?' Rile snapped, his pistol humming into life.

'Iwazar. Something... I can't feel it. Wait, there is–'

'Simlex?'

Esec. His voice was muffled, as though speaking through water. Iwazar was the source of our connection, but I could barely feel our link, or see through its lenses. It felt caged, stifled, its systems and cogitator barely functional.

'Blast it, Simlex, can you even hear me through this ramshackle contraption? You need to bring Shard in. She's lost it completely. I have no idea what she said to that aeldari, but it didn't take him long to retaliate. Vagbon is going to face him, supported by three squadrons. No one-to-one combat this time – we are going to burn

the sky clear. But I need Shard under lock and key until... until I can figure out what I'm doing. Hello? Are you even–'

'Esec has Iwazar,' I murmured, as Shard helped me back onto my feet. 'And he wants you.'

'Why?'

'I'm not sure he knows. He's scrabbling for control. Apparently Cesh did not take well to your challenge. He has already launched an attack.'

'If the path ahead is blocked, perhaps it would be prudent to make for the main hangar?'

'The main hangar will also be guarded,' Rile replied. 'The priority is still the *Aenigma*. It holds secrets that must remain that way.'

'–know if you are listening, but this is your last chance, Simlex. Once this is over and we have control again, there will be a reckoning. You need to make sure you are on the right side. Remember last time? You can only fall so far before you just... stop.'

I glanced to Shard and Rile, still arguing, though thankfully in hushed tones.

'You intend to fight your way through armed only with a plasma pistol?' Shard asked.

'I intend to try. The alternative is–'

'I'll go.'

As one they turned to me. Shard frowned.

'You'll what?' she said.

'I'll go. Esec knows I am close because he has Iwazar. But he doesn't know you are here. I can tell him we separated. Perhaps even persuade him you are headed for the main hangar. Rile, do you have some device with which I can send a signal?'

He nodded, reaching into his greatcoat, his hand emerging clutching a ring with a concealed thumb-switch.

'Why should we trust you?' Shard asked as I slid it onto my

hand. 'Perhaps you intend to turn us in to save your hide? You seemed pretty close to Esec after all.'

'As did you. Close enough to confide in him anyway.'

She stiffened, though her expression was hard to read with the cloth covering her mouth. 'Trusting a propagandist was a mistake. One I am reluctant to repeat.'

I sighed. And said what needed to be said.

'You can trust me because I owe you my life. Both of you, in fact – your brother saved me mere moments ago. And you should know better than most that I put ill-conceived ideals above my best interests.'

'Or you just have poor judgement.'

'That as well. But perhaps I can stall or misdirect them. Worst-case scenario, I am confident I can provide a distraction.'

CHAPTER FORTY-SIX

The Scions raised their weapons as I opened the hatch, hobbling from the doorway, hands in the air. There were half a dozen of them, positioned behind barricades flanking the entrance to the commissar's hangar. Their armour was adorned in Esec's colours, or at least the livery he had adopted from Colonel Surling, their Tempestor identifiable from the skull marking on his helm. But though he commanded the forces, he did not oversee the operation. That figure was a small, flickering thing, sitting upon his distant control throne, domed helm in place, his image projected by one of his xenos-tainted Eyes.

Propagandist Esec. Clearly he saw me, my image no doubt relayed to his barge. He leant forward, smiling.

'*Ah, there you are. I'm impressed, Simlex, a man of your physical limitations surviving this long. Assuming you were alone, of course?*'

'I am now.'

'*Yes. But where is she? I know you were with her.*'

'I was. But we took different paths,' I said, hobbling onwards, the strain clearly visible. The Scions were too disciplined to lower their weapons, but I think they relaxed a shade, shifting their focus to the doorway behind me and the passage beyond, where Rile should be waiting in the shadows. He'd told me to tap my thumb-trigger once if there was an opening, twice if they should retreat.

'So, you don't know where she is?'

'I suspect she is making for the main hangar. She wants a plane. Still thinks she can end this as a hero if she can best Cesh.'

'By the Throne that woman is deluded! Well, she will not make it. I have additional forces there.'

'Is it not worth letting her make the attempt? Perhaps she will–'

'It's too late for that, Simlex. I made a mistake permitting you to send that message. I was caught up in the moment, in what you said about making a real pict. But she is a liability now. I have dispatched our forces to intercept Cesh, Vagbon leading them. When he is defeated, Flight Commander Shard can be awarded credit for the success. It will be her last mission, a neat tying up of loose ends. At this point she holds greater value as a martyr. Then we can move forward with a new project.'

'…You intend to kill her.'

'Not necessarily. But we both know she will not stand down, nor listen to reason, and I cannot let her destabilise the situation further.'

'Destabilise? Edbar is already undergoing an uprising!'

'Exactly! And I will not permit the situation to get worse! I have my orders, as do my troops.'

I stared at the Scions. They weren't his troops of course, their true loyalty to Colonel Surling. But he had presumably instructed them to follow Esec's orders, to enact his will. They were the finest mortal troops in the God-Emperor's armies, renowned for their loyalty and discipline. Perhaps an orator as skilled as the commissar could have persuaded them that Esec overstepped his authority. But they had been trained and conditioned their whole lives to follow orders without question. There was nothing I could do to dissuade them, and even Rile would struggle to overcome such odds. The Scions were like a wall: implacable and impregnable.

I looked back to Esec's flickering image. 'Do you still have Iwazar?'

'It is here. Functional enough, if somewhat redundant.'

I could see it now. A Scion held the device. It appeared to have been temporarily disabled by some arc weapon. But I could feel it awaken as I approached, systems gradually blossoming into life.

'I would very much like it returned. Please.'

'Why? It is nothing more than a crumbling relic.'

'I know. But it reminds me of a time when my future seemed bright. And we were both damaged by our experiences. Please, I have nothing else left.'

'Of course. I see no reason to detain it further. Providing you are still loyal. You are loyal, aren't you, Kile?'

His voice was soft. Almost disinterested. But I felt a ripple pass through the Scions. Their weapons were still primed, their focus shifting back to me.

'I was always loyal to my masters,' I said. 'Before they dismissed me. Or died in service. Now? Honestly, now all I want is to be free from all this. Back behind a screen somewhere far from the front lines. Toil away in solitude.'

'I could perhaps assist with that. Offer a position as pict-scrubber, or continuity enforcer. But I need to know you are loyal to me. Can you do that?'

'I... have a means of summoning her,' I said. 'In exchange for you taking me in and returning Iwazar, I could bring her right to you.'

He looked at me, a tiny, flickering figure on a miniature throne, face hidden by his crown-like helm. Weighing his choices.

'Agreed,' he said, glancing to his troops. *'Someone retrieve the signalling device. Oh, and release the seer-skull.'*

The Scion released Iwazar. Slowly it rose, examining its surroundings as though waking from a slumber. But it did not approach me, instead retreating behind the Scions' line, even as one of their soldiers advanced towards me. I had barely covered half the distance between the access hatch and their forces.

The Scion was scant feet away when I stumbled, falling heavily. Weakly, I tried to rise, limbs shaking.

'Oh help him up,' Esec said. *'Throne's sake, man, you need to do something about your infirmity. Though I suppose it will trouble you less once you are ensconced behind a workstation.'*

The Scion shouldered his weapon, offering his hand. His helmet covered his face, but perhaps we had met before. Perhaps he had protected me from Lanlok, or guarded me as I wound my path through Edbar.

In another life, it could have been Rosln behind that helm.

And, in that moment, I very much wanted to take his hand. Because I wanted to go back to the solitude of my cubicle cell. Back further, in fact, to before I even met her. When I still had faith and believed I served a noble purpose. Before I saw the Imperium for what it was.

But you cannot go back. Not once you have turned from the path.

And I knew what must be done.

As I reached for him, I pressed the hidden switch on the ring, even as I synced with Iwazar, who still hovered behind their lines. I whispered the command even as I sent the impulse to the device.

'Widest shot, panoramic angle. All standing subjects. Full spectrum.'

The seer-skull whirred, lenses clicking as something slid from a metallic sheath mounted beneath the skull.

'Fire,' I whispered, dropping to the ground.

Crimson las-bolts erupted from Iwazar's underslung lascarbine, the volley tearing into the Scions' exposed backs. My would-be rescuer was hit twice, the thuds audible as the bolts exploded against his carapace armour. He grunted, stumbling, even as his comrades fell.

It lasted only seconds before the charge was exhausted, the power pack ejecting from a side port, steam hissing both from it and Iwazar. Without Plient's repairs, without his willingness to attune the weapon, I have no doubt the attack would have failed. As it was, I doubted Iwazar could endure a second volley.

The Scion who had offered assistance rose, glaring over his shoulder to the carnage. He then turned back to me, rifle raised, before a searing bolt of plasma struck him full in the chestplate. The smell of melting armaplas mingled with burnt flesh.

As he fell, Rile was already past me, a second blast striking a rising Scion. A few still lived, for the barrage had been poorly aimed, but they were off balance, having been struck from behind. Shard was suddenly beside me, laspistol drawn, but there was little need. Rile had already dispatched the remaining attackers, the final soldier falling with a combat knife buried in his throat.

Only Esec was left, his image frozen on its throne. He licked his lips, clearing his throat. *'Lucille. Please be assured I–'*

A las-bolt struck the device, his image collapsing as the Eye crumpled. Rile withdrew his blade from the dead Scion, wiping it on the man's uniform before sheathing it, his gaze intent on me.

'A regrettable situation, but a well-played one, Simlex. It might have been useful to know you had such a card up your sleeve.'

'I thought the element of surprise important.'

'It is indeed, depending on whom one intends to surprise.'

'I was unsure who was my ally,' I said, as Shard assisted me to my feet, my arm over her shoulder. 'Shall we proceed?'

'Quite,' Rile replied, before turning his gaze to the hangar door. 'Sealed. Stand by. Once I have it open, we need to relocate Tobia to the *Aenigma* before departure.'

'Wait,' Shard said. 'Tobia is alive?'

'Yes.'

'Someone could have mentioned it.'

'Forgive me,' Rile said, turning back to her. 'It's been a rather frantic few hours, and I was honestly unsure whether you would care one way or–'

The door exploded, spraying metal shards as a massive figure erupted from it. Rile barely had time to turn before a huge fist slammed into his chest, launching him several feet into the air. He landed hard beside us, gasping for breath, the breastplate beneath his greatcoat buckled by the impact.

The towering figure strode through the doorway, cracking his knuckles, the sound reminiscent of an artillery barrage. His skin was scorched, uniform tattered and stinking of smoke, no doubt from Rile's improvised explosive.

Lanlok.

A second Eye hovered beside him, Esec's image once again materialising.

'You made a poor choice betraying me, Simlex. Lanlok, please eliminate these traitors.'

CHAPTER FORTY-SEVEN

Shard drew her laspistol, firing at the hulking ogryn. But he waded through the barrage as though it were pebbles tossed by a child, barely registering the burns it left on his already blackened skin. The brute either felt no pain or was too enraged from his existing injuries to care. He had no means of knowing Rile was responsible for the explosion, but nevertheless advanced upon him, intent on finishing the job.

His fist loomed over the acolyte, just as Rile raised the plasma pistol.

And fired.

I had never heard an ogryn scream. It was closer to an animal's roar. But the shot was wide of the mark, Lanlok jerking aside at the last moment, evading the worst of the blast, though it left an ugly burn across his chest and ignited his promethium-stained clothes.

Rile, still gasping, attempted a second shot aimed for the ogryn's face. But a vast hand closed upon it, and by extension

Rile's forearm. There was a sickening crunch. Rile managed not to scream, though a strangled cry escaped his lips, and I heard the bones in his hand snap like sticks underfoot.

Lanlok released his grip, Rile crumpling at the ogryn's feet. I don't know if he was still conscious, but he did not move as Lanlok batted the flames from his torn shirt, before turning back to the prone figure.

Shard advanced, still firing, aiming for the eyes. She wasn't a bad shot, even outside her craft, but the target was small and protected by an adamantine-like skull. Lanlok had the sense to shield his face with his burly forearm, advancing as she retreated.

I scrambled past as he closed upon Shard, moving to Rile. He was conscious, barely, but debilitated by pain. I rummaged through his greatcoat, seeking a weapon. A grenade, or some other cunning device that might slow our attacker. His pistol was useless, just as mangled as his twisted forearm. I tried not to look at it.

Esec's image drew in beside me.

'This is on you, Simlex. You chose your allies poorly. To think, at one point I respected you.'

I ignored him, still searching, desperate now. But I had no idea what Rile's paraphernalia did. A small silver wand. Three inlaid circles of gold. The grapnel launcher, now devoid of ammo.

Shard suddenly raced past, sprinting towards the hangar's broken entrance and hurling herself through, Lanlok lumbering after, lacking the agility to keep pace. Or perhaps his injuries were slowing him, for I had seen him move far quicker when defending the transmitter. In fact, despite my terror, part of me could not help but note that he seemed less coordinated. Less focused.

He slowed as he passed, looking down at the projection of Esec, slab-like brow furrowed, before his focus shifted to Rile and me.

'Kill them both. Simlex first.'

Lanlok raised his fist. It was larger than my head. Slower or not, there was no way I could dodge it.

But he hesitated.

At least, his hand did. I could see the strain on his face, his desperation to deliver the blow, his arm shaking with the effort. But his fist would not move.

'What are you playing at, you simpleton? Kill him!'

The ogryn redoubled his efforts. But it was as though his wrist were bound by a dozen ropes, and no matter how he strained he could not break them. Even as I watched, his fingers forced themselves open, arm shaking with the strain.

He glanced from me to the dazed Rile, seeking to redirect the blow. His fist surged forward, until I threw myself at Rile, covering him with my body.

And once more he could not land the punch, bellowing in frustration.

'Get out of my head!' he roared, striking his brow with enough force to dent iron, as though seeking to dislodge something from his skull.

'Lanlok, what is wrong with you? Kill him!'

'He won't let me! I have to protect the propagandist!'

'That's me, you cretin. You're supposed to protect me!'

'No! The other voice. The night voice. It told me to protect him. Told me where to be. Like a song in my head!'

Lanlok bellowed again in frustration, straining until his limb thrashed, an errant elbow shattering the Eye projecting Esec's image. It was as if he was pushing against an unseen force, and winning too, at least judging from the foam-flecked curses erupting from his cavernous maw.

But something whistled over my head, and suddenly a dart-like projectile was embedded in his hand.

It was small, barely the length of my finger, and resembled a shard of crystal. Lanlok appeared to have barely felt it, merely frowning at the protrusion before attempting to extract it with his other hand, though his fingers were too large to find easy purchase.

But something was happening. His skin was blackened before, but the spot the crystal protruded from now glinted like onyx, the darkness spreading, tendrils creeping through his flesh, along the knuckle and down the finger. And the hand.

In moments, his fist resembled that of a statue, intricately carved from black glass. But the darkness was not finished, the tendrils now slithering through his forearm, their pace accelerating.

Lanlok still looked surprised. It was not until the contagion reached his elbow that he began to panic, grasping at the limb with his other hand. His forearm shattered under his grip, shards crumbling between his fingers, even as the darkness touched his shoulder and chest.

'What is it? Stop it! Please, God-Emperor, stop it! I was good! I said the words!'

His voice was like a sonorous child's. But not for much longer, for once the blight reached his chest, dark blotches seemed to erupt everywhere, his mammoth heart pumping the toxin throughout his body, consuming flesh and bone. Until at last he was gone, his vast, altered form standing upright but unmoving.

Shard was beside him suddenly, dragging the semi-conscious Rile and me clear. I soon saw why, for the statue that had been Lanlok was swaying. Abruptly, it tumbled back, shattering into jagged shards as it struck the ground.

'Waste of ammo.'

I turned to find Uli crouching in the hangar's shadow, already collapsing his rifle.

He caught my expression and grinned. 'You owe me, propagandist. I have few of those left.'

'You ran to get reinforcements?' I asked, turning to Shard.

'Of course,' she said, her gaze flicking to her brother. 'Rile? Are you still breathing?'

'Seemingly,' he grunted, cradling his ruined forearm. 'But this might prove a problem. I fear the bones are powder.'

He was doing an impressive job keeping his voice level, despite the pain he was in.

'I'll find a medi-pack,' I said, stumbling upright and lurching towards the hangar, picking my way through the ruined door. The *Traderi* and *Aenigma* were both still docked, and I made for the former. The transport pod had already lowered, but before I could access the door's keycode, it slid open.

And there stood Commissar Shard.

His skin was still grey, a veneer of sweat clinging to what flesh was exposed, most of him clad in dressings and rags, though his peaked cap remained pristine.

'Simlex?' he said, blinking. 'What in the Throne's name is going on?'

'I... Sir, I cannot believe you are awake.'

'Who could sleep through that wretched cacophony. Why am I back on the ship? And who is attacking?'

He was intent on the window, and there was no denying the smoke and flames now consuming Edbar.

'Much has happened since your injury,' I began. 'I don't know where I should start.'

He stepped closer, till his face was inches from mine, his stale breath in my face. 'Who shot me?'

'Cesh. He launched the attack. We thought he had slain you, the flight commander too. But she survived, though Cesh's manipulations have since precipitated an uprising. The indentured workers seem intent on retaking Edbar. Esec has deployed his borrowed forces, or possibly launched the first attack, I am unsure. The Láech garrison are involved too, though I don't know about those below. Those in the tunnels where you...'

'Where I was nearly burned alive? I know that part,' he said, pushing past me. 'I see the hangar has been breached.'

'Yes. Lanlok, the ogryn was... Sir, should you be walking?'

He did not reply, dragging himself towards the door, his pace barely faster than mine. He stepped through it, frowning as the spectacle revealed itself. Rile sitting on the ground, examining his injury, Shard beside him. Both met their brother's gaze while Uli, who had only just spotted the commissar, did his best to stay very still and pretend he did not exist.

Commissar Tobia von Shard scrutinised each in turn. He seemed no happier to see them than he had me.

'Lucille,' he said with a nod. 'Rile. It's about time you showed up.'

'Are you well, brother?'

'Tolerable,' the commissar replied. 'I take it you collected your cargo?'

'Yes. Inquisitor Atenbach thanks you for your assistance.'

'Spare me. It was a damn sight more complex than you had made out. Consider it the last time I do your master a favour,' he said, his focus shifting to the flames and smoke. 'So now Edbar burns once more? I think not. Sister, I need your pistol. Unless you intend to lead the offensive?'

She looked at him, then shrugged, rising to her feet before handing him the weapon. He glanced at her bloodied face, but said nothing, merely nodding in thanks.

'Now then,' he said, looking at each of us in turn. 'This is the plan. I will quash the rebellious workers, rally the Láech forces, and ensure Esec's troops stand down. Frankly that cretin is responsible for at least half of this mess.'

I frowned. 'You intend to do this alone?'

'Of course not!' he snapped, glaring at me. 'I have the God-Emperor with me. The only question is what to do with the rest of you.'

Rile opened his mouth to reply. But before he could, Shard stepped in front of him.

'I must face Cesh. Honour demands it.'

'I suppose it does,' the commissar said. 'I am glad to see you taking your role seriously.'

'Forget it. We need to leave,' Rile replied, rising to his feet, arm tucked into the folds of his coat.

'Running away?' the commissar snarled.

'Regrouping and reporting our findings.'

'I do not see the difference.'

'That's because you don't see the big picture. This is more than a squabble over a backwater world. There is a conspiracy beneath it. You must see that.'

'Do you know what I see?' the commissar said, turning to face him. 'I see His city in ruins. I see His soldiers and His servants manipulated into murdering each other. And His precious tithes burning. And while I still walk and breathe, I will bloody well do something about it.'

'I quite agree,' Shard said. 'And that is why I must face Cesh again. Defeat him and prove his words to be lies. In the God-Emperor's name, of course.'

The commissar glared at her.

'Fly well,' he said finally, turning away. 'And now I–'

'Wait a damn minute!' Rile cried, shifting his attention to Shard. 'We are in no position to engage! You don't even have an aircraft. How do you intend to...?'

He trailed off, for she was staring at the *Aenigma*.

'No,' he said. 'There is no way you are flying my ship.'

'Who else is going to do it? You only have one arm.'

Uli, who until now had been easing his cloak over his shoulders in an attempt to disappear, hesitated. He seemed unsure whether to speak, but the commissar stepped in before he had his chance.

'Then it is decided. Rile, you damn well owe me for the favour I did you. If this represents our sister's best shot at redemption, then we should damn well seize it. Simlex, remain here. You will only slow me down. Now I–'

He hesitated, his gaze settling on Uli, who was still only half hidden by the cloak.

'Commissar?' I asked.

'My apologies,' he said, glancing at me. 'My vision is still blurred. I can barely make out any of you. Thought I saw something. Well, it does not matter. Providing these terms are agreeable to you, Rile?'

'I suppose. Assuming you are willing to assist Atenbach in the future.'

'Agreed,' he said, glaring at Shard. 'Get it done.'

'Yes, sir!' she said, offering the crispest salute I had ever seen. Then the commissar departed, striding slowly but purposely in the direction of the thickest smoke. He paused only beside the shattered remains of Lanlok, reaching down and tearing the loaned medal from what was left of the ogryn's uniform.

As he departed, Rile looked at Shard. 'You really want to do this?'

'The alternative is marching to the main hangar and demanding a plane.'

'Esec has probably posted an order to shoot you on sight.'

'Then I suppose it is up to you. Let me fly or let me die.'

She stared at him. He held her gaze a moment before bowing his head.

'Have you even flown a vessel like this?'

'I can fly anything,' she said. She turned to me. 'Simlex, we will–'

'I'm going with you.'

Her eyes narrowed. 'Are you now?'

'If you are facing Cesh, you will need someone to capture the battle. To prove your victory.'

'How do you intend to do that?'

'I can record the inside of the ship. Possibly tap into some of the scanners and–'

'You are not tapping into anything,' Rile warned.

'Then I can record through the cockpit's viewscreen,' I said, looking at Shard. 'Please, I was left behind last time. I don't want that again.'

It was hard to read her expression, with the dirt and scars marring her face. She stepped close, bending her head to my ear.

'Are you sure?' she said. 'Because, between you and me, there is a slim chance I might not make it through this one.'

'Really? Because I heard that Flight Commander Lucille von Shard is invincible. She's never even been shot down.'

CHAPTER FORTY-EIGHT

The *Aenigma* lurched from the hangar and through the skydoor, its passage less than smooth. Shard occupied the pilot's seat, Rile beside her providing guidance. Uli and I were confined to the rear of the cockpit, Iwazar cradled in my lap. The aeldari's arms were folded as he stared sullenly at Shard as she struggled to get to grips with the vessel.

'Insanity,' he muttered. 'I've flown this craft a dozen times. My reflexes and visual acumen are superior to those of any human.'

'Just keep telling yourself that,' Shard replied without looking round. 'Besides, I hardly trust you to complete the assignment. You're xenos. Betrayal is in your nature.'

The craft shuddered, rolling left as Shard accelerated, Rile attempting to coach her through the controls. It was an unusual design, something I doubted was available to conventional forces.

'Oh good,' Uli said, peering at a screen. 'It appears our baby bird has drawn some predators.'

He was right. A score of vessels were ascending from the main hangar some distance hence, visible as miniscule blights on the auspex. Had they been dispatched to attack Cesh or us?

'We need to find him,' Shard murmured, glancing to her brother. 'Any ideas?'

'There are weapon discharges ahead. They appear to be aeldari. Follow the plotted heading.'

'How close are we?'

'Five minutes. Maybe less.'

'Let's make it less.'

She accelerated, smoother now, the force pinning me back in my seat.

'Hmm. More sluggish than a Lightning, but a respectable speed,' Shard muttered, before suddenly dragging the controls to the left. We plunged, the ground rushing to meet us. But she levelled, hurtling over the desert. It was only this low that one really understood the speed of the craft. It seemed impossible that anyone could wage war at such velocities.

'The reinforcements do not seem to be after us.'

That was Rile. Though his ruined right arm was now in a makeshift sling, he was still monitoring the craft's sensors.

Shard frowned. 'Then where are they going?'

'According to vox chatter, they move to intercept Cesh. Led by Shard One.'

'Básk that. Get me a vox-channel. There is no chance I'm letting–'

'Perhaps it would be prudent to follow at a distance. Let them engage first. This craft is designed to evade a standard auspex. If you keep sufficient distance they won't see you.'

'I assume the same can't be said for Cesh?'

'I would suspect not. At least, not for long. But we might momentarily surprise him.'

'What weapons are we carrying?'

'Underslung lascannons. Nose-mounted multi-laser, for the good that will do. There are a couple of missiles, but I'd be reluctant to use them within the atmosphere.'

'Your timidity is noted and judged.'

As they bickered I found my gaze slipping to Uli. Part of me still could not fathom a xenos acting as an inquisitor's agent. I had been taught such creatures should be slain for the sin of existence. Instead, I found myself sharing a cabin with one. Even owing him my life.

'Out with it, propagandist,' Uli said. 'I can tell by the way you are trying to sit still that you are desperate to speak.'

I was. I had so many questions, spiralling like strands in a web. But I knew not where to start, because I no longer had a foundation upon which to build my understanding. And he would no doubt lie, or present a misleading truth.

But when else would I have the opportunity?

'What did you have Shard say to Cesh?' I asked.

'Oh, precious little. The flight commander lacks the nuance to deliver any choice barbs – much of our language is dependent on inflection or body language. I had to settle for a child's insults. Insinuations about his mother's virtue and thus his parentage. That sort of thing.'

'I don't believe you. I do not believe Cesh would emerge from hiding because of a mere insult.'

'Ah, but you forget the aeldari are proud and capricious. We are base creatures who lack your human notions of rigidity and honour, and are enslaved by our base impulses. That is what you believe, isn't it?'

'If that were the case, why would Cesh care if his honour was insulted?'

'Well aren't you the perceptive child,' he said, rolling his eyes.

'All right, propagandist, if you really must have answers, tell me what you know of fate?'

I hesitated. I had heard our preachers declare that humanity's manifest destiny was to conquer the stars. They spoke as if it was ordained, yet in the same breath warned that we must show vigilance and faith, the implication being that a lack of either could subvert this destiny.

'I know very little,' I said.

'A good answer. Very well. To my people the future is... like walking an untended garden. One you can not only visit, but also shape. You clear one path, and it leads to Cesh slaying Shard. You clear another, and she survives. Or died years before. Or was never born. The greatest seers can walk a dozen paths at once, perhaps travel millennia into the future to examine the possibilities. But they do so at great risk, for the further you walk, the more likely you are to stray from the true path, and the harder it is to return. Moreso, the act of observing the future alters it.'

'I don't understand.'

'Of course you don't. You're human. But imagine a seer, or priest, or whomever your kind venerates, informs you that tomorrow you die. Your God-Emperor has foreseen it. There is no way out. Perhaps you would accept your time meekly, praying in church all night, until an unexpected seismic event causes the building to collapse a little after midnight, burying you inside. Or perhaps you decide that, if death comes tomorrow, today you are invincible. You drink, make merry, and take risks. One of which, sadly, leaves you critically injured. Your physicians attempt to heal you, but you succumb to your injuries the following day. In both instances the prediction proved accurate. You died.'

'But neither death would have occurred if the priest had not spoken to me.'

'Precisely.'

'Then it is not a true prediction?'

'Of course it is. You were predicted to die and then died.'

'But only because I was told my future.'

'Exactly.' He frowned, clearly confused. 'What do you fail to grasp? Do you expect seers to merely interpret the future in various ways? The point is to change it. Shape it.'

'And that was why Shard should have died at Cesh's hand? To shape the future?'

'Perhaps. Or perhaps it needed to *appear* that she died in order to lead us down our current path. I merely put this to Cesh, and raised the possibility that his masters may not have been entirely forthcoming regarding his role in manifesting the future. And, if this information was concealed from him, perhaps it was because the intended path does not end well for Cesh.'

He smiled as he spoke, as though indulging the memory. Then his face hardened like marble. He shrugged.

'Something of that nature anyway, the details elude me. And it would seem to have roused him.'

He tapped a screen. Wreckage. Presumably more of our fighters, though it was difficult to say, as all that remained was smouldering metal.

Why had Cesh launched an attack? Surely it would have been prudent to retreat until he had a better understanding of the situation, or confront his superiors. But then the same could be said for Shard. She could have lain low, plotted a retaliatory strike, but instead had launched herself into battle. Perhaps he thought her death was his only hope of ensuring the future came to pass. Or maybe it was simply a mindset they shared, a necessity for any who wished to excel in the role of fighter ace – a willingness to plunge into battle with little thought or care.

Perhaps our peoples were less different than either side might like to admit.

Ahead, faintly, light danced across the sky.

The first explosions registered as we approached the Great Glass Plain.

They were distant, like fireworks, the blasts interspersed by dashes of colour. Vagbon's forces had found Cesh, or perhaps it was the other way round. Her squadron seemed to be working in formation, trying to form a bulwark. It was not a terrible strategy, unleashing such a torrent of firepower that Cesh had nowhere to go. But the terrain did not favour them, the glass beneath magnifying the effect of Cesh's holofield, his flickering alter-images manifesting both above and below.

We were still some distance off, but the view from the cockpit began to shift, glass plain supplanted by sky as Shard began a vertical ascent. Higher we climbed, until the piercing blue receded into the darkening void, its emptiness punctured only by the dimmest of stars.

'You know this is a warp-capable craft?' Rile murmured as we rose.

'Yes.'

'You could simply remain on this course. Leave it behind. Atenbach would have a place for you.'

'I tried running once, didn't care for it and didn't get far. I will not do so again.'

He nodded, tapping a few controls with his left hand.

'Cesh will spot our descent. Even the *Aenigma*'s ability to evade detection has limits, and re-entry tends to draw attention.'

'I know. It's not about stealth. It's about speed.'

She tilted us forward, Deighton filling the viewscreen, and accelerated, hurtling towards the distant planet like a falling star. Firefly-like sparks brushed past, each burning like a tiny ember, the glow rippling out. I was surprised by the colours – oranges and reds flaring as the very atmosphere was ionised by the speed of our descent, the light washing over the craft like ocean waves.

As we hurtled onwards, I could not help but note that this had been Plient's strategy. And it had not been successful.

Ahead, the glass desert suddenly emerged. It was too high for a sense of scale, the only landmarks the ever-mutable light dancing across the plains, Cesh's broken silhouette split between a dozen identical images.

'Magenta. Yellow-green, green-yellow.'

Shard muttered the colours like a prayer. And suddenly I had nothing but doubts. This was her gambit? A fiery descent paired with rudimentary colour theory? I could not look, my gaze falling upon Uli.

'There are some grav-chutes in the back,' he said, jabbing his thumb to the rear door. 'Not that it will help at this speed.'

We were close enough now that I could see the individual aircraft. Their line had faltered, the bulwark bedevilled by losses, the light spilling between and through them, seemingly untouchable.

'Cyan. Yellow-green... Or was it green-yellow?'

I closed my eyes, muttering a prayer to the God-Emperor, but as before, I saw only darkness and felt nothing. We were to be tested. Whatever we faced, we faced it alone.

'Magenta, cyan... Light him up.'

Rile flicked a switch and the nose-mounted multi-laser unleashed a barrage of red bolts. I do not think they were aimed, other than to avoid our own craft, and none were likely to cause much damage even with a direct hit. But Cesh would not have known that. Not at first. For even I could see the colours shift as he evaded the barrage. He must have slowed because, for just a moment, the facets coalesced, before once again exploding into a swarm of bladed diamonds that hurtled towards us.

'Wait for the scarlet. Wait for the scarlet… Where the hell is the scarlet?'

Iwazar chirped in my lap. Perhaps a warning, though there was nothing I could do but watch as the blades of light accelerated and drew closer. A ripple undulated across the swarm, hawk-like silhouettes flickering in and out of focus. There came a flash of scarlet, a bolt of blazing cyan erupting towards us, just as Shard pulled hard to the right.

And fired.

Something burst in the sky, the colours and scattered forms collapsing in on themselves.

And there it was. Just for a moment, the predatory shape of the aeldari aircraft, smoke issuing from its knife-like wing. Crimson. For some reason I hadn't expected it to be crimson.

'Screw you!' Shard exclaimed, punching the air. 'Not so sneaky now, you little bastard. Not when I know where you are!'

The craft shimmered and was gone, breaking into a kaleidoscope of overlaid colours that spilled above and through us, even as we levelled, the images flowing like rain on a rooftop.

We dived, just as twin bolts nearly sheared through the hull.

'No,' she muttered. 'Seen it before. Seen it before. Same old trick.'

She rolled, twisting about and hurtling towards the coalescing swarm. I felt my stomach lurch, and had to keep my mouth clamped shut for fear of vomiting. It wasn't just being thrown about inside the cockpit, but the way the sky and glass plain rolled across the screen, the light refracting in both, until I could no longer tell direction.

'You getting this, Simlex?' she sneered. 'I'd hate to think your presence a waste.'

I could not reply, only clutch Iwazar as tight as I could and pray my grip would hold. Once more we raced to the light, the colours rippling.

'Green-yellow... blue... cyan, cyan... scarlet.'

She fired. The blast clipped something, but we almost instantly surged left, a cyan bolt flashing past the viewscreen. But it seemed we still carried too much momentum from the descent, something which Shard, in her excitement, had neglected to compensate for.

'Throne!' she said, wrenching back, the *Aenigma* protesting as its engines struggled against the gravitational force. We hurtled past an Imperial craft, almost clipping it. I kept expecting us to stall and plummet, but she held us, the craft levelling feet from the gleaming landscape.

Just in time for a blast to strike the ship.

We shook, but the armour held, though I could smell melted metal, and smoke was visible through the screen.

'Oh, he's mad,' Shard muttered as we accelerated. 'Mad and in pursuit. Wasn't really how I wanted this to go.'

She rolled, something flashing past the viewscreen.

'And that was a new move.'

'Because he is done playing with you,' Uli warned. 'Before, his engagement was minimal, sufficient only to achieve his goal. That has changed.'

'He's behind us,' Rile muttered. 'Holofield must be compromised because I'm getting a reading. But I can't get a lock. He keeps flickering in and out.'

'You have any tail-mounted weapons on this thing?'

'No.'

'Decoy flares?'

'No.'

'Why not?'

'Because I do not tend to be pursued.'

'Fine,' she said. 'Then we must improvise.'

The lascannon flared. There was no target beside the ground itself. But the glass-like plain refracted the blast, searing bolts ricocheting in all directions, Shard somehow steering a path through it.

'He's pulled up. But is still in pursuit. He is faster than us. Stand by. Incom–'

We lurched, the blast hurtling by, visible on the viewscreen. Ahead I could see darkness, the yawning maw of a pit we had once traversed in Esec's barge.

Another blast. Closer this time. Cesh had been surprised by our initial assault, but he had recovered and seemed to have our measure. We weren't going to make it.

Perhaps Shard thought so too, because suddenly she dived. I just had time to see a cascade of light scream past before she cut the power.

The ship was suddenly dark, dead, and tumbling into the gaping chasm beneath.

CHAPTER FORTY-NINE

We fell.

I felt the craft tumbling around me but could see little, the only light Iwazar's sensors, which did little to dispel the darkness. It was like Bacchus again, that moment where the green lightning had severed us from realspace, and we had tumbled through somewhere beyond.

It felt that we fell for an age. I kept expecting an impact. Foolish of course, for at that speed we would be dead the moment we struck solid ground. And I would feel nothing, merely be swallowed by the endless black. There would be no record of our loss unless Inquisitor Atenbach would pause to make a brief note in some grimoire. More likely a data-scribe would do it on his behalf. Esec would already be recruiting a new Shard, either an acceptable substitute or a literal replacement.

And I?

I would be as nothing. My work was already censored. What little persisted would be subsumed and trampled by the latest wave of picts forged to preserve an idealised Imperium that I doubted ever really existed. At least I would not be aware of it, for as we tumbled I realised something I had always known deep down. There was no seat at the God-Emperor's table, no respite. Just pain then nothingness. That was all we could hope for.

But, faintly, I could hear Shard counting. She had nearly reached one hundred.

Then light flared. Dim, but sufficient to divide the dark, as the *Aenigma*'s systems arose from their slumber. I felt a shudder as the craft fired its stabilisers, our descent slowing, until we were suspended in the black. Perhaps, far above, there would be a faint halo, the entrance to the pit. But, for us, our view confined to what could be seen through the cockpit, there was only an empty void.

'Did he follow us down?'

Shard's voice was barely a whisper. Somewhat pointless, as her words would never carry beyond the hull. But I understood the impulse. There was a sombreness to the place. I recalled Esec's theory, that this vast expanse was the site of a detonation, some terrible weapon from before the Imperium's founding leaving a permanent scar upon the world.

Rile was intent on the craft's auspex.

'He does not seem to have followed,' he said. 'I do not think his craft is capable of hovering. Not for anything other than a landing at least. If he wishes to descend, it is either slow enough that we could pick him off, or at terminal velocity. There would be no middle ground.'

'He might think we're dead,' I ventured.

'I doubt it,' Rile replied. 'Not after last time. According to the auspex there were still several Imperial craft in the airspace when we dived. I assume Cesh will seek to eliminate them before he heads down here.'

'Returns.'

We turned as one to Uli, who was intent on a viewport.

'Returns?' I said.

'I assume so. Who else would be using a webway gate?'

Shard and I exchanged glances, unsure as to his meaning. But Rile was staring intently at him.

Uli caught the acolyte's expression. 'It's right there. To our left. Do humans even have functional senses? I'm surprised you are capable of dressing without a magnifying lens.'

I tried to follow his gaze, but there was only blackness.

'It's too dark.'

'Try visiting Commorragh. There you will learn to appreciate the true meaning of that word. However briefly.'

Shard flicked a couple of switches, activating the external lumens. It was still difficult to see, but dimly I could identify an arch bound into the crystalline rock. It seemed to encircle us, though the light was insufficient to illuminate the full breadth of the chasm. Whatever this webway gate was, it appeared ancient. Weathered. The figures carved into the edifice lacked features, the detail long since eroded. But, though humanoid, they seemed a shade too tall and slender to be human, and the coiled runescript bore little resemblance to any human language I was aware of.

'A gate to the webway,' Rile said, voice hushed in awe. 'Is it active?'

'Not currently, or we would have tumbled through it.'

'Could it be active?'

Uli shrugged. 'I don't know. There are many that have closed, or lead to nowhere. Or worse. I would strongly advise we keep our distance.'

He too spoke in hushed tones, his hand straying to a gemstone embedded in his armour's chestplate. I only noticed it because it too seemed to emanate a very faint glow.

'But an active webway gate would explain Cesh's ability to appear and disappear?'

'Yes. His base of operations could be light years from here.'

Shard turned to Rile. 'Dare I even ask what a webway gate is?'

'Like a bridge, linking one point in space to another. It was how the aeldari once traversed the galaxy, but most are now lost or destroyed.'

'So, what I'm hearing is that we have inadvertently sought refuge in Cesh's escape route?'

'Possibly.'

Shard closed her eyes and leant back in her seat. 'The God-Emperor really does hate me.'

'In His defence, you give Him good reason.'

'Can we destroy it?'

'Absolutely not,' Rile replied. 'We must preserve it. Atenbach will want to… He would caution that, if it is an active gate, then attempting to destroy it could cause a catastrophic explosion. Indeed, a prior attempt might well explain this pit and the plain of glass above.'

'But is this not a good thing?' I ventured. 'Surely we can arrange an ambush? Wait for his return and–'

'Incoming!'

Shard lurched us to the side, avoiding the burning remnants of an Imperial craft as it hurtled down into the darkness beneath.

'Cesh is dropping planes on us now?'

'Why not?' Shard said. 'We are trapped down a proverbial mineshaft. There is no need to engage directly – gravity can do most of the work. We are fortunate his vessel has no bombs or missiles.'

She then frowned, looking to Rile. 'It doesn't, does it?'

'We'll soon know. Though I suspect, even if he does not, it won't take Cesh long to find another way of casting ruin down upon us.'

'Still, there might be one option,' Shard murmured, turning her gaze to me. 'You remember our ploy last time the odds were impossible?'

'Conjuring a counterfeit armada? That was Plient's work. Iwazar is not what it was, and neither am I. Besides, our foe is not a dim-witted ork. He will not be deceived by a handful of faux aircraft.'

'No. Not a handful. But perhaps just one.'

The *Aenigma*'s airlock was little more than an enlarged dress closet. Sufficient space for Uli and I to stand shoulder to shoulder, despite my ill-fitted pressure suit. His attire was sleeker – the same perfectly moulded undersuit he wore beneath his cloak now topped by a helm tapering to a point at the crown, his face obscured by a smooth featureless dome, lacking either eyeholes or a visor.

Beside and above us, Iwazar waited patiently, its lenses intent on the door.

'You ready?' Shard asked.

Uli engaged his vox. 'Let us just get this charade over with.'

'Stand by.'

The door eased open into the dark. Even with the ship's external lumens and my own shoulder-mounted version, it was like stepping into the void. Only I would not float, suspended like an insect skating a pond. No, it would be a drop into darkness. Rile had supplied me with a grav-chute, more for reassurance than anything else, for it struck me that such a device would not prevent my fall, merely extend it.

'Well, so step forth the expendables,' Uli sighed, before bending his knees and leaping into the dark. He moved an impossible distance, somehow finding purchase on the cracked crystalline walls of our tomb. Perhaps his attire possessed some micro-suction devices at the toes or fingertips. Perhaps.

I made no such attempt, gripping the safety line so tight that were I not wearing gloves, my fingernails would have bloodied my palms. But I had to be close. For while Iwazar needed little encouragement, surging into the darkness, its lenses were immediately intent on the webway gate, assessing its curious architecture. I gave myself a little to it, enough to guide the device without risking my grip.

'Iwazar. Come,' I murmured, even as I willed it to heel. It did, reluctantly, its lenses now focused on the ship, cataloguing its every crevice, mapping the shape. It still wouldn't be a flawless copy. But perhaps it needn't be.

'Shard? I have it.'

'Good. Uli? Are you in position?'

'If I have to be.'

The *Aenigma* lurched forward, its stabilisers slowly taking it to the edge of the pit. Up close it was clear the glass-like crystal was worn, jagged, but Uli had secured a cable. As I drew near he reached out, attaching it to a clasp on my borrowed pressure suit.

'Ready?' he asked. I could hear the grin.

'No. But we lack the luxury of time,' I said, reaching out a hand. He took it, hauling me onto a narrow ledge.

On my departure, the *Aenigma* descended, disappearing into the darkness beneath, its lumens fading from sight.

Then there was nothing. Only the faint glimmer of my suit's shoulder-mounted lumen. A candle against the night.

I waited. It felt an age, but Shard's instructions had been specific. Uli would give the signal.

'Nervous, propagandist?' he asked.

'Do you enjoy my suffering?'

'A little, though less than some. It's more curiosity. I rarely get to see the galaxy through eyes as naive as yours. Even Rile, human as he is, has seen enough to lose that innocence. And as for the flight commander? I do not think I need to tell you how disillusioned she has grown. But you are at the beginning of that journey. It's like watching a child fall in love for the first time, then watching as their heart is broken. It's... refreshing. Almost like experiencing it once again.'

'Glad my heartbreak provides a service.'

'See? Already you walk the path of the cynic. In fact, you probably think the journey complete. But there is so much further you can go. I will watch with great interest. If you survive.'

'If we survive, surely?'

'...Rile just gave me the signal. When you are ready, propagandist.'

In truth I did not know. I had never attempted something like this, despite my earlier bluster. Esec was the one who controlled Edbar's transmitter, who had co-opted the Feed to issue forth his lies and mistruths. I did not even know how it functioned, but I felt Iwazar's connection every time Esec dispatched a vid. It was like an electromagnetic sliver that threaded through Edbar to places beyond my reach. But I didn't need to stretch that far, to broadcast my message across half a continent. All I needed was to send an invitation.

'*Cesh!*'

Shard's voice, her message pre-recorded whilst I fumbled into the pressure suit. Her face scarred and hardened. Esec had been foolish in his attempts to sanitise her image, for the scars gave authenticity.

'*It would seem you have me cornered,*' she continued. '*I imagine you lurk above, ready to strike the instant I emerge. But I found your little secret down here. Your exit.*'

I shifted the image, displaying the dilapidated webway gate, lit only by Iwazar's lenses. The seer-skull was more than happy to trace its confines, relaying it through the data-veil.

'*This is a webway gate, isn't it? Don't be so surprised, we humans are less ignorant than you'd like to think. This is how you appear at will, vanish as desired. A place you can slink away to whenever you need to lick your wounds.'*

I cut back to Shard's grinning face.

'Maybe I cannot best you. Not alone. But I bet even that xenos craft of yours requires some kind of fuel and ammunition. How long will you last without both? Months, for all I know, but in the end your engines will fail, leaving you stranded on this world. I may be trapped down here, but I can ensure you won't escape either. Even if I must sacrifice myself to do it.'

'Wait!'

Cesh. Panicked, I interrupted the playback, looping a few seconds and splicing in distortion, hoping to give the appearance of Shard pausing.

'You cannot do that. You do not understand. If you sever that gate, you could inflict catastrophic damage to this planet. It could be an extinction-level event. And my people… This gate is vital. Stand down, let me depart and this is over. None of us have to die.'

A part of me wanted to believe him. But it did not matter, for Shard could not answer. Unless I interjected? But if I did so, he might suspect the ruse.

I had no other option, cutting the vox completely. Perhaps he thought we were debating his request. It was still possible. I could vox the *Aenigma*, at least present the option.

'He lies. It is too late. This is now our path.'

Uli. I knew his voice, but had never heard him speak so. No mockery or wry wit. He was heartbroken, horrified. He knew what had to happen, had steeled himself for it.

Ants. Cesh had once told me that his people had less regard for human lives than they had for insects. If Uli shared these sentiments, then I could not imagine how it would pain him to sacrifice an aeldari life for ours.

'There is no other way?' I asked.

'There are always other ways. But this is the right path, the only one that has a chance at setting us on the right course. And sometimes a sacrifice is required.'

I nodded, syncing fully with Iwazar. It had been years since I had attempted something this audacious. Not since Bacchus, where the seer-skull had conjured a small armada to support Shard. But this was nothing so ostentatious. I only needed one vessel.

There it was. The *Aenigma*. I doubt it would have fooled an aeldari up close, for even a human would have noted the image was not entirely opaque. But in the darkness? And relayed through the projector of a compromised seer-skull? It might be enough.

I released it through the Feed, giving Cesh a few moments to appreciate the image, before adding the final line of Shard's monologue.

'The Emperor protects!'

Her voice was thunder, and with her cry the faux-*Aenigma* fired, twin beams of light seemingly striking the rim of the webway gate. I let it sit for a moment, before projecting a series of apocalyptic explosions plucked from Iwazar's memory. The Green Storm, the raid on the supply lines, even Cesh's own airstrikes, the scraps of footage bleeding together until the hololithic eruption blazed so bright it lit the pit, the crystalline structure refracting the light and sending it cascading up and down the shaft.

Abruptly, I cut the feed. Darkness.

Would he take the bait? It was a gamble. I doubted he could see through the illusion, for it was but images. But he might possess a means of monitoring the gate. The plan depended on him reacting quickly, thinking his human foes were ignorant and violent enough to risk planetary annihilation just to spite him.

I suppose war is about playing to your strengths.

It seemed we dwelt an age in darkness. Then I saw a flicker. A light. It was impossible to judge its speed at first, for there was no frame of reference, but the spec of light expanded, the thrum of its engines echoing through the shaft.

Cesh.

He was moving quickly, hurtling towards us. In the final moments, he slowed, impossibly so – his vessel should have been ripped apart by the conflicting forces. It decelerated to a near crawl, emptying the xenos equivalent of docking stabilisers, until it sat, suspended a few dozen yards from us.

It was so quiet, its engines barely hummed.

Already, Cesh must have seen through our deception, for the gate was still intact. Perhaps he thought Shard's rash attack had rebounded upon her, the crystalline structure refracting the blasts. Or perhaps he sought his deceiver, for the craft seemed to be slowly rotating, as though scanning its surroundings. I glanced to where Uli should have been, but he was gone, obscured by his cloak.

Then it faced me. A spectre suspended in the shadows. All I could think was how smooth the vessel appeared, the sections bound without rivet or bolt, the hull adorned with glittering gems. It was beautiful. And terrible. And slowly gliding towards me.

It was then I heard the roar echo from beneath.

The *Aenigma*. It was powering towards us, visible only by the light blazing from its multi-laser. Cesh responded immediately, not retaliating but instead fleeing, ascending from the darkness towards the waiting sky, where his speed and agility could be used to best advantage. His silhouette was already fractured into shards, their light mirrored in the crystalline walls of the chasm. In an instant it was impossible to separate him from the infinite alters manifested by his holofield.

But the same was true of the multi-laser.

Its crimson bolts ricocheted between the pit's glass-like sides, the barrage multiplied each time it struck the chasm walls, lighting up the darkness. And no matter how fast he was, how nimble, Cesh could not dodge them all. There was an explosion as one struck his vessel. Then another. Still he accelerated, desperate to be freed from the passageway, to reach the sanctuary of the open sky. In seconds he would be clear.

Another explosion, though faint. Even through Iwazar's lenses I could barely make him out. He was almost there, except smoke now gushed from his rear, his alters flickering in and out of focus.

'Got him.'

Two crimson beams erupted from beneath. They struck, and his craft was torn asunder, its wreckage tumbling down the shaft. Moments later, Shard hurtled past, even as the gate went dark, her passage inflicting a shockwave of sound that buffeted me like a leaf in a storm.

I felt something give, the crystalline glass cracking above, the darkness below reaching out to me. I lurched forward, but stooped suddenly, my fall arrested. I glanced round, the movement impeded by my pressure helm.

Uli.

His cloak thrown back, hand wrapped about the torn clasp that once adhered me to the wall.

'That's two you owe me, propagandist.'

CHAPTER FIFTY

My hands trembled when they summoned me.

But I gripped my cane, steadied myself, and followed the clerk along the passageway, Iwazar trailing in my wake. It was my first time in this section of Edbar. The walls were polished marble, adorned with relics I assumed held some relevance to the population of Deighton. A dusty tome, sealed in amber, apparently containing the words first spoken when the God-Emperor arose from beneath the sands and gifted language to its people. Clay tablets, long since worn smooth, their original decrees a mystery. There were blades and busts, paintings and preserved fingerbones of former rulers.

I passed them all, cane tapping against the stone, my other hand clenched tight to conceal the trembling. The last time I had received such formal summons, the subsequent debacle had cost me my status, reputation and health.

And this time the stakes were so much higher.

Two Scions guarded the door. I faltered as I saw them, for

both wore the ochre-and-midnight-blue heraldry of Propagandist Esec. Except it was not his, of course. It never had been. The colours were Colonel Surling's, his troops merely loaned. But when I saw them, I once more recalled those soldiers who had barred our path to the hangar. I could still picture my would-be saviour shouldering his rifle and offering his hand. Right before I killed him in cold blood. I was thankful I never saw his face, for it would have been one more to haunt me.

Do not think of it, I told myself. *Not for the next few minutes.*

Neither guard acknowledged us, besides opening the doors. The room beyond was a disappointment. I'd expected something ornate, but it appeared to be a scribe's chambers recently repurposed. The plaintiffs were seated in hastily assembled docks, separated by a plascrete partition, but I did not look at them, my gaze fixed on the tribunal itself.

There were four of them – three sitting together, another to one side. I bowed, glanced to each in turn.

Colonel Surling sat in the centre, perhaps indicating his voice carried most weight. Not a good sign, given his prior connection to Esec. On each side were Admiral Desora and Wing Commander Prospherous, all three stony-faced. Unsurprising, given they had been forced to return from the front lines, after Edbar nearly fell to the very workers who had supposedly opened the gates. It reflected poorly on all concerned, except for one man.

Commissar Tobia von Shard.

He was the fourth figure, sitting apart from the others. His uniform was immaculate, though the skin beneath was still marked by flame and blade. He did not acknowledge me when I entered, his gaze cold and hard. And he looked by far the most welcoming of the three.

They were supported by guards clad in three disparate uniforms, perhaps an indication that the trio were far from united. They were supported by a motley collection of scribes, clerks and serfs tasked with ensuring proceedings ran smoothly. A servo-skull in rather better condition than Iwazar hovered beside them, reams of parchment cascading from its underside – presumably a record of proceedings. Iwazar seemed curious, attempting to drift towards its doppelganger until I glared at it. Meekly, it fell in behind me.

'Scribe Kile Simlex,' Surling began, his gaze flicking between me and a roll of parchment. 'You have been called here to provide your... perspective on recent events. I assume introductions are not required?'

'No, sir.'

'Good. This has already occupied enough of our time. Do you so swear to speak only the truth, lest His light scour the flesh from your bones?'

'I do so swear.'

'Right. Then to business,' Surling said. 'We have two accused on trial, Simlex. Frankly, an argument could be made that you should be seated beside them.'

He glared at me. It wasn't hard to guess who thought I should be in the dock.

'May I ask the prospective charges, sir?'

'Murder for one thing. You have been accused of slaughtering a squad of my Scions.'

'I have?' I said, setting my face in a frown. 'With respect, sir, if a man of my limited capabilities were capable of dispatching a squad of the Imperium's finest troops, then we are in dire straits indeed.'

'Perhaps,' Surling replied testily. 'In any event, due to the lack of evidence and a statement of support from Commissar Shard, we have decided not to investigate these claims further. But you should note that decision was not unanimous.'

I glanced to the commissar, who remained stony-faced.

He was perhaps the only one of us who had come through this debacle unscathed, his star ascending. After all, he had single-handedly quashed the uprising, rallied the Láech, and persuaded Esec's forces to stand down. It was apparently a very moving speech.

'The commissar also noted that, during recent events, you were under his employ and had unique access to one of the accused. Is that correct?'

'Yes, sir.'

'Then please enlighten us, scribe,' Surling said, nodding to the docks. 'What transpired that led us so close to disaster? And I remind you to speak only the truth.'

'I understand, sir. As a former propagandist there is nothing more precious to me than preserving the God-Emperor's Truth. That is why it is so painful for me to see a colleague and peer, someone I once admired, having betrayed this principle. In my opinion, Propagandist Esec is guilty of heresy. Specifically, the heresy of undermining the God-Emperor's Truth.'

'Lies!'

The voice came from the dock. I shifted my gaze, and finally locked eyes with Esec. I cannot say detainment suited him. His shaved head was now bristling with stubble, his ornate robes replaced by a prisoner's garb. And his eyes had that hollowed quality that was all too familiar. I doubt he'd slept much.

'This man is a toad!' he continued. 'A bootlicker for the whole wretched von Shard family! He is jealous of my success. Bitter. His word is worth nothing.'

'The accused will be silent!' Prospherous roared, glaring at the man.

'Indeed,' Surling said, shuffling in his seat. 'But I should warn you, Scribe Simlex, that you make a very serious accusation. As it stands, Propagandist Esec is accused of failing to maintain order and wilful misuse of resources. What you describe is something far worse.'

'With respect, sir, I have evidence I would submit in support of my accusations.'

'Fine. Proceed with your evidence. But for your sake I hope it is compelling.'

'Thank you, sir.'

Iwazar's holo-lens flared. Two picts were displayed in parallel. One of Shard from Esec's vids, the second her battered and bloodied face as she issued the final challenge to Cesh.

'These two picts are not the same soldier,' I began. 'Look to the scars, the skin tone. Little amendments to the features. Even the colour saturation. Esec has, since the beginning of this campaign, manipulated his vids of Flight Commander von Shard.'

'By smoothing blemishes?'

'At first. But he soon progressed to crafting falsified images for swift dissemination. That was supposedly how Edbar fell, through Esec's relentless campaign of vids, all featuring the flight commander. A campaign that embedded her likeness within the minds of its citizens. She became a symbol of the liberators, and by extension the greater Imperium. But even that was not sufficient for him. He initiated a programme to have all squadrons flying under her colours, so she was at the forefront of every conflict. Now, I am no expert in the Aeronautica, but I believe that is highly unusual.'

'That is true,' Wing Commander Prospherous said, nodding. 'Aces should have their own heraldry. Assuming another's, even unintentionally, is a tremendous faux pas.'

'Indeed, sir, and I hasten to add I do not fault those who followed such orders – that is a soldier's lot. But once Shard's image was suitably ingrained, once it embodied the very spirit of the war effort, Esec initiated his true plan. It began small – leaking footage of those pilots adorned in her colours being shot down, or slaying the mamutida, beasts sacred to the indigenous population. There were attacks, and deaths, all muddied by conflicted explanations. Soon the citizens of Edbar were unable to discern what was real and what was not, and began questioning everything. Was she even real? Was the whole thing a deception employed so we could seize their land? For if we lied about their supposed liberator, how else were they deceived?'

'That campaign was initiated by the aeldari,' Surling replied. 'We have all seen the vids.'

'But they could not have done it alone. Esec collaborated with them.'

A hush fell over those present, Desora recoiling in horror. Even Surling seemed taken aback by the boldness of my claim. I plunged on before he could interject.

'The aeldari could not breach our data-veil. Not without someone on the inside, someone weak of spirit who could be manipulated. That person was Esec. He traded his loyalty to the God-Emperor for xenos tech to advance his position. He used his influence to manoeuvre our troops so they could be ambushed, then captured the footage to use against us. Why else was his slow, lumbering craft spared during every attack, when dozens of our fighters were lost?'

Surling was staring at me, his eyes blazing but his manner calm. 'Am I to take it you have proof of this?'

'Indeed, sir.'

I reached into my robe, and withdrew a sealed scroll.

'Upon this document is irrefutable evidence that the accused has been utilising xenos technology. His so-called Eyes? Those unpleasant flying devices? They are in fact a crude xenos Abominable Intelligence.'

There were some gratifying gasps. Desora flinched as though

struck, while Prospherous leant in, staring intently at the scroll. Surling was quite still.

'Do you wish to respond?' he said, glaring at Esec.

'Only to damn this as the lie it is! My devices are unusual, innovative even, but that is merely because they are an uncommon design incorporating technology from a distant forge world. I have the documents and papers confirming that the Adeptus Mechanicus have sanctioned the machines.'

'Such documents can be falsified,' I said. 'Or such services bought.'

'Bought?' Surling glared. 'You would now besmirch the tech-priests as well?'

'I can only speak of what I see,' I replied. 'But if your lords would unseal this scroll, I think it covers the situation better than I ever could.'

A clerk was already beside me, reaching for it. But when he saw the insignia emblazoned upon the seal, he flinched. I could not blame him. Even the officers in charge seemed to shrink from it when they caught sight of it. For all knew the mark of an inquisitor.

I cleared my throat, continuing, 'Agents sanctioned by Inquisitor Atenbach, the renowned hunter of xenos, have confirmed that the devices employed by Esec contain xenos technologies. Perhaps Esec used them to spy on the aeldari's behalf. Or perhaps they were merely a gift to buy his loyalty. I do not know, though I hope an interrogator can uncover the truth.'

Esec surged from his seat. 'This is a lie. I never made such–'

'You will be silent!' the commissar roared, now on his feet. Esec shrank before his wrath, and even the judges appeared somewhat cowed. In truth I felt pity for him. Because, on this matter, I did not think he was lying. On some distant world he had simply been given an opportunity and taken advantage of it. Perhaps he had suspected something and decided not to question it. Perhaps not. But the fact his treachery was inadvertent would not save him.

The commissar straightened his cap. 'Apologies for the outburst. I recused myself from these proceedings on the basis of propriety, given one of the accused is my sister. But I will be damned before I let this hack interrupt proceedings again.'

'...Thank you, commissar,' Prospherous said, turning to the scribe beside him. 'Seize everything. The barge, the Eyes. Destroy any you cannot contain. Simlex, you may be required to assist with this.'

'Of course, sir. And, if you have no other questions, shall I take my leave?'

'Not yet,' Surling said, raising his hand. 'There is still the matter of Flight Commander Shard.'

'Ah. Yes, my apologies,' I said, as though this matter had slipped my mind. 'Though I should note that I spent little time with the flight commander during this period.'

'Indeed? You then deny Esec's claim that you are beholden to the von Shard family?'

'Beholden? I would not say so, sir. The commissar is my benefactor, but I only worked with the flight commander once, several years ago. The project was ultimately unsuccessful, though I gather some of the footage was appropriated by Propagandist Esec. And Flight Commander Shard certainly has no fond feelings for me. She made that abundantly clear in the fighting pits. My jaw still aches.'

'Yes. A rather extreme reaction,' Prospherous noted, raising an eyebrow. 'Do you know why she lashed out at you, a lowly scribe?'

I shrugged. 'Perhaps she did not think my work flattering. But that is neither here nor there. Much as I may dislike Flight

Commander Shard on a personal level, I have seen nothing to suggest she has committed any crime.'

'Indeed? Because Esec has presented us with some quite damning footage of her. I will spare a civilian of your sensitivity the details, but there were those amongst us so offended they considered executing her on the spot.'

'I know nothing of this footage. But, if it was presented by Propagandist Esec, then I would suggest it inadmissible. Behold.'

Iwazar's projector flared, a view of Esec materialising, once more sat upon his throne.

'We have so much footage of her. What you shot on Bacchus has not even been used yet. I've done more than one fully functional facsimile. Look!'

The image shifted to a flickering, counterfeit Shard.

'Good day to you, Propagandist Esec. And to you, Scribe Simlex.'

The image was still a little disjointed, but I'd worked hard to tighten it in preparation for the trial.

'I can make her say almost anything,' Esec said, grinning, before the image collapsed.

The three judges exchanged glances. Surling spoke next.

'You believe Esec has falsified other vids of Shard?'

'You heard his boast,' I replied. 'And, whatever else may be said, I cannot fault his skills. Given time and incentive I'm sure he could make it seem like anyone said anything, particularly if he thought casting aspersions would serve his cause. I would postulate that whatever heresies were uttered in this doctored clip are Esec's words, not the flight commander's.'

'That is a lie!' Esec protested from the docks. 'It was all her! She was–'

The guard struck him. Hard. He folded, vanishing from my sight beneath the stand while I returned my gaze to the judges.

'I will submit my evidence for independent scrutiny. That

said, I would note that the accused's assertion I fabricated this evidence is further proof that he knows such acts are possible. Why? Because that is the basis of his work. Lies and deceptions.'

'You have certainly given us much to consider,' Admiral Desora murmured. 'But one thing puzzles me. When questioned about her first encounter with Cesh and her miraculous survival, Flight Commander Shard claimed to have little memory of the events. She said we should speak to you. Why? You claim to have no real connection to her, no knowledge or friendship.'

I sighed, bowing my head.

'Because I did share a friendship with someone close to her. Flight Sergeant Plient.'

'Who?' Desora frowned, turning to the other judges.

'He was a mechanical,' Prospherous replied. 'Served as the flight commander's personal attendant. A good man. Loyal. I gather he was a casualty of the uprising?'

'Sadly, the truth is somewhat more heart-wrenching,' I said. 'In that first duel with Cesh, when she supposedly died? It was Plient who flew in her stead.'

Gasps again, glances exchanged, Surling watching intently.

'Explain.'

'A team of aeldari infiltrated Edbar and attempted to eliminate Shard before she could face Cesh. And they very nearly succeeded. She fought them, slew several as I understand it, but it was not enough. Their foul weapons not only inflicted the injuries you see on her face, but also temporarily clouded her thoughts and memories. A typical aeldari trick, intended to weaken her before the battle. She was left addled, compromised. I am unsurprised she could not remember these events. They must be a blur.'

I looked to Prospherous. 'I suspect you can relate, sir. I gather you suffered an injury on Bacchus that left you unable to recall the previous few days?'

'Careful, Simlex. I am not the one on trial.'

'Of course not, sir. I merely wish to illustrate her condition. In such a state she could not fly, but if she did not her reputation would be ruined, and perhaps our morale broken. Wing Sergeant Plient would not allow that. He forced her to stand down, restrained her and took her place, hoping to fool her enemies into believing their plan had worked, buying her time to recover.'

'Is that right?' Surling said. 'I suppose you have Inquisitorial evidence to support this as well?'

'Alas no, sir. Plient left a message in his workshop outlining these events, which is how I uncovered them. However, I believe the facility was destroyed by Esec's troops? Perhaps they were covering for the aeldari, I do not know.'

'And is this your final testimony? That Flight Commander Shard was but a pawn, a victim of circumstances?'

I rose slowly, supporting my weight on the desk before me.

'My lords, we are all servants of the Imperium. As a former propagandist, I was tasked with speaking the truth so our citizens would know the glory of our victories. I ask you, is not Flight Commander Shard a proven hero? A soldier with countless victories and unparalleled skill? Do we really think a craven xenos could match her in a fair contest? Is that what we think of our best and brightest? No, for if that were the case, what would it say about the state of the Imperium?'

I looked them each in the eye, before turning to the fallen Esec.

'No, the crime here is that a cheap vid-crafter, a non-combatant I might add, conspired with aeldari forces. But despite their attempts to discredit, cripple, and eliminate Flight Commander Shard, they were unsuccessful, because of the sacrifice of a loyal servant of the Imperium. I swear this to be true in the

God-Emperor's name, and when Inquisitor Atenbach's forces arrive I will gladly repeat my testimony to him in person. Indeed, at his agent's request, I have already provided a detailed timeline of events, as well as the hololithic evidence that supports my assertions.'

Surling regarded me for a moment.

'How presumptuous of you,' he said, unsealing the inquisitor's scroll. I knew roughly what it said, Rile having written the charges on his master's behalf. Surling barely glanced at it. The symbol, the signature – that was all that mattered. None present wished to stand in opposition to an inquisitor.

'This seems sufficient,' he murmured, handing the scroll to a scribe. 'I don't suppose you can give me the name of this agent with whom you spoke?'

'I am afraid not, they were unwilling to divulge it. Perhaps Inquisitor Atenbach will provide those details? I have it on good standing he will be here within days.'

CHAPTER FIFTY-ONE

It was raining.

Apparently, this was the natural state on Nephira, though I confess I had never visited the planet before. There was little reason to. It was one of the Imperium's many innocuous worlds, lacking anything remarkable enough to be worthy of fame or infamy. Its tithes were paid promptly, primarily via a greenish wheat that had a bland taste but stored surprisingly well. And its people, of course, for the armies of the Imperium always needed more soldiers.

My footsteps were heavy as I descended the shuttle's ramp. The left, in particular. I was still getting used to the weight of the augmetic limb, but it was a relief not requiring a cane.

Ahead, everything was surprisingly green. There were hab-blocks, naturally, vast looming buildings, and agri factoria for processing foodstuffs. But the fields stretched to the horizon, broken only by hedgerows and tall, spindly trees that seemed intent on piercing the grey sky.

'By the Throne it's miserable.'

I turned, watching as Flight Commander Lucille von Shard emerged from the shuttle. For once she did look fairly resplendent, being clad in her formal attire: a double-breasted tunic of vibrant blue, adorned with bronze buttons and gold thread. One hand rested on the hilt of her sabre, the other holding her hat in place against the wind, its turquoise feather already beginning to droop.

'The rain is good for growing.'

'And terrible for my outfit,' she said with a grimace. 'Perhaps we should postpone for another day.'

'Not possible, I'm afraid. Wing Commander Prospherous is adamant you return to the front lines as soon as possible.'

'Of course he is,' she said. 'Shame the old man forgave his grudge.'

'You did help him assume authority over Surling. Unofficially, of course.'

'That was Atenbach.'

'Perhaps. Have you heard much from Rile?'

'Only his usual nonsense where every other word is redacted. He's enjoying his new hand, though. No doubt it conceals all manner of cunning gadgets.'

'I don't suppose he mentioned Esec?'

'He did not. And you should let it go.'

'I did him wrong. I do not think he realised he conspired with the aeldari when he was issued those Eyes of his. I would at least like to know who provided them.'

'The Eyes weren't aeldari.'

I froze, glancing to her, but her gaze was fixed ahead, intent on the distant hab-blocks.

'But Rile said they were xenos devices?'

'Yes, but there are millions of xenos species in the galaxy. Esec could have bartered with any of them, or their human agents more likely. What does it matter? Whatever scheme they had was thwarted. Or wasn't. But in either event it is no longer our concern. Rile will no doubt investigate. And tell us nothing of his findings.'

I turned my head to follow her gaze, and found our arrival had drawn some attention. The toiling workers raised their heads, elbowing their fellows. I suppose the appearance of an Aquila lander was unusual for such people. Or perhaps it was the occupant that piqued their interest. Even they knew her face, though now it carried a few more scars.

'Everyone is staring,' she murmured.

'Perhaps they've never seen a star of the pict screen walk among them.'

'Do you know where we are going?'

'Yes. I have the dwelling marked. It's in that hab-block over there.'

'Fine. Let's get this over with.'

We walked along the thoroughfare between the fields. It was strangely quiet. No thrum of machines. Just the wind parting the tall grasses, and the sonorous cries of birds in the trees. Even the hab-block felt a part of the scenery, climbing vines adorning its surface. Whatever reservations I held about the Imperium, this felt a world worth preserving.

I felt her slowing and looked back to find she had come to a stop, eyes fixed ahead.

'Are you all right?' I asked.

'Just… give me a moment.'

I nodded, letting my gaze wander over the landscape, watching her from the corner of my eye. She did not move, still staring into the distance.

'May I ask what you are thinking?'

She shrugged. 'Nothing. Just wondering what my life would have been if I were born and raised here. Probably scrabbling in the dirt to make a living. Wedding some dim-witted local and squeezing out a couple of brats before dying of something mundane.'

'Maybe you would have sought adventure and enlisted?'

'Maybe.'

I paused. 'Would you prefer I wait at the ship?'

'No. It's better you're here. Better someone is here anyway, make sure I see it through. That used to be Plient's job. I suppose it's yours now.'

'Lucky me.'

'Would you prefer he never sent you that message? That you were still walled up in a cubicle?'

I shook my head. 'Still you persist with that farcical notion.'

'Well, he is the most likely suspect.'

'Is he now?'

'Well if it wasn't him then I have no idea. I suppose it could be one of my siblings. Josephine is certainly cunning enough.'

'One of *the* siblings, certainly.'

'Oh please,' she said, rolling her eyes. 'You think I'd bother sending you a vid asking for aid? Even if the situation was dire and I had no one else to turn to? Does that sound like something Flight Commander Lucille von Shard would contemplate?'

'I suppose not,' I conceded. 'I just wonder how Plient, talented as he was, found a way to manipulate a vid in so sophisticated a manner. So sophisticated in fact that I have been unable to determine how he did it.'

'Esec must have shown him.'

'They were close, then? Friends?'

'More acquaintances. Though that was before Esec revealed his true intentions.'

'Yes. I'm surprised Plient was so easily fooled into taking Esec into his confidence.'

'Maybe he was struggling, and made the mistake of reaching out to someone,' she suggested. 'Perhaps you were the only person he could think of who might be able to help, or might at least have some sympathy for... his plight. Between the two of us, Plient didn't have many friends.'

I thought of him. The way he moved so easily through the crowd at the fight pit, exchanging jokes and smiles. Even Lanlok had known his name, and for that matter so had Prospherous. I had never heard a bad word against him.

'He did strike me as the unpopular sort,' I said. 'I suppose he was lucky to have you.'

She didn't reply, her gaze on the hab-block.

'I don't think I can do this.'

'You can.'

Her hand strayed into her lapel, emerging with a flask. I said nothing as she raised it towards her lips. At the last moment she sighed, tucking it back into her pocket before advancing towards an innocuous-looking door. She stopped before it, straightening, chest pushed out, head held high, gaze stern, especially given the scars adorning her cheek.

'How do I look?'

'Like a hero.'

'Liar,' she said, rapping twice against the door. It took a moment to open. The woman behind it wore a worried expression. She held an infant to her chest, though given her greyed hair and lined skin she seemed too old to be its mother. Other children stood behind her, one peeking from her dress.

Shard bowed her head. 'Mrs Plient?'

The woman nodded.

'My name is Flight Commander Lucille von Shard. This is my propagandist, Kile Simlex. I am afraid I bear sombre news concerning your son, Flight Sergeant Petre Plient.'

'Petre?'

She knew. You saw it in her face, the way her shoulders crumpled, and the light left her eyes.

'I am afraid your son has passed into the God-Emperor's light,' Shard said solemnly. 'He fought and died with honour and went above and beyond the call of duty. He saved countless lives, and ensured our foes were defeated. May I enter? I would like to tell you of his bravery, and my associate has letters addressed to you and your family.'

'Yes. Of course, my lord,' the older woman said, bowing. 'Petre spoke often of you, flight commander. You were more than a superior officer. You were his hero.'

'…He was my friend.'

POSTFACE

My name is Propagandist Kile Simlex.

I did not reclaim my title so much as have it thrust upon me, the von Shard siblings and their superiors at some point deciding that I should assume Esec's role. Perhaps they believed I was best placed to manage Shard's eccentricities. Already she infuriates me, though less so than the thought of returning to my cubicle.

Saving Rile's life probably helped. Apparently, he was conscious enough to recall me throwing myself in the path of Lanlok's blow, though I'm not sure he knew why the ogryn hesitated. Neither do I, not for certain, though I recall the commissar and Rile noting how the aeldari seers could manipulate the feeble of mind. And who is more feeble of mind than an ogryn? If somehow ensnared in their sorcery, Lanlok would certainly have been a useful agent, seen as too dim-witted to be a spy whilst having access to restricted areas. I can only assume the manipulations he was subjected to involved keeping me alive, for I can see no other reason why he spared me, or saved me during Cesh's attack.

And this is troubling. Because it means the aeldari wanted me alive.

Their forces made no further impact on Deighton. The planet was reclaimed, though Inquisitor Atenbach paid little heed to the conflict; his focus was the webway gate. From what I hear he has, so far, been unable to activate it. He seized Esec's barge too, along with whatever Eyes were still functional. I still do not know who was responsible for their deployment. Were they too simply manipulated by the aeldari, or did another faction have business on Deighton? Or was it neither, simply an unscrupulous trader making a profit from Esec's naivety.

I do not know, but in any event the conquest of Deighton was ultimately deemed a victory for the Imperium, the insurgents crushed and the xenos bested. That's what the picts will say in any event.

But I find myself thinking of pebbles, and the ripples they cast when thrown.

Perhaps thwarting our conquest was not the aeldari's true goal. Perhaps that will not come to fruition for decades, or even centuries. And perhaps my survival was a necessary part of that plan, because in the brief span of my life, I will leave a ripple. It could be as little as a particular pict that inspires another to make a decision. Or perhaps it is simply that were I not to assume my current role, another would in my stead, and their decisions would lead to an outcome unfavourable to the aeldari.

One could go mad attempting to untangle the threads.

Commissar Shard is probably right. It is better to ignore their meddling, impose your own plans. So that is what I did. I ignored Cesh's entreaties to tell the truth, and instead crafted a lie to benefit me and those I favour. After all, is that not what the Imperium is built upon? We are instructed that we cannot permit the xenos, the witch or the heretic to live. Unless the xenos is employed by an inquisitor, or a commissar elects to transport a witch, or our commanders decide that condemning a planet for heresy is just too darn inconvenient and expensive.

For the rules only apply to the powerful if they suit their interests.

And I am hardly powerful. There is little a propagandist can do to change the galaxy. Even one as well equipped as I. Perhaps that is why no one seemed to notice the removal of Esec's control helm. I assume Atenbach paid it little heed, such a trivial detail insignificant compared to the acquisition of the barge itself, the fleet of Eyes, or the webway gate.

But it holds so much. Reams of footage, all contained by something so comparatively small. I have barely had time to review half of it, but I already know much is damning, for it shows how corrupt and incompetent the Imperium really is. How our commanders fail us over and over.

And sometimes I think of what Rosln told me on the *Ilrepuet*. How, when crossing the warp, all it takes is an indentured worker being in the wrong place, or making the wrong choice, for there to be catastrophic consequences.

It is merely a question of opportunity.

Perhaps I will make use of the footage someday. For, if the aeldari taught me one thing, it's how easy a narrative can be forged. Even, hypothetically, one that shows our citizens the true face of the Imperium.

But for now, I will labour as I have always done. I will produce picts proclaiming the glory of Lucille von Shard, if for no other reason than it was Plient's final request. I will hone my skills, I will keep my eyes open, and I will wait to cast my stone. And watch the ripples left in its wake.

And perhaps, in a small way, I will see what I can do to shape humanity's future.

ABOUT THE AUTHOR

Denny Flowers is the author of the novels *Fire Made Flesh, Outgunned* and *Above and Beyond*, the novellas *Low Lives, Da Gobbo's Demise,* and several short stories. He lives in Kent with his wife and son, and has no proven connection with House Delaque.

YOUR NEXT READ

MINKA LESK: THE LAST WHITESHIELD
by Justin D Hill

Cadia has stood in grim defiance against the enemies of the Imperium for ten thousand years, an indomitable bulwark against the forces of Chaos… but now, the 13th Black Crusade has come, and there will be no victory. Here, Minka Lesk will be tested in the very fires of a world's destruction.

For these stories and more, go to **blacklibrary.com**, **warhammer.com**,
Games Workshop and Warhammer stores, all good book stores or visit one of the thousands of
independent retailers worldwide, which can be found at **warhammer.com/store-finder**

An extract from
Cadia Stands
found in the omnibus *Minka Lesk: The Last Whiteshield*
by Justin D Hill

Below them, the planet was poised half in light and half in darkness.

Major Isaia Bendikt could not tell if a new day was coming on, or if the night was falling. He stood with Warmaster Ryse and his posse of command staff on the viewing platforms of the *Fidelitas Vector* and remembered how he'd left Cadia over twenty years before.

In those twenty years, he'd had more than his fair share of benighted ice-worlds, void-moons and jungle worlds with bloodsucking nanobes that dropped onto you from the branches above.

He'd seen the worst of the galaxy and now, looking down upon Cadia, he remembered his last moments on his home world.

A young Whiteshield, without a kill to his name.

Bendikt's father had never got the chance to go off-planet. He was one of the one in ten Cadian Shock Troopers whose draft drew them as a territorial guard. It was his life to stay at home and stand ready to protect Cadia. But war had not come, and that uneventful career was a shame that had discoloured his life.

When the sixteen-year-old Isaia Bendikt drew an off-world draft he was both proud and envious of his son. It was a hard thing for a dour father to express, so he'd done what many fathers had before him – bought a bottle of Arcady Pride and got both himself and Bendikt drunk.

Bendikt remembered the night clearly. They had been sitting at the round camp table that stood in the middle of the small sub-hab central room of their home. His father had drawn up the camp chairs and slammed the bottle down between them, set two shot glasses on the table.

He had forced a smile as he unscrewed the top, crumpled it up in his hand and threw it back over his shoulder, where it had rattled in the corner of the room. His mother had left them a few plates of boiled grox-slab and cabbage on the table. Bendikt had tried to line his stomach as his father poured them a shot glass each.

'Here,' he'd said and held out the brimming glass.

They'd tapped the rims against each other and tipped the glasses high. Shot by shot they'd drunk and slowly knocked the bottle back. When the muster bell rang there was only a little amasec in the bottom of the bottle. 'To your first kill!' his father had slurred. His mother, a thin, worn, earnest-looking woman, had joined in with the last toast.

It was a short walk to the muster point, where other Whiteshields were being loaded onto rail trucks, their apprehensive faces staring out from under their Cadian-pattern helmets. All the tracks led straight to the landing fields outside Kasr Tyrok.

Bendikt and his parents pushed through the crowds to find his truck. Both his mother and his father had last words for him, though he was damned if he could remember them. He was only sixteen and so drunk he could barely stand. There were no tears. It was poor form to show sadness when a Cadian was sent to fight. It was part of the rhythm of life: birth, training, conscription, death. It was natural that a young Whiteshield would go and kill the enemies of the Imperium.

Bendikt had imagined himself many times taking the straight route south, and never seeing his home again. Before climbing aboard, he checked himself one more time to make sure that in his drunken state he had not forgotten anything.

He had boots, webbing, jacket, belt, combat knife, lasrifle, three battery packs, Imperial Primer in his left breast pocket, water canteen in his right. He pulled in a deep breath. He was ready, he told himself, to face anything the galaxy could throw at him.

'So,' Bendikt said. They said goodbye to one another, and his mother briefly embraced him and stuffed a packet of folded brown paper into his jacket pocket. 'Grox-jerky,' she whispered.

She was a tough woman, brought up on a planet where the only trade was war, and little given to expressions of emotion.

'I want to thank both of you for giving me life. I promise you I will be all that a Cadian should,' he said. It was a speech he had prepared, but being drunk he stumbled on his words and left much of it out.

Then he saluted and turned to climb aboard the truck. He looked out to wave goodbye to his parents, but darkness was falling and they had already turned for home. That was the last Bendikt had ever seen or heard of his family. For the next twenty years, other Guardsmen had been his brothers and sisters, and the Emperor his father.

Bendikt found it hard to remember his father's face but had never forgotten the hug his father had given him, and feeling his father's thick arms wrap around him, his broad, rough hands on his back. His mother's voice had never left him; he could recall her whispering 'grox-jerky' into his ear, and those words stayed with him, and somehow came to mean 'Look after yourself', and even 'You are well-loved, my son.'